D1053395

NIGHTWATCH ON THE HINTERLANDS

Also by K. Eason

ARITHMANCY AND ANARCHY

The Thorne Chronicles

HOW RORY THORNE DESTROYED THE MULTIVERSE
HOW THE MULTIVERSE GOT ITS REVENGE

The Weep

NIGHTWATCH ON THE HINTERLANDS

NIGHTWATCH ON
THE HINTERLANDS

K. EASON

DAW BOOKS, INC

DONALD A. WOLLHEIM, FOUNDER
1745 Broadway, New York, NY 10019
ELIZABETH R. WOLLHEIM
SHEILA E. GILBERT
PUBLISHERS
www.dawbooks.com

Published by DAW Books, Inc.
1745 Broadway, New York, NY 10019.

First Printing, October 2021
1 2 3 4 5 6 7 8 9

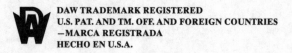

DAW TRADEMARK REGISTERED
U.S. PAT. AND TM. OFF. AND FOREIGN COUNTRIES
—MARCA REGISTRADA
HECHO EN U.S.A.

PRINTED IN THE U.S.A.

To Tan

CHAPTER ONE

The scream sneaked into a gap between a barful of shouted intimate conversations and the Kreeshan Blue cover band. Iari almost missed it. Thought she imagined it. Voidspit band with its two stringy alwar—sibs, guess that by their matching noses, howling like they were on fire—and a wild-haired tenju wrestling with an auto-harp. The auto-harp appeared to be winning. It was a big harp.

Then she heard it again. Or thought she did. Or her ears were ringing. She pitched forward onto her elbows and aimed her voice across the table. "You hear screaming?"

Gaer snorted. Long nostrils clamped almost shut, accompanied by a gusty blast of vakari disapproval that Iari couldn't hear. "They *are* terrible," he said, eyes stabbing the alwar. "But *he's* got talent. The tusky one."

"Not a joke." Iari shoved her chair back, shoved herself halfway to standing. She strained neck and shoulders to catch an eyeful of the door, which was open to the street—to the alley, really—spilling watery yellow light (not unlike the beer) onto waterslick black pavement. One of the bouncers was frowning, staring into the night, with her head tilted, like, yes, she'd heard something.

Not that she'd stuck a toe out to investigate, though, and why would she? Not *her* job, to go stomping around B-town at night looking for trouble.

Technically it was not Iari's job, either. B-town had (civilian) peacekeepers to handle local disturbances. A templar handled Aedian business, Confederate business. And Iari was off duty, in any case. This was time she should've been up in her room, out of the armor, reading, petting a cat (Tinycat, Tatter, maybe Ghost if he'd bothered to stay in). No, here she was, drinking good beer and listening to bad music with the Five Tribes ambassador while someone had an emergency.

Iari took one last, regretful swallow of the former and heaved herself fully vertical. *Now* she drew attention, less for her height and breadth—big, but not outside normal parameters for a tenju—than for the templar armor. This wasn't a real battle-rig, was barely armor at all: no shield, no helmet, no gauntlets, no slagging *axe*.

Iari looked down at Gaer. Only time she could, when he was sitting; vakari were tall. The pigmentation on his cheeks shimmered in the dim overhead lights, bands of happy cerulean against the charcoal dark of his hide. The optic clamped to the bone-and-scale ridges over his left eye caught the light *just so* and flared an opaque, defiant cyan.

Gaer's jaw-plates flared. Flattened. "You're going to investigate."

"Yeah. You can stay here."

His gaze flickered around the pub, gathering up the stares, gauging the attitudes. Reading auras, if she knew him, which she did. He clenched a smile at her.

"*Setat*. No, I can't." His rise was a more graceful unfolding, vakari legs made longer with that extra central joint.

Heads turned.

Truth was, she'd worn the uniform tonight for *this* reason

(besides feeling naked without it). She was one templar, sure, barely armored at all; but the Aedian crest on the chestplate made people—eh, not *think*, maybe, but at least *stop* before they did something stupid. It'd been a generation since the Accords with the vakari Protectorate, and anyway, Gaer was Five Tribes, from the *friendly* side of the vakari front. There shouldn't *be* trouble at all, and he shouldn't need her, or any templar, playing escort.

But truth, come on, he was *one* vakar on a tenju seedworld in the galactic hinterlands. Might as well float a holo-target over his head, walk around saying *express your prejudice here*.

Iari put her hand on her own jacta—to make sure no one else grabbed it, because no way she'd fire a weapon in here—and broke a trail through the bar. Another advantage of that armor: people moved for her, too. Expressions shifted: curiosity for a templar (where was she going?), devolving into a twist of distaste for Gaer (oh Elements, is that a vakar? Really?). A little fear, for her or for Gaer (maybe both). At least one wet-eyed admirer of the Aedis.

And then out, *finally*, past the bouncer, into a late autumn night wet with late autumn rain.

She couldn't hear any screaming now. Just the gush of full gutters, and the soundbleed out of the club following them into the puddles.

Gaer tilted his head one way, then the other. Rain beaded on the long ridges running from his jawline along the length of his skull. Vakari ears were somewhere under that bone.

"You know, if you wanted to leave, you could've just *said*."

"Told you, I heard something."

She kicked into a jog. Slipped in a slick of Ptah-knew-what at the corner, caught herself in the next stride. It was all empty streets out here, but a few streets away, there was a glow on the low-slung clouds that didn't look like streetlamp teslas. Looked almost looked like the flicker of a housefire, but the color was wrong. Fire was orange. This . . . was white. Blue. Looked cold, but Iari knew better.

Ptah had many facets, all of the Elements did. The fire that warmed also burned; the plasma that powered the voidships and made the stars could also liquefy metal and sublimate flesh. And when you took that plasma and bound it with arithmantic hexes and shoved it into a weapon, you got whitefire, which didn't stop for rain or void, burned blue, and was entirely illegal except for templars and Confederate troops and very special permits.

The size of the glow and the brightness (and experience with both) told Iari its origin was maybe a block ahead, sharp right at the corner, and they were rapidly covering that distance. Probably where the screams had come from. No. Definitely.

Gaer pulled up beside her, those long vakari legs finding a path over puddles. "That's whitefire."

"Yeah. I know."

"There are peacekeepers to handle this."

"People down here don't always call. PKs won't always answer. You're armed, right?" She knew he was. Treaty-legal monofil and sidearm jacta fully visible, where treaty said they should be. Arithmancy, less visible, more dangerous.

"Sss."

"Take that as yes. Stay behind me."

Iari wished for her shield and her helmet and her axe, and then charged the rest of the way up the street: into the acrid breeze and the whitefire glow.

No one was shooting now. Someone had been, with a whitefire projectile; there were hotspots on the walls where stone still glowed. Big holes. Big weapon. This was an old part of the city, where they used Chaama's bones for building. Everything since the Accords was plascrete and polysteel, hexed against arson and accident.

Hexes might not stop whitefire. Not much did.

A single lump of *something* burned in the street. Pavement had softened around it, cupping what appeared to be part of an . . . arm, maybe. A very small arm.

It was hard to see much detail in full night, without moons or stars or much more illumination than the tesla street lights. Gaer would see more, with that optic. Gaer would see, oh, all *manner* of things with it. Hexes. Glyphs. Maybe an aura, if the arm hadn't been too long detached.

What *she* could see was a conspicuously empty street, and doors conspicuously shut. Every window shuttered. It was that kind of neighborhood.

One exception: the house *right there*, that had no door. Windows smashed out. Most of the front wall spilled into the street where whatever had done for the front door had taken part of the building with it. Probably the origin of the arm.

"We are very much being observed," Gaer said calmly, clearly. "Every *setatir* window."

"Copy that." Iari dragged her handcomm from its pouch behind her chestplate. A battle-rig kept its comms in the helmet. Blessed Four, she looked like a *civ* making a call, except her handcomm linked straight to Dispatch with a murmured command.

"Dispatch, got a situation. One person down, presumed dead in Midtown. Looks like there might be a whitefire weapon involved. I'm on site with the Five Tribes ambassador. Please advise. Over."

Dispatch said nothing. Iari guessed the comms were out again. The quantum hexes had been skiffy since the Weep, some explanation involving dimensional rifts and dense arithmantic theory. Knight-Marshal Tobin had a report, scrolled thick as Iari's forearm, about why long-range comms couldn't be trusted. He used it to prop his window open on nice days for a breeze. Said he might hear his templars calling for backup that way. Truth was, comms usually did fine over short distances unless there was Brood around.

Which there were not, in the middle of B-town. Not if there was anyone left alive in the neighborhood.

Gaer made one of those little hisses and pointed at a wedge of fallen wall. "Your screamer's back there, I think. Down to heavy breathing. You could go coax them out."

Oh, ungentle Ptah. Almost her whole life spent in the Aedis, first as war-orphan, then templar. What hadn't been either of *those* had been spent in the army. She wasn't good with civilians. Wasn't good with panic.

Or people, Gaer would have said. She flicked a glance at him, where he squatted beside the corpse and made long-fingered gestures that were probably arithmancy and might be just show for the watchers in the windows. He was an ambassador. *He* could talk down a panicky civ.

Or make it worse, being a vakar.

Iari hung the jacta back on her hip—scared civs were afraid of weapons, right? right—and pitched her voice toward the tumbled wall.

"Hey. You, hiding back there. You hurt?"

She waited a beat, then went around the edge of the wall, left forearm raised as if she had a shield gauntlet ready to deploy. The person back there might have a rock, a stick, something.

The person had none of those things. *Did* have a pair of wide eyes, moon round and moon pale, match to the nimbus of wispy hair fluffing off a very small, round head.

Elements defend. A wichu. In *this* neighborhood.

"My name's Lieutenant Iari. I'm a templar." That should be slagging obvious, with the chestplate, but panic made people stupid.

The wichu blinked. Kinda unnerving, the whole monochromatic eyeball thing. Impossible to tell *where* the attention was.

"Lieutenant," the wichu—she? he? maybe one of the other genders—said in unaccented Comspek. Hoarsely. They, she, he, whatever, pushed carefully upright, using what remained of the wall for balance. "No, no. I'm not hurt."

"You have a name?"

"Yinal'i'ljat."

Two glottal stops: that meant a female. "You want to say what happened? Did you see who did this?"

Gaer made a noise from behind her. One of those gravel-click-in-the-throat vakari laughs. Meant the opposite of funny, and also that Gaer had thought of a cleverness he really wanted to say out loud, and would not, being a diplomat. The wichu stared at Iari like drowning people cling to shipwrecks. "I—there was a riev. I came to see my cousin, Pinjat, and there was a riev inside, and it killed him. Then it ran out, and I thought it was going to kill me, but it didn't. People were screaming and running and I just hid."

"A *riev*?"

Leave off the obvious objection: riev didn't kill wichu. If Pinjat had been a Protectorate vakar thirty years ago, okay, maybe; but the wichu had artificed the riev to be shock troops for the Confederation. There were safeguards, both hexed and hardwired, that made riev as reliable as sunrise (more reliable, in systems too close to the Weep). They didn't just go . . . doing this. Any of it.

Yinal'i'ljat sniffed. "You don't believe me."

"Didn't say that."

"But you don't."

"Not my job, rendering judgment." Not her job, playing local PK, either. Murders were out of her jurisdiction. Templars belonged to the Aedis, and the Aedis defended the Confederation against its enemies, external or internal or interdimensional. Since the Accords, when the Protectorate vakari took themselves off that list, the Aedis only worried about Brood surges.

Riev murders, though, were impossible. That might just qualify as templar jurisdiction.

Iari prodded her handcomm. This time it clicked, very faintly. She felt the hexes try to engage, felt them fizzle.

Knight-Marshal Tobin would say, *use your judgment, Lieutenant.* He would mean, *Damn right, get involved.*

"Yinal'i'ljat." Her tongue tripped only a little bit. "Any idea why a riev would go after your cousin?"

The wichu pinched a smile. Tiny little pearls for teeth. "My cousin is—was—an artificer during the Expansion, Lieutenant."

A lot of wichu had been. That was no revelation.

"He worked on riev maintenance."

Ah. Well.

"That's why the riev came to him. They have, you know, problems sometimes. Need repairs."

"You also an artificer?"

"Me? No. I'm a linguist. I'm visiting from Windscar."

"That's a long way for a visit." Not inexpensive, either: a half-day by aethership. "Fond of your cousin?"

"I am. I was." The wichu clasped her hands together, stiff-armed, and stared down at them. She might've sniffled.

Oh, ungentle Ptah.

"Did you see what happened?"

"Not exactly. I was coming down the street. I heard *noises* coming from the house, so I started running, and then there was this flash—"

"What kind of noises?"

"Ah." Yinal'i'ljat blinked. It was like watching two moons go through a sudden, simultaneous eclipse. "Banging. Crashing. Then I saw the riev run out of the house. It dropped something, and—" She was ramping up again. Mouth working. Eyes all moist and panicky. "I saw it was an *arm* and—"

"All right." Iari made what she hoped was a calm-down gesture. She could hear Gaer approaching. Deliberate boot-scuff, so she could track him.

She saw the glint of his optic reflected in the wichu's eyes. "*Lieutenant.* The arm belonged to a wichu."

Yinal'i'ljat made a tiny sound, like she had no air left in her lungs. Another small sound, this one an inhale. Her eyes got even wider, which Iari wouldn't have guessed was possible. "That's a *vakar.*"

Iari grimaced. "Ambassador Gaer i'vakat'i Tarsik. This is—"

"Yinal'i'ljat. Yes. I heard." Gaer bowed, very slightly, and bared a smile. Vakari teeth were etched and dyed with tribe, mothers, local district. Gaer's dye was blue, ranging from cerulean to cyan and all of it black in this light. He'd tried to teach her to read the code once. Lost her at the incisors.

Yinal'i'ljat appeared to be fascinated. Wide-eyed, anyway, though that might be her standard expression.

"Ambassador," she said, and followed his name with a stream of chopped-up Sisstish syllables that sounded a lot like her cousin's house looked.

Yinal'i'ljat had said she was a linguist. Right.

Gaer slid his gaze to Iari's. *There* was his real smile, in the slight narrowing of his eyes. And not a kind one, either. The sort of smile that said *I always wondered how wichu would taste.*

Iari drilled *a look* at him. "I'm going inside."

"Of course you are." He peered down at Yinal'i'ljat. She was on the small side of an already small species. She barely came up to Gaer's chest. "I'll stay here with Yinal'i'ljat."

"Fine." Iari grimaced at him. At Yinal'i'ljat, too—the top of her head, anyway—in passing. "I'll be right inside."

She took another stab at the comms. "Dispatch, listen. We have one dead in B-town, a wichu artificer, and one witness who says it was a riev. I'm going into the house—oh, voidspit."

Blood spattered the walls in broad arcs, almost all the way to the ceiling. In some places, there were wide smears. There was one identifiable limb—a left arm, a hand—near the door. Iari stared down at it. The fingers still gripped a stylus. The wichu had been hard at work when this happened. Unsuspecting. Bits of the wichu's insides dangled from the ceiling, where they'd hit hard enough to stick. Be a mess when they dried and came down. *More* of a mess.

Blessed Elements.

The Aedis had commissioned riev to kill vakari. Hexed them to repel whitefire, hexed them to repel vakari battle-arithmancy. But really, riev were supplemental troops for the infantry, engineered to peel a vakar marine out of their battle-rig, armored to be impervious to vakari talons and spikes and mildly toxic body fluids. Riev were made to take vakari apart.

And vakari were a lot bigger and meaner than wichu. Yinal'i'ljat's cousin wouldn't have stood a chance. At least it had gone fast. Hard to say if he'd even had time to scream.

Hard to say where his head was, for that matter.

Iari clamped her teeth tight. She'd seen worse than this in the last surge of Brood. Or at least, if not worse, comparable. It wasn't nausea crawling up her throat. It was anger. Because *Ptah's burning eye* this was obscene, in the same way Brood attacks were.

Iari picked her way through the wreckage of the front room. It wasn't a living space. Cabinets and storage lockers lined the near wall. There was a workbench, upended and twisted in the corner. Equipment consistent with an artificer's trade—the styluses, the presses, the printing tiles, the small bottles of acid for etching the hexwork—spread around the floor. Some of the bottles had smashed, their contents steaming and hissing their way through the rubber mats underfoot. A tesla generator sparked in one corner, attempting and failing to ignite the acid-soaked tile beneath it.

Iari squatted and dragged a small sheet of plain metal out from the edge of an overturned cabinet. There had been four neat columns of sigils on it, and carefully perforated divisions. A standard hex of some kind, stamp-produced, ready to separate, charge, and sell. She set the sheet aside.

And saw, gouged into a floor tile (local stone from the quarry, flecked and grey and hard, same stuff the Aedis compound was built from), a footprint, as clear as if the floor had been soft ground. Took a lot of force to make a mark like that. Took a *hex* to make stone act like mud, same kind of hexes artificers put on the soles of riev feet, so that big metal bodies kept traction.

There were, now that she looked, more of those footprints. Places the riev had planted its weight to—do whatever it was doing. Bracing to rip a cabinet out of the wall, or upend a workbench, or rip something (someone) into smaller pieces.

Or it'd been looking for something, flinging objects aside, tossing the room like a looter.

An odd thought. Riev didn't have much use for *things*. But riev didn't engage in random acts of destruction, either, or shoot whitefire.

Iari straightened. Took an unwholesome lungful of blood and shit and spilled chemicals and let it out again. The smell turned itself to taste and clung to the inside of her mouth. The blood was appalling, but it wasn't excessive. One body's worth (a small body). That might be another limb over there, in a smear-and-pool at the edge of the room. And there, yes, that *was* most of a head, smashed against a door that presumably led to the back rooms, to a staircase that went up to the second floor. To the back alley.

A closed door. An undamaged door.

She pivoted again to look at the ruined front wall, at the wreckage of door and frame. All of that spilled *out*, consistent with something large and violent leaving the premises. Not tearing its way *in*.

Yinal'i'ljat said her cousin had been an artificer who worked on B-town's decommissioned riev. So a riev could walk up to that front door and get no special notice. The riev could've knocked, and Pinjat would have let it in.

And it didn't make *sense* that—

"Iari." Gaer sounded a little too loud, a little too sharp.

For the love of Hrok and Ptah. Iari whipped her head around, aimed a shout backward. "Keep her outside, Gaer."

"I need *you* out *here*, actually." And then Iari heard the whine of a jacta coming online, and she understood why before Gaer even finished saying, "The peacekeepers have just arrived."

CHAPTER TWO ≡≡≡≡

"I think they might've shot Gaer, except Yinal'i'ljat got in the way. Then they wanted to detain him, and *I* got in the way."

Knight-Marshal Tobin leaned back in his chair, fingers steepled, lips level. A neutral expression, that the unwary or unwise might mistake for detached, disengaged, even disinterested.

"And that settled it?"

Iari had served a long time with Tobin. She knew what that stillness meant. "Might be a complaint coming. I wasn't polite."

He let his breath go gently, and she knew what that meant, too. "No *might*. I already have a protest on my turing."

Oh, sure. Voidspit quantum-hex comms didn't work, but the hard-cable turing-net did. Iari winced. "I'm sorry, sir."

The Knight-Marshal filled the obligatory city council post for the local Aedis representative, which was *always* a templar, which *always* caused tension with local PKs. Tobin made a point of letting B-town do its own enforcement. Of being the epitome of reason, of calm, the velvet glove over Aedian fist, interfering only when necessary.

Looked like Tobin wanted to go bare-knuckle right about now. "You're not, and you shouldn't be. If the peacekeepers on duty were half as prompt in doing their jobs as they were about filing complaints, you wouldn't have been there at all."

"Sir." The knot in her chest loosened. She let her weight shift just a little, heels to ball of foot and back, left to right.

Tobin pointed with his chin. "Sit down, Lieutenant."

"I'm fine, sir."

"My neck isn't. It's tired of looking up at you. Sit down and tell me what happened."

"Gaer's writing the report."

A handsome man, Tobin, as humans went. Square jaw. Medium brown hair streaked grey at the temple. Dark eyes, almost as dark as Gaer's, set deep above cheekbones as high and sharp as an alw's. Those eyes narrowed now. "And when I am desirous of polysyllabic discourse and highly theoretical arithmantic speculation, I will *read* that report. Until then, sit and talk to me."

"Sir." She hooked a foot around the chair and dragged it forward. The office furniture was a matched set, antique, local wood, heavy and serious, decorated with unpleasant ridges that found every knob in a woman's spine, if she wasn't armored. Gaer claimed not to mind, but Gaer had his own set of unpleasant spinal ridges.

Tobin cocked her a wry half-smile. He knew what those chairs were like. His own wasn't much kinder. Wider, with armrests. That was the difference.

Iari sat carefully. "What I think is a riev really killed that artificer. Place looked like an abattoir, but it was—wrecked. Like a whole *platoon* of tenju went berserk in a barfight. Gaer found what he thought was a trail—bits of what was presumably Pinjat, accompanied by dents in the walls, or broken street tiles. Looks like the riev ran into the Lowtown warrens, into the alwar section. Before we could go after it, the PKs showed up. They seemed more interested in detaining Gaer than in following the trail, so." She shrugged. "Rain last night probably washed what was left down to the river."

"Riev don't butcher people. That's." Tobin stopped short of saying *impossible*. "Unprecedented."

"Then I think we need to look into it, sir, because one of them *did*."

Tobin took the first muscle twitch on the road to a smirk. Stopped and held that position. "We. You think this is an Aedian matter."

"I think it has to be. Sir, it's riev. *We* built them. We turned them loose."

Tobin's smirk changed sides and turned grimace. "They were never under Aedian authority. They were never even *leased* to the Aedis. The Confederation commissioned and deployed them as supplemental military equipment, and the Confederation decommissioned them. As such, their management legally falls under local Confederate ordinance."

Heat boiled up in Iari's chest, scalded its way past good sense and propriety and out her mouth. "That means the PKs? Or the city council? Right now B-town treats riev like they're cheap mecha labor. But just because riev can sling cargo or run messages doesn't change what they were made to do. That's kill people."

Tobin raised both brows. "There are members of the Synod who disagree with that."

"That the primary function of riev is killing?"

"That riev can serve in peace as well as war. That they have other purposes. Ranking members, Lieutenant."

"Lots of people outrank me, sir. Doesn't make them right."

The corner of Tobin's mouth twitched. "What makes you think you are?"

Iari started counting off fingers. "It wasn't a rampage. It was a targeted hit. If it was just a single riev's hexes gone bad, it should've killed other people, or torn up other things. It didn't. It went all the way to this artificer's house, it tore up *one* room and it killed *one* person. Either we've got a rogue riev with a very specific grudge, which means they can *have* grudges—and that's something else supposedly impossible—or we've got someone who wanted that particular wichu dead, and who can give riev orders that override their decomm no-kill directives. *And* there was whitefire damage. Riev lost their weapons when they were decommed, so someone's arming them before sending them out to kill people. That person might do it again, so we need to deal with it. The Aedis. Because the PKs aren't equipped to deal with that. Ah. Sir."

She ran out of breath and fingers. Sat back and waited, while Tobin stared at her. Then he sighed. Closed his eyes. Lines spread out from the corners like crazing on porcelain. "Teach me to ask your opinion, won't it?"

"Yes sir."

"No. It probably won't. Because I agree with you." Tobin leaned forward, elbows driving onto the desk, leaving new scuffs on the wood. His armor—polished, sure, but real. The scoring on his right bracer: she remembered the Brood who'd done that. Remembered pulling it off him. "Iari, listen. This incident is still *legally* B-town council oversight. I can't order an official Aedis investigation without more evidence."

"Understood, sir."

"However." He flicked a glance at the turing. "As a consequence of your actions tonight, you're relieved of duty tomorrow. Go find that evidence. Wear a battle-rig and take the appropriate weapons. And be *careful*, Lieutenant. We don't want a panic. And we don't want any more bodies. Especially not yours."

She battered the grin off her face. "Yes sir."

———————

Gaer perched on the top of the Aedis compound, on a wall half-way between watchtowers, and looked for the Weep.

Well, not the *actual* Weep. *That* was an electromagnetic mael-strom, a rip in the actual fabric of the void, and it was a couple of star systems *over there*. Which was fortunate for this little cold rock of a planet. Tanis had missed the worst of a four-dimensional (maybe more than four; the arithmancers argued such things) rup-ture. It still had its star and its sibling planets. It also had a Weep fissure an observant vakar might see from the top of the B-town Aedis wall. On a good night, the fissure would be barely visible. He'd tuned his optic to its limits to detect Weep emanations. Which were really not emanations so much as anti-emanations. An absence of, well, *anything*. It was popular to say void was the absence of matter and energy, but that was so much neefa-shit. The Weep wept *anti*-void. It was a constant leak of nothing-something into reality.

Things—molecules, atoms—tended to fray, where Weep touched them. And the study of that fraying—the how, the what, the what-do-we-do-about-it—was part of why Gaer was here, now, perched on this wide block of Aedian stone on a raggedy planet in the galaxy's hinterland, freezing his spines off.

That was not, of course, the official reason. No, he was an am-bassador, if one checked his credentials. But he was also Five Tribes Intelligence, SPEcial REsearch (SPERE: oh, command did love its acronyms), and what made the little planet Tanis interesting wasn't just its convergence of Confederate species, but its own little Weep fissure that had somehow sliced through the planet without *actu-ally* slicing through anything and which, as all fissures did, vom-ited out periodic Brood surges. All of the fissures did, all along the

Weep, more or less in concert. No one had figured out a pattern, but it was known there *would* be another surge. It was just a matter of when. SPERE wanted reports, through channels other than diplomatic, of everything that went on here. Ostensibly to predict the next surge, sure. Some truth to that. More truth to spying on the Aedis, and figuring out what *they* knew.

Though, admittedly, the view from the top of the wall was pretty enough, if you didn't mind rustic. Little spots of color in the little windows of little buildings. Any one piece of the Aedian compound—temple, garrison, armory, hospice, library, barracks—was larger than the biggest building in B-town.

But the wind was intolerable, opinionated. Tugging his jacket this way and that, jabbing its fingers under his hood and gusting into his ear canals no matter which way he tried to turn.

Iari would say that was because he'd offended Hrok, Element of the Aether, more locally called Lord of the Storms. She might even mean it. Gaer could usually tell what the soft-skins were thinking—*everything* made their faces move—but Iari was almost vakari in her impassivity. And she was from Tanis. *And* she seemed to believe the Aedian Catechism.

"I'm sorry, Hrok," he muttered. "For whatever I've done to offend."

The wind, unimpressed, switched direction and plucked at the spines on his elbows. Whistled around the edge of his jaw-plates. It wasn't a good night for emanations. He hadn't seen any. And really, that absence made it a good night. No one wanted an active fissure, except maybe the stupidest templar recruit (or, be fair, stupid arithmancer academics looking for the next publication. Smart SPERE operatives wanted boredom). Gaer shifted on his perch. Flexed his toes, the tips of which his boots left uncovered ("those aren't boots, Gaer, those are socks"), and found new traction on the stone.

Real stone. *Real* quarried stone, not plascrete. Who *did* that? Why, the Aedis, as a way to honor Chaama, their Element-goddess of Solids (otherwise known as *stone*), just like there was real fire in the temple braziers and water in Mishka's temple fountain.

It was just past Chaama's time now, local midnight. The Aedis quartered the day, marked each quarter with a service dedicated to one of the Elements and a relentless session of bell-ringing before and after. The services were officially voluntary, as duty schedules permitted; but you weren't going to sleep through them, whether or not you attended. Midnight bells seemed especially loud.

And they were real bells, not recordings. Gaer had seen them, on his second official tour of the compound. Iari—he'd known her only as Lieutenant, then, a twice-met stranger—had made a point of marching him to the top of the tower and, while he caught his breath in thin atmosphere, his limbs aching with life in a gravity well for the first time in, oh, *years*, she had recited what sounded like a tourist infodump about the history of bells in the Aedis, the particular calibrations of frequency that made it impossible to say *I didn't hear them* for any recalcitrant initiates.

There was no place, she'd added, watching him try to find breath and dignity and not shiver too much in the wind, that you could go in the Aedis and *not* hear them. Even the library. Even the sub-basements. Even—and here she'd smirked at him, first time for seeing those tenju tusks on display—the ambassador's quarters.

Bells. Who wasted resources on mining and casting big metal conics meant only to deafen with their racket? Who didn't use, oh, *comms* like a civilized people?

But as those first few days bled into weeks, and Lieutenant became more familiar *Iari*, and he actually left the compound and went into B-town, Gaer realized how spotty the comms actually were, outside the Aedian walls and their formidable hexes. The bells were immune to Weep interference, and they were audible throughout B-town, should the Aedis require an alarm system. It was an old-fashioned sort of communication, but it worked.

Also old-fashioned: the Aedian watchtowers, strung along at intervals linking B-town and the smaller, northern Windscar garrison, so that there was effectively a line of Aedian outposts running the length of the fissure. If anything came out of it, the Aedis would know, and mobilize, and deal with it, whether or not they had comms.

That ready-and-willingness was enough to make Gaer forgive the *setatir* bells and their four calls to prayer and, yes, even the capricious, malicious wind. He edged along the wall, mindful of gusts, until he could see the main temple doors. Midnight prayers were sparsely attended. Only priests of Chaama, usually, with occasional crops of templar initiates, who had to attend all the services for one month of their training.

There were a few regulars, though. The devout. The devoted. Iari was one of those.

Gaer had devoted some small effort to figuring out what sort of person he'd been assigned as his escort. The sort who went to every service on purpose. The sort who didn't mind missing sleep. She emerged from the side door of the temple, looking small from this vantage. Looking frail, without either battle-rig or uniform. She wore plain clothes, dull and dark and practical. She tugged her coat closer as the wind gusted. A priest shuffled past her, head down, arms tucked close, scuttling for another doorway. Iari looked up instead, as if she expected to see Brood coming over the walls.

Gaer waved, to be sure she saw him. She was always looking. She didn't wave back. Folded her arms instead, in a way that had nothing to do with keeping warm, and cocked her head. Waiting, but not for him.

For—*him*. The Knight-Marshal, one of the other midnight regulars, emerged from the door. Most nights (because Gaer was up
here most nights, he saw things) Tobin and Iari walked back to the
officer quarters together, a monkishly proper distance between
them. The officer and her mentor-superior. Gaer wondered what
they talked about. If they talked at all. If they did more than walk-
without-speaking when they got back to quarters. He thought not;
mammalian sexual signals and protocols were tricky, but the whole
Aedian fraternization rules, now, those were explicit and clear.
And *those* two, of everyone, would follow them.

Tonight, however, Iari and Tobin didn't walk together. He said
something to Iari, and then they both looked up at Gaer, and then
Iari turned and started across the courtyard, alone. While Tobin—
oh, *setat*. Tobin was coming *this* way, heading for the nearest of
the staircases bricked onto the side of the wall. Looking up at
Gaer, making very clear his intention.

The Knight-Marshal wanted a conversation. Now. That couldn't
be good. The man's aura was as hard to read as an arithmancer
with a full hex-shield, all stoic and muted and steely blue-grey. But
there was a spidering of chartreuse tonight.

Gaer spread his jaw-plates. Tasted woodsmoke (because of
course these rustics burned organic matter for heat, never mind
the pollution) and the threat of autumn rain. Tasted his own suspicion, sour and thin in the back of his tongue. Tobin wanted to
talk about something to do with tonight's drama, no doubt. That
dead artificer, the witness and her improbable tale, Iari's emphatic
refusal to let the peacekeepers arrest him. Tobin might be unhappy about that. Might want to suggest the ambassador confine
his spiny posterior to the inside of the Aedis for a time.

But no. Chartreuse in the aura meant *worry*, not anger.

Gaer slid off the wall, leaned against it, and watched Tobin limp up the stairs. The Knight-Marshal's right leg glowed to Gaer's optic, from the hip to just past the knee, in a throbbing fusion of hexwork and metal. The prosthetic hadn't mated up cleanly to bone and muscle. That kind of scarring meant Brood damage, something too awful for Aedian priest-healers or templar nano-mecha to completely repair.

Something that probably should've killed Tobin outright, and hadn't, probably *because* of that Aedian nanomecha. Gaer thought about meeting him halfway down the steps, sparing him the climb. Discarded the idea in the next exhale. The Knight-Marshal could've summoned him to his office, whatever the hour. That he wanted to talk on the walls meant something unofficial, off the record. Something worth the discomfort to Tobin of climbing up here.

Something *interesting*.

"Knight-Marshal," Gaer said. Best to fire the first volley. That was the vakari way.

"Ambassador." Tobin didn't smile. Barely even a bow.

"Iari did nothing wrong tonight."

Tobin cocked his brows. "The peacekeepers think otherwise. You are, in their words, *a person of unknown motive*."

"That just means I'm the xeno no one likes."

"I know what it means. So did the lieutenant. She's not in trouble with me and that's not why I'm here."

"No? Well. It *is* a nice night for a walk on the wall. Join me?"

Tobin looked back, unblinking, unspeaking, and Gaer clipped his teeth together. Felt a ripple of heat in his chromatophores, was glad that human eyes wouldn't notice the color change in the dark.

"I need you to do something for me."

Gaer noted the omission of his title. Tobin didn't just forget things like that. Oh, the interesting things were just stacking up. "A personal favor, Knight-Marshal? I'm happy to help where I can."

Tobin's eyes narrowed. "A personal favor. Yes. Which you're free to refuse."

Which about guaranteed that Gaer wouldn't. He grinned, vakar-style. "Just tell me what you need."

CHAPTER THREE ═══════

Although the B-town Aedis was the second largest on Tanis, possessed of a finer library than even Seawall, B-town itself was considered a bit of a cultural backwater. Mostly human and tenju, agricultural, not even a working wall, the city squatted on the banks of the Rust River, flanked by the Barrowlands on one side and a coniferous forest that spiked into rocky foothills on the other. The Weep fissure sat at a comfortable distance, carved deep through Chaama's bones. Its emanations were visible in the aether only on clear nights from the top of the wall. They got brighter before a surge. Plenty of warning. Plenty of time to prepare.

It had been almost nine years since the end of the last surge. The fissure vomited up only the odd slicer or boneless these days, almost all of which were detected and dealt with in Windscar. And still, every templar initiate in B-town prayed one would get through, come to B-town, be discovered on *her* watch.

Iari prayed otherwise, having been a fighting part of that last surge. And because she (and the Knight-Marshal, and a handful of clergy) actually *attended* the inconvenient midnight and dawn prayers, she hoped the Elements gave her wishes a little more weight. She prayed for no Brood, obviously and always, but this morning's prayer had included an addendum:

Let me find this riev fast.

Then she spotted a tall shape leaning on the wall just inside the gate, a distinctly vakari shape, and Iari amended her prayer again:

Let that not be—oh hell.

So much for the power of prayer.

Gaer wore a vakari battle-rig, a motley collection of what looked like fins on both gauntlets and greaves where armor tented and angled to cover the spikes. The jacta for which he had special diplomatic permission hung off his hip. Dressed for business, Gaer. Dressed for trouble. Dressed to go with *her*, clearly. He detached himself from the wall with lazy grace.

"Iari." There was an implied *good morning*.

Iari kept walking, chin up, eyes front and fixed. The very junior templars staffing the main gate snapped to attention. Iari scowled and snapped a return salute and waited, soul of patience and fortitude, until she and Gaer were out of their earshot.

"What are you doing?"

"Taking a walk on this fine morning—"

"Gaer."

Condensation gleamed on his rig like frost. Vakari ran a little bit hotter than the other sentients. Steam leaked through his teeth and from the gaps in his jaw-plates. "Going with you, obviously."

Iari took her own lungful of early morning. Humid, cold, smelling like yook trees and the river and wet pavement and maybe rain, later. "Dear Ptah. Please tell Gaer to go back to his apartment right now. Tell him I'm working on something *other* than escorting him around B-town today."

"Do you actually expect your imaginary personified plasma to talk back?"

"How many imaginary vakari void-lords are there? Remind me. Nine or five?"

"There are *five*, you degenerate mammal."

"Some of your fellow bird-lizards say otherwise."

His nostrils squeezed flat, turned breath to a trickle. "*Setat i'mekkat* the Protectorate."

That was real anger, cold and sharp and reflexive. The civil war among the vakari was over, officially. After the Weep opened, no, get the word-order right: *after the Protectorate opened the Weep*, priorities realigned. But that didn't mean forgiveness on anyone's side. Not the Five Tribes, not the Protectorate. Not the Confederation, either, who'd fought all vakari during the Expansion, and then, after the Schism, found their work somewhat easier with a heretical Five Tribes third of vakari as allies.

Allies. Huh. "Knight-Marshal Tobin."

"Is that a question?"

"Not really. He asked you to come."

"Yes." He dragged the word out. Clipped it off on a puff of breath and blew. "If there's a rogue riev out there, something's gone wrong with its hexes."

"You're not an artificer."

"No," like the very idea smelled bad. "I am an *arithmancer*."

"Riev are resistant to arithmancy. And they like killing vakari."

"Which is why I have this." Gaer patted the jacta. "And you. Tobin asked me accompany you and assist the investigation, which I take to mean *read auras as necessary*. In exchange, he will grant me full access to your library and the archives. Anything not classified, anyway. Though I am disappointed. Your library is woefully deficient in riev technical manuals."

"That's proprietary information. The wichu won't release it, even to us."

"*Setatir* wichu." Gaer sounded more contemptuous than angry. The wichu had been Protectorate clients (read: annexed, colonized, two steps above *slaves*) once. They'd switched sides partway through the Expansion War, joined the Confederation, loaned their considerable expertise to the war effort. Their defection had made the first crack in the Protectorate's alliance. Had led to the Five Tribes heresy and the Schism, which had led to the Protectorate arithmancers ripping a hole into another layer of the multiverse.

And, in a very roundabout way, to Gaer's presence here on Tanis: ambassador and arithmancer (and probable spy, if Iari thought it through, which she had). Point was, Gaer wasn't inconspicuous, and B-town's streets weren't empty, even at this hour. People would note a templar and a vakar walking together, both battle-rigged. People would wonder. People would talk. And it was a very long walk to get where they needed to go.

B-town had been built on a hill. In the very earliest days, it'd been a tenju village, a collection of yurts surrounded by neefa herds and the piles of dung that came with them. You could imagine the chieftain's yurt on the crown of the hill, that eventually turned into a hut, then a fort, as the tenju mastered the art of stonework. They'd even built a wall around the hill, partway down.

Then came agriculture, industry, and before the tenju had managed to drag themselves out of Tanis's gravity well, the first alwar landing. (Though not here: in Seawall, where the town-building endeavor had gone rather more largely, and thus been visible from orbit.) Then the humans, and the voidport in Seawall, and peace-and-trade. B-town's wall and the city gates fell into disuse. And *then*, when the Protectorate ripped the multiverse, the fissure had arrived, and suddenly what had been a fistful of yurts and some neefa herds became the Aedis compound, which occupied the top third of the hill. B-town spilled down from there in concentric spirals and raggedy lanes of varying width all the way to the river's edge. Hightown, Midtown, Lowtown, unimaginative in their designations. The Aedis had widened the streets immediately around itself, had carved a straight line to the four gates of the city, built into the old tenju walls. Those streets could, in emergencies, accommodate vehicles (troop carriers, to get templars in and out); but the bulk of B-town was still a pedestrian zone.

Iari led Gaer across Hightown until she got to the East Road. You could see the Rust River from here, looking silver if you felt poetic, grey if you favored realism. The river mirrored the dull pewter sky, the red clay bed for which it'd been named invisible from this angle. The bleeding sunrise had gotten lost in the clouds. The aetherport's silhouette hunched like a sulking cat, partly obscured by the curve of the hill. The aetherport had largely replaced the docks as a source of transport before the Weep. Now since aetherships were still legally conscripted to Aedian service, and since Seawall had the only functioning off-world voidport, the docks in B-town were making a comeback.

Or, if you didn't want to float your commerce: on the other side of the Rust stretched the grasslands, rippling with the barrows of a thousand years of tenju chieftains, crosshatched by highways. Some of those were overgrown now; the Weep fissure, which split the northern plains and curved down like a knife scar toward Seawall, had disrupted more than aether-travel. You could build bridges over (through? Iari wasn't sure of the physics) some of the smaller fissures. Most of the time you just went around them, wide as possible, to avoid their unpredictable effects.

Gaer, who had mercifully held his opinions about B-town's

architecture this time (having waxed loquacious about the superiority of vakari cities, spires and towers and glass and steel, during previous visits), appeared to have reached his limits on silence.

"Where exactly are we going?"

Iari considered a terse, "You'll see." Considered not answering at all. Considered the half-dozen visible heads with visible ears who were already side-eyeing the templar-vakar combination with curiosity. This was still Hightown. Rumors floated up slower than they ran down, as a rule.

She drifted to the edge of the street and pointed with her chin. "There."

"The river."

"The docks. *There.*" She flicked her eyes at him. Snagged his attention and turned and pointed with her stare. "See? That open area, that's where the decommed riev go and stand around waiting for someone to offer them work. Records say we've got twenty-seven, although sometimes they sign on with caravans going overland. A few might be out of town. Or we might have a few new ones."

"Ss." Gaer's optic shimmered. Turned briefly opaque, pale and blue as a cataract. Then it cleared, and Gaer's void-black eye rolled back her direction. "Twenty-*seven*. The Confederation's best weapon, and you have them unloading boats and guarding boxes."

"War's over. So's the surge."

"Yes. But they're not exactly *retired*, are they? Decommissioned isn't the same as dismantled." His jaw-plates flared wide. "Why do docks always smell like rotten fish?"

"Because there *are* rotting fish."

"You'd think somebody could find them. Clean them up. Feed them to stray cats or something."

There was Gaer-normal-running-monolog, and then there was Gaer-clearly-nervous-and-babbling. No, this was more than nervous. Say *terrified*, just not out loud. Vakari pride was pricklier than vakari silhouettes. What Gaer hadn't asked yet was the obvious *why are we going down here*, and not back to Pinjat's to try asking his neighbors what they'd seen. Maybe Gaer had figured the answer to that part out already: that this wasn't an official investigation. She couldn't ask civilians anything without aggravating the PKs more than she already had.

But riev, now. Riev, she could ask. And maybe Gaer had followed that trail of thinking right to the edge of the cliff, to that vast emptiness of *ask them what* and *what do you think they'll be able to say*. Because, truth, she'd fought *with* riev all her life—two years regular army, ten more after turning templar before the end of the surge—and she'd never held conversation with one. It hadn't occurred to her try. Riev were not quite mecha, one step up from that, but they were still not quite people, either. Not legally. They were former people. Repurposed people. Whoever they had been, before the rieving, had been artificed out of them.

Maybe she'd just start with *hello*.

They were past the last inhabited streets of Lowtown now, well into the warehouses that lined the riverside. Everything was brick, made from local mud. Reddish brown, worn and pocked with weather. Slick, too. She felt the rig's traction-hexes ripple through the needle-socket at the base of her skull. The streets were wider here, crowded with all manner of traffic, from a-grav lifts to conventional hand-carts to the occasional mecha.

Iari tried to imagine how Gaer would see this place, with so much manual labor. Vakari didn't tolerate invasive personal biotech—Gaer's optic bumped right up against heresy, with permanent surgical hardware, but it had nothing neural—no, but they did love automation. For transport, manufacturing, agriculture, all sorts of industry. The vakari had perfected mecha while the alwar had still thought combustion engines marked the pinnacle of engineering.

Riev weren't mecha, though. Riev were . . . well, *riev*. Metal and dead meat held together with alchemy and reanimated with galvanics. Protectorate doctrine said they were abominations, further proof of the Confederation's moral pollution. The Five Tribes, with its gentler regard for heresy, excused the riev as a by-product of war, and certainly less horrific than the Protectorate battle-hexes that created the Weep. The Confederation had, after all, ceased production of riev after the Accords were drawn up in rare political haste, when everyone decided the Brood were more of a threat than doctrinal disagreements. The remaining riev stock proved useful for killing Brood, which was enough to overcome all but the most orthodox Protectorate squeamishness, and even then—no Protectorate force had ever said, oh, no, we'll handle this Brood, keep your riev to yourselves.

Gaer, of all vakari in the poor, tattered multiverse, was among the least orthodox, the least hidebound, the most curious. Iari thought that curiosity might've gotten him down here, gotten him to agree to Tobin's request, as much as any promise of library access.

Ask if he was regretting that now.

Gaer had gone silent. His head moved in little jerks, responding to sound, to motion. Reminding everyone looking at him that vakari had been (still were) their native biosphere's apex predators, before they'd found arithmancy and literature and art and the stars and become apex predator to the galaxy.

The B-town riev were congregated into a vacant lot that had been a warehouse, before the last surge. The Aedian forces had met the Brood here by the river, turned them back from the city, and in so doing, turned most of the dockside district to cinders and mud and pockmarked eruptions of stone. Commerce had come back, along with the buildings. But *this* place remained vacant. It was almost a pen, a corral—almost, because there was no gate or barrier to keep riev in, or people out. Just a line where the street's pavement ended and packed clay began, and the windowless walls of occupied structures around on three sides.

Iari's neck prickled. It felt like Brood back here, that gut-sense that you learned to trust even when your HUD said *all clear.* That hollow, cold, acid-up-the-back-of-the-throat certainty something was about to go very wrong.

But there were no Brood. Just twenty-odd riev turning their heads in near unison, all looking at Gaer. Eyes and eyestalks and varying sensory structures, all angling toward him. Riev basecode said *protect the Confederation,* and vakari had been a threat before there was ever a Weep.

Iari's heartbeat kicked up and her syn responded: lightning sheeting under her skin, behind her eyes, as the nanomecha in her blood came online. Those nanomecha, in turn, talked through the needle in the base of her skull to the battle-rig on the other side of that needle, and the arms-turing in her right gauntlet began searching targets. She took a deep breath and locked the syn back down. Sent the arms-turing back to standby.

Say hello.

"Hi," she said. "Ah. Good morning, riev."

One of the riev—a big one, built on a tenju frame-core, missing most of a right arm, detached its attention from Gaer. Riev couldn't help but stand straight. This one seemed to draw itself up even straighter as it squared to face her. "Lieutenant. Good morning."

Iari blinked. "Stay here," she told Gaer, and went over to talk to it. Ptah's ungentle regard, but it had seen battle. Its plating was scarred, patched, scuffed in places and worn bright in others. Its artificer had remained faithful to its biological source: its features were tenju, stylized into flat planes and sharp edges. Cheekbones, wide jaw, what were clearly meant to be tusks jutting up from the curve of a lower lip. That kind of artistry marked the riev as old, dating from not long after the wichu's break with the Protectorate. Void and dust, this one might've *really* killed vakari.

But that arm, gentle Mishka, that was Brood damage. It looked like something had snapped the limb off just above the elbow. Big Brood could do that. The ones with the scythes for hands, the ones with the disproportionate jaws. There were deep gouges above the riev's arm-break, the metal blackened, pocked and corroded that way polysteel got when exposed to Brood guts and pure void. That would've been the riev's weapon hand. That wound must've come late in the last wave, or the artificers would've grafted another arm, or grown a replacement from the stump and fused new armor onto that flesh. Instead, they'd capped the damage, a rude patch-weld, and proceeded with its decommission.

End of the surge. Huh. Iari rode a hunch and jabbed her chin at the stump. "Where did that happen?"

There was no expression possible on the riev's features, or in the steady plasma-blue glow of its eyes. But there was something in the deep, machine-sexless voice—coming out of Elements, *somewhere* between throat and mouth, some hidden speaker—that sounded like shame.

"The Saichi peninsula."

Almost ten years ago, give or take a month. Autumn rains giving way to winter sleet. Mud halfway up a battle-rig's knees. Tobin—only a knight-captain then—and a newly commissioned Private Iari and the rest of a unit that was all ghosts now. They'd crossed the Rust to go after one of the Brood generals. Twenty against, well. A lot more than twenty.

Iari blinked the memories back.

"Saichi," she said. "I was there. West rim."

The one-armed riev looked at her. "Southern shelf," it said finally. "Fifth Army, Third Battalion, First Company."

First Company had taken the brunt of the Brood assault. "And the army didn't repair you." Not asking, because void and dust, proof was right there that they hadn't.

The riev took a beat too long to answer. "The objective was achieved. The Confederation won the battle. There was no need for repair."

Iari ground her teeth together. Tobin had said that same thing, *we won*, the one time he'd talked about Saichi with her after everyone else had been—not buried, there hadn't been anything left to bury—but after they'd put up the marker. It had been just the pair of them at the end, once the priests and the families had gone home.

We won.

She'd thought then—sure, call it winning. Tobin's new Knight-Marshal rank on his dress uniform, the long skirt of which hid the casts and the bandages and the hex-and-patch ruin of his hip and thigh. She hadn't had a name for the feeling, then. That hollow, corrosive heat in her chest. An amalgam of grief and anger and a grim satisfaction. This was the job. This was the price for it.

All of that might be beyond riev capacity to feel. Or it might not. Iari lifted her chin and saluted, right fist to left shoulder. Riev had no rank. Didn't *get* salutes. But soldiers did, should, and what else was this riev if not that?

Another silence, for long enough Iari's ears ached. The sun was making some progress on warming the world. It punched a hole through the overcast and cut a blinding swath through the square. Dropped a curtain of watery light behind her and blasted the one-armed riev into harsh relief. Every scar on its armor, every scuff, turned suddenly visible. The Confederate stamp on its breast, almost like a templar's crest. Almost.

Then the clouds reasserted themselves, and the riev lifted that ruined right arm and reached the stump for its left shoulder. "Lieutenant. How may Char serve?"

Iari let her breath go in a plume. Huh. She hadn't supposed riev would have names. Alphanumerics, for easy record-keeping— but names would make more sense on a battlefield, if you had to shout. She wondered if it was the artificers who named them after their forging, or if there was some bureaucratic office of riev name generation. Didn't really matter, though, did it? Riev had names.

"Char," she repeated. "I'm Lieutenant Iari." Templars gave up their surnames, their ties to family. Only Iari. Only Char. "I'd like to ask you some questions, if that's all right."

Char's attitude shifted again, from defense into neutral. Maybe a centimeter's adjustment, a settling up and back. No one asked riev for permission, either. Bet on that.

"Please ask, Lieutenant."

And now what? Void and dust, she hadn't thought this far. Like how you ask, *Which of you ripped a wichu apart last night?*

So start safe, for some value of that word. A question for which she knew the answer, because she could count. "Is this all of the riev who live in B-town?"

"No. Three are not present."

That matched Iari's numbers. "And do you know where they are?"

"Yes. Neru has accepted employment with a caravan which departed this morning to Windscar. Swift Runner has been absent for five days, and Sawtooth has been absent for three. Their locations are unknown."

Two riev unaccounted. Elements defend.

"Do any of you know the artificer Pinjat? Wichu. Workshop in Lowtown."

The back of Iari's neck prickled again, an eyeblink before she heard the riev moving. Converging. Surrounding her in pneumatic whispers of joints worn out of true and the subliminal whine of power cores in want of recalibration.

"We know the artificer Pinjat," said Char. It—no, *they*, because Char had a name, that made them some kind of not-it—seemed like they were about to say something else, but their attention shifted.

"Excuse me. Coming through." Gaer drifted into Iari's periphery. Back and to the left, to leave her weapon arm clear.

"I told you to stay back in the street, didn't I?"

"You did. I chose to ignore you. Odds aren't good for you, surrounded like that."

"Char can remove this vakar." The big riev's voice dropped and softened. "Char would be *happy* to do so."

Iari's heart lurched again. The syn sent plasma-hot fingers along her spine. An offer.

"No. This vakar is"—*a pain in my ass*—"with me. He's an ambassador to Aedis. An ally. Hear me? *Not an enemy.*"

The riev tilted just a little bit back toward Iari. "Understood, Lieutenant."

Iari let a little breath go. "Good. Char, this is Ambassador Gaer i'vakat'i Tarsik. Gaer. This is Char."

"Hello, Char." Gaer had his teeth bared. A vakari greeting. A vakari challenge. Hands conspicuously clear of his weapons, but then, he was an arithmancer. He didn't *need* weapons.

Char said nothing. But Char's remaining hand, which had been curling into a fist, uncurled. "You are Five Tribes."

Gaer drew up, straight and startled. "You read vakari cipher?"

Char did not answer. Their body canted again toward Iari. "Lieutenant. Riev visit artificer Pinjat for repairs. His fees are reasonable."

Repairs. Shame twinged in Iari's chest, and then anger, and then just cold grim. Minor repairs, bet that. Replacing an *arm* would cost, and how hard would it be to earn enough without that arm in the first place? "Did Sawtooth or Swift Runner visit Pinjat recently?"

The riev did not answer. None of them. That creeping dread feeling returned, like the silence had something waiting on the other side, wanting to rip through.

Then Char said, with obvious reluctance, "They did."

"Were they damaged?"

Expecting a yes, which would lead to a query about the sorts of damage, and then—

Except Char did not say *yes*. Instead, Char said, "No," closely followed by, "They were attempting to reacquire Oversight."

You could hear the capital letter. And you could see that Char expected *something* for having used the word. Like they thought Iari would punish them, or, or yell at them. Or something.

Iari felt like an idiot asking, but she hadn't served with riev. Just near them. "What's that? What's Oversight?"

Char turned their head slightly. Then slowly, every word ground out at the lower limit of their volume, "Oversight made riev *we*."

"You don't just mean a common comm channel, do you? You mean an actual *link. Sss.*"

Iari was about to ask what that even meant, but Gaer held up a finger, *hush, wait.*

Vakari faces didn't have much in the way of expression. Plates open, plates closed, nostrils flat or wide, teeth showing or not. The second set of eyelids, once in a great while. Gaer was expressive, for a vakar, always flapping this or flattening that. But now his face was entirely still, classic vakar. His optic winked as he turned to Iari.

"A mystery of the war," he said. "Solved. We always wondered why we couldn't disrupt riev communications. Yours, we could, but never theirs. And that was because they had their own *setatir* network. Probably quantum, linked up to those power cores of yours. Am I right, Char? Was Oversight some kind of quantum hex?"

Void and dust, yes, please, evoke the Expansion in front of riev. Ask them about their own engineering. "Later," she told him.

Whatever Oversight was, the Synod, the Parliament, *someone* had decided riev couldn't keep it. Riev had lost their armaments after decommission, sure, that made sense. But removing their communication network seemed . . . cruel. Or paranoid. Oversight, capital O, was something like wartime weaponry. Something dangerous. Something proof against arithmancy. Or something that, without small-o oversight, might be dangerous. Riev as we. Riev moving together. Collective intelligence, maybe.

And whatever the case: "I don't care about that," she told Char. "Whatever Swift Runner and Sawtooth were trying to do with Oversight and Pinjat. I just need to know where they might be now. The artificer was murdered last night, and it looks like a riev did it."

She paused, waiting for a protest. *Riev couldn't. Riev don't.* A chorus of *no*, or *that is impossible* or whatever passed for strenuous objections among beings whose basecode discouraged complaint. Instead, silence. Stillness.

"I need your help. I need—" Iari pivoted on her heel. "Any information you have. I can ask the Aedis for compensation, usual rates, whatever you usually ask for."

A ripple passed through the riev. Then one of the smaller scout-class models worked their way through the ranks, came and stood beside Char. The artificers had replaced the top of their skull with an array of flexible sensor stalks that waved a little bit like grass in a breeze, if grass were a deep pewter-black. Half of the array aimed at Iari's face, the other half drooped and dipped in what felt a lot like a once-over.

"Lieutenant," the riev said. "This one is Brisk Array. Swift Runner finds regular employment in the deep Warren. Two days ago, Swift Runner asked Sawtooth to go with them. Brisk Array saw Swift Runner and Sawtooth meet with an alw."

"An alw! Well. There aren't many of *those* in B-town, are there?"

"Gaer. Shut it.—Could you identify that alw again, Brisk Array?"

"Yes."

"Then—"

"Wait, now." Gaer put a hand out. "Did Pinjat *succeed* in restoring Oversight?"

"Gaer. That doesn't matter."

"It does." Gaer turned to look at her. Tilted his head in the direction of all the riev. "If they're on a network, they could be talking right now."

"There is no Oversight." Char's voice deepened, slowed. Sounded both thoughtful and condemnatory at once.

"Thank you." Iari shot a *shut up* look at Gaer. "Brisk Array. Will you show us where you saw Swift Runner and Sawtooth meet the alw?"

"Yes."

"Iari." Gaer leaned over and put his mouth near her ear. "That's all very fascinating. But it might be good to know *where* Brisk Array wants to take us, before we commit to going. There are parts of this city where I'm, ah, even *less* welcome."

She resisted an urge to prod him back with her elbow. Ducked her shoulder instead, and turned her head to make eyelock. "Parts where I am, too. And probably that's where we're going."

"There are *two* of us."

"And Brisk Array to lead us. So three. You're rigged and armed. So'm I."

Elements, the look on his face. Every orifice clamped down until she wondered how the hell he was breathing at all. His chromatophores had turned almost black. "Against a possible *two* riev who have already killed someone. Perhaps we could even those odds."

All right. Point. Iari pivoted back to Char. "Will you accompany us? A request, Char. Not an order."

Char took a careful step. The ruined left arm drifted up. "Lieutenant. I am—"

"A veteran of Saichi. Yeah. So you said." She wondered what it'd cost to get that arm repaired. If there were mecha parts back in the Aedis, or if Tobin knew where to find an artificer licensed for riev repair. "Will you come with us?"

The riev hesitated. Then, "Yes, Lieutenant."

"Good. Then Brisk Array, you've got point. Let's go."

CHAPTER FOUR

Gaer opened his mouth, vented his plates, and got a taste of the Lowtown air, which was tabac smoke and urine from at least two species and vomit from three and an eddy of rotting fish off the river. He kept his gaze on the glassless, shutterless holes in the walls that masqueraded as windows in this derelict canyon of buildings. There were people up there. The ambient aura glowed red orange, like embers. Like a fire just waiting to happen. Or a rain of jacta bolts.

"You might've been right," Iari muttered. "About coming down here."

"So we turn around now."

"No."

Of course, *no*. Iari had a void-be-damned mission. The street—an alley, really, clearly an artifact of B-town's rustic origins before, oh, pavement—was empty, except for him, Iari, the riev.

"It's too quiet," she said. "Middle of a workday. Where *is* everyone?"

Movement flickered at the next corner. Gaer got a glimpse of someone's foot and leg as that someone darted across the intersection. "They're avoiding us."

"The gangs don't run from the templars. Or the PKs. Or *anyone*. This is their district."

"If you want me to say, *then it must be a renegade riev making them run*, I'm saying it."

"What do you see?"

He cocked his head, got her square in his optic. "A tenju templar." With remarkable eyes. The color of strong tea, and clear, flecked with gold near the pupil.

Those eyes narrowed into viridian slits. "Funny. I mean auras."

"I know what you mean. *You* are a little worried. *They*—" He whipped a glance forward, at Brisk Array. "Seem unconcerned. The other one—" He glanced over his shoulder at Char. Blinked.

Riev auras had a greyness to them, all the colors bleached and muted. That had to do with their levels of cross-contamination, how much metal and artifice had permeated their (dead) organic core. Char was the brightest riev Gaer had scanned. Almost alive in their vibrancy.

"Also worried." He resisted the urge to reach up and reboot his optic. It was fine. It was Char who was different. And, more importantly, "All the auras I can see—and there are quite a few, glowing up behind those windows—are hostile."

Iari cut him a sharp glance. "Huh."

They reached the crossroad. Brisk Array paused, as if reorienting, then turned right and starting walking again.

Gaer pitched his voice to the edge of audible. "Are you *sure* about our guide? *If* there are compromised riev, they could be one of them and we're following them into a trap."

"Thought of that." Iari's gaze scaled the walls, skipped over the broken teeth of blank windows. She nudged Gaer toward the center of the street, fingertips of her left gauntlet just touching his elbow above the spikes. "That's why Char's with us."

The one-armed riev, veteran of—what had Iari said? Saichi. The name sounded familiar. Somewhere local to Tanis. Gaer had a skull-full of vakari war stories, battles and generals and victories and oh, yes, so *many* defeats. This Saichi was not among those stories. It must be a strictly Confederate event, and of sufficient import that Iari trusted Char on the strength of that name alone.

Iari took her hand away. Gaer watched her fingers flex. His optic showed him the ripple of shield-hexes on the gauntlet. A templar's battle-rig was a marvel of arithmancy and alchemy. Unorthodox by vakari standards, but effective.

An alarm flashed in the top edge of Gaer's optic. He'd set the display for auras, expecting, well, to see *auras*. But the passive scan had caught something else, something it read as a battle-hex. He cycled the display.

And there in the middle of the *setatir* street was a battle-hex, all right, and one Gaer recognized (any vakar trooper would). Roughly a meter square, intricate glyph-work, glowing bright about the filth of the not-really-pavement. And Brisk Array was about to walk into it.

"Wait," he said. "Stop—"

Brisk Array's foot came down. Lightning sheeted out from that point of contact, spread to the glyph's limits and lit their frame white and blinding. Lightning climbed Brisk Array, too, like electromagnetic vines. White light, that Gaer could see with both eyes, as well as wavelengths he could see only with the optic.

Brisk Array shuddered. The trap's charge wasn't quite enough to take the riev offline, but Gaer guessed they wouldn't be moving far until their systems recovered.

Alwar materialized from the shadows, ranged themselves across the width of the street. A gang, clearly. Five, by Gaer's count, armed with sidearm jactae and *maybe* some gutter-trained arithmancer. The one on the far left was wiggling fingers like she thought that was necessary to throw a hex.

Iari made a fist of her left hand and deployed her shield. White-fire edges, blinding bright, the center muted and tinted Aedian red.

The alw in the center, clearly the leader, raised empty hands. "Templar. Our fight's not with you. Or the veek."

Gaer could *hear* Iari's eyebrows go up. Her hand came down on the axe. Not drawing it yet. "Gaer, get that trap off *our* riev. Char. Make sure no one interferes with him."

Five pairs of beady little alwar eyes landed on Gaer. His heart kicked against his ribs. He bared his teeth, the vakari way to say *hello, I'm about to kill you.*

"Yes, Lieutenant." Char stomped forward. The line of alwar wobbled, bending back from the leader, who stood like his boots had fused to the pavement. That was, Gaer thought, because the little neefa-shit couldn't see auras. Char was all reds and purples and almost as bright as Iari. *Please, dear dark lords, let that riev remember he was an ally when they started smashing people.*

Gaer blinked the optic's setting from passive to active scan as he edged up to the trap. The auras winked out. Plain angry riev, plain angry templar, plain nervous alwar. The trap's perimeter blazed into view. It was already starting to spark, would come down on its own soon enough in ten, twenty seconds. He squinted through the plasma-glare at the hexes themselves. The trap wasn't military issue; these hexes weren't vakari work. But it was a good forgery, good enough to stop a decommed riev. Although. Gaer glanced at Char. Might be a fortunate thing that the trap had gone off on Brisk Array. He didn't think it would've held Char, even *with* Char's damaged hexwork.

"Well?" Iari said.

"A moment, Lieutenant." He made a show of flaring his jaw-plates. He lifted his right hand and pointed at the glowing hex. Counted down, in his head, as the hexes unraveled, and at the last heartbeat, curled his fingers into a fist.

The trap died. Brisk Array, caught in mid-step, slammed their foot down and made a noise not unlike water on hot metal.

Two red-auraed riev within arm's reach. This just wasn't safe.

Something on the ganglord's face said he'd just realized the same thing. He retreated a step.

"Templar—"

"My rank's lieutenant," Iari said gently. "And that trap's illegal. Way I see it, I can arrest you and take you up to the Aedis for questioning, or you can cooperate and answer a few questions here. You choose."

The ganglord slapped a sneer on his face as if he'd just put on a mask. Stiff. Unconvincing. "Not your business, where I got it. Self-defense isn't illegal."

You had to admire that kind of audacity. You just didn't want to be standing near it.

Iari lifted the left corner of her mouth, revealing the capped tusk. Dull metal, brushed and muted, meant to absorb light so it didn't draw attention. Funny. Everyone's eyes always went straight to it anyway. "That wasn't my question. Right now I don't care where you got it. I want to know about riev. Might be one of them came down here last night from Hightown. Late. Might've been bloody. You see something like that?"

The alw closest to the ganglord—female, a little round in the gut, with a face that'd rival a tenju for ugly—turned and said something in a rapid street-cant Gaer couldn't understand. The tone was clear enough, though. Ugly wasn't happy.

The ganglord held up a finger, and Ugly shut up. His sneer settled, made itself at home. "You're asking about who killed the artificer, templar, then you want Tzcansi."

"Tzcansi." Iari tried out the syllables.

"That is not a riev designation," said Char.

The alw puffed up a little. "Tzcansi's a *person*."

Iari stared at the ganglord. "Rival gang leader, maybe. You trying to get me to settle a turf war for you?"

The leader's sneer slipped. "No. I'm telling you, Lieutenant, no
lie. Tzcansi's the one who killed the artificer. Or *had* him killed,
you know what I mean. She's been expanding." He thrust his chin
at the riev. "Used *them* to do it. That's *why* we need traps. *Them*
running around. Used to be gang muscle was *people*."

"Gaer."

He flipped the optic's setting. The alw bloomed into a palette
of yellows and anemic blues. "He's sincere that he wants you to go
after this Tzcansi, and sincere in his belief she is responsible, *and*
sincere in his fear of riev."

The alw bared his teeth. "Not *afraid* of them, veek."

"*Setat* you're not."

"Thank you, Gaer." Iari raked the ganglord head to heels, wearing a face like she wasn't sure she liked what she saw. "Huh. And
where would I find this Tzcansi, then?"

The alw pointed. "That way. When you get to the fountain,
you're in her territory. Ask there. Someone'll know."

"Brisk Array. That the direction you saw Sawtooth going?"

A fistful of eyestalks inclined the direction the ganglord had
said. The rest pointed at Iari. "Yes, Lieutenant."

"All right, then that's where *we're* going."

The alw turned an unhealthy shade. "You can't take *them* with you. You'll end up like that artificer and Tczansi'll have two more of *them* on her side." He stabbed eyes at Gaer. "Last thing we need, 'specially now I'm down a trap."

Iari stared hard at the alw, like she could see into his skull. She could, Gaer thought, if she'd just use the axe. But she turned to Brisk Array and Char instead.

"I'll take point with Gaer. You two stay behind us. Come on."

"That's neefa-shit," Gaer said, when they'd gotten another fifty meters down the street, well clear of alwar earshot. "There's no arithmancy that can hack riev. If there was, my people would have figured it out already."

Iari side-eyed him. She twisted her wrist, and the shield disappeared in a breath of ozone. "Maybe one of you did. Vakari arithmancy gave us the Weep."

Gave was the wrong word. *Misfired* was more accurate. An arithmantic attempt to turn back Confederate forces, to end a war the Protectorate was losing: the best arithmancers working together, feeding their hexes through quantum-linked turings across the whole Protectorate front line, trying to disappear the Confederate fleet into the void. A simultaneous working, momentous, ambitious. Ultimately disastrous.

"*Protectorate* arithmancy," Gaer said primly. "And no vakar on either side ever cracked riev artificing."

"Someone has." Her tone said *shut up, enough*. She had infinite patience with him until she just didn't, and he'd learned, after almost a year of association, when to stop pushing.

The fountain was just up ahead, partly visible around a curve in the street. (No one built anything *straight* in this place, it was maddening.) Gaer got a mouth-and-noseful of humidity, heard the faint spatter of running water. Heard voices, too, for the first time.

A buzz of Comspek and Dwerig, the most common alwar dialect, in varying pitches and volumes. Normal, in other words, in a day that had been anything but.

Gaer traded a look with Iari. She thrust her arm out like a bar, *keep back*, and slowed down. It was Iari's right side, her weapon side. There were scuffs on the gauntlet. Gouges on the forearm that'd been polished, you could see that, to disguise the worst of the blemishes. A line of scoring jumped from forearm to chest, ran the breadth of her on a diagonal up to the left shoulder. Two not-quite-parallel lines, patched at the shoulder joint where something had punched through the plating.

No, not *something*. Brood had done that. Brood effluvia (all Brood fluids had the same composition and effects, whether they came out of orifices or injuries) had discolored the rig there and there, too, streaked the armor's dull black with swirls of pink and green, like an oilslick burned into the alloy.

"Gaer." She was looking at him, frowning a query. "You see anything?"

He brushed her frown aside, hid his own scowl in a head-tilted squint through his optic. "There's . . . something here. Not exactly a barrier, but." He blinked. "Check your visor. Maybe your Aedian unorthodoxy will see something I don't."

Her mouth stretched and flattened, baring the upthrust islands of her tusks. Iari tended to carry her jaw pulled back, the artifact of what had clearly been some attempt to minimize her tusks behind her lips and pass as what, human? Those tusks were still as visible and as obvious as her nose and her eyes and those wide flat wedges of cartilage she called ears on the side of her head.

This particular twist of her mouth was a grimace, differentiated from a grin only by the narrowness of her eyes. Then the helmet's visor deployed in a soundless slide. Gaer was left looking at himself reflected in featureless black. Not much of a reflection—the alloy, like the cap on Iari's broken tusk, was meant to absorb light. But he did see a hint of his own brow ridge and jaw-plate and the rectangular glow of his optic, faint blue-white and translucent.

That same optic showed him the dusting of hexes along the helmet's seams. Aedian glyphs, which Iari would call *blessings*. To Gaer, they were proof against Elemental incursion: plasma, liquid, aether, solids. Proof against void, too, in short bursts, though this particular rig didn't carry a rebreather. Most Brood needed atmosphere as much as any other organic. Brood who swam the void, well, you met those in ships, because they were too big for planets (unless you were on a planet where the Weep had opened, and then you met those Brood and died.)

And *why* was he thinking of Brood now? The closest tangible danger was nervous Confederate citizens, mostly alwar in this district, whose pointed features of various pigments peered from doorways and windows with more open dismay (their auras yellow and orange, mostly, shot through with pinks) than the gang had done. Well, of course there was dismay. How many of them had seen a vakar before, except in a vidcast, or as the villain of some third-rate drama?

Except. *Look*, you *setatir* idiot, don't assume. Arithmancy revealed auras. It didn't diagnose causes. That was a task for eyes and brains and sentient judgment. And the sightlines of those peering alwar aimed mostly at Brisk Array and Char. So.

"Gaer." Iari's voice leaked out her rig's external comms, all the usual rough depth squeezed flat and thin. "Get your visor down. I need reads on all the auras in the area, and anything else arithmantic. Don't want to walk into another hex."

He did as she asked with a cold twist in his chest. His optic, sensing its arithmantic superior in his faceplate's hexwork, switched to transparent standby. His HUD bloomed into a border of status reports. His biometrics, rig integrity, a whole spectrum of electromagnetic feedback. The ubiquitous hex-scans, which flashed pure alarm at the number and disposition of riev in proximity.

And his rig comms, which flashed *incoming transmission, accept y/n* in the lower left.

"Yes," he murmured. Iari wouldn't have to speak to *her* rig comms to activate them. It was a matter of Aedian heresy: that needle-socket in her spine, the implants, the nanomecha permeating her body that linked biology to machine and made the battle-rig an extension of her nervous system. A synthesis. *Syn.*

The idea of machines inside his skin was revolting, horrific, rather eat spoiled meat than *do* such a thing. But void and dust, the convenience of that connection. Gaer made a face Iari wouldn't be able to see behind his faceplate, and molded his voice to match. "I know why you people won the Expansion war."

"Yeah. Because the Five Tribes split off from the Protectorate, which interrupted the Expansion and allowed the wichu to defect and bring us the riev. Listen. What're you seeing, for hexes? Because my rig thinks there's major arithmancy around here, except *not* arithmancy."

"What does that even mean?"

"It means my HUD's lit like the Double Moon Festival without any directional indicators."

"My rig's more upset by the nearness of two riev." One very large, flashing frame on his HUD, and his arms-turing trying to come online and acquire targets.

"Fantastic. Big help. Thanks." Iari thrust her faceplate back toward the fountain. Lowered her arm and began walking again. Hands open, loose, but not swinging.

Whatever normalcy was happening in the fountain stopped

the instant two battle-rigs and two riev came walking up. Conversations stopped mid-syllable. Faces turned like anxious flowers to a capricious sun. It was good, Gaer realized, that he'd lowered his visor. The optic did fine for general reading, even detail for a single subject, but it didn't have the processor to handle this volume and detail.

And oh, there was a full spectrum of auras sparkling through the fountain square. Curiosity—from children, mostly. From adults, the expected suspicion, the expected hostility. Fear, sunbright-yellow, when eyes passed over the riev. But then they saw Iari, marked the Aedian battle-rig, and the auras splintered bright blue with hope. And that hope lingered, despite his own presence. Despite the riev.

It was a surprising thing, no matter how often he saw it, the trust and *faith* the bulk of the Confederate citizenry had in the Aedis. How Iari could walk under all that weight defied reason.

"They're remarkably happy to see you."

"Huh. Can you tell why?"

"Not from their auras. But at a guess, I'd say they expect you to save them from something."

He couldn't see through her visor any more than she could see through his. But he sensed the look she cast at him. Felt it, punching through armor, scorching the side of his face.

"Then let's see if they'll tell us what I'm supposed to save them from." Iari pivoted neatly and aimed at the fountain and a cluster of citizens—alwar, mostly, but there was a tenju street vendor selling something formerly living, now thoroughly charred, from a handcart whose phlogiston tank needed adjustment. Gaer's HUD told him the parts-per-million on the exhaust were above safe regulation, and being heavier than aether, those particles weren't dispersing neatly.

"Iari," he said. "Avoid sparks."

"Huh."

He rolled his eyes and trailed after her. *Yes, of course, Gaer, I understand* would be too many syllables. And he said aloud, softly, trusting the riev's audio feeds: "Don't do anything flammable. There's a phlogiston leak."

"Acknowledged," Char said, in a surprisingly quiet voice. He looked at them, startled. The big one-armed riev was holding position, scanning the crowd, the square. Presumably surrounding buildings, too. Brisk Array stood in their shadow, eyestalks waving like wheat in a summer breeze.

Splinters of hope and expectation or not, the food vendor's customers weren't sticking around. The last one snatched up her flat-bread-and-dead-thing roll and darted sideways, leaving the vendor alone with her cart and her leaky tank. Gaer noted the pair of monofils hanging from her belt, one of which might be within legal regs for civilian, but probably wasn't.

Iari's rig hissed and her visor snapped up. The vendor jerked, surprised. Then she straightened. The vendor had much bigger tusks than Iari's, much sharper, jutting out of her block of a lower jaw. Buttery-pale skin, contrast to Iari's sepia-dark.

"Help you?"

"Hope so. I'm Lieutenant Iari. Need to ask you a couple questions. That okay?"

The vendor shrugged. "Ask."

"You know the name Tzcansi?"

"Know *of* her." The vendor shifted back on her heels. She looked at Gaer again, then past him. *Not* at the riev, he realized; they were still behind him, back the direction they'd come. She didn't offer her name. "Why?"

Iari's aura bristled with scarlet. Her tone stayed steady. "What can you tell me?"

"Not much. She's not someone you mess with. Alw, you know? Not my problem."

"Oh. I think she is. I think she's this whole neighborhood's problem. It's her territory, isn't it?" Iari propped a casual elbow on the edge of the cart. Pretended great interest in the rack of roasting meat. "She's got you scared. This little alw."

Gaer rolled his eyes. It was a baldly obvious jibe. The Aedis made a very public deal about inclusivity and equality and strength coming from difference. Legally, that held true. *Socially*, well. That was another matter. All the old inter-species prejudices were alive and well.

The tenju's aura fractured into bands of red and violet, with a band of lingering, sickly yellow. Physically, she stiffened and thrust out her lower jaw like a weapon. Flat-footed, wearing no armor, she was eye-level with Iari, and equally as broad without the *setatir* rig.

Iari stared back, unblinking, impassive, and the vendor's eyes skated sideways. They landed on Gaer and burned, having no easier target. "She's got riev working for her. So *yeah*, she scares me. You cross her, you end up—" The tenju shook her head. "Never mind."

"Smeared all over a broken shopfront?" Gaer interjected.

The tenju curled her lip. "Something like."

"You seen very many of those? People smeared on shopfronts?"

"Couple. Davan's bar, just down there. This one ganglord, *his* house, couple streets over. Maybe some others."

"When did this start? Tzcansi enforcing with riev."

"Maybe three weeks ago. A little less."

"And you never reported it?"

The tenju twitched a shoulder. "Davan did, to the PKs, after Tzcansi smashed up the ganglord. You want to see how *that* turned out for him, go look at his pub. No one's cleaned it up yet. Tzcansi said leave it. It's a message."

Iari leaned forward. "I find her, that neefa-shit stops. Help me do that."

And there, that splinter of blue hope again, stabbing bright through the food-vendor's aura. She made her hands busy on the cart, moving meat, rolling it. She laid a set of fresh raw strips on the rack. Leaned forward, and said through the burst of smoke and fresh sizzling: "I don't know where Tzcansi is. Swear that, Lieutenant."

"Then tell me where Davan's place was."

"You want to see it, just keep walking. It's up the next street. You won't miss it."

The vendor wadded a strip of meat and flatbread together, thrust it at Iari. "Take that. Take one for the vakar, too. Walk with the Elements."

She kicked the cart's wheels, disengaging the brakes. Then she shoved it hard, so that Iari had to sidestep or be hit. The cart jolted over the cracked pavement.

Iari watched her go. Then she sauntered over to Gaer and offered a meat-roll.

"Got us lunch. Eat it. Be polite."

Gaer took the roll. Retracted his visor. Ate the roll in two unsavory bites and thanked his ancestors for an evolutionary legacy of eating things mostly whole. Iari was forced to chew.

"PKs know about this Tzcansi person, and they don't do anything," she said, between mouthfuls. "Those neefa-shits."

Gaer nostril-hissed disapproval. "Maybe they're taking bribes."

"No maybes." Iari stuffed the rest of the roll into her mouth and frowned at the grease on her gauntleted fingers. Her gaze unfocused a little. Doing something with the rig, no doubt, through that unholy connection. "Huh. My long-range comms are down. Try yours."

Gaer did. Once, twice, *setatir* error message. *No signal. No signal.* He tried rig-to-rig. "You copy?"

Her rig crackled obediently. Iari frowned at him. "Yes," echoed in his helmet, match to the word coming out of her lips.

"Right. Well. I've got no long-range, either." It wasn't unusual. He knew that, and still his gut coiled and dropped. "What about the riev? Can they—?"

"Negative," said Char, at the same time Iari said, "No."

They looked at each other, riev and templar. Then Iari said, slowly, "When the riev were decommed, their transmitters were removed."

Gaer noted that Iari hadn't named a single agent in that sentence, which meant there was a someone, or someones, behind the decision to rip out riev-comms, and Iari's opinion of those someone(s) wasn't Aedian-protocol-polite. He wondered what she thought about Oversight's removal. Probably didn't approve of it, either.

"What about all the warning lights on your HUD?"

Iari pressed her lips in a line. "Still there."

"Are they, oh, *worse?*"

"No." Her aura sparkled chartreuse. Oh, that was a rarity. Iari, undecided.

Or lying.

She gazed narrow-eyed at the riev. Then: "Let's keep going."

"Iari." He thrust out his own arm, not quite a grab. "Look at these streets. This is the perfect place for an ambush."

"Yeah."

Look at her aura. All that brightness. "That's what you're hoping for. Void and *dust*."

She looked at him with a vintage blend of exasperation and pity. "Gaer, what did you think I was coming down here to do?"

"Investigate. Gather evidence. That's what Tobin thinks you're doing."

Half a smile. "No, he doesn't. He sent me down here to use my discretion."

CHAPTER FIVE ═══════

Yeah, the vendor hadn't been wrong. The ruined tavern was obvious: a rotting tooth in a jagged smile of weatherworn wooden storefronts. The cracked sign that dangled from two of its four bolts spelled out *Davan's Brew and Chew* in Comspek and Dwerig and broken teslas. The door itself was missing in action. Iari put a tentative hand on the doorframe. The top layer of wood smeared away onto her gauntlet. The wood itself seemed pretty solid, though. The fire must not have burned too long, or too hot.

"That's a terrible name." Gaer was hanging back by the riev, like he'd decided they weren't as dangerous as whatever might be inside. Well. He might not be wrong.

"Yeah," she said, because Gaer expected some kind of response. Probably needed it. "You see anything?"

"Damage. No hexes."

"Right. Stay behind me."

Iari poked her head inside. The helmet sensed the change in the ambient light and turned on the headlamp. It was a narrow space, close-ceilinged. It had been cramped, once, crowded with tables and chairs. Now it was scattered shards of wood and slivers of polymer. The bar took up most of the width of the place. There were swing-doors behind it, leading into what must be a store-room. Those doors sagged on their hinges, mostly intact. There might be stairs back there, too, to the level below. Sixty years ago, there'd been a massive flood in B-town when the Weep fissure had opened. The Rust had jumped its banks, torn its bed loose and brought it along, filling the streets of Lowtown with three meters of mud. The priests of Chaama had offered to help clean it up, but moving that much earth took time, and most of surviving Lowtown had decided to build new doors on the second level.

Iari slid a foot inside, tested the floor. Real wood plank, probably old. Maybe pre-flood. It *seemed* stable enough, but—

She stuck her head back outside. "Char. Brisk Array. You stay out here. Floor's rotting."

Brisk Array's eyestalks rippled. "Yes, Lieutenant."

Char, however, took a half step toward Iari (and startled Gaer, who flinched aside and out of their way).

"Lieutenant." Char sounded . . . terse. "It is unsafe."

"The floor, yeah. I'm not sure it'll take your weight."

"Char does not mean the floor." Riev didn't—weren't supposed to—argue. Truth, Iari's personal experience of riev was limited to her two years of army service, and even then, it'd been only circumstantial. The Aedis didn't use riev, and she'd never had cause to hire one, and none of that mattered, because Char (big, *massive* Char) was clearly unhappy.

So, "Why? You sensing something?"

Char hesitated. "There is something wrong in that place, but there is no data to support that assumption."

"Oh, void and dust." Gaer stared at Char. "A hunch. The riev is having a *hunch*."

Iari ignored him. "What kind of something? Can you be more specific?"

Char shifted their attention past Iari, like they could see in the dark. Probably could, for that matter, the whole spectrum, with those artificed eyes. "No, Lieutenant."

"All right," Gaer said. "*Now* can we leave? The *setatir* riev is spooked."

"Spooked." Char tried out the word. "That word is adequate to describe this discomfort."

"Understood." Iari's scalp prickled. Well, now she was spooked, too. She resealed her faceplate. The hex-warnings blinked on her HUD's perimeter: unspecified, still, but persistent. Sometimes that happened in proximity to a Weep fissure, when the Weep bled contaminants into the aether. Sometimes it happened near Brood, for the same reason. And sometimes it meant hostile arithmancy at work.

The nearest fissure was well out of range. No Brood.

But Char was spooked. Iari unclipped her axe-shaft and balanced it in her palm. The rig's arms-turing came online, sent a little jolt through the needle-socket at the base of her neck. The syn was ready. A single instant's intent, a jump from nanomecha to rig, and the axeblade would deploy.

"Gaer? I could use you. Take a look."

Vakari rig headlamps were bluer than their Aedian counterparts. Where Iari's light brushed over things, Gaer's stabbed, blasting details into sharp relief, making darker shadows.

"Door was bashed in. Scorch patterns on the floor make it look like the fire started in the middle of the floor. Are you asking me if I see any organic remains? Because I don't. Only traces."

"Anything left after the fire would've gone to rats by now."

"Sss. Thank you for that image. Then why am I in here?"

Iari prodded a broken chair with the axe shaft. "I want to know how this fire started. There should've been protective hexes."

"So let us assume there were not, or someone got through them." Gaer folded his legs into a crouch and nudged the rubble aside with the muzzle of his jacta. "I don't see any lingering hex-work. However, I do see traces of phlogiston, so I'm guessing conventional explosives. A small bomb could produce this kind of damage. Or a group of large, angry tenju with rags stuffed into bottles of flammable liquid. Or a riev, armed with the same. Although that seems like overkill."

"*Setat.*" Iari tried out the vakari expletive. Satisfying collection of sibilants. Easy to see why Gaer overused it.

"Your accent's improving. Yes. *Setat.* Though I'm not sure why angry tenju are more distressing to you than rampaging riev."

"First, because Yinal'i'ljat didn't mention anything hitting Pinjat's place except a single riev, and that looked . . . well. Like a riev tore the place up. This looks more, what, conventional? More like a gang war than an assassination." Iari moved another few steps into the pub. "If Tzcansi's responsible for Pinjat *and* this place, why not just burn them both with the same materials? Or have the riev trash them both the same way?"

"Assuming our single eyewitness wasn't lying—"

"Why would she?"

"Because she's wichu." Gaer's voice shifted into that breathiness that meant both jaw-plates flared, teeth bared. No love between wichu and vakari; that grudge was older than the Accords, the Schism, the Expansion that'd started it all. "But assume that she's telling the truth. Pinjat was an artificer, and that means he would've had protective hexes over every centimeter to protect against Elemental damage. Presumably he'd've gotten those hexes from *you*. Or not you personally, but—" Gaer waved a hand, three fingers, one thumb, too many joints. "Your Aedian priests, since they are the Elemental experts. So he'd've had the very best. Some little burning rag in a bottle wouldn't destroy his shop. Whitefire's about the only thing that would."

Void and dust, his prejudices. "Not every wichu works for the Aedis."

"No. But all artificers are wichu, which means they've all worked for the Confederation during the war, which includes doing work for the Aedis, and I am reasonably certain that association entitles those artificers to a level of benefits most people won't get. Think a more inclusively plural *you*." Gaer drifted back toward the front door. "This place didn't need whitefire to burn. Pinjat's workshop did. Where's it say a ganglord has to use the same method twice?"

"Nowhere. But people have habits. Seems to me Tzcansi's are changing. She's getting more serious, if she's going from phlogiston to whitefire."

"Yes. Now she's arming her murderous riev with better weapons and sending them into the nicer parts of town. She might go for the Aedis next."

Ungentle Ptah. There was a thought.

"Let her try." Iari leaned around the bar. Broken glass sparkled like frost under her lamp. Every bottle on the shelves had come down, along with most of the shelves. Wood. Glass. Polymer. A jacta, short-barreled and five kinds of illegal, its muzzle bent like a big hand had grabbed and squeezed, lay on the top of the pile. Davan had fought back, then. Hadn't done him much good.

Iari passed her headlamp over the walls. A cheap knock-off print of Gock's "Nightflower" hung askew, the frame cracked, but no sign of burning. The fire was remarkably well-behaved, to confine itself to the room's center. Iari was turning away when she noticed a hole in the wall beside the painting. A particular discoloration around the edges. Looked very much like someone's head had gone through the plaster there. The reddish-dark stains on the paint seemed to support that assumption.

A templar's rig was designed for basic scan-and-identify. Hazmat, mostly: excess phlogiston, radiation leaks, toxic alchemical compounds. You didn't want to put a foot into a puddle of corrosives or walk into a fire too hot for the rig's shielding. The panoply of warning lights on the HUD had been all for conventional alerts. But as Iari got close to the wall, the whole HUD redshifted, so that it felt like looking through blood.

There were two reasons a HUD would do that. A suit-breach in void, which this wasn't, or:

"Gaer. I'm picking up Brood emissions."

Gaer sputtered shards of High Sisstish in which *setat* figured heavily. But he didn't challenge her. He'd argue the color of the sky, or the wetness of water, but not whether an Aedian templar knew when to call Brood.

"Stay back," Iari said, and deployed the shield in her left gauntlet. It would turn solid projectiles, whitefire, battle-hexes, some of the lesser Brood. Which, please Ptah, there weren't any of in here. In this pub. In B-town at all.

Except the HUD *said* Brood, and so there were. Take that with the same faith as Ptah's very existence.

Iari moved forward. Brood didn't like daylight. They were probably hiding in the storeroom behind those saggy swing doors. Her arms-turing tried and failed to get a lock on the Brood. That didn't worry her. It'd happened before, Hrok's breath, it happened most of the time when you found Brood. You told recruits that, they never believed you. You survived your first few encounters, you stopped worrying about it.

She deployed her axe in a shimmer of whitefire. It was hexed *especially* for Brood, who could warp honest physics out of true and send a jacta bolt skewing into an ally, or make it explode inside the weapon. The axe relied on muscle and aim. And proximity.

She stayed close to the wall to minimize herself as a target and poked the right-side door open with the tip of one boot. The back room was an extension of the front: maybe three meters long, made narrower by stacks of boxes propped on each other and all available walls. Some of those boxes had come down, shattered, spread their broken, seeping guts across the floor. The door to the back alley was still closed, intact and poorly sealed. A thin strip of light leaked along the seams.

The arms-turing began finding targets, marking them on the HUD. Small shapes. Brood swarm.

Oh, ungentle Ptah.

Her syn responded to the surge in her heart rate. Tingling like electricity in her spine, down her limbs. All those little nanomecha, coming online and waiting for her trigger.

"Counting ten or so swarm inside," she told Gaer. "I'm going in."

"Copy." All business now, Gaer. "On your six."

A pause, a breath. Then she eased over the threshold.

The first Brood peeled itself off the ceiling. It dangled, three sides loose: a boneless, vaguely trapezoidal mass of what looked like gelatin. It had legs, about a thousand of them, very small, very hooked. *Very* sharp. A priest she'd known once, half-alw named Mikanasan, told her that the shape of those legs was more reminiscent of teeth than locomotive limbs, designed to sweep food into the orifice on the belly. More like cilia, Mikanasan had said. Like, like *teeth-legs*.

Iari aimed for the center of those teeth-legs and struck.

The edge of the axe blade threw purplish sparks when it touched Brood-skin. Iari knew from unvisored experience that there was smoke curling up from the contact point. This particular sort of Brood was flammable.

And there, yes: three-point-five seconds of contact. The swarm burst into flame—

Thank you, Ptah.

—and fell the rest of the way to the floor in a flickering bundle of don't-ask-what.

The ceiling rippled. The sides of the shelves. Moving, all moving.

She had time to trigger the syn—the searing rush of nanomecha along the length of her spine, through her muscles, into what felt like every cell, and then back through the needle and into the rig, a faster-than-thought link between armor and body—before the swarm swooped at her.

She flung the shield up, slinging swarm aside, keeping them *off*. They clung to the shield, all those teeth-legs trying for purchase on battle-hexed whitefire and sparking, burning, *smoking*. Too many to hold, too many to cut, *but—*

The crate nearest to her had a shipping label which featured a logo for a local distillery. Please, Hrok, Lord of Aether, let that not be an empty crate.

Iari planted a foot and swung the axe low. Whitefire could make a surgical cut, smooth, easy, slice the crate in half and leave it standing. She wanted a little better than that. Put force behind the swing, dragging the blade through the crate's polymer, through its contents, a list of which marched up one side of her HUD, tiny letters greyed to be more easily ignored unless the blade touched something reactive.

Like, oh, alwar whiskey.

The crate crumpled. Smoke curled behind the blade, then the first licking of fire.

"Go left," Gaer said suddenly into her helmet, and, "Stay low."

Iari dropped, crouched and pivoted, as beams of bright not-quite-white light speared past her, over her. Sunlight, that was *sunlight*, bent and focused by arithmancy into lethal beams that Gaer wielded with a sniper's accuracy. He cut a swath across a shelf on the far end of the back room, nearest the door.

More swarm erupted from dark corners, flapping. *Burning*, adding to the light in the room, adding to Gaer's ammunition. He built a lattice of beams ever more fine, more focused, searing whatever they touched.

Polymer. Swarm. Flammable liquids. Wooden walls.

Gentle Mishka, Gaer was going to bring the whole place down on her. Except Gaer was a skilled arithmancer, and this lattice-light show was her cover.

So she used it.

Iari bulled into the room and smashed her shield against one of those walls. Swarm had no skeletons, they didn't break, but they could (did) rupture in little sparkling bursts of corrosive liquid that chewed past the hex-shields and left little smoking pits on her armor.

She pivoted and put that burning wall at her back. Alcohol fire wasn't hot enough to crack through her rig's hex-wards. Even if Gaer managed to ignite every bottle, she'd be fine.

Gaer, however—oh *voidspit*. The swarm had figured out he was the problem, had redirected en masse. They converged on him, a burning, flapping, spattering blanket of teeth-legs and sucker-mouths. Gaer met them head-on: swiped, right-handed, to knock them aside. He had a monofil blade in that hand, which would cut almost anything. He caught one swarm with it, sliced it in half; but then there were three more on him, then four, dragging his arm down. One of them jumped for his chest. Landed and began to slither-run across his torso.

For a moment Iari thought it'd go for his left arm, straight for the light-hex, and commit noble suicide; but then it surged up, at the last, and slapped itself across his faceplate. Because if he couldn't see, he couldn't aim the light-hex, which made him as much a danger to her as he was to the Brood.

Not stupid at all, for flying gelatin blobs.

"Drop the hex," she shouted. "Let it go, let it *go*."

He did, with a snarled *setat*. The beam-lattice vanished. The smoldering swarm converged on him, trailing fire and burning bits of themselves. Iari swiped at several in passing. Killed two, wounded one; but swarm were *fast* and *many* and they'd piled themselves on a part of Gaer she didn't want to swing at with an axe. Miss, cut through the swarm too neatly, she'd take off his head.

"I've got a rig breach," Gaer said, breathless. "Iari—"

Might be kinder to decapitate him than let swarm eat his face. Or she could think of something better.

She pivoted hard and drove for the back door. Raised her shield and *rammed* and noted, a blink before she hit, that there was a bar, a padlock, *and* a voidspit keypad, all engaged—

—and then she hit. The shield absorbed the brunt of the impact, fed still more to the rig, and *still* she felt the shock in the bones of her forearm. Her HUD flashed a report, eyeblink quick, the contents of which went straight to her implants. The bar on the door hadn't broken. The padlock had. And the keypad, which meant electrical locks—

Sparks erupted, blinding, that became a crackling shockweb spreading over her shield, her arm, making the arcing jump to her chest. The lightning tangled itself in the Aedian crest, jumping angle to angle, winding itself into a sizzling ball as her rig's defenses responded. Lethal ward-hex, she noted, black market, anyone unrigged who'd been trying to break it would've been fried.

The bar across the door, though. That was plain, brutally tough polysteel. She staggered back, *fuck* balance, and slashed in with the axe. Not an optimal angle, but whitefire sliced through the polysteel like it was butter. She ducked her shoulder and rammed again. Her HUD flashed an alert as momentum overtook balance, and then she burst through the door and skidded and finally fetched up on her back, top-of-her-skull first into the opposite wall of the alley.

The syn blanked the pain, all those little nanomecha intercepting her neural reports, redirecting that bioelectrical energy to more useful projects. Like getting her upright, more or less.

She looked back at the storeroom. Daylight spilled through the broken door—watery, strained through clouds, but still brighter than Brood ever liked. The swarm burst off of Gaer like a flock of startled birds (slimy geometric birds, without wings).

And then, to her surprise, the remnant-survivors came right at her. *Into* the light. She lurched to her feet, rode the syn's boost and got her shield up and ready; but the swarm slewed away from her, surprisingly graceful, and skittered-fluttered a hard right up the alley. They moved fast—not running, exactly, flapping and scuttling, smoking where tendrils of sunlight found their way into the canyon of shop-backs.

She hesitated. Looked back at the dark guts of the storeroom. "Gaer!"

"Fine." He sounded breathless. "Go after them."

She started to run, scared she'd lose them. But it turned out there was no need to worry: they slewed into an open cul-de-sac, where a ring of buildings backed on the alley and made a dead end. There were two other alleys emptying into that cul-de-sac, wider than Iari's own, which meant major streets on the other end of them.

Elements, *please* don't let the swarm split up—

But again, no need for worrying. The swarm aimed themselves at a set of red double doors and skated beneath them.

Iari stopped. Swarms were vanguard Brood. First wave. Little and terrible and so much *less* awful than what came after them. Or with them. There could be—*what*, exactly, in that building? It looked bigger and wider than its neighbors, like a warehouse. Like it could hold, oh, a great many Brood of various sizes. There could be more swarm, or a couple of boneless, or even something bigger inside.

Assuming her comms stayed offline, worst case: at a run, synning to stay at full speed, fastest route, she was a quarter-hour at *least* from the Aedian gate, and another quarter-plus before she'd have people rigged and ready to follow her back. So say an ungenerous hour before she returned with reinforcements.

Swarm could go a long way in an hour. And even if she ran only until she had long-range comms again, assume, oh, ten minutes: that was still a lot of time for swarm to relocate. It'd take *weeks* to sweep all of B-town, and the panic that'd cause would be epic, plus political fallout, void and dust, it'd be like a season of *Jacta: The Last Defender* without the required victorious resolution.

And if she went after Brood *now*, alone, she might end up outnumbered by worse than swarm.

Protocol said report this (and she would). But her oaths said something else, about stopping the Brood, being the shield between light and darkness. Pretty poetry, very inspiring, from the first page of the Catechism. Those lines got recruits through the Aedis door. Sometimes it carried them through their first couple of fights, until their training turned into reflex.

And sometimes those pretty words sank all the way in, deeper than even the nanomecha, so that you went to midnight prayers every night, and not just on festivals.

"Iari!" echoed in her helmet, and she turned to look at Gaer finally hauling his spikey ass up the alley. He *looked* mostly intact, no bits of his rig hanging off. The riev pounded behind him. Brisk Array held the lead but only just. Char was behind him, bits of the tavern floor jammed into the various crevices and crannies in their armor. Char shed them as they ran, little clouds of ash and wood.

"Where did they go?" Gaer asked, a little breathless.

"In that building. Red doors." She pointed with the axe. "I'm going in."

She heard the hiss of inhale, Gaer ready to argue. But then Char said, "Yes, Lieutenant," and Brisk Array repeated it, and they split around Gaer like a river around an inconvenient stone.

"*Setat*," he said, aggrieved. "I'm with you."

CHAPTER SIX ≡≡≡

The warehouse doors, unlike every other slagging thing in this section of town, weren't wood. Voidspit polysteel, according to her HUD, and likely locked on the other side. And, because of *where* they were in Lowtown:

"Gaer. Check for warding."

His left hand drifted up, fingers spread, the gauntleted tips of his talons pointing at the door. "Oh, yes. Couple of nasty ones. One's locked to particular biometrics, and it's scribed on the back side of the left door. The other's alchemical. I can get that one. It's on the locking mechanism itself. The first, however, will take time."

"Which we don't have." Iari's shield could absorb the hex's damage. Probably. "Kill the alchemical. I'll deal with the other one."

Gaer's left hand clenched. Something popped. Smoke began to bleed from the seam between the doors.

"Done."

"Good." She hesitated. Wouldn't ask another templar this, but Gaer wasn't. She was supposed to be *his* security. "You all right?"

"Unhurt. Pissed off. *Not* green, Iari." He took an impatient bite of air. "The seal on my visor is damaged, but it will function. Just don't submerge me."

All right. Her ambassador wasn't just an arithmancer, he was

NIGHTWATCH ON THE HINTERLANDS   71

something with combat skills. File *that* for later. But for now, just a nod for acknowledgment, before she turned back to the door.

Her arms-turing found the weakest spot *there*: the seam between the two doors, at just about midway up. She hefted the shield. There might be a bar on the other side, like there'd been in the pub's storeroom. She'd have to hit hard.

"Lieutenant." Char thrust out their stump. "Let me."

Massive Char, all over hexwork, and built for exactly this: bashing into closed spaces and taking what was inside apart.

Iari stepped aside. "Go. I'm behind you."

Char slammed their right shoulder into the door and—polysteel or not, bolted or not—it folded like paper. There was a second's delay, and then the hex went off: a shower of sparks, then a *bang* that blew part of the door inward. Iari's HUD registered intense heat, *alert alert*, and then a fireball blasted the door back out again, knocking both panels off their hinges, and rolled over Char.

Iari jerked aside, riding the syn's mecha-induced adrenaline spike for speed. Her HUD's temperature displays spiked high and red. But the battle-rig's hexwork held. Iari let her breath go as the fireball dissipated in a ripple of superheated air.

Char was still standing in the door, framed by splinters of glowing scorched polysteel. The hexwork on Char's body throbbed the same sullen orange as the shattered door. The stump of their right arm glowed, tip to shoulder. The patchwork cap on the broken end had partially melted. A drip of semi-molten metal gleamed like blood on the pavement, even as the heat warped the stone and sent cracks spidering across the tiles.

Void and *dust*.

"Char. You all right?"

"Yes," they said, with what couldn't be, but sounded just like, satisfaction. The riev's head turned slightly. Their teslas gleamed brighter than any fire. Then Char swung their ruined limb and stabbed the doors aside, and Iari saw jagged shards of plating in the stump like shattered bones, as if something had bitten through. It was old damage, its hexwork gone dull and dead. Saichi damage.

If they lived through this, *if*, Iari was going to make fucking sure Char got repaired.

She followed the riev into the warehouse. Expected an on-slaught of swarm, an immediate mobbing of teeth-legs and flapping bodies. But it was quiet in there. Empty. Teslas on auto-sensors popped into life overhead, one-two-three, until the whole space was daylight-bright. It was a larger version of the tavern's store-room, except stone-floored. Shelves on one wall, empty, floor to four-meter ceiling. A line of crates bisected the room. Iari could just see across the tops of them. She spotted an office space toward the front right part of the room, what looked like a three-by-three cubicle added onto the original interior structure, beside a second, smaller set of double doors facing what was presumably a main street entrance.

"Where the *setat* are the swarm?" Gaer sounded indignant. Iari tracked him, a friendly green dot on the translucent map in the HUD's bottom left corner. Brisk Array, the other moving green dot, came behind Gaer through the doors, then immediately an-gled away toward the warehouse perimeter.

"Don't know." Her HUD still read Brood emissions. "They're still close."

"There will be an alarm on the door we just destroyed," Gaer added mildly. "Someone will know we just blew our way in. Maybe Tzcansi owns this place. Maybe she'll just walk in here."

"Huh. We can't get that lucky." Iari took a careful step. The syn made her legs shake, all that energy stored up for leaping, slashing, rolling, and she was locking it down to a creep.

"Lieutenant." Char had stopped. Was standing, tilted forward, looking—down? Elements bless.

Iari moved that direction. "What?"

"The Brood are here."

Iari squatted beside Char. Her knees shook a little less in this position. That was nice. There was a grate set into the floor that was dry, mostly, except for a little slickness between some of the bars. The HUD confirmed her suspicions. Brood effluvia, which meant, "That's where the swarm went."

"Into the *sewers*. Fantastic." The green blip that was Gaer's rig moved on the HUD map, a sudden and rapid diversion in her direction. "Do you still want to go after them?"

"Yes. But we can't do it—"

"Oh, thank all the dark lords."

She shot him a glare he couldn't see. "—from here. Someone'll have to get down into the tunnels. There's maintenance access."

And the swarm could be *anywhere* by now, in that network of drains under B-town. There might be plans in the city records. A map with access points, a way to get templars and priests down there. Hunting Brood in the dark. Well, some of the bored initiates would be a great deal *less* bored in the coming days.

Iari stood. Refused an urge to stomp on the grate. Her syn still wanted a fight. Her HUD told her one was coming. The sensors were acting like she was surrounded, but there were just walls and a ceiling, no extra floors and—

Wait.

Iari circled the grate. The overhead lights didn't get much past the metal grate. Solid black down there. But her HUD said, among other things, the nearest Element past that grate was aether.

"There's no water down there."

"It hasn't rained especially hard lately."

"That's not the point, Gaer, listen. My HUD's still lit up like there's Brood all around us, but I'm thinking they're not *around* us, they're *under* us. This part of town was flooded during the last Brood-surge. All the first floors became basements and cellars. There's got to be another level below this one. Or a partial level. Maybe sub-basement."

"Well, there is nothing in *here* worth the security on the doors." Gaer had pried the top off one of the crates, was stretched up on his toes and peering inside. "Anything deserving those hexes must be elsewhere. Your hypothetical sub-basement would be a good bet. Maybe we'll find some contraband."

Irritation prickled through her chest, hot and spiky and urged along by the syn. "I don't care about smugglers or fucking contraband. I care about the Brood."

Gaer slid the crate's lid back in place and turned to face her. The light broke on the alien planes of his visor like oil on water, purple and blue running over the black. She felt his stare through the layers of armor, cool and hard as the visor itself. "I know that." He picked his way around his accented Comspek like there might be venomous snakes in its syllables. "I'm only adding to the available information. Someone wants to protect something inside this place, and it's *not* shipments of alwar undergarments. It's something very valuable."

Iari's irritation soured. She spun away from Gaer and glared down the way she'd come at the shattered double doors. The hex still smoked. Hell, *Char* still smoked. Gaer was right about the security. That kind of arithmancy didn't come cheap. Certainly wasn't legal. So whoever owned this place had something to protect.

And Brood in the basement. If there was a basement. Which

there was. There *had* to be. And in the absence of obvious base-ment access—no lift, no stairs—then the way down must be con-cealed. She closed her eyes. Took a deep breath of rig-filtered aether. Tasted like ozone, a little metallic. The syn buzzed behind her eyes, under her skin. Didn't make thinking easy; the Aedis gave the syn implants to templars, not priests, for a reason: to fight well, to fight *fast*, mated up with a battle-rig. Priests got a different set of nanomecha. A gentler set.

Point was, the syn wasn't meant to help thinking.

Another breath. Iari forced the syn back to a hum, a bone-deep itch.

Gaer started speaking again—

Of course, always talking.

—and Iari squashed the syn down, and held it, and listened.

"We were down here looking for an alw named Tzcansi," Gaer said, still enunciating and therefore still angry, "who might or might not be involved in the death of an artificer. We are not look-ing for smugglers. Brood are a source of alarm, *yes*, which is why we should get somewhere the *setatir* comms work so you can re-port to. The Knight. Marshal."

Except this was Tzcansi's territory. Tzcansi was very likely in-volved in smuggling. The ganglords usually were. Tzcansi, who had neighbor gangs scared because she had riev enforcers. And now some association with Brood. Brood *and* riev? That seemed impossible, but all of this did.

Iari realized Gaer hadn't said anything for too long. He was waiting for her to—what, agree with him, likely, *okay, you're right, let's go call Tobin.*

Her irritation was entirely gone now. *This* buzz was anticipa-tion. "There were Brood in that tavern, which we know Tzcansi hit. They ran *here*. That's not random. They knew where to go. That means they've been here before. That's a link between them and Tzcansi. And they're underneath us right now, so there's got to be a, I don't know, a trap door hidden somewhere in here. Some kind of access. We need to find it."

Gaer raised hands and visor toward the ceiling. "Dear imaginary plasma-god, please tell this templar—Sss. He's your god. He won't listen to me. He'd probably tell you to do *exactly* what you're doing, which is look for a fight we're underequipped to win."

"Ptah doesn't talk to me. Maybe to the priests, I don't know. They've got different implants." Iari dismissed the axeblade and clipped the shaft back to her rig. "A trap door would be under something. And something not too far from the door. So one of these stacks of crates is my guess. Char. Help me move these. Brisk Array, you're our sentry."

"Understood." Brisk Array moved to the ruined door and snugged themself into a gap they shouldn't be able to fit into. They didn't quite disappear, if you knew where to look; but your eyes wanted to slide off.

"Huh. Stealth-hexes." Present Gaer with something new, he forgot to be angry. "That's a nice bit of artificing."

"Great. Admire it later. For now." Iari put her shoulder to a stack of crates. "Help me shift this. See if there's something underneath."

"A patch of floor, I bet," he muttered. But he came and took the other side of the stack. "Which way?"

"Left. On my count."

Char found the trap door on the fifth try—the *collective* fifth, Gaer noted, since he and Iari had moved only two stacks so far, and Char was a *setatir* riev. Even one-armed, Char was more for-midable at crate-shifting. Not that it took *arms*. Hips, mostly. Weight. Of which Iari had the balance, in their pairing.

Iari was almost to *three*, time to shove, when Char said, "Lieu-tenant. There is a hatch."

Which meant Gaer got to stop, and straighten, and lean against the stack. Meant he got to find his breath again. He spread his jaw-plates as far as the helmet allowed and dragged rig-tepid air through his mouth. The rig did most of the load-bearing, but it took all its cues from him. Where to bend. How much effort to spend.

Aedian rigs ran on some unholy combination of bioelectric interface through the needle-socket and Aedian—oh, call it al-chemy, lacking a better, more accurate term. (The Protectorate had one: heresy. But the Protectorate were a bunch of neefa-eating egg-breakers, so.) Vakari rigs used a very tiny on-board plasma core, hexed and engineered against breach or overload. Neither system was perfect, but the Aedian model was more—and Gaer hated to think it, but it was the right term—more *efficient* at sus-taining high-intensity bursts over time.

And oh, be fair: some of it was just Iari. Tenju physiology was formidable. Heavy bone, dense muscle. Dense brain to go with it, the joke ran (alwar and vakari told similar versions); as without, so within.

Tenju weren't stupid, in Gaer's experience. Iari certainly wasn't. But she *was* stubborn, sometimes to excess. She'd've spent the next hour shoving crates around, looking for that door.

So thank Char for finding it first.

"Gaer." Iari trotted over to Char's summons. Didn't look back to see if he was coming, but Char did. Cold blue teslas in a face that looked artistically, generically tenju. There was an actual dead tenju under there. An *actual* body under all that grafted alloy and armor, however alchemically altered. Unsettling thought.

Gaer came over, *not* trotting, because a vakar actually approaching a riev seemed unwise enough without rushing.

Iari was leaning over Char. "Huh. It *is* a hatch. A real hatch. A voidship hatch."

Gaer gathered breath to argue, because a voidship hatch had no place on a warehouse floor, but no. Char and Iari were right. A hatch made of metal, with a hollowed indent and an actual wheel, set to be flush with the floor and easily covered by crates.

"There's reinforcement under that floor," Gaer said. "You don't just bolt metal into a wooden frame."

"Huh. They'd've had to shore up the basement after the flooding. It's probably stone. Maybe more alloy." Iari extended a hand toward the handle. Stopped. "Is it hexed?"

Gaer sighed, audibly and for effect. His rig's scanners, more acute than his optic, could see that it was. But the hexes' exact nature required a little more finesse. He took another breath, and then sank his awareness, just a little, into the first sublayer of aether, under the skin of the world.

Everything solid shifted just a fraction out of true, acquiring hazy edges, a blurriness that might be translucence if you didn't stare at it. That was the first skill an arithmancer learned, that soft-eyed unfocus. Look at nothing, but see everything.

Information collected on the periphery of Gaer's vision. Iari and the riev were all over Aedian hexwork, those distinctive (and wrong-headed) crypto-matrices of correspondence, both limiting in their possibilities and limited by the implants and, yes, extremely effective for all that.

He floated his attention back toward (and not quite toward) the hatch. Blood and burgundy alphanumeric equations swirled like eddies in a river, fracturing and reforming. These hexes were not Aedian. Not vakari, either Five Tribes or Protectorate. There was an inelegance to them, an imbalance that could've been merely dynamic but instead was *ugly* with a side of *unpredictable*. Particularly those two alphanumeric strings *there*, chasing each other around the lock, flickering like a shorted-out tesla.

A palpable chill prickled behind his eyes. A matching chill further down closed fingers around his heart and squeezed. If he could catch one of them, just for a moment, he would *know* what they were.

Gaer shot his awareness out as one passed close, caught the tail. Willed it *still*, so that he could look at the alphanumeric sequence, identify familiar parts. Arithmancy had formulas, patterns, there had to be *something*.

And just as he thought he saw a familiar pair of symbols linked by the symbol for—*no*, that wasn't right, a *tesser-hex* had no place on a ward, tesser-hexes were for moving ships very great distances, straight through aetherless void—the whole string writhed and doubled back on itself like a worm dodging a bird's beak. He had a moment's premonition, perhaps his subconscious, perhaps years of arithmancy, perhaps simple luck. His mind flexed and he let the string go just as it realigned into a very familiar sequence, blue-white and blinding.

Gaer pushed his awareness away from it. Felt his body stagger back, like an afterthought.

One layer of aether away, where things had hard edges, the hatch crackled with a fine web of plasma. A ward. On that same, hard-edged layer of reality, Iari grabbed hold of Gaer's rig and set off the proximity and impact alerts and kept him from falling into a stack of crates.

"Gaer. Hey. You all right?" He noted the sharpness of her voice, squeezed as it was through the comm speakers. Worry. Maybe anger. It was hard, without auras or even faces, behind armor, to tell.

"Fine," he tried to say. Coughed instead. His mouth tasted sour, like—oh, *setat*. Blood. He backed out of the aether. His skin fit around him again. He coughed a second time, and sniffed hard and twitched away from her.

No. He *tried*. She kept a grip on him. "Gaer."

"It's a nosebleed. Minor. Nothing."

"How did it get through your rig? You didn't touch it."

"I did, actually. Just not with my hands." He sniffed, swallowed. Grimaced. Wished to all five dark lords he could spit. "I was trying to get a look at variables in the hex. I'm not even sure I was seeing actual letters from any real alphabet, but I *am* sure I saw part of a tesser-hex equation in the mix."

Iari was staring at him, the attitude of shoulder and hip more eloquent than any scowl hiding behind her faceplate. "I didn't say to hack the hex."

"And I *didn't*. I just looked. Did you hear me? I saw a *tesser-hex*. On a hatch. In a warehouse. Quantum hexes do information, that might make sense if it was some kind of alarm, but a tesser-hex is for, for voidships. There are other ways—"

"Doesn't matter what it's supposed to do." Iari grabbed his rig by the elbow fin and jerked him around to face the hatch again. "Because you got it open."

The hatch was ajar, not quite open, as if someone had dogged the wheel and popped the seal and walked away.

Gaer blinked. "When . . . ah. Did that happen?"

"Just now. When you went flying backward like a slagging bomb went off in your rig."

"I didn't *fly back*." But his HUD was flashing unhappily, now that he paid attention to it. Minor damage to the shielding, like he'd been in an actual blast. Elevated biometrics, straight across. Gaer swallowed. Grimaced. "All right. Maybe I did. I wasn't trying to hack, though. I was trying to look."

"You." Iari didn't so much let him go as snatch her hand back. She flexed her hand into a careful fist. Gaer found himself running the probabilities of just how hard she could hit someone.

Then she turned a shoulder to him, and managed to insert herself between him and the hatch at the same time.

"Well, since you did open it, I'm going down. Stay behind me and don't touch anything. Or think about touching anything. Or whatever you just did." She moved toward the hatch. "Char. Can you open the hatch for us?"

"Yes." The big riev leaned over with surprising grace—the torso *looked* solid, all those tubes and plates, but flexed like living tissue— and grabbed the hatch with their (now he was doing it, thinking of Char as a person) remaining hand.

Gaer expected a sizzle. Some repeat of whatever had happened to him. But there was nothing. Not even a creak as Char dragged it open. The floor was unusually thick, about a meter, and stone, so it was more than enough to support the hatch.

Gaer had expected a ladder, some spindly collection of rungs, leading into an ominous, light-swallowing darkness. Instead, there was a perfectly innocuous set of stone-and-tile stairs leading down into, yes, well, darkness, but it was the ordinary sort that gave way to wedges of light and Iari's headlamp, when she got far enough down. A faint crosshatch of light came down from the grate in the ceiling, maybe four and a half meters *that* way.

Iari canted her shield down, to catch any swarm coming up the steps. Nothing.

"Lieutenant." Char sounded unhappy.

"It's all right. Looks like the stairs descend maybe three meters."

Gaer cleared his throat. "We've set off two sets of wards, Iari. That's two sets of alarms. No one's come yet. Maybe think about why."

"I am. They reckon we're dead, so why hurry, or they reckon we're going to be, so why hurry." She was almost flush with the warehouse floor now, crouched and descending behind her shield. Alone. Into a cellar full of Brood.

Idiot templar.

Char looked at Gaer. The riev's aura flared a deep, expectant cerulean. "Will you follow the lieutenant, Ambassador?"

Like that was even a question.

"Just don't let that hatch close behind us," he snapped, and went after Iari.

The basement was clearly a product of reconstruction. The stonework was smooth, seamless—Aedian work, probably, priests of Chaama and Mishka sent in to clear earth and water and help rebuild. It was the sort of thing the Aedis did, as part of duty and calling.

It pissed Iari off, to think the Aedis had helped rebuild this place just so some voidspit smuggler could move in, take over, start murdering people. No *way* Tzcansi was working without PK collusion, and that was expensive. So was the hexwork. So was the slagging hatch. Whatever Tzcansi was storing down here, it had to be *big*. Given the hexwork on the door and the hatch—and, truth, after Gaer's explosive moment as a projectile, she'd had a moment of pure red-line biometric panic—Iari was expecting a basement full of weapons.

Instead it was . . . empty. Or at least, not full of interesting contraband. The whole place was a series of low half-domed arches with pillars running to the ground for support. Iari's rig started pinging, building a rough map on her HUD. It wasn't quite as big as the warehouse, by width and breadth. Seemed like there might be a meter missing on all the edges, which'd make the walls the same kind of thick as the ceiling. That suggested more than Aedian repair work. Whatever this place had been before the flood, it'd had stone walls originally. An old temple, maybe? Wasn't much else that would've rated shape and dimensions like this. Might be records in the Aedis she could consult.

Right now, that didn't matter. It was dark. No motion-activated teslas down here, and she didn't see any switches on the walls. There were pinpricks of light spangling through the grate, and the open hatch behind them spilled a sliver of light in their wake.

"Gaer." Knowing he was behind her: the green dot on her HUD said as much. "Can you light this place up?"

He didn't answer with words, for once, and she thought he might've taken more of a hit than he wanted to own. But he did respond: light sliced down from the hatch, rays and beams finding their way through the dark like a fistful of headlamps. They dragged across empty floor, brushed empty walls. Illuminated the fine swirls of dust like diamond fog. And settled, finally, on the room's centerpiece, which appeared to be some kind of wrought iron—

Oh, Mishka's left *tit.* That was an altar.

You didn't become a templar, didn't sit the vigils and *do the work* and not know a focus for worship when you saw one. This, though, was not of Aedian construction. It was squat, a matte black metal that Gaer's light hex couldn't gouge a shine out of. Ornate spikes and spires jutted out of the corners. It seemed to have six sides. No, seven, and not symmetrically proportioned, covered with designs and carvings. Two of the points crowded together, one taller than the other, with a fine mesh of wire draped between them like a moth-spider's web.

"Gaer—"

"I have no idea what that is."

"It's an altar. And it's setting off all my alerts." And more than setting off: it was the source of the Brood readings. Iari angled behind her shield, feeling a little bit like an idiot—*it's a chunk of metal, templar, what are you afraid of?*—and edged forward. The alert flashes on her HUD got brighter, the readings smearing into one glowing mass. "It scans just about like a Weep fissure."

"Yes," he said grimly. "It does. So maybe don't walk up to it."

"I'm not going to touch it." Except maybe with her axe tuned all the way to immolate. She willed her muscles loose and ready and breathed around the hot *thump* in her chest. The syn hummed under her skin like live current.

"Iari. Seriously. Just stop. There could be hexes. I might not *see* them."

"I'm not getting any closer."

She could see the altar's surface more clearly from this range. Asymmetrical bodies—clearly bipeds, that was all she could identify—with mismatched limbs (that one had a single vakari leg, and two short arms) and disproportionate features reached out of the metal. Instead of a single offering surface, the altar had seven, one for each side, but they were all empty. No vessels of any kind.

No candles, or cloths, or burners. Nothing of the usual altarish trappings.

The hell else did you use an altar for, though, except as a focus for prayer? Aedian altars had the Elements' symbols on them, one in each quarter, with a physical representation of that element for meditation. You shifted your focus and position in the sanctuary based on which set of prayers you were attending: Chaama in the north at midnight, Hrok in the east at dawn, Ptah in the south at midday, Mishka in the west at dusk. You could do that with *this* altar, too, and its position in the center of the room seemed to suggest that was the intent. But the symbolism wasn't there. Just these flat, irregular platforms covered with grotesque figures and— Oh. The surfaces weren't entirely irregular. They all sloped, very slightly, toward the center of the altar, where there seemed to be a little hole.

Iari had been largely ignoring the march of readouts on the periphery of her HUD. Alchemical composition, density, all of that was data for the report she'd owe Tobin. Now she *did* look. And yes, there. Organic residue.

Well, sure. You could use an altar for *sacrifice*.

"There's blood on this thing," she told Gaer.

"Of course there is." He sounded grim. "But there *isn't* any warding. None. And that seems odd." His voice sharpened. "I'm getting Brood readings."

"Yeah, me, too, from the altar. You think they're inside?"

"Not from the altar. From the northwest corner of this cellar."

So that's where the swarm had gone. How civilized of them to wait this long to attack. Iari peeled her lips back, a grin Gaer couldn't see, and activated her axe.

"So light it up. Let's see."

Only it wasn't swarm that Gaer's arithmanced beams found in the dark. It was dark metal, brushed and dull and meant not to reflect, carved and channeled and molded into interlocking plates of armor, segmented, over two arms and two legs and a standard bipedal frame. It was a pair of teslas that should have been steady, cold blue, and were instead a throbbing amber.

Oh, ungentle Ptah. It was a *riev*.

CHAPTER SEVEN ▰▰▰

Gaer blinked through the info-splash on his HUD. Scout-class, built on an alwar frame, small and light, probably fast. So guess: that must be the missing riev, Swift Runner, there in the basement's furthest corner. Not quite sitting—riev weren't well-suited for that position—but not standing, either. Propped. *Slumped*, really, head tilted a little bit out of alignment. One shoulder a little too low.

And those tesla eyes, which might be looking at him, or at Iari, or at nothing. Pulsing, like a heartbeat.

Riev still had those, though, didn't they. Hearts that still beat, however hexed and coerced into service.

"There's no aura. There's no—*anything*, except Brood readings. What does that yellow mean for the eyes?"

Iari had stopped, with one foot raised. Now, slowly, *slowly*, she began to set that foot down. "Don't know. But light at all means offline, not dead."

Oh dark lords, riev were nothing *but* dead. Gaer forbore to say it. The finer points of what made someone deceased could wait for a civilized venue. Far more worrying now: "What does that mean, offline? Can they come back *online*?"

"Not an artificer, Gaer, I don't know. I don't see any damage. No ruptures. You see anything?"

Gaer forced a swallow down a dry throat. Wished he could blink himself somewhere else. No: he wished he could blink *that thing* somewhere else, say behind a good barrier. Iari was too close to it, if *offline* decided to become *online*. "No smoking hexes. No. Do riev just . . . die? Of old age, or hex-rot?"

"No idea. Ask Char."

It wasn't the worst idea. Gaer flipped comms to external speakers. Pinned all his attention on the dormant Swift Runner and called, "Char?" into the dark.

A moment, a beat, and then, "Ambassador?" echoed off the metal hatch.

"There's one of you down here. Yellow eyes. What does that mean?"

"Amber optics indicate either hex failure or breach."

Iari swung her faceplate Gaer's direction. Her voice boomed out of the rig, bodiless. "There's no visible damage. Hex-failure, then."

A Char-shaped silhouette cut into the light from the staircase as they leaned over the open hatch. "Do you require assistance?"

Gaer ground his teeth on a *yes, please, go kill it.*

"Negative," said Iari, predictably. "Hold position."

At least she kept her shield up, Gaer thought, even as she sidled up to that monstrosity and peered over the rim. "Brood could've done this." She sounded doubtful. "I don't see any swarm, though. Or effluvia. Is there another floor-drain down here? Gaer? By the altar, maybe? Somewhere they could've gotten out?"

Gaer looked and yes, *there*, another grate. "Yes. There's a grate under the altar. Hard to see from my angle. Impossible from yours."

"Figures."

Gaer gave lip-service to the five dark lords because that's what you *did*, that's what everyone did; but imaginary personifications of elements, superstitions about ancestral ghosts, that was all neefa-shit. The multiverse was numbers, that was all. Numbers didn't need blood to function. Numbers didn't *want* blood.

But someone's god or gods or ancestors did, clearly. Or someone *thought* they did, which was worse. (Or, worst thought of all: someone had decided to worship Brood, and this altar was for them.)

It was hard to talk with his jaw-plates clamped this tight. He forced the words through. "So who builds altars these days, besides the Aedis?"

Iari grunted. "Don't know. You see anything on it?"

He didn't want to get close enough to try. Made himself take the necessary steps, toes clenched so tight in his boots, with his talons fully deployed, that they cramped. "Symbols. They—huh. That looks like old k'bal script."

"K'bal? They're extinct." Wiped out by the Protectorate during the Expansion, Iari did not say; she didn't have to. "Long way from their territory, though."

"They visited a lot of worlds." Gaer leaned a little bit closer. The script seemed to squirm on the altar. He blinked himself into the first layer of aether, but the sense of the equations *just* eluded him, like grabbing at wisps.

"There's arithmancy involved, but I can't say what it's doing without a closer investigation."

"Don't touch it."

"No intention."

"Lieutenant." Char's voice sounded sharper. "Brisk Array reports activity in the alley."

"Acknowledged," Iari started to say. All that Gaer heard was *ack*, appropriately, before a crash that sounded like something large slamming into something larger, followed by a metallic scream like (exactly like) the sound warehouse doors might make if they came suddenly and violently off their tracks.

The ceiling shivered. Then came another clattering, and a bang as the vault door slammed shut. Gaer whipped toward the hatch. His prism-hex, deprived of its source, winked out and dropped the cellar into darkness.

Betrayal spiked through his chest, cousin to panic. The *setatir* riev had shut them in. Gaer skeined a new hex from the meager teslas on his headlamp and the pinpricks of light bleeding from the ceiling grate, and turned to gather more beams from Iari's headlamp.

Just in time to see Swift Runner come online. The right arm snapped up, and Gaer watched, horrified, as the riev's hand *retracted*, fingers peeling back, exposing a hollow wrist and a cloud of hexes, ugly and patchworked and effective. A whitefire cannon, where there should've been reanimated flesh and bone. Decommed riev didn't carry weapons. But someone had made Swift Runner *into* one.

"Drop," Gaer shouted, and followed his own advice with a hard kick-and-roll. He came back into a crouch in time to hear the shriek of whitefire, to see Iari's shield take the blast. She staggered, recovered, lunged at Swift Runner and managed to knock the cannon-arm out of line with the rim of her shield. The riev's second shot sizzled past her helmet and splattered on the far wall of the cellar. The stone melted where it hit, dripped and cast the room into a flickering orange glow. Iari snapped the axe into her hand, blade materializing as she swung past the lower edge of her shield. Not a clean shot, not good: but it caught the riev on the knee, splitting metal plate and hexwork alike.

Swift Runner kept their momentum, even as they collapsed on that damaged knee. They punched a fist under the edge of her shield and knocked Iari off her feet, no, *lifted* her. She took momentary flight, arcing up and back, before she crashed into a nearby pillar. Her armor's hexes flared, dispersing force across the rig in a ripple of static. She kept hold of the axe, somehow. But she lost her balance and slid sideways, off the pillar, down onto a knee.

Swift Runner leveled their cannon arm and paused. The artifice patterns in their metal skin glowed first red, then white, then blue. Charging the cannon, Gaer realized. That took *time.*

Which told him, first, the riev had two shots to a charge, and second, that the cannon had a wicked power-draw, which led him to third: that power-drain would be straining the riev's galvanic core. It wasn't a native weapon. It was a graft. It was a *weakness.*

Iari was getting up, graceless lurch and stagger, raising her shield. Gaer's optic, amped by his visor, showed him gaps in the shield's hexwork. It wouldn't survive another hit from Swift Runner's black-market cannon.

The light coming off the semi-molten wall was suboptimal as a source for a prism-hex. Iari's headlamp wasn't much better. The two together made complete neefa-shit, but you could throw shit and have it stick, and so Gaer did. He wove the numbers and made a little flare that he tossed into Swift Runner's face. The riev turned again, twisting from the torso: a reflex, maybe leftover from their days as an actual living person, maybe just a matter of *identify what just happened.*

And in that moment of distraction, Iari moved—so *fast*, that must be the templar syn—and sliced through Swift Runner's outstretched forearm. Aedian axes (and swords, and occasional pole-arms) were meant to deal damage to Brood. They worked just as well on the riev. Gaer saw, with an arithmancer's awareness, the way the equations meshed. How the whitefire insinuated itself into the riev's artificed defenses, split them as neatly as the blade itself split the riev's metal shell. The blade didn't even hitch on its way through.

Swift Runner jerked their ruined arm up as Iari shouted, hoarse and wordless, and lunged again. She took another low cut that swept the bad leg out from under them. And this time, there was no shower of sparks. The riev's hexes ruptured, and something *else* came spilling out—a smoking slime that triggered every hex-alert in Gaer's rig. His HUD flared, and his optic, tuned to the first layer of arithmancy, adjusted, turning briefly, defensively opaque. He suffered a moment's half-blindness, during which his HUD flashed again, this time with good old-fashioned *movement detected*.

Behind him. The hatch.

Let it be Char, he wished, but then daylight came gushing in and he turned and he saw it was *not* Char, no, although it was a very big riev. This one had both arms, and a head with a single optic wrapping the skull's circumference, glowing that same corrupted amber as Swift Runner's. This riev was missing most of the lower jaw, but enough of their jagged namesakes still jutted out of the splintered metal that Gaer knew which one they must be.

Sawtooth didn't bother with the stairs. They jumped the distance to the floor and crumpled upon landing, collapsing down onto one knee. Sparks sprinkled down from the other. The riev had taken some damage, then. Probably Char's doing. The wound in their jaw sparked and oozed—that same awful something Swift Runner had bled. *Setat* if Gaer knew what to call it. Not blood, riev didn't *have* that particular fluid. This was Brood-tainted, corrosive, undeniably toxic, almost-but-not-quite Brood effluvia to his sensors.

Riev were blasphemy bordering on horror on a *good* day. Whatever had been done to this one was simply obscene.

This, all this—altar, corrupt riev, Brood in B-town—was more than coincidence. It was news; it was, oh, maybe *epic* in its implications. It needed to be known, reported and dealt with. Preferably a unit of templars and a few of those Aedian witch-priests and a great *many* whitefire weapons, plus every SPERE arithmancer on Tanis.

It was a bigger problem than a single vakar with a very small jacta, whose job (and oaths) it was to observe and report to SPERE command. Gaer owed no oaths to the Aedis. Certainly no oaths to a single templar fool enough to come down and pick fights with Brood (those were her oaths, he knew that, not really foolishness). Gaer measured the distance from self to stairs and the circle of light beaming down. Step aside, step back, and let Sawtooth charge at Iari (who would not step back, who would give the riev cause to attack her, sure as the sun rose in the east). Then he'd have time to cross that space, to climb. To get *out*, so that he could report what he'd observed, and fulfill his duty.

And likely earn the Knight-Marshal's contempt, even if Tobin never said anything. (*Setat* on Tobin's good opinion.) But Iari would die thinking he had betrayed her, if she got to think anything at all before Sawtooth ripped her apart. Maybe she wouldn't hate him for that; Iari understood *duty*.

That he'd hate himself if he left her: that was a certainty.

"Sawtooth!" Gaer shouted, in case Iari hadn't noticed. Then he unclipped his jacta. Oh dark lords, he'd trade his immortal soul for a longcaster; but this poor little sidearm was the best diplomatic dispensation could provide. His arms-turing came online, found a target, and locked. Gaer emptied the jacta, the entire charge, into Sawtooth's face and chest. The riev's hexwork, that slagging wichu artificer bastard cousin to arithmancy, held. The whitefire bolts glanced off its armor, careened and ricocheted and peppered the walls and ceiling with fresh spots of heat and light and molten stone.

Sawtooth slammed both fists into the floor and lunged onto their good foot. All Gaer had, when Sawtooth charged, was a depleted jacta and a slagging *monofil* clipped to his rig.

And arithmancy.

The ganglord's riev-trap in the alley had been amateur work. By the time Gaer had completed his mandatory military service, the Five Tribes had been decades past setting riev traps in actual combat. But the *exercise* of doing so—the need to build a complex hex in high-pressure combat conditions—remained part of the training. They'd even had actual riev at his training facility, part of the exchange program with the Confederate regulars. One of Gaer's fellow trainees had spent a week in medical after his trap failed and the riev broke four ribs and an arm.

Because he—that trainee, what was his name? Kerik? Kerask?—had panicked, had misaligned two equations. It was an easy mistake to make, with your hand shaking, with half a ton of riev coming at you (even when that riev was friendly-ish, participating in joint operations, with no-kill orders).

So don't *let* the hand shake. Steady the limb, steady the breath, steady the mind.

Gaer dipped just under the skin of the world, past that first layer of aether, just far enough to see the patterns of hexwork of Sawtooth's armored skin. Whatever had been done to fill them with Brood had also damaged their hexes. Some of the symbols had slipped out of true. A little off. Just so *very* little.

The part of Gaer's mind still entirely inside his body made note, on his HUD, of the rapidly shrinking distance between him and the riev, of the rapidly shrinking time to impact. That part of his mind directed his body to crouch and to extend his left arm. The part of his mind in the aether traced this symbol here, that equation there, aligned them with Sawtooth's weakened hexes.

Iari would say, now pray, as if the multiverse cared. No, the multiverse obeyed its own laws, and those laws were *math*. Gaer grinned, all teeth, as he slashed the final symbol.

Steady.

The equations flared and locked, and then Sawtooth crashed into them.

The syn and the rig were the only things keeping Iari upright. Her HUD was all over alarms, from yellow to red. Shield damage, hex-damage, an actual physical breach in her chestplate where Swift Runner had punched around her shield. The plating had split, just there at the bottom of the ribcage, driven inward. Broken a couple of her ribs, by her reckoning. It felt like knives and steel bands every time she drew breath, and that was through the syn's damping.

And she was breathing hard, fast, little bites of humid air because the rig's cooling system was one of the HUD's yellow alerts. At least she wasn't breathing *wet*. No blood bubbling up her throat, both her lungs fully inflated. That was something.

Void and dust, though, it hurt.

She reckoned Swift Runner was dead. Looked like its optics were grey, like most of its insides were outside, and that meant—

A new rash of alerts scrolled across her HUD, just as Gaer's voice cracked through the comms. "Sawtooth!"

Her eyes blurred, sweat or tears, didn't matter. She didn't need to see with hard edges. She knew where the hatch was, and the stairs. She aimed herself that way. Saw, with hazy edges, as Gaer unclipped that little whitefire jacta, pointed, fired. Sawtooth was damaged, something with the knee, something else with the jaw; but they were fast, and they aimed straight at Gaer. Iari wanted to scream at him, *just go*, but the syn wouldn't make room in her lungs. It sheeted under her skin, threaded muscle and nerve. *Moved* her, in cooperation with the battle-rig. A conspiracy of nanomecha and implants that, please Elements, would get her across the room in time to keep Gaer alive (but it wouldn't, not fast enough).

Then Gaer knelt and slapped his palm on the floor, and Ptah's plasma erupted from Hrok's aether. A vakari battle-hex that lit up every seam in Sawtooth's armor, made every hex flare up into the visible spectrum.

Sawtooth stopped.

"This won't hold long," Gaer said, brittle and cool in her helmet comm. "Hurry—oh, *setat*."

The riev-trap burst. All the force went flying outward, an expanding shockwave bubble of lightning and superheated aether. The shockwave hit Gaer, spun him like leaves in an autumn gust. He kept his feet only because he slammed into a pillar. He clung to it one-armed, and with the other, dragged his monofil out of its sheath.

The shockwave had thrown Sawtooth a fortunate meter or so in the opposite direction. For a heartbeat Iari thought the riev was down, dead—not moving, a heap of metal and leaking slime. But then *whir-click*, Sawtooth dragged their legs under themself, and their fists.

"Gaer. *Gaer*." Please, Elements, he hadn't broken anything. "You need to move. You need to get out. Get back to Tobin.—*Hey you fucker, I'm over here.*"

She banged the axe shaft against the edge of the shield. The hexwork shrieked a protest, sent a corona of angry plasma radiating off the rim. Damn sure *that* got Sawtooth's attention. The riev adjusted their aim and started to charge, a hands-and-knees scrambled launch to upright.

Her biometrics were edging up red. Fine. You could run in the red for a while. That's what the implants and the nanomecha were for. Iari cycled the syn one more time. Something broke in her nose. Hot rush down the back of her throat, out both nostrils. She licked blood off her lip.

Sawtooth—whose jaw and knee leaked (impossibly, but the HUD was sure) Brood-slime, whose hexwork glowed and writhed like snakes, thundered at her. Iari braced the shield, reckoned that it, she, could take at least one hit from a riev that size, which meant she'd get at least one strike on Sawtooth, too. She *might* cut that knee in half, if she hit it right. And if not, well, she'd wreck the joint badly enough it wouldn't be charging. Gaer would be able to evade and escape.

"Go, go, *move*," she screamed at him.

A shadow spilled through the open hatch. Her rig's motion-sensors sent out an alert, one more flash, one more wailing drag on her attention. *Silence*, she wished the rig. Die in peace, couldn't she, or at least fucking *quiet*. Her ears were already ringing.

But then shadow resolved itself into a silhouette—one-armed, massive, icy blue teslas like stars. Char—trailing smoke, bleeding sparks from their forearm, their fist, their chest, came down the stairs in two leaps and crashed into the crippled Sawtooth from behind. They went over together in a tangle of metal-plate limbs.

Gaer was shouting something, competing with the alarms in Iari's helmet and with the noise of two massive riev beating all five vakari hells out of each other. Char was losing the fight. Sawtooth was *just* that much bigger, had both arms, and Sawtooth was *biting*, or trying: jabbing that mangled face at Char, spattering Broodslime all over. Smoke curled off Char's plates where the slime touched the hexwork. Char clubbed at Sawtooth with the shattered arm, clawed at Sawtooth with the other; but Sawtooth had one fist on Char's throat, the other hammering Char's chest, over and over, same spot, a seam between armor plates. It was a Brood trick for getting through armor, which Iari had seen work before on templar rigs. At Saichi, where Char had been, too.

Iari made the syn drag her back onto her feet. Then she charged. She aimed at the back of Sawtooth's skull and raised the axe and swung it for the seam in their wrap-around optic. Chopped, and again, and *again*, the same dogged violence Sawtooth was using on Char. It was a matter of whose armor gave first, that was all, and whether syn-strained muscle gave out before artifice.

"*Setat m'rri*," Gaer hissed, and then he shouldered her aside, which shouldn't have worked and did only because she was tired, the syn tailing off and taking her balance with it. Her rig managed to keep her upright. Gaer climbed up on Sawtooth's back and jabbed down, burying his monofil to the hilt in Sawtooth's optic. Her HUD added another weary alert

arithmancy

to the litany of warnings already flashing.

"—clear," Gaer was shouting, Comspek gone thick with a vakari accent. He snapped the monofil off at the hilt and jumped at her. "Get clear, get *back*."

The syn tried to relaunch, but all it had left were slivers of ice and lightning. So Gaer managed to snake past her shield and smack one spiked forearm across her torso, to lend force to his directive.

Right on the voidspit crack in her armor, right *in* it. She lost breath with the shock of it, feedback slinging between rig and nanomecha already stripped bare by the syn. She landed flat on her back, Gaer on top, just as Sawtooth burst open with a shriek of metal and raw riev agony.

Gaer squirmed, shifted his weight to look back at his handi-work. Iari took advantage of that, bucked her hips and used the shield to scoop him sideways and off. She got herself mostly up-right, stagger-stumbled back to Char.

Who was, somehow, still moving, under what remained of Sawtooth, the top of whose skull was just gone, the plating open like petals, the contents—

Iari clamped her jaw in a grimace. The insides of things were always slimy. She popped her faceplate. Got a faceful of cooler air that smelled like Brood-slime and scorched metal and the not-quite-ozone nothing of spent hexwork. Sawtooth's limbs still twitched. Smoke curled up where their squishy bits touched Char's plating, thick and eye-stinging. Iari heard the hiss of corroding metal.

"Gaer, help me." Iari deactivated her shield. Dropped the axe outright. Then she wedged a shoulder against Sawtooth and shoved. "Get that off Char."

Together they rolled the dead riev clear. Iari dragged Char back on their feet. Like pulling on a building, hard to say how much help she could give. "You all right? How bad is it?"

"I retain basic function." The riev sounded surprised. Char touched one of their chestplate splits with careful fingers. "The damage is extensive." Char's teslas moved in their sockets, the only motion in that mask of a face. "Lieutenant. You are injured."

Iari licked blood off her lip. Hard to tell where that came from. Nose. Mouth. "Yeah. I also retain basic function." Iari paused. Looked hard at Char. "You called yourself *I*, just now. First person. Not third."

Char straightened. Stepped carefully clear of Iari. The riev's remaining hand flexed, then relaxed. "Yes."

"Aha. Look." Gaer had gone over to examine Sawtooth. Now he came trotting back, something gore-smeared and foul-smelling in his palm. "I got this out of Sawtooth's head. I don't think it's standard—what?" His visor swung between Iari and Char, throwing back distorted reflections.

"Nothing." Iari decided to leave Char's personal pronoun for later investigation. She poked at Gaer's palm. "It's a—what is that?"

His visor retracted. "I'd like to say it's a chip of some kind. Some version of comms, maybe? Assuming I am correctly interpreting the interior structure of riev-skulls. I'd guess Pinjat got Oversight restored after all, but this chip also stinks of Brood. And alchemy. And arithmancy."

She couldn't tell the chip's Brood-stink from the rest of Sawtooth. She *could* smell Gaer quite distinctly: like burnt sugar, which was vakari fight-or-flight chemistry, their version of adrenaline and stress chemicals. Her syn prickled. Aedian implants had been made first to combat vakari reflexes, to give templars some kind of edge in close-quarter combat. It was only after the first field tests that they'd discovered the biochemical side-effects to both species. She'd read about them. Never experienced it before. The burn in the back of her throat, the prickling under her skin that was neither fight nor flight and just as primal.

Gaer's nostrils spread. His pupils flexed. He didn't look at her. Didn't comment on whatever he smelled. Instead he bent all attention on that chip. He lifted his palm and stared across it, and the chip, at Iari. "I bet Swift Runner has one like it, too, if we crack them open."

"That is not standard hardware." Char had drawn up to their full height, like they wanted distance from the thing in Gaer's hand. "It is a contamination."

"Interesting word. Yes. And appropriate." Gaer turned the chip over. "How does one get something like this *into* a riev, Char?"

"With permission."

Iari snorted. That was both funny and not. One thing to imagine someone had hacked Sawtooth and Swift Runner. Another to think they'd agreed to . . . this insertion.

Riev didn't kill civs. Riev couldn't be hacked. Riev didn't use personal fucking pronouns. Betrayal was on that list of riev-don'ts, too.

Iari cut a glance at Swift Runner. A spreading puddle of noxious slime slid toward the drain under the altar, draining from the ruptured limbs. "Well, bring Sawtooth's chip. We'll leave Swift Runner's in their head, for the moment. We need to secure this site. See if we can lock the hatch back down. Once we've got comms, I'll ask the Knight-Marshal to send people down here."

"Iari." Gaer was looking at her, narrow-eyed. "You all right?"

"Functional. Yeah." She touched the split in her chestplate. Looked back at Gaer and made sure she had eyelock. Then: "Thanks. You didn't have to do that. You made a deal for library access, not to fight with corrupted riev."

The vakar's gaze broke. His chromatophores warmed, then chilled again, emotions locked down. "The dark lords know who the Knight-Marshal would assign to my security next, if something happened to you. Someone more humorless. Someone—" He waved his fingers. "Who doesn't appreciate music."

She stopped the laugh before it had a chance to really hurt. Confined it to a shallow, wheezy snort.

Char took a step toward the stairs. "Someone is coming."

Gaer's head snapped up, cocked. His plates flattened. He rolled a thoughtful eye at Char. "It's outside my rig's range."

"Mine, too." Iari heard only ringing in her ears. She sniffed back a mouthful of blood. "Brisk Array? Or did Sawtooth get them, too?"

"Unknown. I." Char paused. Then, firmly: "*I* told Brisk Array to deliver a sit-rep to the Knight-Marshal. Sawtooth was more concerned with gaining access to this cellar than with preventing Brisk Array's departure, so it is likely he survived to complete the mission."

He. Ungentle Ptah, did all the riev have personal pronouns? "So it could be templars up there."

"Or not. Could be your Tzcansi, or a horde of tenju enforcers armed with phlogiston bombs." Gaer quietly scooped up his jacta. "This time, maybe *you* stay behind *me*."

"No." Iari checked the charge on her shield. Within functional parameters. "You're vakari. If it's *not* templars, if it's PK again, best they see me first."

"And if it's some ganglord enforcer?"

"I'll leave you something to kill."

She took the deepest breath she could manage. The edges of what was possible marked themselves out in knives, steel hooks, the cold triangle of a staved-in rig pressing on her ribs. She climbed past Char (ungentle Ptah, walking hurt) and lifted her shield head-height (which hurt worse). It would deflect any incoming shots, if they weren't whitefire. It would also announce who she was, in case that mattered.

"Iari."

"Got this, Gaer, hold position."

She cleared the lip of the hatch. Daylight—was it really that bright?—had invaded the warehouse interior from the hole where the doors had been. Bounced off the walls and the pavement outside and sent beams criss-crossing through the dust. No one *in* the doorway, which meant they were already inside. Iari reached for the syn, tasted the metallic backwash that meant over-strained nanomecha.

"Lieutenant!"

Oh, merciful Mishka. Iari let her breath go in a shuddery gust. She knew the voice. Turned to meet its owner, who stepped out from behind the cover of crates, and lowered her shield.

"Corporal Ren."

"Lieutenant! Are you all right?"

Youngish woman, Ren, part of Peshwari's unit. Iari counted a squad behind her, more of Peshwari's people, all privates and initiates. All human, because that was Peshwari's (bigoted) preference, and Peshwari's Seawall aristocracy that made that preference stick over Tobin's less politically connected objections. "I am, and please tell me you're not all the help there is."

"I—yes sir." Ren flushed. "The riev you sent found us on patrol. Its report sounded urgent."

So Brisk Array had gotten through. Good. "Did Brisk Array keep going for the Aedis?"

Ren blinked. "The riev? Yes sir. It said it had orders to report to the Knight-Marshal. We thought we should investigate. But, sir, we haven't called the report in yet. We lost comms at the end of the block."

"Just *one* block? That's promising. Perhaps the Brood are

getting further away, or there's just not that many of them," Gaer said from behind and below her. And then here he came, with much more grace than she had, climbing the steps from the cellar two at a time. "Char would like to come up. Move over, Lieutenant."

Someone's jacta whined. Several others clicked as their wielders raised them.

Voidspit privates.

"Stand *down*," Iari snapped. "It's just G—the Five Tribes ambassador."

Ren's face settled into that careful, professional mask as she took in the state of Gaer's rig. "Sir. I didn't know the ambassador was with you."

"No reason you should have." Iari moved over and made room as Char limp-thumped up the steps.

Ren's head tilted up, and up a little bit further as Char climbed all the way out. Surprise slivered her professional mask: wide eyes, lips *o*-ing. "Sir, what *happened* down there?"

Iari grimaced.

These kids would be looking for some action. They watched her now, caught between curiosity and envy. None of them, not even Ren, had seen Brood. And if Iari said compromised riev, said unknown, non-Aedian altar, said hostile arithmancy, she'd have four sets of nervous fingers on whitefire jactae in a neighborhood where human wasn't the typical resident. Tell the *whole* truth, she'd set this entire squad off.

So, "Brood incursion," she said. "Swarm. They escaped down the drain. We need to make sure they don't come back up. Secure this warehouse, Corporal, until the Knight-Marshal sends reinforcements. *No one* down those stairs until you've got a priest on site, or without the Knight-Marshal's explicit orders. Clear?"

Ren nodded sharply. "Sir. Yes sir. Understood." She snapped a salute.

Iari returned it, a little less crisply. "Char. Ambassador. With me."

Then she turned and marched (no limping) for the doors and the alley, outside and into the sun.

CHAPTER EIGHT ▬▬▬▬

Iari didn't look good. The split in her chestplate had stopped leaking smoke. It leaked EM instead, a power core hemorrhage that lit up Gaer's optic. Her hair was drying into spikes where the wind touched it. Still dark and wet at the roots, though, which meant she was still sweating, which meant—pain? Her armor's cooling system offline? *Setat* if he knew.

Gaer's jaw-plates spread reflexively. The tang of Aedian syn tingled in the back of his throat and all the way into his sinuses and then south from there, pooling in his gut and further down. Dear dark lords. That was going to be a distraction.

"Iari. The Aedis is *that* way." He pointed, for effect; he could feel the Aedis brooding behind them, on the top of the hill. "Shouldn't we be going back there? Report to the Knight-Marshal?"

Iari side-eyed him. "Eventually. What you did back there in the cellar. That's not a diplomat's arithmancy."

"And there are those who wonder *why* trust is so difficult between our people."

She snorted. "We've got a Weep fissure running through this planet. I'd be surprised if the Five Tribes *didn't* send someone military. What are you? Intelligence?"

"Sss. Let me keep my illusion of professional camouflage and refuse an answer."

"Special Research, I bet."

"I should have let Sawtooth smash you flat."

"Yeah." Her mouth bent. "Glad you didn't. Are you coming or not?"

Gaer raised his hands in vain supplication to whatever imaginary persona looked down from above. "Yes. Fine. Safer than staying here with a bunch of jumpy young templars. Seriously, though." He pointed. "Your nose is bleeding. And I don't think it's arithmancy."

She sniffed. Wiped and frowned at her glove. "It's the syn. Overdid it."

"If you collapse down here, I'm not sure I can drag you all the way back."

"Char can. And I won't collapse."

"You want to say where we're going?"

"We're not going to find Tzcansi now without some help. She'll've gone to ground. Just so happens I know a guy."

"You—now you know a guy? Why didn't we ask him earlier? Oh. *Oh*." Her aura looked like a stained-glass window, colors thick and solid, nearly erasing the sparkle that came from those Aedian implants. Gaer sifted through the kaleidoscope. Dark, intense, streaks of orange, the whole thing laced with black like webbing. No. Like fracture lines. "I see."

"Doubt you do—oh voidspit. You reading my aura?"

"*Reading* suggests some interpretation would be required. What I'm seeing is quite definitive. This is not a happy association you are eager to renew."

"His name's Corso Risar. We served in the army together.

Infantry." Iari's mouth twisted. The expression drew attention to the scar crossing her lips and the capped tusk. Gaer wondered, not for the first time, what had made that scar, and, not for the first time, did not ask.

Whatever history Iari had with this Corso fell into that same just-don't-ask category, and staring at her aura was too much like asking those questions. Gaer found somewhere else to look. Look, there: the scrap of someone's lunch wrapper. Waxy paper stuffed with the remnants of bread and a few strings of onion, smeared with something viscous and orange.

"All right," he said carefully. (Was that orange business meat? Surely not.) "Then why go find him now?"

"Information." She shook her head carefully, like the motion hurt. "We've got Brood in the city. People are going to hear about that. And if people start connecting Brood and *riev*, we're going to have a mess. So the sooner we find Tzcansi and end it all, the better. I was hoping we could handle it ourselves. Tobin wanted to keep this investigation need-to-know. Talking to Corso, well. Tobin also said use my discretion."

"I'm not criticizing your choice. But, you know. You're bleeding, you're limping, you look like a three-day-dead neefa. You could do this *after* we get you checked out."

Her mouth bent again, this time in a new direction. "My nanomecha will deal with the worst of my injuries. But when I come back with the rig looking like *this*, there will be reports to file. The more I can get done before there's a requisition for massive repairs to a battle-rig, the better. Things like that get questions, and attention, and that's what the Knight-Marshal doesn't want." Iari's expression twisted again. "*That's* why we're going to see Corso now."

———

Truth: Iari wasn't sure she'd be able to find Corso. He might've moved in the intervening years. Might've, oh, gotten killed.

No. He was too fucking stubborn for that. And the pain in her chest when she thought too long about him being dead, well, that was a cracked rib. A bruise.

Gaer had gone uncharacteristically quiet. She wondered about his hurts, under the layers of his armor and pride. They'd stopped at a public lav to clean up. He'd been more successful. Emerged from the stall with no sign of nosebleed, no visible scuffs on that dark vakar hide. No limping, either.

She had a bloodspot in one eye from a burst capillary. Under the armor, well. Just a guess, she hadn't looked, but it'd be colorful. A pulpy mess. A match on the surface for how it felt every step, every breath.

Gaer might feel like that, too. Maybe that's why he was so quiet. Or maybe he was taking his cues from her aura. Or the neighborhood—tenju now, and so the residents were larger—had him on edge.

Or maybe—she closed her eyes. The blood-spotty one felt hot, scratchy under the lid. Gaer was a distraction, something for her mind to play with. Truth was, Char was more of an eye-draw than he was. And truth, anyone who decided to indulge anti-vakari prejudice would think twice, three times, just give up the idea, with Char there.

And with her there. Templar. Rigged. Shield deployed, axe in her right hand, like she expected (more) trouble.

She did. Just not the sort she'd have to chop up with whitefire. "Gaer. Where we're going—don't take offense."

"Ominous. All right. Though why I'd be—*oh*," as they rounded the corner.

The Vulgar Vakar sat in the belly of the cul-de-sac. It was a collection of code violations—non-standard additions on the third floor that made it lean over and touch its neighbors, a saggy roof patched with sheet metal—protected from a PK crackdown by virtue of both location and patronage.

"Ah. Iari." Gaer cleared his throat, which in vakari sounded like a prelude to spitting. "We're not going inside that place. Right?"

Void and dust. *Now* he got squeamish. The alwar ganglords liked to play at respectability, suits and nice things and everything little inside the law. It was the big things where they stepped out of line: smuggling, drugs, all the voidspit that templars weren't supposed to involve themselves in. Tenju anarchist-collectives maintained a more general disregard of PK order. Their dishonesties ran smaller: illegal gaming, illegal fighting rings, illegal—

"It's a needle-den, Gaer. Specialty's cross-species porn. Told you, don't be offended."

"I'm not offended. I'm afraid of being crushed under the ceiling's inevitable collapse."

She laughed. It hurt. "Don't be. We're not going inside. We're going this way." She pointed at the side of the building. Corso's office was a walk-up on the second floor, one set of crumbling brick steps and an indifferent railing from street-level. The flood hadn't got this far up; the ground floors were original masonry, pockmarked by years of uneven erosion, scarred by acid rains during the last surge. A door to the building's interior sulked at the top of the landing, peeling blue paint and a missing handle.

Gaer sighed. "Oh. *Steps.* Excellent. I can fall to my death instead. Or perhaps fall through the floor. The ceiling collapse scenario from the *other* angle."

Iari eyed the masonry. Patches of concrete like scabs. The railing was a tangle of bolts and braces and wire. She imagined the floors inside, and looked at Char, and winced. "Char. You should wait down here."

The riev cocked their head side to side, like each tesla saw something different. Maybe they did. "Acknowledged, Lieutenant."

"Is that wise?" Gaer bared a sliver of blue-etched fang. "We might need Char with us."

"Thought you didn't want to fall through the floor."

"Rather that than being shot."

Iari started up the steps. "You can wait down here if you want."

"Sss." But he followed her, gingerly, as if soft steps would lessen the weight of his battle-rig.

The door at the top of the steps wasn't locked. It swung open on surprisingly quiet hinges, into a claustrophobic hallway of scuffed wooden floors and peeling plaster walls and yellowy teslas doing their best against pervasive gloom.

"The floor will hold Char," Gaer said from behind her shoulder. "It's all over hexwork. So are the walls."

"Huh. What kind of hexes?"

"Second-rate. Meant to keep existing structures intact." He grunted. "I'd *guess* no one wants jacta bolts going through the walls or the floor. And some of these hexes are also resistant to surveillance."

No surprise there. The floor made a sound like snapping bone from the landing's direction. Iari paused, mid-step. "Sure about the hexes?"

"Yes." Gaer bit the word off.

"All right. Char. Come up. Be careful."

There were doors on either side of the hallway, about halfway up and facing each other, and a third door where the hallway dead-ended facing the outer door. It looked sturdier than its fellows, some kind of amalgam instead of plain wood. A small metal plate hung in the middle like a single, polished eye with letters etched on the metal plate, stencil-stiff Comspek.

Corso Risar, P.R.I.S.

Iari walked the length of the hallway, past the other two doors, made herself ignore the prickling urge to bash them down and clear the rooms. This wasn't a raid. There weren't Brood back there, laying ambush. There was just Corso behind that fancy door with the nameplate, maybe, assuming he wasn't out on some errand and this hadn't been a wasted trip.

Her rig beeped a warning as Gaer leaned over her shoulder, brought with him a gust of burnt-sugar smell and the natural heat of vakari. "The *setat* does that stand for?"

"No idea. Used to be *P.I.S.* Private Investigation and Security."

"Piss?"

"Guess we know why he added the R." Iari eyed the door handle. It looked somewhat newer than the rest of the door. The surrounding material—wood-looking, but clearly not *just* wood—had visible patches, daubed with fresh paint.

She traded a look with Gaer. Then she brought the shield up and reached right-handed around the rim and tried the handle.

Nothing blew up. The handle moved, the door clicked open. A wedge of light escaped into the hallway, its diffusion and white-fading-grey suggesting a single source from somewhere chest-height, rather than an overhead tesla.

Iari nudged the door open with a boot and stepped in behind it.

A chair skidded back. Then came a second, more hollow bang, that might've been someone's knee hitting something more solid than itself, and a rattle of metal. The light wobbled.

"Veek-licking *fucker*—!" Iari heard the whine of a whitefire weapon's power core. A voice, *Corso's* voice (her skin prickled with recognition), followed. "It's customary to knock, but all right. Come in."

She cast a quick eye around the apartment, in case he wasn't alone. There was the desk (askew, now, to the square of the room); shelves on one side, books competing with clothing and oddments for space; a pallet in the back corner partly cordoned off by a battered screen. A rudimentary kitchen, cookbox and coldbox and sink, all crammed into the opposite side. A small collection of crockery on the counter, stacked and filthy. The smell of pickled greenstalks and pepper sauce lurking under the stale oppression of old laundry and dust. A single window, smeared grey with dust and Elements knew what else, let a smudge of watery light in from the alley.

No one else. Good. Because voidspit *Corso* was half-crouched behind that desk, holding a whitefire longcaster, old miltech issue, all the lights primed and ready to fire. An equally old miltech-issue lantern lay on its side on the desk, half its light scattering across the desk's surface, the other half getting lost in the ceiling shadows.

The battle-rig sent a jolt through her socket, a near-reflexive need to drop her visor. She gritted past the urge. "Put the voidspit weapon down, Corso."

He blinked at her. Same old Corso she remembered. Same slab features, jaw like a brick, eyes that remarkable tesla-bright blue. His hair had gotten even longer since the last time she'd seen him, even further away from army regs. Multiple braids glittering with hooks and bits of bone and Elements knew what else.

"Iari." His gaze dropped to her shield. "Still wearing the shell, I see."

Good thing she'd overworked the syn already. Corso made her want to trigger it again. Beat that grin off his face. She drew a slow breath through clenched teeth and reminded herself what Jareth had said in *Meditations* about acting from passion instead of reason, about that which differentiates a sentient person from a beast. Void and dust, that chapter could've been about Corso.

It was *not* about her. She pitched her voice to dealing-with-scatterwit-recruits levels. "I mean it. Weapon *down*. Whitefire's illegal for civs."

Now he looked at her. "Since when do I count as civ?"

"Since you took your discharge."

He grunted. Flicked his gaze past her shoulder like a whip. "There's a veek behind *you* carrying whitefire."

"The *ambassador's* got clearance to carry. You don't. Last time I'm telling you, put it down."

"Or what? You shoot me? Arrest me?" But Corso lowered the weapon and powered the core down with practiced, very clearly *not* civ motions. He set it down on the desk, muzzle pointed politely away. Raised both hands and waved empty palms at her.

Iari stowed her shield with a wrist-flick. Now Corso could see the damage on her rig, and his expression changed again. Thoughtful now. No outpouring of concern. A measuring look, like *what could've done that*?

There weren't that many things on the list. His eyes narrowed. "You want to come in, then? Shut the door?"

"Don't know we'll all fit."

"The veek's not that big—ah. I see," as Char filled the doorway.

"There is room enough, Lieutenant." Char ducked under the lintel, surprisingly soft-footed, and, just as gently, pulled the door closed.

Corso's gaze came back to Iari. "Lieutenant, is it? Congratulations. Not surprised you'd make officer."

"Thanks." Ungentle Ptah, Gaer had to be getting an eyeful of aura, hers and his. Pyrotechnics. More drama than a wichu opera. "Not here to be social, Corso."

"Yeah. Figured. So what do you want?"

"Need your—" She routed her tongue around *help*. Be a cold day in Ptah's particular hell before she'd use that word with him. "—your services. We need to find a ganglord named Tzcansi. Alw, I think."

"Alw, definitely. I know her. Know *of* her," Corso amended. "She's an enforcer for one of the big houses. Runs their day-to-day street operations. Has a reputation for efficiency, if you know what I mean." He retreated around the desk, one hand within snatching distance of the longcaster, and lowered himself into his chair. He dragged his turing pad front and center and tapped the screen. "Sec. Let me see if I have a 2D of her on file. Yes. There." He spun the tablet.

Iari leaned in to look. So that was Tzcansi. Pretty, if your tastes ran to pinch-faced and dainty. The 2D had caught her mid-conversation, looking out of frame.

Gaer made one of those rattle-click-hisses. "And do you know where we might find her?"

"We." Corso snatched the tablet back. "Tell me, Iari. The Aedis's making nice with the veeks, now?"

"Yeah. Called a treaty. We've had one for, oh, what? Sixty years? Long before either of us was born."

Corso sneered. "That hardware on your face, veek. You an arithmancer?"

Gaer looked like he might answer that with a demonstration.

Iari interposed her voice, her shoulder. Damn near thrust out an arm. "He's an ambassador. Ptah's own *sake*, what's your problem? You find some ancient pre-Landfall poem someplace says *traditional* tenju have to be assholes to everyone else?"

This was old ground, old argument. Old pyrotechnics happening in her aura. Please, Ptah and Hrok, Corso decide to let it drop. Her ribs hurt. Her head was starting to. It was hot in the rig, with the vents half-functional. She wanted to get home and out of the damned thing (and probably land in Tobin's office, but even so: that prickle-backed chair was better than standing here).

Ptah and Hrok seemed to be listening (and oh, Corso would hate the very idea some Aedian upstart Element could affect *him*). Corso let his gaze drop and drift past her, past Gaer, until it settled on Char.

"What *have* you been up to, Iari?"

"Today? Talking to the riev. Tracking a ganglord to a burned-out tavern, in which we found a Brood swarm. Tracking *them* to a warehouse, in which we found—" She grunted as Gaer slammed a foot sideways into hers. "Something else. But we're *here* because a wichu artificer got murdered last night by a riev on Tzcansi's payroll."

"An *artificer?*" Corso barked laughter like jacta bolts. "Good for the riev. About time they took a little revenge. I don't blame 'em."

Char took a step closer to Corso. "I do."

"I? *I?*" Corso squinted up at Char, unconcerned by the riev's greater dimensions. "Since when do you lot self-identify?" But Corso was frowning now. "Your damage. It's fresh and it's too extensive for swarm. *Big* Brood, maybe." He rubbed his chest. An absent gesture, the thing you did when you had a scar running shoulder to hip and most of your guts had spilled out. (Iari knew the geography of that scar. Winced in memory.) "But I'm *guessing* it was another riev. Am I right? Same one who killed your artificer?"

Char looked at Iari. Waiting permission to speak, clear enough. Iari nodded. "You can answer."

"Yes."

Corso waited, clearly expecting more of an explanation. When it was clear Char was done talking, he shook his head. "Okay. You're not going to tell me anything else."

"Your affiliation is unclear."

"That means you don't trust me?"

"Correct."

Gaer made that throat-clicking sound again. Waved off Iari's glare and, oh Elemental miracle, kept his cleverness behind his etched, dyed teeth.

Corso met Gaer's smirk, matched it, added a pair of tenju tusks. Of course that was what their species shared in common custom: dominance measured in dental displays.

Iari wanted to muzzle them both. She rammed her foot into Gaer's, no attempt at hiding the gesture. She put both hands flat on Corso's desk, not quite slamming, and leaned forward until he had to look up at her.

"Listen. I need to know what Tzcansi did to the riev to get it to kill someone. I need to *ask* her, personally."

"Yeah, she's going to *love* talking to you." Corso jerked his chin. "That shell you're wearing. That shield. She'll open right up."

"Just set up a meeting."

"If I can find her. Whatever you did today—if she's behind it even a little bit, she'll have gone to ground."

"You saying you can't find one little alw in Lowtown?"

"Oh, fuck you. I can find her." Corso leaned back. "What do I get?"

"Your usual fee." Iari gestured back at the door. "P.R.I.S. What is that, Private *what* and Investigation Services? You've got a fee schedule, right?"

"Reconnaissance. And right."

"So give me your account number. The Aedis will set up the payment."

"Like I want to be in the Aedian accounting system as a fucking vendor."

Probably meant he *had* no account. All right. "We can work out cash, then." Not convenient for paperwork, and Iari would have to deal with Sister Rie, quartermaster and head bitch (no, not quite *head*—Sister Diran had that title), but she'd get Tobin's authorization.

"Iari," Gaer murmured, and she realized she'd drifted. That she needed to say something.

She gathered the threads of the last few moments. Corso should've said yes to cash payments. Assume that he had. She guessed what came next in the conversation. "Fee schedule," she said. "Need a copy."

Nope. Not the right thing to say. Corso was looking at her, defiance at war with voidspit worry, like he was still corporal to her private, like he hadn't been playing civ for the last ten years while she'd put on *that shell* and helped push back the last surge. He'd been on his *ass* here in B-town while she'd been at Saichi. Fuck him for worrying.

"I'll invoice," he said. "Waive the advance. I reckon the Aedis is good for it."

"You mean, you'll overcharge."

"That matter?"

"Not if you get results." Iari pushed off the desk. Her elbows ached. Definitely something off with her implants. The nanomecha should've effected at least *some* repair by now. "Comm the Aedis when you have something. Somebody will know where to find me."

CHAPTER NINE ═══════

C orso sat for a very long time staring at the door through which Iari had appeared after damn near a decade, and through which she had disappeared again (without looking back. Iari never looked back). He could still smell the hot metal of her battle-rig, the acrid fumes leaking out of it. It left a little burn on the back of his throat, sour and sharp-edged. That was a power-cell on its way out, cracked and leaking. She'd be lucky if she made it back to the Aedis. With that kind of damage, a rig could just quit. Oh, she'd be fine (she was always fine). That one-armed riev could probably carry her. Or the veek, who smelled unexpectedly like burnt sugar, gritty and confusing on Corso's tongue.

Voidspit *veek* in his office. He wondered if anyone else had seen. Mak or Devi. They wouldn't let him hear the end of it. Veek and a voidspit templar and a riev. The whole neighborhood had probably noticed. *Tzcansi* probably had. He wouldn't have to look for her if she came looking for him.

That could be a problem.

Corso's jaw ratcheted tighter. Hard to say if he'd get more judged for the veek or for Iari. That templar shell of hers. Fuck. He'd known she'd survived Saichi; he checked. He'd known when she ran a check on *him*, when she'd discovered his association with the Vulgar Vakar. He had friends in the peacekeepers (the kind you could bribe); they always told him when someone from *up there* ran his name. Corso had thought then—eight years ago, after that check—that she'd come see him. That maybe she'd be ready to give it up, this templar voidspit, and come back.

Looked like that wasn't going to happen.

Corso leaned forward, finally, and dragged his longcaster back across the desk. Call *him* civ, would she? Void and fucking dust. He'd taught *her* how to use 'casters, jactae, all of it: how to change the cartridge under fire, how to field-strip and repair. Civ. Right.

Iari had said *civ* to him, but Corso had heard *gutless*. Because he'd quit when his enlistment was up. Because he'd decided someone else could deal with the fucking surge—like the fucking *Aedis*, because they had the templars and the priests and the funding to manage. Confederate marines, regular army—what he and Iari had been—were just there to slow the Brood down, and the best way to do that was by dying. So no, thanks, he was done with that.

Iari had said only, *The surge isn't over. Someone's got to deal with it.* And then she'd walked out.

Corso popped the cartridge and checked the longcaster's charge, let his fingers move through patterns as familiar as eating, drinking, fucking. He stowed the weapon, finally, butt-down in the corner, and heaved himself out of the seat. His knee hurt a little. Bruised from a collision with the desk, which was fucking *heavy* and which he'd sent skidding across the floor by a good half meter. He replaced it now, gripped the corners and dropped his hips and *pulled*.

His heart was beating a little too fast still, but that wasn't because he was civ and gone soft. She'd surprised him, that was all. He folded his knuckles onto the desk. His tablet stared back at him from the desk's surface, its screen dimmed to power-save, but he could still see the outline of Tzcansi's 2D. He leaned hard onto his fists and flexed the muscles in his arms and shoulders. His gut might be a little softer—regular meals could *do* that—but *he* wasn't.

Heat prickled under his skin, a flush rising and ebbing again, like spring runoff in the Rust. Iari called him civ because to her, that's what he was. Because she wore that slagging templar shell, because she had that socket in the back of her skull and the little machines in her blood, because she'd *chosen* those things. Because she'd wanted, she said, to *do something* about the Weep and the surge, because she'd wanted to fight Brood.

And then she'd darkened his doorway years later, bloodspot spreading in one of her eyes, crusted blood on her nose, that templar armor beaten to a vakari hell, talking about Brood. In B-town. Now.

Corso's chest tightened as his heart kicked into way-too-fast. He rubbed the heel of one hand across it, as if he could press the pain out. Hard muscle, hard bone under that. But it was the skin he was feeling, the raised ridge of keloid, where a Brood slasher had opened him up—through regular army-issue armor, through skin and bone.

Brood in fucking B-town.

He shifted his weight to one fist, reached the other forward and tapped his tablet awake. Tzcansi's image brightened. Sharpened.

That was a good word for Tzcansi. *Sharp.*

She wasn't hard to find, if you knew where to look. Tzcansi owned a fistful of cafes scattered through her district, any one of which might serve as an office or a meeting place. For someone coming in cold, there would be surveillance work, identifying patterns. Putting the reconnaissance in P.R.I.S. A few days, if Tzcansi was predictable. A few weeks if she wasn't.

Corso wasn't coming in cold, though. Corso knew exactly where she'd be, on any given day or hour.

Iari hadn't wondered how he'd found that image of Tzcansi so fast on his tablet, or why he'd had one at all. Iari hadn't asked for an estimate how long it'd take him to set up a meeting. Hadn't done *any* of the things a normal client did, when they retained his services. Corso couldn't decide if that meant she didn't care how long it took, or if the Aedis didn't, or if the two things were equivalent. Or—and this was his suspicion—she had no idea she was supposed to ask. Maybe she thought a good P.R.I.S. kept files with 2Ds of all local ganglords on his tablet. Or maybe she thought Corso just knew every ganglord in Lowtown that intimately.

He didn't. But he did know Tzcansi. Corso had been on *call me if necessary* terms with her since she'd bought half the Vulgar Vakar two winters ago, after Mak had gotten arrested for being stupid and Devi hadn't been able to cover the PK bribes.

So Corso felt a little bit bad, but only a little bit, taking a fee to find her.

Iari's power core flat-out died twenty meters outside the Aedis gates. Then she had a choice: let Char haul her inside the gates like a broken doll or strip on the street. Gaer, Ptah bless him, figured out a third option. He jumped power from his rig to hers, some arcane tangling of cables that weren't meant to mate up and a fistful of hexes to make sure they did.

Once inside the gates, once Gaer untangled their rigs, Iari grim-stomped her way to the armory—Char in tow, Gaer peeling off to his own quarters, one of the guards stabbing comms and saying *Yes, sir, she's here.*

Comms. Right. She keyed her own. "Dispatch, this is Lieutenant Iari."

And before she'd even gotten a *copy that* acknowledgment, she got Tobin.

"Lieutenant." He must've been hovering over his comm. "You're back."

"Yes sir. Heading to the armory, sir. Rig took some damage. I'll be up to your office as soon as I'm clear."

"Are you hurt?"

Much as she wanted to say otherwise, she didn't lie to Tobin. Ever. "Minor injuries, sir."

And much as he wanted to see her, she knew what he'd say. "Then you come see me *after* you see medical. Clear?"

"Yes sir."

Then Tobin cut off, which was good. Iari wasn't sure she could do more questions. She was all over cold sweat under the rig, heart beating a little too hard, lungs just a little too small. She cleared the armory door with one hand on the jamb pulling her through.

Most times you got out of a battle-rig with a wall-mount. Hooked the torso in place, cracked the seals, got the top half of yourself out. Then you anchored the boots, reached up for the overhead bar, and pulled yourself the rest of the way.

The times when the rig was too damaged for the wall-mount, you just got out however you could. Iari unsealed the torso—didn't take too much work, slagging Sawtooth had cracked most of the seals for her—and took the rig off panel by panel, until she had a little pile of plating stacked around her. Then she anchored her lower half, reached up. Almost gagged when she reached overhead for the rack, it hurt so bad.

Ribs. Right. She muscled her way out instead (still gagging). Climbed out of the bottom like a fucking green recruit, human or alwar or some other frail species without shoulder strength to just lift. She regretted the tile floor's chill. It soaked through her skinsuit's soles like water. Turned her whole body to shivers.

Char observed from the armory doorway. The riev offered no comment about their own condition, no complaint.

Of course not. Char was riev. They *didn't* comment or complain. They also didn't use personal pronouns or get Brood-poisoning and try to beat templars to death. And until the decomm, they'd all been a *we*, and *us*. That Oversight-with-a-capital-O, or whatever, that Pinjat might've been trying to restore. *That* was why all of them referred to themselves in the third person. The way other people saw them, because they didn't *have* a self.

Except Char. Char was an *I*.

Iari leaned on her elbow. She typed, one-handed, the repair order into the wall-console turing and tagged it *priority*. That would route the request up to Tobin's office. Assuming he approved it, it'd bump her rig to the top of the queue.

And if Tobin didn't approve, well. She could take a day or two off, or however long it took Corso to find Tzcansi (she should've asked). She was sure, though, that Corso would find her. So if Tobin was pissed about how today went, at least Iari could take *that* information to him. Show him she'd made some progress. This alleged Oversight repair, this corrupted riev, it was too big to just *drop*.

Iari closed her eyes. Pressure throbbed behind her eyes. Sensible, then, to close them and lean her forehead against the cool wall and let Aedian stonework hold her up. It was very, *very* hard to breathe. Ribs. But the thundering in her ears, that wasn't ribs. Neither was the nausea and the absolute certainty that if she tried going anywhere, she'd fall down.

Char said something. Rumble-rumble-Lieutenant-rumble. And then she heard Char coming, little tremors through the stone floor, as her vision went from grey on the edges to black, all black, like void.

Iari fixed her stare on the wall and pretended Sister Diran wasn't doing unpleasant things to her needle-socket. That there wasn't a squad of test tubes on the counter, racked and standing at attention, all of which gleamed redly, and that her arm wasn't crooked around a soggy gauze square soaking up the leftovers.

She could ask Dee how much blood she needed, sure, but she'd get voidspit for an answer. So instead, she asked, "What happened to Char?"

Dee's breath smelled like cinnamon and cloves, warm on the back of Iari's neck. Contrast to her frigid fingertips as she jabbed Iari's needle-socket with a diagnostic wire. "Who?"

"The riev. One-armed. Brought me here?" Iari dredged her memory. Flashes of corridor between armory and hospice, an unyielding pressure across her back, under her arms. The cool hardness of riev plating, except for where the armor had split; those crevasses were hot, hotter than fire, hot as Ptah in his purest form. The heart of a riev. Iari touched her shoulder through the hospital robe, and felt the fresh raw of a burn.

A gust of cinnamon exasperation, and Diran withdrew the wire. "Last I saw, it was scaring the interns in the hallway. I told it to wait outside in the courtyard. It declined."

"Char. *They*, not it." Iari unbent her elbow. Under the gauze, a faint bruise radiated out from a central hole.

"Whatever. I think *they* would've waited in here, if I'd've let

them." Dee made that little sniff that signaled a general dissatis-
faction with the current object of her attention. "I don't see anything wrong with your needle-socket. All the diagnostics are
coming back fine. That tells me there's something wrong with
your nanomecha, and I need to run more—*where* are you going?"

Iari slid off the cot and stood up. Floor in the hospice was cold
as the armory's, but worse, because it was bare skin to tile now.
She was in an actual room, though, not the curtained and partitioned triage unit. Whatever was wrong with her, it didn't rate a
med-mecha's constant surveillance.

Iari looked around for her skinsuit. Saw it draped over a stool
by the turing console like shed skin. It was what, half a meter
across the floor? Iari reckoned a couple of steps, if her legs held.
Seemed like they might; her knees were steady, and the first step
went well enough, anyway.

"You don't need me here to run tests. You have all my blood
already."

"You've got cracked ribs."

"Yeah. And I have to give a report to the Knight-Marshal."

"You're *not* fit for duty."

"Dee. Ptah's own sake. My battle-rig's in pieces. I'm not going
anywhere off-compound. If there's something wrong with my
nano, you can come find me." It sounded braver after saying it
than it had in her head. In there, *something wrong with my nano*
had sent all kinds of cold shivers through her gut.

Dee's face said she shared that feeling. "There shouldn't *be*
anything wrong. That's the point. You're certain you didn't ingest
Brood fluids? No contact with open wounds?"

"You find any cuts on me?" Iari shrugged out of the hospice
robe. Let it fall in an off-white puddle onto the tiles. Yeah. She'd

reckoned it'd be ugly under there, all that bruising. She probed gingerly at the spongy, hot skin. *That* was clearly the point of impact, where the rig's seals had buckled; but even that was just a welt rising up out of the sea of purple-red. The skin itself was unbroken.

"No." Diran took a short, nervous-energy step. Her hands flexed and fluttered. She had nice hands. Long fingers. Fine bones. Skin darker than Iari's, warm and creamy brown. You could see the shadow of her tenju grandmother in the squared-off stubborn of her jaw, if you knew where to look, if you'd ever got Dee to admit that grandparent's existence.

Iari had.

Jareth said, in *Meditations* Book Six, Chapter Five, that all experience led to knowledge. That even mistakes, *especially* mistakes, were necessary and valuable lessons. Iari reckoned she'd be happier with a little more ignorance about Dee. But then, Jareth had a lot to say about happiness, too.

Diran lifted her chin. Narrowed her eyes. Clenched her jaw and made that tenju grandmother that much more obvious. "I can *make* you stay."

Oh, for the love of the Four. Iari shook out her skinsuit. Raised a cloud of stale sweat, a spangling of skin-flakes. She grimaced and shifted (careful, *careful*: lose balance now, and Dee would have real cause to keep her), and started to put the foul thing back on. "Medical order? Sure. You want to do that, go ahead. Then we're both miserable. Or I go report to Tobin, and I take Char with me and you get your hallway back. We both win."

For a fistful of heartbeats Dee stood there, not really blocking Iari's path to the door. Then she stepped aside. "I'm going to make sure the Knight-Marshal knows you're leaving against my advice."

"Void and dust, fine, whatever. If he tells me to report back here, I will." Iari paused long enough for the door to retract. Took forever. Slagging thing, creep-creep-creep in its track. She eeled through as soon as she had enough space. And yes, there was Char, taking up more than their share of the corridor, even pressed against the wall, slumped and trying to be as compact as possible.

They straightened. "Lieutenant."

"Char." Iari was eye-level with the rent in Char's chestplate. "Got to get you repaired. Come on."

The way out was—Iari blinked, oriented, aimed herself down the hallway—that way. She damn near flattened a junior healer who slewed out of a room with a trayful of vials full of—oh, Ptah's fiery breath, looked like piss—and into Iari's half of the corridor. Little alw, eyes the size of plates and blue as summer skies.

Iari folded out of the way (let Char do that, too, please, oh Elements). Muttered, "Sorry," and kept her hand on the wall for support. Every step made her knees ache. And her hips. And every joint, toes to skull. Too much synning. Let the nanomecha rest a little (Rest? What did that even mean to little machines?), and those aches would recede.

Should've already, Iari thought. It'd been hours now. That wasn't impatience talking, either, that was experience. Something *was* wrong with her nanomecha. Dee wasn't lying about that.

She felt stupid asking, but, "Char. You feel all right?"

"I am within operational parameters." The riev made a grinding noise not unlike one of Gaer's laughs. "Barely."

"Okay." Iari had to give up the wall as she came to the hospice's main door. The door that led up the back stairs to her quarters was *just over there.* She could see her slagging window, shutters open to the breeze and the ledge the cats used to get in and out. And she had to cross the courtyard to get there.

The Aedis courtyard was a massive piece of real estate, ringed on all four sides (one for each Element) by barracks, offices, offi-cers' quarters, the kitchen, the library, laboratories, the hopper hangar, *everything*. A whole little city with mooring to land an aethership in the center (two, in emergencies). The temple domi-nated one end of it, furthest from the main gates, massive doors thrown wide to daylight. So a single riev, scout-class like Brisk Ar-ray, didn't stand out immediately.

Except for the eyestalks. Those were distinctive. So was the sudden burst of movement, from absolute stillness to brisk trot, straight for them.

There were usually templars training in the yard; it was mostly empty now, with Peshwari's unit fully deployed in B-town. The handful remaining paused in their exercise to watch Brisk Array, to notice Char, to notice *her*.

Fantastic. There'd be gossip all over the barracks by midafter-noon. Lieutenant Iari and the riev.

Brisk Array squeaked to a sudden stop and snapped a salute, right fist to left shoulder. "Lieutenant."

That wasn't going to help the gossip. Neither was this: Iari re-turned the salute. "Brisk Array. I'm glad you're all right. I was afraid Sawtooth might've gotten you."

A trio of eyestalks bent toward Char. "Brisk Array was ordered to avoid engagement and to alert the templars." He sounded faintly accusatory.

Char made that faint rumbling noise again.

Iari cleared her throat, forestalling—what, a riev squabble? Was that even possible? "You saved our lives. Mine and the am-bassador's. You and Char both. I know riev collect fees for their service, so." She bounced a look off Char. "Any repairs you need, in addition to whatever your regular rates are for this morning, I'll see you get them."

"Lieutenant," said Char. "Brisk Array and I have determined that we wish to remain in service."

"In service. What, on retainer?" She could make that argument to Tobin.

"In service," Char repeated. "As templars."

Iari blinked. "Oh."

Brisk Array tilted an eyestalk at Char, what passed for trading looks. "Please," said Char. "Lieutenant. Will you take our petition to the Knight-Marshal?"

Supplicants usually did that themselves: appeared at the gate, requested admission, requested an audience with the resident Knight-Marshal. Except supplicants had to be Confederate citizens, and riev were—what *were* riev, legally?

That wasn't her decision, though, was it? Hers was a lot simpler. Tell them *yes*, or *no*.

She stared at the rent in Char's chestplate. At the stump of their right arm.

"I will," she said. "I'm going there next." After a shower, a change of clothes. Iari took a bite of breath. "Char, I can't promise what he'll say."

"I know. *We* know." Char saluted again. "Thank you, Lieutenant."

Iari drew a deep breath, regretted it, compounded that regret by waving her arm and shouting, "Corporal!" at a dark-haired human in the training yard.

Iari didn't know her well. Another of the unassigned who kept to herself, rotating through unloved and unpopular nightwatch shifts. Young, and markedly *not* one of Peshwari's unit. Which made her available right now, and that was all Iari needed. Luki might be dull as a stone (apologies to Chaama), but even stones could serve.

Luki turned out to be unstonelike. Her eyes were sharp, flicking back and forth between the riev and Iari. But she didn't stare, didn't stutter, didn't hesitate when Iari said *take Char and Brisk Array to the armorsmith, get them patched, tell Jorvik it's priority one.* Said, "Yes, Lieutenant," and then, "Come with me, please," and suddenly Iari was alone.

She marched—carefully—across the courtyard and braved the steps to her quarters. Two flights, which lasted forever and hurt every slagging step. She was breathless by the time she got to her door, vision all grey on the edges (and no Char to catch her, so don't fall). She leaned hard on the wall as she pressed her palm on the door lock and wondered, not for the first time, what happened if a templar lost a hand, or scarred her palm past reading. Did they reset the lock for the other hand, then?

Keep picking fights with Brood-corrupt riev, maybe she'd find out. Iari ducked inside, shut the door and leaned briefly against it. Locked it again as an afterthought.

"There you are."

Her heart lurched, damn near triggered the syn. Sent a whole new surge of misery into her limbs. She whipped around (too fast, void and dust) and there was voidspit *Gaer* perched on her workstation stool. Spiky knees drawn up, feet hooked on the rungs. Vakari didn't do toes on their casual footwear. Bare talons. Had to be miserable in the winter. Stone floors were cold.

She hoped he was a little bit miserable now.

"*What* are you doing here?"

"Waiting." He held up one hand, palm out and open. In the other, he clutched a tablet with a Five Tribes Embassy logo embossed on the back. "The Knight-Marshal is worried about you."

"Tobin did *not* send you to wait in my quarters."

"No. But I am also worried, and so I showed some initiative."

"By hexing your way through my lock? Don't answer that." Iari shook her head. Regretted the sharpness of the motion. Got angry at that regret and repeated the gesture. She started peeling the skinsuit off, rapid gestures that minimized the time spent balancing on one foot. "You needed to see me, I was down in the hospice."

"I know. I don't go there." Gaer leaned back, folding his arms in some origami of spikes and joints that managed to look graceful, careless, unconcerned. He tucked the tablet against his chest.

She didn't need to be an arithmancer to see *nerves* all over him. "Neither do I. But you were bleeding, before. You should get checked out."

He sniffed. "Nosebleeds happen with arithmancy. Nothing serious."

"Don't be a neefa. The Aedis healers know what to do with your physiology."

"Yes. I'm sure. I'm sure *everyone* with a hint of military background does. You were right, before. I'm not just an ambassador. Special Research. SPERE."

"So? War's long over. Isn't that what you say all the time? No one's going to crack you open, even if you're not really a diplomat." She kicked the skinsuit off and took the long way around her bed—on which there was a cat asleep, a patchwork fluff that looked like Tatter—and ducked into the tiny WC. Officer's privilege, getting private facilities, even if she'd seen bigger field privies. But the water was hot. Hell, there *was* water, not that alchemical mist that did fine for the dirt and did nothing for comfort or warmth.

Gaer was still there when she got out, a fistful of minutes later. Watching her, eyes narrow, second lid half-drawn in. Probably waiting for her to ask him to leave, or look somewhere else, or some other indication of the taboos he knew he was breaking. The

Confederation had a lot of different customs, even within species; but they had a few uniting features, and one of those involved wearing clothes when dealing with foreign ambassadors.

Well. Let Gaer learn a new thing today, then. Iari had redefined what naked meant to her a long time ago. Her skin pebbled in the chill. She stalked to the fireplace, activated the hexes. Stood there, as fire bloomed on the hearth. The Aedis compound had central heat. But there was something about fire that made warmth seem more real than hot water piped under stone floors. And, well. Fire was an aspect of Ptah. Every living quarters had a representation of the Four, in one aspect or another.

The warmth felt good on her skin, anyway. She rubbed her hair carefully. Finding new bruises every second, wasn't she. "Seriously, Gaer. Cut the voidspit. Why're you here?"

"Tobin is expecting a report. I wanted to talk to you first. I believe Tobin will be less likely to shoot me if his favorite lieutenant is there."

Iari paused, mid-toweling. There were a couple things wrong with what he'd just said. She picked the only one she intended to argue about. "Why in the name of the Four would he shoot you? Gaer. Make sense."

"He sent me along with you to prevent *this*." Gaer waved a hand at her.

"What, you think you were there as my protection? Flip that around." Iari laughed, *hell* with her ribs. Raw sound, wheezy, scaring Gaer a little. She choked it off. Panted until she caught enough breath to say, "Seriously. What's the matter?"

Gaer flared every appendage on his face that *would* flare. "The riev. Could they do that to you, when you die? Make you into one?"

Huh. That wasn't what she'd expected to hear. "There's a ban on creating new riev. So no."

"Could they have, *before* that ban? Is this what you people did with your dead?"

"Some of them." She glanced sidelong. "Wouldn't have minded. Used to be you could sign waivers in the army. I would've done that. But once I joined the Aedis, it's impossible. Something about the nanomecha and the syn implants makes it so the artificing doesn't work."

Gaer's facial orifices did a full reverse, narrowing and flattening until his head looked a third smaller. His chromatophores, ordinarily so relentlessly neutral, faded yellow, then red, then soaked back to a dull sepia. Only his eyes widened, that second lid retracting to invisibility, leaving his eyes round and dark and gleaming.

Oh, blessed Ptah. This was the expression for offended vakari orthodoxy. Which was fine for the civs who never left their own gravity wells, but she'd expected better of Gaer. Iari teetered between irritation and embarrassment. She turned her shoulder to him and got on with dressing. Whatever she'd told Dee, she wasn't really off duty (unless Tobin said otherwise). That meant a uniform, and *that* meant armor. Just not a battle-rig.

Still heavy, though. Still required concentration to settle the chestplate over the uniform shirt and trousers. Required squaring off with herself in the mirror and not looking at an offended vakar.

He was watching her, though. She felt that attention, heavy and pointed and still somehow fragile, like a massive rock teetering on the edge of a cliff, half a breath of wind from a rockslide.

"Gaer. I'm losing patience."

"It's just—you have no idea how terrifying they were during the war. How terrifying they are, even now. How they moved together, how we could never intercept any comm signals. They had to be linked in a quantum network, we knew that. But there's *knowing*, with facts in hand, and then there's what you *believed* when riev ripped through the hatch of your ship, or five of your squadmates. *Then*, it looked like magic." He flashed her a vakar grin: narrow eyes, lips sealed, nostrils flared wide.

"You talk like you were there."

"Of course I wasn't. I'm too young for *that* war. But I studied a great deal. Vakari—Five Tribes, Protectorate—we all love a good war story. Half the war-vids produced are about the Expansion or the Schism, and if they're about the Expansion, there's always riev in them because we're always fighting the Confederation."

"And the other half of the war-vids?"

"All about the Weep, of course. Brood. Then, it's mostly you lot getting torn apart while our arithmancers save everyone. The point is—*knowing* that there was a signal connecting the riev is like finding out the strange noise in the dark is just a neefa, and not, oh, a pack of Brood boneless. And *that's* why I'm here. The chip we pulled out of Sawtooth. While you were sitting in medical, I was looking it over. I was expecting, given the levels of Brood contamination, for it to be covered in the same marks we found on that altar. But it isn't. I think that it's got hexwork like an *Aedian* implant. I cannot *confirm* that, since I don't have official access to that data. Or the hexwork. Or the arithmantic theory underlying them. But whatever it is, it successfully circumvents riev security measures." He shifted on the stool. Moved his face out of her sightline.

"So . . . ?" She tugged the chestplate ungently into line. "We knew that already. Sawtooth and Swift Runner wouldn't've attacked us otherwise."

"Iari." He said her name a little bit desperately, like a prayer that meant *please hear what I'm not saying.*

She wanted to spin around, snap at him, *I've got two cracked ribs and I'm missing a half a pint of blood and Diran thinks my nanomecha are compromised, so just say what you mean.* But that would all be—well, true, yes, but also an excuse. There wasn't anything wrong with her brain. Nothing wrong with her wits, whatever the stereotypes about tenju intellect.

She adjusted her chestplate, more gently this time. Centered that crest. Lined up her lieutenant's pips. Angled herself so that she could see Gaer's face again in the glass, scrunched up as he was on the edge of the stool. "*Circumvent.* You're saying someone didn't cut through the safeguards. You're saying someone went *around* them. That's significant?"

"It is. This chip was meant to leave a functioning riev after its installation. That suggests someone with an intimate knowledge of riev hexwork. A wichu artificer certainly would have that expertise. I'm not sure who else would."

"You're saying a wichu did this."

"I am."

Iari turned around, *hell* with exactly where her pips sat, and locked eyes with Gaer. "Except the only artificer we've had cause to know about is Pinjat, and he's conveniently dead. He could be responsible for this circumvention, or he could've discovered someone else was doing it. Either way, that'd be a reason to kill him. Except that would change who'd have a motive to do it. If Tzcansi commissioned the hack in the first place, seems damned shortsighted to kill him. She gets no more evil riev."

"Pinjat might have tried, oh, I don't know. Raising his prices? Maybe he thought he was too important to kill. Or he was going to sell the technology to someone else, and she found out. *My* government would pay for the knowledge."

Iari's gaze snapped to Gaer's tablet. "But they don't have to, do they, because you've got the chip already. You can just tell them. Report."

"You understand my dilemma." Gaer turned his tablet over in his hands.

What she understood was the more nervous Gaer got, the more syllables he deployed. Like adjusting the bolts-per-second on a jacta, except his vocabulary just got more accurate, where a jacta's aim went to shit. "I don't, actually. You know I'll report what you say to me to Tobin, so you can't mean to keep it secret. You also know I won't stop you from sending the information to your superiors. And if you were worried that Tobin *would* stop you, you'd've kept your mouth shut and sent your report, the end."

"Right. I would have. This is the sort of thing careers are made on. I report it, I am off this little rocky seedworld with the next voidship. I'm—" He bit off whatever he'd meant to say next. His face flowed through another chromatic shift of distress. "Brood contamination in riev, a mysterious altar, hexwork I don't recognize. A *setatir* swarm in B-town that isn't killing random civilians, but appears to be attacking targets. And this planet's got its own Weep fissure. That can't all be coincidence. There's got to be a connection. Figuring out what that is . . ." Gaer cast a frustrated glance up, as if the answers hung on the ceiling. "That's *bigger* than making reports, isn't it? Or seeking promotions?"

Now she got it. Like a mallet between the eyes. "So you want to tell Tobin and *not* Five Tribes Intelligence? Because you're *curious*? That's treason, isn't it?"

"That's discretionary reporting. *Yes*. That's treason." Gaer grinned unhappily. "I need Tobin to work with me on this. I need access to Aedis data. *Need* it, Iari, because I *need* to understand how this works. Now do you understand?"

What would make a man turn on his oaths, just to *know* something? Arithmancer. Scholar. But priests got like that, too, sometimes, with knowledge. "No," she told him. "But Tobin might. You can ask him. I'm going to make a report. Come with me."

"Now?"

"Yeah. Now." She dragged the word out. "Unless you have a reason to wait?"

"No. But I hope you're right about Tobin's reaction. If I get killed over this by *your* side, I'm going to be disappointed."

CHAPTER TEN ═══

s Knight-Marshal of the B-town Aedis, Tobin was entitled to a double-chambered office in the administrative
wing's first floor, sharing a corridor with the Reverend
Mother (or, occasionally, Father) as a symbol of their joint gover-
nance. He was also entitled to a secretary minding his schedule
and guarding his doorway from frivolous distractions.

When Tobin had first been assigned, there'd been a mix-up
with the departing Knight-Marshal, an overlap of several days that
departing Knight-Marshal's office had not been entirely packed
when Tobin walked (limped) down the aethership ramp. And
since he had duties to assume, and no leisure to wait, accommodations had been found: on the second floor, somewhat recessed, an
office usually relegated to assistants and ranking subordinates. Although the inconvenience had been labeled officially uninten-
tional, there were some (among them the head librarian) who had
seen a petty malice in the departing Knight-Marshal's tardiness,
so that her successor would begin his duties sandwiched between
Sister Aren of Procurements and Brother Fin, Assistant Alchemist
and Associate Director of Chirurgery.

That Tobin had chosen to stay there once his rightful office
was vacant was interpreted as a sign of his humility and

approachability (or, alternately and incorrectly, a signal of disunity with Mother Quellis). Iari reckoned he just wanted the quiet and privacy of the second floor, and that he *didn't* want a secretary. Tobin's office was open to anyone who cared to climb those steps and knock. And it was a matter of physical knocking. The B-town Aedis had keypads and updated locking mechanisms, but the doors themselves were hinged monstrosities that required manual effort to open, and so Tobin generally left his ajar when he was inside and willing to talk. Iari had climbed the stairs more times than she cared to count. Ordinarily she didn't mind.

Now—*now* she wished Tobin had taken that first-floor office. Late afternoon sunlight spilled into the hallway from a series of high, narrow windows, horizontal like the pupils of goats' eyes. It made the hallway seem oddly bright and dim at the same time, light reflecting from the ceiling and washing down to the floor and sifting through dust along the way.

Iari paused at the top of the steps. Leaned on the wall and chased her breath and ignored Gaer's concerned stare. She thought her ribs might be hurting a little bit *less*, finally. Maybe that meant the nanomecha were working and there was nothing wrong with them.

The other office doors were closed and the hallway was empty. She suspected Tobin's hand in that. A politely worded *be elsewhere this afternoon*. She also suspected he could see who came up the stairs from his desk, which meant he'd've seen her leaning on the wall. Maybe.

"Lieutenant," Tobin said, before she could even knock. "Come in."

Shit. She pointed at a stiff wooden bench on the wall between office doors. "Wait out here," she told Gaer, and pushed the door open.

Tobin wasn't even pretending to work on the turing or shuffle documents around on his tablet screen. His stylus sat, neglected, beside his folded hands. "Come in. Shut the door. Sit *down*."

"Sir." She did all three, choosing the chair closest to his desk. Hrok's breath, it'd been, what, eighteen hours since the last time she'd sat here?

Tobin's face said he was thinking the same thing, and he didn't much like the changes to her person. He frowned, eyes narrow, looking a little too closely at her face. Probably the eye. "I know what you're going to say, but I'll ask anyway. Are you all right? And before you answer, know that Sister Diran just sent me a strongly worded message regarding your fitness for duty."

Of course she had. Iari blew out a breath. "Bruised. Sore. That's all."

Tobin's lips flexed. His eyes stayed serious. "Sister Diran thinks there's something wrong with your nanomecha."

"There might be. But Dee—Sister Diran doesn't know what, yet, and she's got a bucket of my blood to run tests on. When she figures it out, she'll say. Until then." Iari let herself sag, just a little bit. The chair reminded her why that was a poor idea. It also helped her find a new bruise, just off-center on her sacrum. Delightful. "I think there *is* something wrong. I think it's related to what we found in the warehouse, and what's happened with the riev. That's why I'm here, sir."

And that fast, Tobin shed *Tobin* and became the *Knight-Marshal*. "Tell me."

She did, a brisk march through events and pertinent observations that ended when Gaer finished off Sawtooth.

Tobin did not interrupt, even when his turing beeped. Only after she finished did he glance at the screen. "Ah. It's Peshwari's initial report."

Iari sat up straight (too straight, void and dust). "What did he find?"

"Nothing yet. The warehouse is secured. There's been no attempt by anyone else to access it. He's cordoned off the basement, and he's conducting a sweep of the immediate area for further Brood, but so far he concurs with your assessment that the swarm appears to have fled into the sewers. There don't appear to be any remaining." Tobin arched a brow. "How fortunate that Peshwari's comms appear to be functioning. I thought there might be a problem with that part of town."

Iari felt her skin warm. Hoped Tobin thought it was fever, or the patch of sunlight trying to bake her in her armor. Might as well hope the sky would open up and rain beer, while she was wishing for the impossible. "My comms came back up after we neutralized the riev. I, ah. Didn't report back right away. I wanted to chase down a lead before too much time passed."

Tobin nodded. She might have been telling him that B-town winters were cold. He waited for an explanation. No, a reason. Because he trusted she had one. So she told him about Corso. Waited, while he accessed his turing to check the name. His eyes reflected the flickering march of data on the screen. "Corso Risar. Former sergeant in the Second Fleet, Second Division. Resigned his commission after most of his company died holding the line at Windscar." Subtle emphasis on *most*. Tobin knew her prior service record, too.

"Yes sir. After Windscar, there wasn't enough of the company left, so they offered us reassignment or retirement. Corso was . . . not handling it well. He chose retirement."

Truth was, Corso'd been tired of fighting. Tired of *losing*, which is how he'd seen the whole surge: the Confederation throwing its military at Brood, void and dirtside, winning sometimes but mostly just holding a line, while the Aedis made surgical strikes and *did things*, having the alchemy and the arithmancy and the equipment the regulars just didn't.

"I should've asked permission before talking to him, sir, and I'm sorry for that. But I didn't want to wait on Tzcansi."

"And you think Corso can find her?"

"Yes sir. We need to know what she knows. Whatever's happening here, Brood's only part of it. Corrupted riev are not something PKs are equipped to deal with. *Maybe* vakari troops, but no one's going to ask the Protectorate for help, and Five Tribes would ask *why*. This is the conversation I didn't want to have over comms, sir. I think we need help, but—from the Windscar garrison, maybe. Not Seawall."

"All right, Lieutenant. You're forgiven."

Iari let her breath out. "Yes sir. There's more. I, ah, promised the riev compensation in trade for their cooperation. Their usual fee. But then Char said they and Brisk Array wanted to become templars, and asked if I would bring their petition to you. That *could* be because they're trying to secure permanent employment, so they can afford repairs—so that *we* repair them. But that seems like pretty convoluted reasoning for riev."

Tobin's sharp look settled and sank into her. Prickled under her skin like barbed hooks. "Does that mean you think they're sincere in their request?"

"I do. The charter *says* a templar is called to serve the Aedis, but what that means depends on the supplicant. People join for all kinds of reasons. Fight Brood, serve the Elements. Serve the Confederation. Protect people. Steady salary, fancy armor." Iari shrugged, spacer-style, a gesture she'd learned from Tobin. "We don't ask anyone else for a motive."

Tobin leaned back. Steepled his fingers and tapped his chin with the foremost pair. "Riev have no legal status in the Confederation, *or* in the Synod."

"No sir. But they aren't classified as mecha, either. And Char uses a personal pronoun. Char is *I*. That makes them . . . a person."

Tobin blinked. "Does Brisk Array also use a personal pronoun?"

"Not that I've heard, but Char didn't either, until Sawtooth almost killed us both. I think they slipped up."

"You think Char was . . . concealing their preferences?"

Iari twitched an eyebrow, the corner of her mouth, in lieu of a more painful shrug. "I think so."

"I'll talk to Mother Quellis."

"Thank you, sir." Iari squirmed on the chair. "There's something else. Char said Pinjat was trying to restore 'Oversight.' They made it sound like an official thing. Gaer thinks it's some kind of network. Riev-to-riev. The way they were controlled during the war. Quantum, he said. Immune to vakari attempts at hacking. But that's not what I wanted to tell you. Gaer pulled a chip out of one of the riev." Iari tipped her chin sideways, vaguely in the direction of the door. "He's waiting in the hall, sir. You should probably hear this from him."

"I'm not going to like this, am I?"

"No sir."

"Oh. Well." Tobin sighed. "Better go get him."

"Wait out here," Iari had told him, and so Gaer did: skipped that hostile bench and remained standing in the hallway outside Tobin's office, at first at a polite distance from the door and then, when it became clear no one was watching, a scant handspan from its surface.

Before Tanis and B-town, Gaer had been in exactly one Aedian compound. *That* one, on Tr'Lak, far from the Weep, shared a planet with the Confederate Parliament and the Aedian Synod, and so it had been far less rustic. The doors there had been a sleek, polished chrome and steel, with an inlaid Aedian crest in the center. Tobin's door was hinged and wooden and unmarked and very good at absorbing sound.

Gaer gave up on dignity and pressed the side of his head against the gap between door and frame. The wood smelled faintly of oil and dust; the stone wall, of *more* dust with a tang of damp. Voices hummed on the other side, distinguishable mostly by tone and level. He heard his own name a few times. Heard Tobin's voice lift and sharpen, followed by a flood of Iari again, lower and rapid. He imagined her leaning forward and her hands, with those sad and useless little keratin talons (nails, they were called, though an *actual* nail was much more useful and formidable), gesturing like she did whenever she felt strongly about something.

Then came a small valley of silence, during which Gaer's guts knotted and chilled. Tobin might be sitting and thinking, or he might be typing an order for Gaer's detention. Gaer cast a glance down the hall, toward the stairs that led down to the main hall and the templar barracks. If an arrest came, it would be from *that* way. And if templars did come, well. Iari wouldn't do anything. She couldn't. Argue, yes, but actively interfere? Gaer didn't think she would.

He didn't like how that knowledge curdled in his belly. Didn't like the hard bang of his heart in his chest, either. Tobin was sensible. Iari trusted him. And so Gaer just had to trust her and her instincts and, by extension, Tobin, too.

He almost missed the footsteps on the other side of the door, *right* there, *setat.* He recoiled as the latch clicked and the door swung open.

Iari stood there. Noted his proximity to the door, likely noted the kaleidoscope of his pigments—no, *definitely* noticed. She quirked a brow at him.

"Ambassador," Tobin called. "Do come in. The lieutenant says you've got something to tell me."

Gaer tugged his jacket a little bit straighter. Then he pinned his best neutral expression in place and went in. Offered a polite bow to Tobin, and then offered his tablet.

Tobin didn't reach for it. "What is this?"

"My notes on the chip removed from the compromised riev, Sawtooth." He offered the tablet again. "Knight-Marshal. You'll be interested."

Tobin took the tablet like he expected it to bite him.

"Sit down, please."

Gaer did, in one of those chairs, all bumps and canyons in all the wrong places. There were jokes to be made about torture and diplomatic immunity and oh, no, this was not the time.

Gaer had gotten quite skilled at reading soft-skin expressions— such mobile faces, almost as revealing as auras—but the Knight-Marshal's lips and brows remained level, immobile, unhelpful. His aura was probably a stunning display, but he had some kind of hex running that rendered his aura a uniform and patently false bird's-egg blue.

Gaer realized, with some belated embarrassment, that he'd never imagined the Knight-Marshal would employ a concealment hex in his office. But he'd never tried reading the Knight-Marshal here before, either, because he'd never been invited this far into the templar administrative wing. All his meetings with Tobin had taken place in the public parts of the Aedis. Reception. Mess halls. Courtyards. And yes, that one little assignation on the battlements.

Gaer was glad of his own facial rigidity, because if he had brows and lips that would pucker and droop, his would be doing so. *And* he was glad of Iari's presence. She sat beside him, her chair a little closer to Tobin's desk, watching the Knight-Marshal read Gaer's report. No sign of impatience, no fidgeting. She might as well have been a part of the wretched chair.

A less charitable, less informed person might've attributed her stoicism to her tenju heritage, and the downright bigoted would say that stoicism came from a basic lack of intellect. The tenju were the shock-troops of the Confederation, without whom, it was widely accepted, the fragile alliance wouldn't have survived its first decade. Certainly it had been tenju infantry that had gone toe-to-talon with vakari marines most often. Oh, the Confederates didn't segregate their units, not officially, of course not. But it hadn't been *alwar* units making landfall on Driss, in the last days of the Expansion war.

It was also a fact not lost on Gaer, or SPERE command—or anyone else who spent any time studying the Confederation—that alwar made up the bulk of seats in the Confederate Parliament. In the Synod, it was humans who held most of the titles. Tenju had a higher percentage membership in the templars, but even there, their total numbers did not constitute a majority. And that might be coincidence; tenju spacers were organized around clans and battle-fleets. Tenju seedworlds showed a trend toward tribal organization and limited industrialization, which seemed to suggest a cultural disinterest in large-scale empire-building. No tenju seedworld had ever developed void-travel on its own. Certainly *this* little rock, Tanis, had been just figuring out explosive powder when the first alwar dropped into its gravity well.

Humans, now, like the Knight-Marshal—clever mammals. Flexible genetics, able to breed successfully with alwar or tenju. They had, as a species, spent less time in the void, and so they were at some disadvantage with void-travel trade routes. The tenju spacer-clans had been the humans' natural allies (being somewhat natural pirates) against the pre-established alwar web of galactic trade.

It was a fact much bemoaned in Protectorate history that, had the Protectorate kept to its borders another century or so, the tenju-human alliance might've taken care of the alwar altogether, the tenju clans allying with the human leagues and consortiums, acting as a counter to the old alwar Harek Empire, eventually outspending it, overwhelming it, either financially or militarily. Had that happened, there would have been no alwar left of any socio-political-economic consequence to join the Confederation to oppose the Expansion. Without the alwar, the Confederation, lacking formidable alchemy and arithmancy of its own, would have been too weak to oppose Protectorate forces.

The Five Tribes was more agnostic in its judgment; without the Expansion, there would *be* no Five Tribes, no reason to rebel, no chance that their heresy would succeed. But there wouldn't be a Weep, either, if the Protectorate hadn't felt cornered and desperate.

It was the sort of historical irony that kept academics on all sides occupied.

What Gaer knew was that had Knight-Marshal Tobin been alwar, not human, Gaer would be politely confined to his quarters already, and the contents of his tablet would be triple-encrypted and already quantum-hexed to the Knight-General on Tr'Lak. Of course, had Iari been alwar, he wouldn't have gone with her into B-town at all, whatever favors or access to libraries and data the Knight-Marshal had offered. Chase down riev with an *alw*. As if.

Which meant—in that alternate plane of the multiverse—proof of a massive security breach to riev by an unfamiliar, hostile arithmancy *and* a localized Brood incursion would have remained undiscovered until it was possibly too late to do any good.

So. There was a lesson there, about xenophobia. Maybe he'd include that in his report, too, assuming he ever got round to sending it to Commander Karaesh't in the Seawall embassy.

Assuming Tobin didn't do all the things Iari swore he wouldn't.

What Tobin was doing now was rereading, for the third time or the thirtieth, the contents of the tablet. Gaer leaned back in the chair, and then forward again when some knobby protuberance jabbed into his spinal ridge.

Iari flicked a glance at him, and the smallest half-hitch of a sympathetic smile.

And when he looked back, Tobin was staring at him. The Knight-Marshal's face had sunk all the way back to neutral. Some soft-skins got *very* still when they were most angry. Iari, for one. Gaer thought Tobin might be one of those, too.

"I'm not completely sure I understand every technical detail," Tobin said, and his voice confirmed Gaer's suspicion. Cool, quiet, briskly contained, and furious. "But what I'm seeing here is that you've discovered that riev have in fact been compromised, with what you allege is contamination akin to Brood, but using a vector, what did you say, *not unlike Aedian implants*, and that we have a person, or persons, in Lowtown who possess this skill, using it for purposes as yet undetermined. Is that right?"

Gaer wished his chair was the chair closer to the window, in case he needed a quick escape. One jump to the desk and he'd be there. Simple mechanical latches. Then he let the fantasy go, and his regrets that he'd come here at all, and made eyelock with Tobin. "Correct. But Char—and I imagine Brisk Array, too, if someone asked him—says that the installation of such a device requires co-operation on the part of the riev. The implication being—the riev *asked* for this chip, but whether they knew they were getting *this* or not, we don't know. It's unclear whether the contamination is a feature of this chip or a side effect."

"Do you know whether the affected riev shared some sort of communication?"

"No. We know that Brood appear to communicate with each other without equipment. Pheromones, some sort of deep-aether entanglement, telepathy, magic—there are a great many hypotheses. *I* hypothesize that this chip is meant to employ a similar mechanism to what Brood use to connect the riev. I hypothesize that the altar we found might be some sort of transmitter or central point. But to be sure, I would need to examine it in some detail."

"Yes. The altar. I note your report makes a detailed mention of it, but draws no conclusions as to its origins or purpose, except to say that the script on it appears to be k'bal. Is that because you really don't know, or . . . ?"

"Or am I trying to retain some information for my superiors that you don't get to read first? I really *don't* know. Even if I had not come to you with this data, Knight-Marshal, I *would* be here asking to examine that altar. K'bal artifacts are rare. What one is doing here, on a tenju seedworld, I can't even guess. I suppose it was smuggled from offworld. We did find it in a ganglord's warehouse."

"And I suppose SPERE wants to find out why it's here, and who brought it."

"Of course they will. So does the Aedis. Obviously, sir, because here we are in your office having this conversation."

Iari moved, on Gaer's periphery, an audible squeak as the chair scraped the stone tile. Take that as a kick in the ankle, long-distance.

"They will, future tense." Tobin spun the tablet on the desk and pushed it back to Gaer with a fingertip. "You haven't sent this to your superiors yet."

It wasn't a question. Gaer cocked his head. "I haven't."

"Why not?"

Gaer leaned forward slowly, hands open, empty, hopefully non-threatening. "My assignment here is, among other things, to observe the fissure, to report Brood activity, and to report signs of a new surge. If there is a new surge, then I am authorized to assist the Aedis at my discretion. I have a lot of latitude, as a SPERE agent, in how I fulfill that assignment."

Tobin's lips broke their stiff line, drawing together in an expression Gaer knew meant *thoughtful*. "Including when you file this report."

"Yes." He felt Iari's stare scorching the side of his face. Please, oh dark lords, she didn't call him *liar* right here, and throw the word treason around the Knight-Marshal's office. Because he was committing that, to some reckoning (his political enemies', certainly), but also not, dependent largely on how circumstances resolved. "If I am to be of any use to my superiors, I need *your* confidence to operate. I don't get that confidence if I send SPERE command proof that someone has breached riev security. That sort of information will delight some, and disturb others, and generally sow chaos as people scrabble about trying to figure out how best to *use* it. I think that would distract us from bigger problems."

"Such as?"

"Why there are Brood in B-town. How they got here. Why they aren't killing everyone they encounter. *And* the potential for breaching and corrupting Aedian hexwork. If *you* go down, the next surge will be the last one for all of us."

"Could you replicate the arithmancy on the chip?"

"Me personally?" Gaer flared his plates. The room's aether tasted like stone and wood-oil and the constant presence of mammals. Most vakari couldn't distinguish human from tenju from alwar. Soft-skin was soft-skin.

No. It's not that they *couldn't* distinguish. It's that they didn't bother to try.

"Perhaps, with time and access to documents the Aedis won't thank you for giving me."

"Only perhaps?"

"I'm unfamiliar with Aedian techniques. It's not strictly arithmancy, as *we* understand it." Careful, careful use of pronouns. Differentiation without judgment. "You are more inclined to, ah, diluting the purity of the equations with galvanics and alchemy. And the nanomecha, of course. They replicate and, if I understand correctly, self-repair."

Tobin's gaze flicked to Gaer's optic. His mouth flexed into a smile that could've been gently amused if his eyes hadn't been anything but. "What about repairing riev armor? Jorvik is going to need some help with Char."

Gaer glanced at Iari. Found her looking back, a smile curdling around her capped tusk. The light coming out of the courtyard made that scar on her face seem especially livid. Iari was the sort to run face-first into trouble. And since he was intending to go with her into that trouble, well, best he helped where he could.

"I'm an arithmancer, not an artificer. But yes. If Char's willing to let me try, I think I can repair their hexwork."

"If Char's *willing*." Tobin's face said he'd never thought about *asking* riev anything before. Then his expression twisted into something like shame's younger cousin. "Then we'll ask them."

Gaer wasn't sure what'd just happened, what shift in Tobin's worldview had occurred. But whatever it was, it wasn't making his stare any more comfortable when it returned back to Gaer. "What about internal defenses? Do you think you can work something up for Char and Brisk Array against whatever the chip does to riev?"

"Char said a riev would need to consent to the chip's installation, which they and Brisk Array have not. Although, *sss*. If someone re-establishes Oversight, that might not matter, if they can hack straight into the riev *collectively* across a quantum hex. Which means no, I can't work anything up. Not without access to a great deal more proprietary data than I think you have, Knight-Marshal. I understand the wichu don't part with their secrets."

"No. They do not." Tobin's jaw flexed, the first crack in his near-vakari mask. "I can't *order* you to do anything. Let's be clear on that. All I can do is trust you and *believe* that you share a mutual interest with us in preventing whatever's happening out there from spreading."

"I won't betray you, Knight-Marshal. Not Lieutenant Iari. Not the Aedis, in this matter." Gaer bared his teeth. Tribe, mother, *everything* in those blue etchings. Tobin couldn't read them (*probably* couldn't); but he would understand what the gesture meant. Templars swore by the Elements and the ideals of the Aedis, not family lineage, but the effect was the same.

Tobin and Iari traded a look that was really a whole conversation. Then Tobin rummaged around on his desk. He found a blank chit and stuffed it into the side of his turing. He struck a sequence of keys, and caught a faint ozone smell, accompanied by an even fainter hiss, followed by the chit's ejection.

Tobin pushed it across the desk. "This pass will get you into the warehouse. Give this to whichever of Peshwari's people is on duty. Those are my orders to let you down to examine the altar. And whatever you find—"

"I report to you first. Yes." Gaer started to reach for the chit. Stopped when Tobin's finger showed no signs of moving. "Knight-Marshal? Is there something else?"

But Tobin was looking at Iari. "Lieutenant," Tobin said softly, reluctantly. "I'm sorry to ask, but I need you to act as the ambassador's escort. You're familiar with the situation. Anyone else at this point would *not* be, and I want to keep knowledge of this altar as limited as possible. Therefore, I'm going to authorize a temporary replacement for your battle-rig and clear the medical hold on your records."

A medical *hold*? And the Knight-Marshal overriding that. Gaer failed to control his surprise. Hissed, then stopped breath altogether. Tobin ignored him. Iari did not. Shot him a *don't* setatir *say anything* glare diluted by fear.

Iari's lip curled around that capped tusk. "I understand, sir."

Tobin slid the chit across the desk toward Gaer. "All right. Be careful. Both of you."

CHAPTER ELEVEN

"You can stop pacing." Gaer's voice leaked from beneath the altar, muffled and distorted by depth and angle. "You think I'd be down here on the floor if I thought Brood might crawl up out of the drain?"

Iari didn't bother answering with the obvious: that all the arithmantic optics in Five Tribes territory—of which there was one here already, strapped into a certain vakar's face—wouldn't detect Brood incoming unless they were pointing at the source, and Gaer wasn't looking at the drain.

She stopped beside him and stared down at his lower half. It looked like the altar had fallen on him, not like he'd crawled underneath it. Disturbing idea. "So what is under there?"

"I'm not sure. Every *setatir* scrap of this surface is marked. Most of it looks like k'bal script, but I'm also seeing fragments of other languages mixed in. I am scanning those into this tablet, in hopes that your mighty Aedian turings can help translate. Or, failing that, your library might be of use. There are *also* some equations, mysterious and likely dangerous and definitely out of place here."

"Equations, what, like arithmancy?"

"Yes. No." He made one of those overheated-plasma seal noises. "Shall I explain the nuances of the Ringelt Mean to you?"

"Yeah. Go ahead."

"No, because you wouldn't understand. *I* don't understand. It's obscure theory having to do with quantum properties and tesser-hexing, and what that is doing on a dirtside chunk of metal, I have no idea—*setat!*"

There came a hollow bang, the sort a vakar's bony skull might make bouncing off iron.

Iari sighed and squatted, arms balanced on her knees. It felt like breathing knives. "You all right?"

Gaer had his nose damn near pressed to the metal, the glow from his optic bouncing blue off the iron. "This thing has an *interior*. It's *hollow*. I can see the seam, but I can't find a latch or any way to open it."

Iari imagined an unvisored Gaer getting a faceful of violated wards. "Don't touch it."

"Sss. Of course not. I am entirely certain I don't want to open this without more than just you in attendance, particularly since you aren't entirely well." He began extracting himself from beneath the altar without actually touching the metal, until he was clear and as flat on his back as vakari spines permitted. The glow off his tablet dusted his chin and jaw-plates with silver, like frost. "What's wrong with you, exactly? The medical hold."

"My nanomecha are being a little sluggish doing their repairs."

"What does that mean?"

That Diran was furious, mostly. And: "I'm not healing fast as I should be, and I don't have the syn right now. So don't start any fights."

Gaer turned far enough to see her square in his optic. Bet he was reading her aura, and seeing whatever color *scared* was. She braced for some clever remark.

But all Gaer said was, "Understood," in a quiet voice, and then went back to making notes on his tablet.

He was SPERE, she reminded herself. Five Tribes special ops. The chattery scatter-wit arithmancer-ambassador had to be an act, or at least partly so. That made her feel better and not at the same time. He'd backed her in a fight. That was something.

And still. She was an Aedian templar. She should have, oh, *other* Aedian templars at her back. Instead she had a pair of decommissioned riev and a vakar commando. Fortunately she *also* had nothing to do except watch Gaer root around under a piece of metal. It was a little like being on nightwatch again, both wishing for something interesting to happen, and dreading that something might.

Her comms beeped. "Lieutenant Iari. Go ahead."

Peshwari's unit had set up a relay just outside the warehouse, with a little transmitter booster to banish any claims of *dead comms* next time Tobin tried to call her.

"Lieutenant?" The voice wasn't Tobin. Someone young and male and probably spacer-born and human, from the depth and pitch of his Comspek. "Someone named Corso Risar called for you. Wants to be patched through. Said it's urgent."

Oh, blessed Elements. Saved from Gaer's curiosity by Corso, of all people.

"Do it."

The comms clicked. "Iari?"

"Corso. You find Tzcansi?"

"I did." His tone sounded like a man talking through a locked jaw. Iari's guts did a dive-and-roll. "What?"

"She's—you'll want to see this. How soon can you get here?"

"Where are you?"

He gave her an address farther up the hill, almost to Hightown. Mostly residential, post-war reconstruction projects that didn't defy fire codes and rely on Chaama's mercy to stay standing.

"Understood. Give me ten. Iari out."

Gaer got to his feet and came and stood beside her. Iari got a noseful of warm vakar, less burnt sugar this time, more like scorched metal. "Well? Where are we going? I didn't quite hear the address."

"Corso's found Tzcansi. Not far from where we found Pinjat." Hrok's breath, two nights ago. Only two. "You're not coming. I'll take Brisk Array with me. Leave Char here with you."

"Sss. Don't be stupid."

"No. Whatever *that* means"—she stabbed a finger at the altar—"is important, and you're the closest thing we've got to an expert. You stay. Figure it out. Don't think it's going to help, dealing with some ganglord, if I bring a vakar with me."

The address turned out to be a row house in the middle of a street of row houses that looked like a post-surge reconstruction initiative. Everything with the same basic hinged doors and latching windows, the same steps, same facade. The ones on this side of the street were shuttered against the sunlight slanting into the street. On the other side, where the houses sat in shadow, the window stared like vakari eyes, black and blank.

Her needle-socket ached. This borrowed rig felt like someone else's skin, all of it just a little too large, the proportions just a little bit off, and there was chafing in three places, one of which made her grimly grateful that she was currently celibate. The voidspit thing was still default settings, not battle primed, not adjusted to her particular nanomecha frequencies because they were voidspit offline.

Iari stopped at the foot of the front steps. The front door hung just a little ajar, scratches in the wood of the lintel. The edge of the lock was blackened, like someone had overloaded the electronics and fried their way inside.

Corso wouldn't be that stupid, please Ptah and Hrok. Someone else had been here first.

She glanced at Brisk Array. The riev stood behind her, sensor array stiff and pointing every direction. He didn't seem alarmed. (How would *alarm* look, on a riev?) Just alert.

Brisk Array noticed her looking at him. Two, three, five stalks canted her direction. "Lieutenant?"

She considered leaving him outside for less than a heartbeat. "With me. Stay close."

Iari made a fist of her left hand. The tesla's steady glow in the gauntlet said her (borrowed) shield was ready to deploy. She used that hand to push the door open. Dark inside, except where the sun leaked around the shutters: bars of dust-beam brightness that turned the whole room to twilight.

It looked like a post-surge project floorplan inside, too. Square front room, stairs to the second floor at the back, adjacent to the hallway that led to a kitchen. There were rugs on the floor, not especially clean. Tables. A pair of chairs, a wide sofa, a vidscreen mounted on the wall with a small array of electronics beneath it. A console 2D player, a bulkier, older-model 3D player. A lingering odor of grease hung in the air. Someone had been using the kitchen recently. The coldbox whined, audible all the way out here. Probably a motor on its way out.

She took a careful step into the living room while Brisk Array filled the doorway. The room went dimmer with the riev blocking the light. Iari waited, listening past her own breath. Trusting Brisk Array's augmented audio-visuals. Trusting her own gut, which tensed up at a house this quiet, this *empty*.

"Brisk Array. Anything?"

"A person at the top of the stairs, Lieutenant."

A floorboard creaked. Iari snapped her shield out, marked with one part of her brain the fractional delay between crackle and actual *shield* (the rig relying on physical signals, nerves firing through her implants, rather than a nano boost) and the faint ozone smell that came with it. Then a familiar silhouette bled out of the shadows at the top of the stairs.

"Corso," she snapped, for Brisk Array's benefit. She shook her wrist and sucked the shield back into her gauntlet.

"Took your time," he snapped back. "I thought you were the fucking PKs."

"Those your scorch marks on the front door?"

"What? No." Iari could just make out the glint of a tusk as he smiled, the flutter of movement as he pointed. "I came in through the kitchen window. Over the garden wall," he added, when she stared. "*This* district, all the labor—grounds, domestics—is tenju. Shuffle around like you belong, people look, no one *sees*. Not like you two. Probably a hundred posts on the local grid by now about the templar and the riev walking around the neighborhood."

Iari moved to the bottom of the steps. From this angle she could see Corso more clearly. He wore the shapeless coveralls of a day-laborer, unmarked by any brand or logo. He slid a jacta into one of the pockets as she watched. The way his arm moved, the shoulder, the way the coveralls creased, said he had more under that plain grey canvas than just himself.

Ungentle Ptah. No wonder Corso was nervous about the PKs. Bigger wonder he'd gotten through a window at all. "That armor you're wearing is illegal."

"Rather pay the fine than have a bolt in my chest."

"That something you worry about a lot? Bolts in your chest?"

"When I'm hunting ganglords, it is. We don't all get fancy battle-rigs when we go to war. *You* remember."

She did. Army standard-issue field armor was a lot like templar uniforms. All physical armor panels, no needle-sockets, no hexwork. Cheap to make in large quantities, like this rowhouse. Like the soldiers.

"We're not at war anymore."

"Huh." He straightened. A stray band of sunlight glanced off the beads of sweat on his cheekbones. Yeah. Standard armor was hot. She remembered that, too. "You come up *here* and tell me that."

"Yeah? What'll I see?—Stay here," she told Brisk Array. She took the stairs faster than her ribs liked. "Whose house is this? Not Tzcansi's."

"No. Belongs to her sister. She's got kids, two of them. Tzcansi bought them the house, so I figured she'd know where I could find her. Only I get here, and—no sister. No sister's kids. Only one I found is Tzcansi." Corso laughed without humor or air and started down the hallway. "Good thing, I guess."

And then the smell hit, stronger than the grease or dust, right in the base of her skull. Thick and metallic and clinging to the back of her throat as she breathed. There was something sour under that, something rancid, that her brain remembered before her rig lit up with Brood alert. She killed the alarm before it got a chance to start howling.

Corso was watching her, eyes flat and knowing. His jaw was knotted again, screwed tight. Fresh sweat dotted his forehead.

Nerves, not heat. "Your shell says it smells Brood? Well." He gestured through what looked like a bedroom door. "I already knew that."

"You didn't say over comms."

"I wanted *you*, not the whole fucking garrison."

"You go in there?" Iari asked, and poked her head around the jamb before he answered.

Oh, blessed Four.

Tzcansi hung half on and half off of the bed, over there under the window. Her hips were still on the mattress, one leg partway up the wall. Her torso spilled over the side, twisted and bent in a way that suggested many broken bones. Her arms stretched overhead, wrists on the floor, head dangling. She had several massive wounds to her torso. Iari guessed they went all the way through, given the amount of blood on the bed, and the spattering up on the walls and the ceiling. Bone poked up. Sternum, ribs.

The rug underfoot had been rucked up to show long, visible gouges in the floorboards. Iari could think of at least three types of Brood that could've dealt this kind of damage. Not swarm, though. Big ones.

Brisk Array's voice floated up from the foot of the stairs. "Lieutenant? Do you require assistance?"

"Found evidence of Brood up here. You sense any?"

"Negative."

"No," Corso said, and Iari threw him a *the hell?* look, before she realized he was answering her earlier question, not Brisk Array's.

"You asked," he said. His eyes were glassy and screwed down to slits. "No, I didn't go in."

"Right." Iari made herself look around at something other than Tzcansi. Kid's room, looked like. A shelf had come off the wall, spilled trinkets onto the desk, and from there to the floor. Some stuffed animal, a set of little army figures, a pair of model void-ships (Protectorate cruiser, Sissten-class, she noted. And a Confederate corsair. Expansion war models). There were 2Ds on the walls, a model of the local solar system on the ceiling, nudged in its orbit by vagrant drafts from the—yes. The *vent*. Or rather, the hole in the wall above the door, conspicuously empty and black and *not* covered by a metal grate.

Gaer would've been able to stretch up on his stupid-long toes and unbend those extra joints and get himself nose-to-grate, tell her if there was any residue or indication Brood might've escaped that way. But lacking Gaer, well. She sealed her visor. Banished the redflash alarm and upped the magnification instead.

"What is it?" Corso had edged over the threshold. "What do you see?"

"An open grate on the heating duct. What looks like slime on the edges. Like something a little too fat squeezed through that opening." She retracted the visor. The world retreated to its proper distances. She turned her attention to the floor and poked along the rucked-up edge of the rug with her boot—aha. The vent cover. "I'm guessing," she said, because Corso seemed to be waiting for her to say something, "that it was a boneless that did this. That kind of damage to Tzcansi, it sure as voidspit wasn't swarm. And boneless would be able to get through the ducts."

Corso made a little noise in the back of his throat. Iari looked over her shoulder. Tzcansi was a *mess*, sure, but she wasn't guts-coming-back-up awful. They'd seen worse, she and Corso, in their army years. A dozen Tzcansis in a slagging *morning* during the worst days, people whose names they'd known.

She scraped up some patience. "You been in any of the other rooms up here?"

"Yes." He was still hovering in the doorway. "Told you. I looked through the house. It's empty."

"Vent-covers on the floor? Or in place?"

"I—fuck. Stand by." His footsteps retreated. The floorboards creaked an audible map of his progress. "Vents are intact."

He reappeared in the doorway. He looked a little less nauseous. A little more focused. "That kitchen window, though. *That* was open. There could be Brood *out there*."

"It's still daylight, so if there's Brood, they're still *in here*. Brisk Array! Clear the downstairs. Make sure there's no Brood."

"There aren't." Corso was not looking at Tzcansi as hard as he could. Scowling, apparently furious, drilling his stare through Iari. "If there were, they'd've got me."

"Maybe they don't want you." Iari took a lungful of blood-soaked air and gestured at what was left of Tzcansi's body. "Maybe they just wanted her. Maybe someone got to her before we did."

"Brood did this, not some damn gang enforcer. They aren't picky."

"They have been lately. Last death was at Tzcansi's orders, so why come here now? And where'd they go?" Iari thrust her chin at the window and the late (very late) afternoon light. The residents in this neighborhood might ignore tenju in coveralls. They wouldn't ignore a boneless in the yard. Assuming they saw it. Assuming it didn't just slice its way through the whole neighborhood the moment the sun dropped.

That was the stuff of bad dramas and scare-the-kids-into-behaving stories, not experience. Someone had gotten the boneless in this house in the first place. Those things didn't just *walk* anywhere.

"Lieutenant!" Brisk Array's voice boomed up from below. Vibrated through the floor, echoed off the plaster. "There are three more casualties in the cellar. Female alwar, one adult and two adolescents. There is also another drain in the floor. The grate has been removed."

Iari clamped her teeth tight. "Thought you said there was no one else here, Corso. You remember any fucking thing they taught us about clearing a building?"

Color crawled up his cheeks. "I *did* look. I checked all the rooms."

She raised both brows, and his skin darkened.

"I fucking checked! I didn't see a damn cellar door!"

He was still standing in the doorway. Bigger than her, broader, some of his muscle turned soft, maybe, but still strong. She had a battle-rig, so she'd win any kind of shoving match; she just didn't want to have one. He wasn't infantry anymore. Wasn't, well, *anything*. P.R.I.S. That meant civ. Templars didn't hit civs. Find Tzcansi, she'd told him, and he'd done that. He didn't deserve her anger, or her contempt.

"All right. Fine. You did fine. I got it from here." She raised her arm like a bar and Corso yielded ground, retreated backward into the hall. She keyed her comm. "Dispatch. This is Lieutenant Iari. I need Knight-Marshal Tobin. Code red."

"Copy, Lieutenant, this is dispatch—"

And a searing crackle as the comms died.

Ptah's left fucking *eye*. "Dispatch! You copy?"

A tremor rippled through the floor. Not the sudden twitch of an earthquake, but something slower, more deliberate, like the coils of a massive serpent sliding past each other.

Iari dropped her visor. The HUD was lit with Brood alarms (those hadn't changed) and comm-out alert (no surprise) and directionless proximity alert as if trouble was coming from all sides, or was just too big to pinpoint.

Or, third unhappy thought, it was coming from underneath the house. The cellar with an open drain in the floor.

Plasma shot down her spine, hot and awful and oh blessed Four, that was her nano clawing back online, finding the needle in its socket, making contact with the rig. Firing the syn. Her limbs moved and never *mind* the ribs, the aches, the solar-flare agony where her needle linked up with a rig not calibrated to her nervous system. She shook her wrist and deployed the shield (against what, templar? *what?*) as she took the stairs in a single rig-rattling jump.

She skidded across the living room rug, gouging new lines in the floor, and through the doorway into the kitchen. There was a narrow door at the far end, looked like a pantry—and obviously wasn't, because that was where Brisk Array must've gone. So forgive Corso for not opening what looked like a pantry. The floors and the walls vibrated in here, accompanied by the occasional *boom* of Brisk Array's frame hitting metal. The hell was down there that was metal, though—

Oh. Shit. This was a post-war house. It'd have central heat, which meant a phlogiston furnace in that cellar. Metal, those furnaces, scribed with protective hexwork to keep them from blowing up.

Brood emanations wrought *hell* on civilian hexes.

She glanced down at her shield. Its whitefire was hexed *not* to react with phlogiston or other flammables, but if the priests who'd been scribing that day had been just the littlest bit wrong in their hexwork, she could set the whole kitchen off. And if whatever was beating all five of Gaer's hells out of Brisk Array in that cellar ruptured the riev's shields, well. Same effect, fireball; but there'd be a dead riev, too.

Dear Ptah, ungentle Ptah, lord of fire and plasma and things that burn: stay your hand.

Her rig beeped a proximity alert. The HUD display showed Corso coming up on her flank. He clutched his jacta in his right hand, fingers as tight as his jaw. Her chest spasmed, partly the syn shooting her full of adrenaline, partly because that jacta was a projectile model and therefore five kinds of useless against Brood and Corso knew that. He should be running out the front door right now.

Whatever he'd forgotten about clearing buildings, *don't leave your squadmates* was burned too deep to forget.

Then the floor heaved, spars jabbing up like broken bones. The wall of the kitchen adjacent to the cellar door collapsed, spilling inward and down into a gaping wound in the floor. Darkness welled up out of the hole, bruise-black, EM bending and warping, refusing to show the details of what was moving there. Brood, the big ones, did that: warped this layer of the multiverse, subjected it to their own plane's physical laws. Tiny fingers of plasma arced from point to point, as if the aether itself was charging (it might be; that happened too, sometimes, with Brood). Brisk Array, though, she *could* see: flashes of limbs, the brighter blue lines of riev hexwork, all lit, all glowing, all engaged.

She whispered another prayer to Ptah:

Stay your hand.

And one to Hrok:

Help me now, lord of the aether.

And jumped.

CHAPTER TWELVE

I t was, Gaer reflected, creepy enough being halfway under an altar so reeking of Brood he could *taste* it. But to be sitting right next to a Brood-soaked altar while a large, one-armed riev stared at him was just a little too much.

"You don't need to be down here."

Char ignored him. Or at least, they didn't answer, but Gaer thought he saw their tesla-eyes snap toward him.

"I mean, unless you can help with this." He turned his tablet. "Not the k'bal itself, because I don't think you're that old, but maybe you can tell me who *did* write it, because I would bet my optic and the eye underneath no k'bal ever touched this *setatir* thing."

If Char heard his sarcasm, they ignored it. They leaned over the tablet. "The k'bal language predates the Aedis, and you are correct, it predates me. But there are discrepancies in the formation of the third and fourth double-s variants in the script that suggest whoever wrote it was educated in the last forty years and was also wichu."

"How the *setat* do you know that?"

Now he did feel the weight of Char's stare. *Setatir* unpleasant, that cold and unblinking blue. "I have served with many wichu.

Their fingers are smaller than other people's and so the flourishes on the k'bal double-s will be flatter and less full than another hand would produce."

"Perspicacious of you. Now perhaps you have a theory why a *wichu* would be writing in ancient k'bal dialects?"

Char's aura shifted slightly, banding oil-slick pink and blue. "Because whatever she needed to say could only be expressed in that language."

"You're being clever. I didn't think riev could do that."

"It is a day for discovery, Ambassador." Char's aura settled again. Deep purples, a cobalt core. A band of worried chartreuse on the border like the healing edge of a bruise. "To offer explanation to your initial complaint: I am down here because in the lieutenant's absence, I have assumed her post."

"I would think another templar should do that. I mean, you're not technically part of the Aedis."

Char's aura spiked briefly sienna. The color told Gaer that the feeling was old, and deep as a scar. "But you *want* to be."

An organic—all right, a *fully* organic—might've objected, or protested, or blustered. Char said only, "The templars above do not understand the possible threat to you down here. I do."

"You mean Brood coming out of the drain. Funny. I thought that's what templars are *for*. Dealing with Brood."

That stylized tenju face—so unlike Iari's broken features, and yet so familiar—could not purse its lips or roll its eyes. Char gave that impression anyway, with a subtle dimming of their teslas, with a new sharpness to their gravel tones. "In event of a Brood incursion through that drain, the templars would respond, but first they would have to come down the stairs, and the delay could be fatal to you."

"So you're protecting me, not keeping an eye on me."

"There is no distinction."

"Because I thought you were down here to hurry me along."

Char's eyes brightened slightly, from a merely bright blue to searing. "Is that likely?"

"My progress does not depend on your presence, no. However, it *does* depend on the resources in the Aedis library."

Char's regard was as flat and heavy as a voidship's polysteel deckplate. "So you are finished in this location."

"Not quite. I'm under orders to *secure the altar*. You did read that part of the order, too, right?"

"Corporal Heph's rig was blocking that particular passage from my sightline."

"Well then, you will have to trust me."

Char was summoning the wit to retort, yes, Gaer could *see* that. But then the drain under the altar gurgled. Wet sound, which would be normal for drains, except this drain had not made any watery noises at all in the hours of Gaer's observation. It emptied into the run-off tunnels, and was not part of the network of plumbing and sewage. And since there was no rain falling, and the Rust wasn't cresting its banks, there should be no noise coming out of it.

The drain gurgled again. The liquid—please, five dark lords, it was just *water* down there—sloshed further up the pipe.

Char made a noise in their chest like crumpling metal. "Brood."

Oh, *setat*. Of course it was. There was hexwork on Char's face, he realized: a dusting of glyphs and equations on their cheeks, around the sockets of their eyes. All glowing faintly, to his optic, all throbbing and angry and red.

Gaer twisted around until he could peer down the drain. Warnings spangled his optic like faint stars.

"It's an echo," he said. "Like shouting in a tunnel. Something large and unpleasant is down there, but it's someplace else, and the displaced water is washing back this way. I'm seeing effluvial particles *in* that water, not any actual Brood."

"You are certain, Ambassador?"

On another day—yesterday, actually—the idea of a riev asking any question would've been a source of amusement. Now Gaer just thought *Oh, of course, it's Char* and snapped, "Yes, I'm certain."

He stood up and waved his fingers. "Give me room. I was going to ward this *setatir* thing anyway. I'll just make it proof against something coming up from the *inside*, too."

Char stepped back almost delicately, certainly soundlessly, and watched with head-tilted interest as Gaer sketched a perimeter around the altar with the stylus from his tablet. It left no visible marks to an organic eye. What Char could see, with their artificed sight, was Char's to know. Gaer, looking one-eyed into the third layer of the aether, saw a bright white line composed of equations. *His* equations: hexes to prevent penetration in either direction by liquid, by plasma, by solid. By Brood and void. And, after a moment's consideration—by aether, too, in case something noxious came wafting up out of the drain. Brood didn't usually bother with aether-borne toxins, but *usually* didn't seem to apply lately.

The altar began glowing. Faintly at first, so that it looked like a trick of bouncing light, something to blink away and laugh at oneself for imagining. Until that glow turned pronouncedly crimson, like live coals, around the altar's base. Gaer knew better than to interrupt arithmantic workings to *stare*, so he didn't; he finished his final circuit, sealed his circle, and *then* looked.

One set of symbols was brighter than the rest. One set, repeated at intervals in the script. He hadn't noticed the pattern before, black scraping on black iron, no spaces between words, a dialect of a dead xeno language (oh, make *excuses*, he should have seen it). He cycled the optic back to the shallower layers of the aether. His hexwork receded from bright white to faint grey, a lattice-work dome around the altar, the drain, sinking just a talon-tip into the floor. The symbol-set on the altar kept glowing—brighter, even, on this plane than in the deeper aetheric layers.

Gaer tilted the tablet at the altar. Cycled special filters, took a 2D, stored it. Then he looked at Char. "All right. *Now* we're done."

Char gestured him toward the stairs. The riev remained where they were, all their attention pointed at the altar. Call it suspicious glaring, with their unblinking tesla eyes and their unmoving mask of a face. Call it a scowl. Char waited until he was halfway up the steps to leave off and follow, in case something should come boiling out of the drain, or the altar itself should do something.

If it did, Gaer wanted to say, his hexwork would hold it; but there was something comforting in the big riev's suspicion, and *definitely* something comforting in their bulk at his (very unarmored) back.

Comfort. From a riev. Reality was crumbling.

He climbed up into the warehouse expecting—well, if not fanfare, at least notice. But Corporal Heph had his face pointed elsewhere. Voices trickled up out of Heph's comms, out his open faceplate. Human, sounded like; and pitched up and sharp.

"What is it?" Gaer dusted his palms together in what he hoped was a casual *no threat here* gesture. "Something wrong?"

Corporal Heph was within his rights to say *slag off, veek* (and Gaer expected it, though with a more polite phrasing). It was Heph's aura he wanted to see. Mouths lied. Auras did not. Heph's was a shifting palette of sunset and fireballs all threaded through with a yellow, twisted worry.

"It's not your concern," said Heph, dry-voiced, and the aura slivered green.

"It is," said Char. "I heard the lieutenant call in a code red."

That meant Brood contact. Oh *setat*.

Gaer powered down his tablet, rolled it, and jammed it into a hard-sided hip-panel on his skinsuit, which tented over a particularly inconvenient set of spikes. That extra reinforcement was only fabric. Not armor, nothing *like* armor. It would protect the tablet from casual impact. It would not protect anyone or anything from, oh, *Brood*.

"All right." Gaer looked at Corporal Heph. "You'll need an arithmancer. That's me. Where are we going?"

"Sir. *We* aren't. We've got orders to hold *this* location. There are more templars en route to the lieutenant."

"You're closer than they are. Oh, *setat*, never mind. Char! With me."

"Yes," said Char. They moved for the door, all stomp and momentum. The templars gave way like sensible beings. No one even reached for a weapon.

Gaer attempted to follow. Heph made a grab for him. "Sir. You can't—I mean, you're not authorized—"

"To walk out of here? I am. I am an ambassador from the Five Tribes, and you, Corporal, cannot detain me."

Corporal Heph was too young to have been weaned on anti-vakari sentiment. Only standard-grade Confederate, Aedian superiority in his eyes, no particular fear or loathing, no particular need to thwart and dominate, just a deep puzzlement when someone didn't respect his authority. "Sir—"

"I'm going after the lieutenant to render aid. Yours would be welcome. But if you can't, well, *that*"—and he pointed at Heph's hip—"would be helpful to me."

Gaer did not expect Heph to hand over his weapon. He did, however, expect Heph to reach for it on reflex, for his eyes to drop, for his whole attention to shift that way, just long enough for Gaer to get past him. Long vakari legs had their uses.

He caught up to Char in a double fistful (the vakari finger-count) of strides. The riev was moving at the infantry trot, a gait between jog and march.

He matched it easily enough. "Do you know where we're going?"

"Yes."

Gaer waited through thump-thump-hard-right-around-a-corner before he realized that no more explanation was forthcoming. *Where* was the obvious question; but follow Char, and he'd find that out. Which left:

"How do you know?"

Thump. Then: "I heard the address Corso Risar gave to the lieutenant."

Through comms in someone else's helmet. Gaer revised his understanding of riev aural sensitivity. That the Confederation hadn't repurposed riev into spies was a tragic waste of resources. Or a very fortunate one, for the Protectorate and the Five Tribes. Something else for his reports, if or when he ever sent them.

If he didn't die this afternoon. He was running *at* Brood for the second time in one day, only this time without a battle-rig. He should've worn one down here, except then he wouldn't've fit under the altar. The five dark lords did have their sense of humor.

He followed Char for(ever) at least a kilometer, until at last they turned into a residential street hardly wider than an alley, a row of identical facades and uninspired architecture. Gaer didn't need to wait for directions; the Brood emanations coming out of *that* one made it pretty clear where Iari's code red originated.

And not just Brood emanations. Gaer's optic scrolled out a new set of numbers. Oh, dark lords.

"Char, *wait*," with all the breath in his lungs.

Not expecting they would—but they did, and stopped much faster than something that big should've been able to, at the base of the house's front steps. Char's hand flexed into a fist and back out again, all the fingers stiff and furious. "What?"

"Phlogiston leak," because that was the most important bit. The basic structural instability of the house was the other part.

The door was partly ajar. *Not* a good sign. Also not good: the crashing sounds from the interior. There were micro tremors in the structure, which Char might or might not detect. The Brood-emanations were rising almost as fast as the phlogiston levels. And there was the faint whiff of hexwork to all of it, one worrying icon in the bottom right of his optic. Arithmancy at work. Some-one was hexing right *now*.

He thrust his hand out, as if to hold Char back from a dash up the steps. The riev's chest felt like a small furnace, uncomfortably warm even through the intervening layer of aether. Gaer slid a nervous glance sideways. The templar armorer Jorvik had welded a patch onto Char's chestplate, but there hadn't been time for hex-work. Examine the altar: that had been the priority. And that meant Char had nothing to shield and contain whatever galvanic atrocity passed for a riev power-core from hostile arithmancy. Or Brood. Or a well-placed jacta bolt.

"You need to stay out here. The house is not stable." Though if the whole building came crashing down, Char was most likely to shrug it off and keep going. But if the whole building came crash-ing down, Gaer wanted Char outside to pull it off *him*. He dropped his voice to breathless. "And I think there's an arithmancer out here someplace. You're vulnerable."

Char made a rattling noise. Rage, fear, acquiescence. But their voice was deep, steady, almost soft. "Acknowledged."

Which left the shaky house full of Brood (and Iari, who *must* still be alive) for *him* to manage. Fantastic. He bounded up the steps. Flattened himself against the door. The locking mechanism was a charred mess. Not a jacta shot, though. An ugly hex-job, meant for speed. Gaer toed the door open. Let it gape wide for just long enough to be sure nothing was coming out—no jacta bolts, no whitefire beams—before he ducked around the edge and inside.

The noise was much worse in here. Splintering wood, shattering polymer. The high-pitched whine of whitefire, which, *dear dark lords*, with these levels of phlogiston was asking for explosion. Gaer blinked in the shade-drawn dim and saw Corso in the middle of the hallway fumbling with a jacta.

Gaer lunged forward and swatted the weapon aside.

"There's a phlogiston leak," Gaer snapped. "You shoot, you could set it off."

Corso actually growled. He shoved bodily against Gaer (who was braced for it, toes dug in, and still he felt himself slip a few centimeters). He was intensely and uncomfortably aware of how very little resistance his skinsuit would offer a bolt from this range. Oh, sure, firing the weapon might set off the phlogiston and incinerate everything in a fiery explosion—but not before a high-velocity bolt hurt a great deal tearing its way through his body. And Corso was willing to do it. With Iari, most of her temper was noise, surface, flickers of crimson lightning over a cool, stoic cobalt. Corso's aura was all boiling reds, and he was slowly muscling his arm—and that *setatir* jacta—back around. Gaer spared a moment's consideration for the monofil clipped to his hip, and whether he could reach it (yes), and what Iari would think if he stabbed Corso with it.

This, Gaer thought, is what the Expansion war must've been

like in the early days, tenju on vakar, before the Aedis and its *setatir* nanomecha and syn implants and templars. The vakari had been *winning* that fight. Remember *why*.

Gaer clamped his jaw shut, plates and lips, flicked his second lids closed, and slammed his forehead into Corso's face. And in the moment's respite he carved out—because it didn't matter how tough a tenju was (or a human, or even some stringy little alw), a vakari skull in the nose stunned the neefa-shit out of you—Gaer jammed his (spiky) shoulder into Corso's chest and steered them both out the front door.

Corso missed his footing as he went down the stair and slammed flat on his back on the front walk. Gaer made no attempt to soften his own landing. Twisted elbows and knees to drive his joint-spikes into Corso as much as he could. The skinsuit's panels would keep the spikes from doing blood-letting damage. Bruises, stunning—that was fine. That was the *point*. There was that phrase in Comspek about knocking sense into someone, as if violence and injury could produce reasonable discourse. Gaer expected when Corso recovered—already he was sucking the air back into his lungs—he'd be even *less* inclined to reason. Best strike now, before that happened.

Gaer dropped his face blurry-close to Corso's. "What's happening in there? Tell me. *Report*."

Corso might indeed have found sense through contusion and impact. He blinked up at Gaer. "Tunneler came up in the cellar. Iari went after it. In the hallway off the kitchen. Whole place is coming down right now." Then a heave as Corso tried to shove him off. "She needs help, *get off me*."

Gaer was close enough to see the little web of blood vessels in Corso's hot blue eyes. Close enough to smell the remnants of lunch on Corso's breath, and his sweat, which was not a *bit* like Iari's, all male musk and sour with fear.

"I'll get her." He levered up off Corso—hard push, contributing to another gust of lost breath—and wrenched the jacta out of Corso's hand and passed it to Char, who had come close enough to cast them both into shadow. Then Gaer stalked back through the front door. He drew his monofil on the way, left-handed, reversed his grip and folded the blade back against his forearm, *careful*, because a monofil would cut skinsuit and skin and everything else it touched.

A monofil and his arithmancy, against—oh, *setat*. Against a tunneler.

Against—*that*.

Coils thick as an adult tenju's torso, maybe a little bit thicker, clogged the hall to what must have been the kitchen. Looping and segmented and sliding past themselves, slicked with corrosive slime. The whole caved-in hallway was thick with smoke as the tunneler's excretions chewed through wood, plaster, whatever cheap materials had been used in construction. And out of that mess—a riev's arm, rising and falling and *tearing*, followed by a riev's shoulder and head. Brisk Array's sensor cluster had taken damage, wilted on the edges (burned, broken). The rest of his hexwork blazed blue and white and solid.

Then another part of the floor buckled and Brisk Array, who'd nearly pulled himself loose, slid sidelong into that hole. And then, *then*, Gaer saw something squirming down there, something that wasn't tunneler coils or a furious riev. A battle-rig—smoke curling off it, the headlamp dim and grey in the Brood's light-eating effect. The Aedis shield emitted its own EM, red and furious, in defiance of Brood-effects as it scythed into the tunneler. Plasma burst from the point of impact, a little forest of finger-length lightning bolts that ignited the surrounding phlogiston in brief bursts of orange, yellow, blue, like stars burning themselves out.

Gaer's throat felt too small, too tight for breath. Don't panic. He was a *setatir* arithmancer.

Mathematics was the language of the multiverse. Equations described how reality behaved. A mathematician stopped there, imagining that the numbers only reflected what was. An arithmancer knew better: the numbers also described what might be. An equation was a request to which reality would try to conform. It was the alchemists (the alwar: be honest. They were best at it) who focused on changing *things*. The four states of matter— Aedian Elements—were fluid. One could become another, with the proper external conditions. Aedian implants skipped past arithmancy (or incorporated it; SPERE intelligence was uncertain) and allowed direct interface with the material states. An Aedian priest could transmute mere oxygen into phlogiston and *make* fire. Gaer could only nudge substances into doing what they did naturally.

Phlogiston did love to burn.

Gaer cycled his optic to a different layer of the aether, until he could see the drift of phlogiston particles on the breeze blowing from the partly open door, the infinitesimal straight jumps the plasma made from particle to particle. Until he could see tiny matrices of solids: wood, polymer, Aedian polyceramics and steels. Iari's rig resolving itself, layer by layer, into its components.

He calculated a possible gap between Iari's rig and the surrounding phlogiston. Phlogiston contaminated normal, breathable aether. He could calculate the smallest possible percentage of phlogiston in that aether, and enforce that percentage improbably and completely, until he'd wrapped her in a combustion-proof layer.

In the layer of awareness marked *reality*, part of Gaer marked the tunneler arching into the ceiling, recoiling from Iari's shield and a matrix of Aedian hexwork. He marked the trail of sparks made by Iari's shield as she swung a follow-up strike. He'd be done with his hex before she finished.

But Gaer was only halfway through when a counter-hex eeled through his equations like oil, smearing across numbers and variables. Shifting decimal places and warping his carefully crafted reality and *changing* the formerly benign and unburning aether into phlogiston, *just* phlogiston, pressed up against Iari's armor.

Gaer had just enough time to throw up a warding hex before all that phlogiston exploded.

CHAPTER THIRTEEN

The explosion lifted Gaer and *threw* him backward across the living room and out what would've been the front door, if that door or surrounding wall remained. He hit Corso on the way down, Corso having decided to try the stairs again, and they both tumbled back into the street. A rolling wave of heat followed, which might well have included a fireball, or fingers of flame, or *setatir* plasma—but which was also uncontrolled, so Gaer's defensive hex deflected most of it. One searing second of awfulness, and then it was past.

Corso had landed on the bottom, lost all breath and capacity for violence—and he was intending the latter, obviously, with his hands balled into fists. Gaer put an ungentle, spiky knee into Corso's midriff (surprisingly solid) and bounced to his feet. Oh, *mistake*. He didn't have all his balance back yet, ears ringing, *skull* ringing. His vision hazed on the edges, threatening a retreat to full blackout. The optic rebooted, taking one eye asymmetrically dark, prompting a rapid, violent blinking, both sets of eyelids flapping out of sync.

He staggered, one arm flailing for balance. The other— miracle!—still held his monofil. He'd flexed it a little too far back, and the blade had sliced through both his skinsuit and his forearm's flesh beneath it. Blood—bright! so very bright—welled up in the gap. Didn't *seem* serious. But you couldn't always tell with a monofil, you could cut all the way through bone sometimes without feeling it—

Blink, *focus*. Breathe, which had the twin benefits of chasing the fog out of his vision and reassuring him that nothing was broken. He shook his head, hard and perhaps unwisely, and looked for the house—oh yes. There. Fire and smoke and shattered walls. There was glass on the street from the windows. But as Gaer watched, the shards began sliding back toward the house. Slow at first, then skittering faster.

Gaer had never seen the phenomenon, but he'd read about it. When some of the larger Brood died, sometimes you got what they called the singularity effect (which led to the rise of a joke ending with the punchline, *Killing Brood Sucks*, versions of which were found in some form in the Five Tribes and Protectorate *and* Confederate forces). *Theory* said the effect was the result of tunnelers returning through the void to whatever layer of the multiverse spawned them, essentially punching through the layers like a tesser-hex. Little Brood—swarm, slicers, boneless—didn't generate the effect, or generate it strongly enough to register.

This tunneler was sucking mightily as it died, dragging smoke and fire and even the shattered walls back in on itself. The effect plucked at Gaer's knees, at his hips. Tentative fingers, nothing he couldn't resist. For now. But if that Brood didn't finish dying, oh, *soon*, it'd drag the whole *setatir* street in behind it.

Gaer let himself sag back into a crouch, not entirely an act; standing was hard right now. His optic was coming back online, reporting up an excess of Brood emanations and dissipating levels of phlogiston. And—oh, no. That was just Char stomping past, flinging debris aside, wading into the wreckage.

And possibly more pressing, there was a *setatir* arithmancer somewhere out here who'd just blown up the *setatir* house, and was likely to interfere with any attempt he made to suppress the fire or help Char.

Gaer lifted his chin and squint-scanned both rows of houses. The windows had filled up with faces, with auras as bright as the fire. There was no way to pick out a single *anyone* in that ambient noise. Much less an arithmancer, who would be shielded, especially knowing what Gaer was. Because she, he, it, they—*did* know. They'd countered his hex too neatly for accident. And they were still there, watching their handiwork. Gaer knew it, *felt* it.

So draw them out.

Gaer closed his naked eye, took a breath, shifted his perception into the nearest sublayer of aether. A simple matter to tune the optic to see the underlying hexes: equations describing the motion of heated air, the rate of phlogiston consumption, how fast the surrounding air heated. The force of the tunneler's singularity-drag, the distortion of light.

And there, *yes*: brighter than its surroundings, a battle-hex concealing itself in an overlay of variables and constants and symbols. Gaer sketched out his equations, quick mental strokes aided by the optic's pre-loaded list of components. You could make up wholly original hexes, yes, and arithmancers did—but not generally outside of a sealed laboratory (at least until the effects were cataloged and predictable). Gaer had the Five Tribes' usual battle-hex library to draw from in his optic; but he had a few of his own, too, developed in those sealed labs.

He built a counter-hex, a standard hunter-seeker, and loosed it, and yes, *there*: a flare as it found its quarry.

The enemy hex was fast, oiled-eel quick in its response. It went for immediate evasion, throwing junk code in its wake. Chaff, to confuse Gaer's hex. Which worked—annoying, but not unexpected. *Useful*, because that told him the arithmancer was still in range, and he had another chance to go code-to-code with that neefa-eater.

Gaer altered his attacking hex, trimming variables, eliminating the chaff's ability to distract it. Then he pivoted hard and visibly, there on the street, made a dramatic *I'm throwing a hex* gesture at the burning house. He sketched out a standard ward that any damn fool watching would be able to see. Equations describing a limit to the fire's reach, equations ripping the remaining phlogiston into atomic components. Equations to dissipate heat away from Char's unshielded chest-patch. The riev's remaining hexwork flared, sensing arithmancy; but the red-hot rim of that patch cooled a fraction.

And there, yes: another incoming battle-hex. Char's armor flared again, repelling a new attack, even as the fire under their feet flared up as if they were standing on oil. The enemy's battle-hex had come back around for another go.

And in the same instant, Gaer's hunter-hex found its target, and tore the enemy code into fragments. The fire guttered and slunk away from Char's artificed warding. Gaer let his breath go and chased sparks from the edge of his vision; stupid, to hold your breath like that, *amateur*, but he was upset, he was angry, that was *Iari* under there. He started to hex the air itself, strangling the currents that would bring oxygen to the fire. There was a risk there to Char, if he was too effective—even a galvanic heresy still needed to breathe—but if he kept the airless layer low, just over the fire, he might drive the fire back.

Then the enemy arithmancer struck again, an onslaught of

code that tore through Gaer's equations like shrapnel through bread dough. A nice battle-hex, very effective. You could admire that. Gaer grinned and countered, shoring up his constants and tangling the whole thing in infinite, repeating prime. It was like one of those clever slip knots that got tighter the more someone struggled, cutting into not flesh, now, but calculations, hexes.

The fire flared up again, burst against Char's hexwork. And then *didn't*, suddenly, as a piece of that hostile battle-hex sliced into the riev's artificed shielding. Sliced *through* it.

Gaer traded a lungful of stale air for fresh (smoke-laced, Brood-sour) and countered. Slapped his own hex-ward across the gap in Char's wards. Not that they noticed. Not that they missed one debris-tossing beat. This time, his modified counter-code worked less well, sliding off the enemy equation with little effect.

And—it should be working. The enemy's constants were the same, he could see that much. One of the variables had changed, but given the order of operations that shouldn't matter.

But it was mattering. And that made no sense. Not from an arithmancer's aesthetic sense, either, but just plain *logic*, theory, the underpinnings of arithmancy itself. Arithmancy ran on rules that this person wasn't bothering to follow, and somehow their code didn't care.

Which meant—void and dust, Gaer didn't know what, exactly, except nothing good. Someone could break the *setatir* laws of the multiverse, or someone knew a set of laws no one else did. It could be an effect of the tunneler—Brood disrupted all manner of natural orders—but that seemed unlikely. Riev were effective against Brood precisely *because* artificing was so resistant to their warping effects.

Gaer switched strategies, then. He partitioned off a slice of awareness, awaiting the return of hostile battle-hex, and began to hex protection for Char. He started to layer equations that described stagnant aether, all gaseous motion slowing, chilling, maybe condensing some of the molecules into liquid (water might be helpful, what with the fire). A *setatir* Aedian alchemist-priest would be useful, about now. Two priests, one for liquid Mishka, one for solid Chaama. (One for Iari's beloved Ptah, because if anyone deserved death by plasma, it was that *setatir* arithmancer.)

Char continued to fling debris aside. A twisted bit of metal. A scorched and black lump of wood. (Please, let it be wood.) Gaer started imagining the force and the heat of that blast, weighing it against what he knew about Aedian battle-rig tolerances. He shut it down. Wouldn't *help*, no, he kept thinking like that and he'd be joining Char up there, soaking up Brood emissions and getting third-degree burns and *not helping* Iari because he'd be killing himself.

So trust his wards, pray (*Chaama, right? Stone mother and all that? I think this is your province*), and *wait*. At least it seemed the *setat-m'rri* Brood-loving, pyromaniac, murdering arithmancer had stopped throwing hexes. Had maybe run off.

Corso was just now dragging himself onto hands and knees and coughing like he might have something cracked in his chest. The dying Brood's suck was working on him, too, pulling the shredded remains of his coveralls into a waving fringe of canvas. Gaer lurched over and grabbed a fistful of that coverall and hauled Corso upright. He expected—not thanks, Corso was tenju—but at least a few more moments of man-folded-over-and-hacking. Instead Corso twisted in his grip like a furious cat, fingers clawing for purchase on Gaer's skinsuit. Cracked nails snagged on the polyhide.

"You veek fuck, *you did that—*"

"I did *not*." Gaer forced his jaw-plates apart. Forced his vision back to wide-angle from tunneled hunter-lock, *stand down*, however much he wanted to show Corso exactly what a vakar could do in close quarters to a soft-skin with delusions of formidability. "Listen, you rabid mammal. There was another arithmancer here."

That stopped Corso. Wide-eyed, "What?" and a sudden surcease of struggling.

"You heard me. That person blew up the house. And I think they're gone, but if not, *I* am the only one who can stop them from taking out Char. Until the templars get here, that riev is Iari's only help."

Corso's face changed when Gaer said Iari's name. All that rage taking a sharp turn, finding a new focus. Gaer tightened his grip, anticipating the—ah, yes, *there*—sudden jerk and pull.

"Let me go!"

"Listen. I can protect Char. Riev have their own hexwork, all I have to do is support that. But there is not enough arithmancy in the multiverse to render you fireproof, you hear? And there's a *setatir* tunneler dying in there. You get that? You go after Iari, you die."

"I—feh." Corso stopped struggling. His eyes were wide, round, white on the edges; but sense was beginning to leak back. "But we can't just *stand here*."

"We can. Iari's rigged. She called a code red. Templars are coming. If she's not dead yet"—and Gaer's chest hurt like someone had put a fist through it—"then they'll get her out. We *can't*. We're not armored. We're not shielded. The riev is both of those things, so let Char do their job."

Corso grimaced and batted at Gaer's hand. Surly with anguish: "Fucking let me go. I hear you, all right? I'll let the riev handle it."

The whole world shivered suddenly. The ground underfoot, the air, like a curtain moving in a sullen breeze. And then a stillness, a sense of *right* returning.

"The tunneler," Gaer said, because Corso looked like he needed to hear something reassuring. "It just died."

Corso did not look reassured. Corso stayed stiff and still, ribs heaving like he'd sprinted all the way from the Aedis. The look on his face matched the contours of Gaer's guts.

"Fuck you," Corso muttered, without direction or force. "Fuck you, fuck you. You know where that arithmancer went? Because I want that fucker's *head*."

"If something happens to Iari"—*and even if she's fine*—"you'll have to share that head with me. Deal?"

"Deal." Corso sagged back a step, feet braced wide, shoulders sloped. He watched Char with bleak, grim eyes. "I found Tzcansi dead in that house. Brood killed her. Boneless. Not the tunneler."

Gaer looked both ways up the street. There were residents coming outside now, trickling out to their steps. Faces visible in the windows. Human, mostly, with a few alwar mixed in. They seemed disinclined to venture far from their doorways. Their auras marched between bright bands of alarm and more muted curiosity and fear.

Those weren't the auras of people who'd seen Brood. "Very well-behaved boneless, then, to stay inside one house. To kill exactly the person we needed to see."

Corso's shoulders tightened. He turned, very slowly, and tried to pin Gaer with eyes almost as black as Gaer's own. "What are you saying, veek? I know what I fucking saw."

"I'm sure you did." Gaer touched his skinsuit pocket. Felt the contours of his tablet, *please* it had not gotten smashed or corrupted or otherwise compromised. He glanced up at the Aedis, brooding on the hilltop. There weren't *that* many templars inside its walls. One full-strength unit that belonged to Peshwari, a portion of whom were at the warehouse already. A scattering of others, like Iari, not part of a formal unit. That didn't leave many to send on a code-red rescue.

Whereas the PKs were plentiful, and likely closer, and *very* likely to arrive first. Someone would've called them by now. And what would they see when they got here, hm? A vakar and a tenju dressed like a service worker standing in close proximity to a burning, exploded structure, with a one-armed riev standing *on* it and throwing debris into the street.

"PKs will be coming," Gaer murmured. "How do you think they'll like us?"

Corso blinked. "You better not be saying we run."

"No. *We* won't. You, yes."

"Fuck that."

"*Listen.* They can't do much to me." Not entirely true. They could shoot him. The group who'd shown up to Pinjat's had seemed so inclined. "I'm a *setatir* vakar. I have diplomatic identification. The templars will show eventually, they'll bring priests, *someone* will know who I am, and I'll be fine. You, however—you're *Iari's* agent, and she's somewhere under that rubble. You want to help her, you keep chasing leads. And the only way you do that is by staying out of custody."

He could always send Corso after the arithmancer. Get him to start looking around, at least, though if he found his target, he'd probably die. And while Gaer didn't anticipate shedding tears on the tenju's behalf, Iari might be perturbed (if Iari survived, but don't think about that). And more than that, being *practical*, Corso was an asset, and you didn't waste assets just because they were bigoted neefa.

Might be Corso's not the only one of those, Gaer, think of that?

"Listen," Gaer said again. "I have someone for you to find. Yinal'i'ljat. Wichu. The dead artificer's cousin."

Please, Corso didn't ask why.

"Why?"

Of course. *Setat.* "Because whoever our unseen arithmancer is, he knows a little bit about artificing." *And bending natural law like warm noodles, but never mind that.* "That says wichu to me. Maybe Pinjat had a friend or an apprentice. His cousin might know. *I* can't go looking for her. She's in PK jurisdiction. I'm betting you have friends there. And you know wichu. They'll all go hide under the bed and call for help if they see a vakar. But *you* can look. You can ask around. So find Yinal'i'ljat, get her a message that I want to talk to her, and *call* me. Can you?"

Corso was looking at him now, narrow eyes, red-rimmed eyes, sense seeping into them. His aura flared, sullen with fear and fury and a bitter joy at the chance to *do*, and not wait.

"All right. Find Yinal'i'ljat." Corso handled the syllables well enough. "Pass on a message. Call you. But you call *me* when Iari's all right. Hear?"

"Done. Deal." There were sirens approaching now, thin, mecha-voiced wailing from one end of the street. "Go."

Corso started walking the other direction, smoothing his braids with their hooks and ornaments, tugging his shredded coveralls into order.

Gaer gritted his teeth. Hissed through his plates. His skull felt three sizes too small already, and he was about to do *another* hex. He sliced off another wafer of awareness. This equation, at least, was relatively simple. He bent the light around Corso. The shadow rolled up first. Then the tenju's legs blurred, then his hips. Then he smeared into fuzzy obscurity, like a flicker in the corner of an eye that you couldn't identify when you actually looked for it.

The hex wouldn't work if someone was actually watching Corso, and it wouldn't last much past the end of the block. Gaer was contemplating some sort of public performance—screaming, collapsing, something to draw everyone's eyes to him, but without distracting Char (if such a thing were possible)—when the peacekeepers rounded the far corner. Jogging, longcasters held ready, a sharp-legged battle-mecha clicking in their wake like an overfed and overly large insect.

Oh, *setat*. The PKs who'd responded to Pinjat's murder hadn't had one of *those*.

Gaer jammed his monofil back into its clip and set himself square in the street. He held his arms out, hands splayed and empty. Let there be no doubt he was a vakar, let everyone see his hands nowhere near his weapons. Let that actually matter; the PKs were heading for *him*, not the smoldering structure, and they were raising their *setatir* weapons and shouting at him to stop, hold, don't move. The mecha, which *clearly* had emergency medical equipment on it, and fire-suppression hexes, raised a forelimb tipped with prongs strung together with quivering bolts of electricity and waved it at him.

"I'm the Five Tribes ambassador," Gaer called. "There's a templar in that burning house."

He might as well have been speaking Sisstish, or not speaking at all, for all the effect his words had. There was a joke somewhere in there, about a diplomat for whom talking failed. Iari would laugh, if he ever got the chance to tell her. Or at least she'd grunt and roll her eyes.

And if she died because of these neefa-brained *m'rri*, so help him, all dark lords. So help *them*.

The PK's mecha was getting closer now, edging wide, like it

meant to creep up on his flank. The PKs themselves held back a little. At least they weren't running after Corso.

"Listen," Gaer started to say. But then a shadow blotted out part of the street, at the same time his optic—stretched to the limits of its hardware—warned him of incoming hexes, major arithmancy, alert, alert.

An Aedian hopper crested the roofline and began its descent to the street, its belly glowing with hexwork, its side panels folded down and gleaming with templar shields (one, two, *five* of them!) and, oh thank you whoever is listening, at least *two* armored (but not battle-rigged) priests. The hopper stopped maybe one and a half meters off the pavement, deliberately positioned between the advancing PKs and Gaer.

That was what Iari's code red conjured up, evidently.

Gaer almost let his hands drop, he was so relieved. He took a deep lungful of ozone and soot. The hopper didn't make noise, exactly; it throbbed and vibrated and made his ears feel both over-warmed and wrapped in padding.

Whatever communication was going between Aedis and peacekeepers, it was happening on closed comms. One of the priests—small-framed, petite, probably alwar, her armor sashed with healer blue—wormed past the hedge of templars and squatted on the lip of the hopper and then, after a teetering moment, dropped down. She landed in a hard crouch. The flexible panels of her armor, so much lighter than a battle-rig, caught the fire-glow and gleamed like chrome. Then she stood up and, with barely a look at Gaer or the PKs, trotted toward the burning house and Char. Gaer could feel the cold in her wake as she slowed down the roiling aether, condensed it. Could *see*, through his optic, her alchemical heresies drawing the oxygen out and choking the fire to ashes.

You forgot, sometimes, that the priests were almost as formidable as the templars.

He noted, with half an eye, the PKs falling back (and their mecha with them, in a flutter of limbs).

And then Char shouted, "Ambassador!" and Gaer snapped his whole body that way. And saw the upthrust forearm, laced all over with glowing hexwork and ash and Brood slime. And at the end of that forearm: a hand, flexing. *Reaching.*

Iari was alive.

CHAPTER FOURTEEN

For the second time in the recent past (without a chrono, she couldn't say *how* recent), Iari woke up in medical. Not a klaxon-alert, jarring wake-up out of deep sleep, but a slow slide into focus, like blinking through fog until everything acquires sharp edges.

Smooth stone ceiling overhead crossed with tracks so the med-mechas could go where they were needed. She turned her head. Curtains on three sides. Stone wall on one. No window. She rolled her head on the pancake of a pillow. A single, lonely stool stood vigil near the bed, beside a metal stand with a bag of clear liquid hanging from it. Tubes leading—ugh, into *her*. Antiseptic burned in the back of her nose. And it was cold, because she wasn't wearing anything under the ungenerous blanket and rough-spun sheet, not even one of the wretched gowns.

All of which told her that this was the hospice trauma wing, adjacent to the courtyard, so that when the hoppers and aether-ships delivered the severely injured from the front, there wasn't far to move them. Close to the main gates, too, in case of a more conventional delivery of wounded. Which way she'd come in—

She didn't know.

The first hint of panic soured the back of her throat. She

breathed past it. Steady, *solve* it. Work backward, from what she did know. She'd been injured, badly enough to end up here. But it was quiet in here. No voices, no beeping mecha, which there should be. Templars didn't fight alone.

Unless everyone had died. Saichi had been like that. Just her and Tobin left, two of twelve.

Except—remember!—she was not part of an assigned unit now. This was peace time, between surges (everyone knew there'd be another one; *when* was the point of disagreement). The last time she'd flown in by aethership had been after Saichi, with Tobin (then Captain, not yet Knight-Marshal). And he'd been the one in the bed, staring up at the mottled stone and the hovering med-mecha, while she'd slept on a pallet on the floor. A shortage of beds, in those days (a lot of noise in the trauma center, voices and sobbing and screams), and her injuries had been minor things. Bruises, burns, exposure: what you got, fighting Brood in the field.

No. What you got most often was *dead*. She and Tobin had been lucky.

Iari couldn't remember coming in by aethership this time. Couldn't remember much of anything. She *hurt* like she'd been through a battle, but the surge was over, and templars didn't get into street-brawl fights. Serious injuries were confined to training accidents or the mundane damage that people did to each other with jacta and monofils. Or accidents: rockslides, avalanche, people caught out in winter. And the nearest med-mecha hung two meters over, on the border between curtained cubicles, its limbs drawn up like a dead spider's, its optical array blinking on standby. If she were *really* serious, it would be on her, over her. *Involved*.

Iari gritted her teeth, braced for pain, lifted her head, was pleasantly surprised when that didn't hurt. Encouraged, she levered up on her elbows and oh, that did. Ribs, loudest and sharpest. A smaller twinge in the crook of her left arm, which had a fat patch of bandage on it, holding a needle in her flesh, trailing a tube leading into that bag of clear fluid. She squinted at the bag's label. It was written in alchemical, priest-speak Comspek, which might as well have been High Ancient Sisstish for all the sense she could make of it.

She studied the afflicted arm. Seemed intact, except for the needle jammed into her vein. Some bruising on the hand and the wrist. She turned her head carefully and looked at the other arm. It seemed to be in similar condition. The blanket had slipped a little bit off her shoulders, showed her the leading edge of a gorgeous palette of bruises trailing down her torso. Probably be even prettier if she sat all the way up. Probably hurt a lot more, too. She took an experimental breath, deep and slow and *voidspit daughter of a neefa*, she had a lungful (left side) full of knives. But she could inhale fully. And she could stay propped on her elbows. So she was probably fine, or on her way to it.

She *remembered* the ribs. A gift from Sawtooth in the basement of the warehouse, where she and Gaer had found that altar. And after that, she'd come back to the Aedis and reported, and then—back into the city, back to that altar, and then—?

And then something had smashed her flat a second time.

Corso. *Corso* was involved, somehow. Her memory painted an image of him, wearing gardener's coveralls and holding a jacta and pointing it—

At her? No. That didn't make sense. Nor did the coveralls. He'd resigned his army commission after the Windscar campaign, before the surge was even over, before Saichi, and sank himself into the B-town slums to be angry and live on the fringes of law and society and not, no voidspit *way*, to take care of other people's gardens.

So he wasn't a gardener. He was a P.R.I.S. *Right*. And she'd asked him to help her find Tzcansi. And somehow that'd ended her up *here*, in a windowless room in the hospice. Because—because . . .

Iari gritted her teeth, held her breath, and shoved herself upright. Her vision tunneled down to a single white light. Sweat prickled hot, then cold, all over her skin, and her gut indicated it might want to heave up whatever might be left in it. But a couple of cold, disinfectant-bitter breaths and it settled, and her vision widened, settled back into color.

Good thing. The bruising on her torso was awfully pretty. Hate to miss it.

The blanket and sheet puddled at her hips. She traced the silhouette of both legs to the end of the bed. Good. But the shape of the left one was wrong, too bulky.

She dragged the bedclothes aside, found her left leg in a mobile boneset below the knee. The knee would flex, so that was good. Bonus: the leg didn't really even hurt. (Painkillers. Probably the contents of the drip-bag). The boneset's timer said twelve hours remaining of a programmed twenty-four. So that meant an accelerated cycle, which suggested a fracture rather than an actual break. Or maybe her nanomecha were working again. Maybe both. Also meant she'd been out at least twelve hours so far.

A flare in the corner of her vision caught her attention. She looked, and the med-mecha was looking back, its multi-faceted array lit up like her HUD had been, at the end (another memory). Well, not quite like that. No red-flash and in-rig siren telling her she'd breached seals, Brood was leaking in.

The med-mecha slid along its track and stopped overhead. It scanned her. Rays of translucent light, red and green and yellow, crisscrossing over her skin.

Iari eyed it. "Hi."

It beeped. And then, unsurprising, she heard slapping foot-steps. Getting louder. Too light to be Diran's, too quick. Iari looked past the blanketed peaks of her feet at the curtain-door. A pair of very small feet appeared underneath, and then the curtain twitched aside.

It was that little alw priest, the one Iari'd nearly run over in the corridor last time she'd been here. Sister what was it? Iphigenia, Iphigeniaria, something polysyllabic and pretentious and very al-war. Sister Impossible-Name hesitated a fistful of seconds, staring at Iari. Then she pasted a healer-sweet smile onto her face, and dropped her eyes to the tablet in her hand as if she'd just happened to walk into an otherwise empty trauma partition by casual coin-cidence. She hooked the stool with her foot, dragged it over, climbed on top.

"You're awake, Lieutenant. How are you feeling?"

"Naked. Cold. Like I might've broken something. Sister . . . ?"

"Iphigenia. Call me Iffy. You broke a few somethings." She didn't look up from the tablet. "Two ribs on the other side of your torso, joining the two you cracked in your last adventure. And you broke your left tibia."

"Yeah. I saw the boneset. Short program. Couldn't've been a *bad* break."

"Any break is serious." Sister Iffy pursed her lips. "But yes. You're healing quickly. Your nanomecha seem to be working again."

A tiny knot let loose in Iari's chest. "What made them stop?"

"I can't say for certain." Iffy pretended great interest in her tablet.

"Sure you can. You're reading my file."

"They *appear* to have repaired themselves, but we still aren't sure what caused the initial interruption in function. Sister Diran would know more about that, so don't ask me."

"You mean she's not telling you, so you can't tell me. Sounds like Dee." Iari ran careful fingers over her chest, over skin hot with bruises. More memory leaked back. She'd gone into that house with a working battle-rig. She'd found Tzcansi inside, very dead. And then—"What happened? I mean, why am I here right now?"

Sister Iffy's busy stylus stopped, mid-stroke. "You don't remember?"

Too high-pitched for sincerity. Iari sighed. That hurt. Scowling hurt. Her head hurt. "No. And you're not surprised."

"Memory loss is consistent with concussive trauma. I know that there was an explosion and a fire and that a building collapsed on you, Lieutenant. I know your rig was breached. I don't have all the details, I'm sorry." She tried a smile, tight and nervous and guilty. *Someone* didn't like lying.

"Then who does have the details? Sister Diran? Maybe I'll go ask her."

"You will *not*." Iffy threw herself off the stool and pressed a small hand in the middle of Iari's bare chest. "You can't go walking around in a boneset."

"I can hop." Iari wasn't sure about that. Whatever excellent painkillers she'd had were starting to wear off. Little twinges in her leg, bigger ones in her chest.

"You should lie down." Iffy pushed firmly. Frowned, when Iari did not yield a centimeter. "Lieutenant."

"I'll stay in bed, but I'm sitting up. Find me a tunic. Or you'll treat me for hypothermia next."

"Fine." Iffy did a credible Diran imitation, a heaved-from-the-guts sigh and eyes rolling. She made a point of stowing the tablet in her pocket—out of reach, unreadable—and ducked back through the curtain. She left it open, the width of a particularly petite female alw, which meant just wide enough someone could see in from the corridor, but that someone on the bed wouldn't be visible if she held still, even if she *was* halfway naked.

That open curtain was probably supposed to be a deterrent. Or a test. Iari side-eyed the med-mecha. "Stop me," she whispered. "Just try."

It beeped softly. Shuffled those spider-limbs, rattle-click. Its array of tesla-optics held steady and green.

Right. Her co-conspirator.

Iari leaned over carefully, slowly (it hurt), and looked where Iffy had gone. Polished corridors. A row of curtained chambers, all open.

The med-mecha whistled. Not an alert, like *come in here, the patient is dying*, but a *hey, heads up*. Iari glanced at it. It extended one of its limbs partway, pointing over the curtains, toward the interior wall of the trauma unit.

And yes, there, now she heard them: footsteps on that polished, hygienic stone. An uneven gait, both in meter and weight. A limp. A *hard* limp, the kind you got with mecha prosthetics and a rough initial graft, which only happened when Brood slime sat too long in a wound, because you were far from the front line (or behind it), a day's march and an aethership's flight from the nearest priest, and even Aedian nanomecha couldn't repair all the damage.

That was Tobin.

Iari tugged the sheets up over her chest. Iffy could hurry up with that shirt. *She* didn't care about naked so much; but Tobin was a spacer, human, born and raised on the *Darmak*, and that lot was weird about privacy. Damned, though, if she'd lie down and pull the sheets up under her chin like an invalid.

And oh, thank you swift-running Mishka: a second set of foot-steps detached themselves from the Knight-Marshal's metallic tread. Faster, skittering on the stone, propelling a breathless Iffy through the gap she'd left in Iari's curtain. She had a bundle of washed-out colorless fabric clutched against her chest like something precious.

"The Knight-Marshal's coming." Iffy shook out the tunic—one of those boxy things, open on one side and held together with strings. "Let me help you with this. You'll have to sort of drape it, you've still got the needle in your arm—"

Iari pinched the needle in her elbow gently, held her breath, *pulled.* On a scale of current injuries, that pain barely rated. She offered the needle to Iffy. "Trade."

She thought, for a beat, Iffy wouldn't: outrage sketched out in round eyes, round lips, the rise of color in her cheeks. Then she snatched the needle out of Iari's hand with enough force to rattle the whole metal stand. She dropped the tunic onto Iari's lap like one might drop a sodden rat.

"Thank you, Sister."

"You're *welcome.*" Iffy started a vigorous rolling up of the needle tubing, not looking at Iari as hard as she could.

Iari smothered a grin—she'd offended enough already, no need to provoke—and slid her arms into the cavernous tunnels that passed for the tunic's sleeves. She shrugged it over her shoulders. Tried raising both arms and discarded any idea of actually *tying* the thing.

Iffy left off harassing the needle stand. "Let me."

Iari leaned forward carefully. Held herself up on stiff finger-tips, denting the mattress, as Iffy did the ties at her nape and between her shoulder blades. Tobin's tread was very close now, deliberately loud. Deliberately slowing down.

Iffy whispered something foreign—was that Dwerig?—and obscene. "Sorry. I can't reach this last one."

"It's fine," Iari muttered. "Thanks," as Tobin paused outside the curtain. She could see a pair of armored boots. Greaves. He wore the full formal uniform, every damned day. That was *so* Tobin.

As was the quiet, polite, sincere, "Lieutenant? May I come in?"

And if she said no, he'd leave, Knight-Marshal and her superior or not. Which was exactly why Iari straightened (which hurt) and took a deep breath (which hurt worse) and let it out as slowly and steadily as she could manage. "Yes, sir. Of course, sir."

Tobin pulled the curtain open. His gaze flicked around the perimeter of the cubicle. Paused at the med-mecha, on the needle stand. Dusted over Iari without stopping and landed on Iffy.

So serious, Tobin, pure Knight-Marshal, face stiff as a vakar's. But his voice was gentle, courteous.

"May I have some time alone with the lieutenant, Sister Iphigenia?"

"Sir. Yes sir." Iffy bolted in a flutter of scrubs.

Tobin waited until her footsteps receded to silence. Then he blew a breath through his nose, not quite exasperation, and dragged the stool to the bedside in a jarring shriek of metal on stone.

"Lieutenant."

"Knight-Marshal."

"You do realize that this is the second rig you've destroyed in a day."

"Yes sir. Have to dock my pay."

"Or give Jorvik a raise." Tobin leaned forward and his smile dropped off. "Sister Iphigenia says you don't remember what happened."

Iari frowned at a blank spot of blanket. "Not entirely, sir. I know there was an explosion. Phlogiston, I'm guessing."

Another slice of memory: a roiling mass of coils, arcing plasma where Brood and riev collided. Her HUD bleeding alerts, her rig (her?) screaming as the seals ruptured. Brisk Array going down in a spray of Brood slime.

"Oh, voidspit. Brisk Array." More memory crashed back: coils in slick blackish violet, plasma sparks, her whole rig flashing alerts. "There was a tunneler, sir, in the house, Brisk Array took it on. He okay?"

"No. He is not. We can't find his remains—we *assume* he was pulled into the void after the tunneler after it killed him."

Or there wasn't enough left to find, Tobin did not say, but Iari understood anyway. She'd gotten lucky. She found her fists rolled up tight. Made her fingers uncurl, one at a stiff time. "And Corso?"

"The ambassador got him out before the explosion. He is, as far as I know, fine."

Iari's eyes flicked past Tobin, as if the vakar was lurking out in the corridor. "*Gaer*? What was he doing there?"

"Exactly what I asked. Evidently when you called your code red, Char overheard, demonstrated initiative, and went to render assistance. The ambassador chose to go along." Tobin's face settled back into *you can't read me* lines. "Is any of this sounding familiar?"

"Some, sir." There were big smears of nothing where that fight should've been. The back of her neck ached a little, right at the socket. She reached back. You had to know where to find it. Flush with the skin, tucked between vertebrae. Cooler than the surrounding flesh, most of the time. Hers felt hot. "Sister Iffy said the memory loss was trauma-related."

"Iffy?" Tobin's eyes crinkled, and the edge of his mouth. Then his features crashed sober again. "She might be right. But I think it's more likely you're feeling rig feedback. Iffy wouldn't know about that. She's too young to've been in the surge. It's something you get from too much synning. I lost most of what happened at Saichi."

After he'd killed the Brood hulk, he meant, after it had damn near ripped him in half and dropped him into the mud. There'd been a lot more of that *after*. Iari remembered the cluster of templars around him, the remnants of Tobin's rig like petals peeled away from flesh and winking bone. The look on Sergeant Neem's face, doing the calculus of lives and risk and chances.

The sergeant had never said, *leave the captain behind*. That decision had killed her, and Corporal Uesh, and Beren, and—ungentle Ptah, Hrok's freezing breath—*all* of them, except Iari.

The march back to the Saichi plain, back behind allied lines—that had been the real *after*. And what, Iari wondered, must that have been like for Tobin: to yield up consciousness (or have it taken, rig feedback and injury conspiring together) and come back ten templars down, missing most of a limb, missing *how* those people died and only knowing that they had done, and for his sake.

Iari had all those memories. Rain slashing down, mud pulling at her rig. The hike out of the ravine, the howls of the pursuing boneless. Tobin's body across her shoulders, because of the remaining templars, she was the one big enough, strong enough, *whole* enough to carry him. The rest of the unit, her friends, buying her time to haul Tobin out.

And afterward: a curtained space (in this very room, but closer to the door) and a med-mecha hovering over Tobin, touching and monitoring. Tobin's profile, eyes pointed straight up (at this very ceiling, speckled and smooth). His quiet, raw, *what happened, Private?* and her quiet, raw recitation.

Mishka's mercy that he *didn't* remember it.

Tobin's throat moved (then and now). Human males could grow facial hair, you could see where it would go, the dark shadow tracing jaw and throat and cheeks. It looked like a bruise in this light, from this angle. He stared somewhere else, some*when* else.

She steered them out of that place.

"Sir. Here's what I do remember. Tzcansi's dead. Looked like a boneless did it. That's bad enough, Brood in B-town—a boneless, plus the swarm from before. But the boneless *only* went after the people in one house, and the swarm stayed in the tavern until we flushed them out. I've never heard of Brood doing targeted assassination before. That suggests they're controlled."

"Gaer insists there was an arithmancer present at Tzcansi's house, who was responsible for the explosion. He might be the one responsible for the Brood, too." Now Tobin's anger showed, if you knew where to look. The cracks around his mouth. Around his eyes, themselves gone glittering and sharp as splintered polysteel. "The Brood presence and the attack on Aedian personnel give us cause for an *official* investigation. I've already informed the peacekeepers that we expect their full cooperation." It was Knight-Marshal Tobin looking down at her now. "When you've recovered, you'll assume responsibility. You report to me, and me only, for the time being. Clear, Lieutenant?"

Damn good she was already on her ass. "Sir?"

His brows stabbed upward. "That surprises you?"

"I've broken two rigs, lost a riev, *and* gotten our prime suspect killed."

"On the contrary, Lieutenant. Tzcansi *might* have killed Pinjat, but her murder suggests there's another killer out there. If someone's controlling Brood, I think it's more likely the arithmancer who tried to kill you. And then there is the altar in that warehouse." The Knight-Marshal—because this man was *all* rank right now, all armor—looked at her with that mask he'd perfected after Saichi, whenever anyone asked how he was. "This is a multifaceted investigation, Lieutenant. We might be dealing with the beginning of a new surge, which is cause enough for alarm. But the murders, the altar, the arithmancy Gaer is investigating, and the possible breach to riev security, all appear to be connected. We don't know how, but until we do, we need to limit the number of persons involved. The uncertainty of events, coupled with the novelty of our suppositions, would invite speculation from people less well informed of the situation. Do you understand?"

Oh, ungentle Ptah, this was above her rank and pay grade. Probably five levels of classified to which she was not entitled. And there was only one way to answer. "Yes sir."

"Good." Then the Knight-Marshal splayed his fingers, spacer reflex, spacer shrug, and became *Tobin* again. "I'm putting you in charge of the new initiate. Char," when she stared at him. "Mother Quellis could find no doctrinal reason to refuse their enlistment."

Mother Quellis was a small woman, human, gentle-voiced, a priest of Mishka by temper and calling. An excess of pastries had rounded her silhouette. But you thought *soft* about her at your peril. A priest didn't get her own Aedis, even on a backwater tenju seedworld, by being lax with doctrine. Tobin must've argued himself hoarse on Char's behalf.

"Thank you, sir."

He raised a brow. "There's more work in it for you. Ordinarily we'd send Char to train at the facilities at Windscar, but given their unique circumstances, Mother Quellis and I agreed it would be better to handle them here. She and I will devise a curriculum, and I will oversee the implementation, but I will delegate their direct oversight to you. You'll have to find a way to make that fit in with your current assignment. I'm going to give you Corporal Luki to help."

Void and *dust*. Gaer had alleged that she was Tobin's favorite (and she *was*, she knew that), but that didn't mean failure came with no consequence. She'd expected a reprimand, or temporary reassignment to nightwatch. And here Tobin was giving her a tacit promotion.

With a riev initiate. With a civilian contractor and a SPERE operative. With poor Corporal Luki, who probably didn't deserve this notoriety. Not exactly a *conventional* command, not the sort of thing that got notice from the Synod, or led to offworld postings. But better than patrolling the walls on nightwatch for the next six months.

Also politically dangerous, if someone up the chain decided Tobin should've done something different.

Her mouth felt full of sharp stones. She swallowed them. "*Yes* sir. Thank you, sir."

Tobin took a small bite of air. "Don't thank me yet. I also agreed that you should spend the next thirty hours here in the hospice for observation."

"Sir." Iari hoped she kept the look of horror off her face. Knew she'd failed when Tobin's eyes wrinkled up at the corners.

"I sympathize, Lieutenant. But Jorvik insisted that he needs that much time to get your rig repaired, and it was the briefest span Sister Diran would agree to." He rolled eyes at the curtain-walls, the monitors. Then his gaze snagged on the med-mecha. Any lingering humor seeped out of his features. Only memory left, hollow and brittle. "I'm sorry to leave you alone in here."

Felt like another building had collapsed on her, not enough room for lungs and heart and breath. "It's fine, sir."

His eyes closed for a little bit too long for a blink. "In the meantime," he said, and slid a hand behind his breastplate and produced a flat, slender volume, bound in leather. "I brought you something to help pass the time."

There weren't many places to stash-and-carry in non-combat armor. A part of her mind imagined the sharp-cornered discomfort of storing that book between poly-plate and uniform tunic. The rest of her mind recognized the pattern on the cover, without needing to see the title, or the author, or anything else.

"*Meditations*," said Tobin, as if she might not recognize it. "I didn't want to rummage your quarters to find yours, so . . ."

So he'd brought her *his* copy.

Iari took it with careful fingers. The book had seen rougher handling: had traveled with Tobin, she knew, since his own initiation, through each deployment. A memory surfaced of Saichi, rain rattling down on the tent before—*before*. Soft-lit interior, the lantern teslas throwing their blue-white glow into all the creases and corners. Bright enough a young captain could read, there on the periphery, while his even younger unit diced and bickered and tried to pretend the next day's mission didn't worry them. While Iari, who'd done time in the army already, who was no stranger to night-before jitters, sat on the tent's other side, trying (and failing) to meditate and envying Tobin his calm.

And after, so much *after*: bringing that book to him here, his request, while the med-mecha prodded the ruin of his hip and leg. She had watched his hands smooth the cover, trace the title. Watched them shake.

Have you read this?

No sir.

And a breath. Ragged. *Read it to me. Now. Please.*

Iari rubbed the edge of the cover, smudged and discolored and ungentle Ptah, don't think about why. "Thank you, sir."

"You're welcome." Tobin stood up, equal parts stool-on-stone squeak and the rattle of armor. Under that, where bone and joint should have been: the whine of the mecha graft, faint as whispers.

CHAPTER FIFTEEN ≡≡≡

Corso rearranged himself on a stool just a little too small and a little too short for comfort and sipped good, bitter tea out of a cup he could, well, *cup* in his palm. There were dimples in the side, meant for gripping by fingers both smaller than his and one fewer. Like, oh, *that* wichu over there. Moon-eyed little man, cup balanced in his fingers just so, the third and smallest held out straight like a perch for birds, sipping with his little narrow lips at the delicate little rim.

Corso considered for half a breath trying to imitate him—it was etiquette, obviously. But the only reason to try to match wichu custom would be to blend in, and *that* was slagging impossible. He couldn't even hold the cup right. So he just held the whole cup in his palm instead, and poured hot liquid into his mouth that way. It was actually a little unpleasant; the tea was hot, and so was the ceramic. Reminded him of drinking tea in the field, out of metal cups. *That* had been an exercise in minimizing burns. And when they'd been deployed east of Windscar, on the northern line—then it'd been a wages-on competition to drink hot tea in that zone between scalding and tepid, while the metal cup gave up its heat to the crackling cold and the wind and the snow. Lot of coin changed hands back then, between him and Iari. Lot of bets won and lost.

Corso grinned at the memory. The wichu—you could never tell where they were looking, with those featureless eyes—flinched. Corso grinned a little wider and slammed the rest of the tea down his throat (hot, straight shot to gut, where it hit and spread out). Then he put the cup down with a little more force than necessary (made the other man flinch again, earned a glare from the barista) and got up to leave.

The veek had said, *find Yinal'i'ljat*. B-town was a big place, but sure as sunrise, you wanted to find a wichu, you went to Wichutown (except for that dead fucker Pinjat, but he was the exception that proved the rule). Wichutown had taken over about ten square blocks of B-town, carved out of what had probably been alwar neighborhood; the buildings had alwar dimensions, which already made them a little cramped and narrow for Corso's comfort. Wichu had made renovations, and they'd been at the exteriors, painting and shaping, slapping wood and plaster onto honest bricks. Voidspit *pink* on that wall, yellow on *that* one, like a slagging field of wildflowers. Banners fluttered on storefronts, printed and painted in wichu script. More conventional signs, in conventional Comspek, stuck out like stones in a stream, flat and grey and *useful*. Like that one, over there: *Lodging*, it said, in simple block text, beside some elaborate foreign scribbling that probably said *This Place Is Very Proud of Its Bedbugs*.

It was also the place Yinal'i'ljat had listed as her place of residence on the official PK report, which Corso had gotten by means the Aedis wouldn't approve. Chief Inspector Elin had taken her sweet slagging time giving him the address. Two days for a voidspit sliver of information that probably took five minutes to access from the PK turing net. *It's been busy*, Elin had said, *there's shit going down, fucking Aedis has half of Lowtown behind barricades, templars crawling all over, asking for our fucking files.*

And Corso had made sympathetic noises and didn't ask details, same as his contact didn't ask what he wanted with Yinal'i'ljat. But then Elin *did* say, *Aedis wants everything we've got on who killed that other moon-eye. If you're involved, you watch your back.*

Which Corso had done. He was very good at back-watching. What he had not done, and what he did feel a *little* guilty about, was report to Gaer that he had an address; but then, the veek had said *find Yinal'i'ljat,* not just *find where she's living.* So he was only half done with the work, technically, and besides: the fewer times he was logged comming the Aedis to report to the veek ambassador, the better. Shit like that got out, his reputation would suffer.

So, get the address, check; *find* the address, check; and now to put the R in P.R.I.S. Corso had been sitting in that tea shop for the better part of a day, waiting for Yinal'i'ljat to come out, or go in, or even confirm her existence. It was better, he thought, to approach a subject on the street, keep it public, since all he needed was to pass on a message. But he was sick of wichu tea, and he was sick of little wichu stools, and he had a headache throbbing behind his eyes because of all the bright wichu colors.

And really, he was starting to think she wasn't there at all, in that hostel, and if she'd moved, he needed to figure out where she'd gone before the veek called him for a progress report. Or, void and dust, *Iari* did.

Gaer had said, last communication they'd had: "Because you asked me to call you: our mutual friend is alive and recovering, no permanent damage."

Mutual friend. Mutual *friend.* Corso ground his teeth hard enough that they squeaked. He wasn't sure what Iari and he were, anymore, but *their* relationship and whatever association she had with some slagging *veek* wouldn't fit in the same word.

Gaer. Ambassador. Arithmancer. The reason Corso was down

here right now, instead of—void and dust, what? Lurking outside the Aedis gates, gathering the guts up to go inside and see her? Or more likely, holing back up in his office with a bottle of whiskey and worrying there.

The veek had done him a favor. Given him something to do. Given him a *target*.

As for what the *veek* was doing, well. Corso looked in the Aedis's direction (invisible, behind walls and architecture, but you could feel it up there). Hopefully finding the fucking arithmancer who'd tried to kill Iari, so someone could go kill him.

Corso gathered his braids out of his face and tucked them behind his shoulders, careful to avoid the hooks threaded through them. That'd taken practice, learning not to snag himself. Now it was easy as breathing. Easy as checking his weapons, too. He wasn't wearing a laborer's coveralls this time. Wore his usual canvas coat, oiled against autumn drizzle, meant to blur his outline and hide a very illegal whitefire sidearm tucked up under his shoulder and a monofil in the left sleeve. The coat made him look even broader, which he usually liked. Intimidation was useful in some investigations. In *this* one, less so; but damned if he'd leave his weapons home this time, even if wichu crossed the narrow lanes to avoid him if possible, and if not, drew back against the brightly colored walls and stared as if he were an iotun from pre-Landfall legend, come to crush them with stone fists and stone feet.

Corso *felt* a little bit like an iotun as he ducked into the hostel. The ceiling in here was a just a little too low. Beams crossing over his head with a handspan's clearance. The desk in the foyer, in the middle of a little patch of colorful carpet, might come to the top of his hips. Maybe. If he crouched.

The wichu behind that desk—palely round-eyed like all his

species, wispy hair gathered up in a knot—glanced up from his turing. Frowned. Raised a finger in universal *just one moment* gesture.

Corso hunched a little bit deeper into his coat and tried to take up less space. Maybe this was how Char had felt, squeezing into his office behind Iari and Gaer.

The clerk, having finished whatever neefa-shit he was doing on the screen, looked dubiously up at Corso. "May I help you?"

Thus invited, Corso approached the desk and loomed over it (like an iotun). "I'm here to deliver a message to Yinal'i'ljat. Is she in?"

The clerk blinked. "I can take that message for you, sir."

Confirmed she was on the register, anyway. Clerk hadn't asked, *who's that*. Corso grinned and leaned forward a little. "Yeah. Sure you can. But I need to deliver it to her personally. So, she in?"

The clerk's head cranked back on his skinny little neck. Fucking creepy eyes. You couldn't see a reflection in them. "I'm afraid not."

"You know when she'll be back?"

"No, sir, I'm sorry."

Now, that slagging veek arithmancer with his fancy optic, he'd've been able to read the clerk's aura and tell truth from lies by the colors he saw. Corso didn't pretend to understand what the fuck that really meant, or how it worked, but he knew it was real enough. Seemed like a slagging waste of arithmancy, looking at people's colors, though, when it was easy enough to tell *liar* from *honest* from the outside.

"Listen." Corso spread his hands on the desk. "I got orders it's got to go straight to Yinal'i'ljat. My *boss* says. So, I can wait for her *here*"—he gestured at the lobby, and the clerk's eyes widened and rounded, taking his mouth along for the ride—"or you can let me go up *there* and leave it for her. I can shove it under the door."

"That's not our policy." The clerk's voice was thin as steam coming off a teacup in a Windscar spring morning. "Only guests go upstairs."

"Then I guess I'll wait." Corso made a show of looking around the little lobby, which was not equipped for waiting by someone Corso's size (two little chairs, that was all). "Maybe outside," he said. "Right by the door. That way she'll see me right away. That okay?"

The clerk blinked rapidly. You could see the calculations march across his face. Tenju standing outside, scaring everyone. Gossip piling up like shit behind a neefa.

"I. Um. Perhaps I can make an exception in policy, sir, just this once, and allow you to go up."

Corso grinned in the clerk's face. "That'd be *great*. Thanks."

The clerk sighed. Tapped something into his turing with the force that said *logging off*, and then came around the desk. "Follow me, sir."

He abandoned Corso at the top of the stairs. "That way," he said, and pointed. "Room Seven."

Which begged asking *why* number to seven when Corso counted only four doors, but hey, they were wichu. Probably some numerological voidspit involved. Wichu were almost as bad as vakari for seeing the world in numbers and equations.

And color. Void and *dust*, magenta walls shading to violet at the floorboards, doors in eye-bleeding yellow and orange, and yeah, that was number seven, in terrible teal. Corso grunted at the clerk—thanks, fuck off, however you wanted to interpret it—and started down the hallway. Thick carpet underfoot, masking boot-steps and creaking floorboards. Almost as quiet as stone. That was fucking *weird*, after the rattle-trap Vulgar Vakar.

And it wasn't just the floor. Corso slowed as he passed Room Three (yellow door, plasma-blue trim). There was no sound coming out of any of the doors: No voices, no rustling around. No sound *anywhere* up here. Corso turned slowly, tilting his head at each door in turn. This was exactly like Tzcansi's sister's house had been, when it'd been so quiet he was sure Tzcansi was waiting upstairs for him with a whitefire longcaster, laying ambush.

Instead she'd been Brood-gutted and dead.

Corso's heart ricocheted off his ribs and got stuck in his throat. P.R.I.S. wasn't *safe* work, especially not the districts he worked; but it wasn't, until very fucking recently, going to put him in the way of Brood, either. He should turn around, get the fuck out of here—*why* had he taken the veek's job, anyway, after what he'd seen in that house, Tzcansi split open and guts everywhere and—

—and Iari's face, when she'd walked in and seen what'd happened. She might've been cast from the same alloy as her battle-rig. He remembered her face before the scar and cap on her tusk, remembered the day she'd got both (lot of blood, shattered visor, serious swearing). The Iari he remembered had always been cool, but she'd never been fucking *ice*. Templar Iari was a whole slagging glacier.

It wasn't the ice that stuck with him. It was the look she gave him after, when the riev had shouted up about finding Tri and her kids dead downstairs. A flash of anger—*that* Iari he recognized—and then a dawning disappointment. Like she'd expected better of him.

Fuck if she'd look at him that way twice. Ever again. No matter how slagging quiet this hallway was, how *wrong* it felt, like the very silence was pushing him back, plucking at coat-tails, urging him *go back*. He'd said he'd do a job. And he would. Right now.

Corso adjusted his sweat-slick grip on the sidearm. The charge-light was green, ready to fire. He crept up on door seven, *listened* (to nothing). He knocked, lightly, with the back of his left hand (right hand and jacta still ready).

More nothing. More aggressive silence. More *get the fuck out of here* wrongness.

Explain to Iari why he'd walked away now. Explain to that bone-faced veek. Or put a hand on the panel and expect (explosion, fire) an earth-shattering beep of *locked, no entry*. At least there'd be a noise.

The panel chimed—polite, demure—and turned green. And before Corso could entirely summon his wits and conceal the jacta, the door slid aside.

"Sorry to disturb you," he started. But there wasn't anyone on the other side of the door. Not a maid, or a maid-mecha, and certainly not Yinal'i'ljat. An empty patch of floorboard carved out in a square of bright from the corridor teslas. The room itself was all dimness and gloom. Corso ducked his head a little and peered in. Curtains drawn tight, with only a little leak of light from the gap in between.

He stepped over the threshold. His shadow blotted out the light from the corridor and merged with the room's shadow. The air felt markedly cooler inside. There were reasons it might: this was the northeast side of the building, it was autumn, and raining, and late afternoon. But it was stale, too, and close, like the ventilation was off. And the room's teslas, which should've lit up when the door opened, stayed dim. The remaining light-bleed from the hallway teslas showed him a cramped little entry corridor, a shut door to his immediate right. That'd be the WC. In the dim beyond that, he mapped out the rest of the room: the smudged line of light around the window. A hard-cornered shape, tall and flat to the wall, that must be a wardrobe. A partition wall jutted into the room, squeezing off any view of what else the room held. He guessed, from prior experience in places like this: a bed, a desk, or a table on the other side of that partition.

Corso's scalp prickled tight. He raised the jacta, one-handed, and slapped for the tesla panel on the wall. He found the switch. The teslas flared bright as the sun for a second. Then came a *pop* and a smoky smell and the dark slammed back down like a fist.

Corso brought his left hand up, stabilized his grip on the jacta. *Sense* said come in quiet, walk soft. But he'd already tried the slagging lights. Anyone inside would know he was there. Best give them a chance to:

"Come out."

The room snapped up his syllables. Corso strained against the pressing silence to hear breath, or any whisper of friction: fabric or flesh on the floorboards, on the bed. Maybe the whine of a jacta, whitefire, or old-style bolt-thrower. He held his breath. Waited. *Listened.*

"Yinal'i'ljat? My name's Corso. P.R.I.S. Not PK. Hear me? Just want to talk."

And still—nothing, except his own heartbeat thumping in his ears. He slid a foot forward. Felt the sole of his boot glide over the polished floor, felt it catch on the edge of a rug.

And heard . . . nothing. Not even a whisper.

That wasn't right. And when something wasn't right like *that*, it meant arithmancy. A silencing hex, the kind you got for abattoirs or machine-shops or brothels, so that the neighbors didn't hear. The Vulgar Vakar had, like, a dozen of those for the needle-rooms. None this good, though; Corso could still hear things through his flat's floor. These hexes were excellent, and that meant expensive.

There weren't many in his clientele whose targets could afford hexwork, but there were a few. Ganglords, mostly, people with money. Tzcansi had been one of them. A wichu—what had the veek said she was? Oh, right—linguist, something fancy, might have that kind of capital. Clearly she *did*.

Though what she was doing staying *here*, in a second-rate hostel with first-rate arithmantic silence-hexes on her room, might be worth investigating. The veek might pay for that knowledge.

For now, though, the arithmancy. A hex for silence made no sense, unless it was *that* kind of establishment—which this wasn't—or unless the people inside the room wanted no sound to escape. Tzcansi'd had rooms like that in a few of her cafes, for business meetings. Had a cellar like that, too, in a warehouse in Lowtown, for a different sort of business meeting.

Corso sniffed the dead air. Stale dust, maybe some mildew. But there was no metallic blood smell. No dead-meat. He took a small bite of breath. Held it and came all the way into the room.

The door shut as soon as he cleared the threshold, taking the light from the hallway with it. He couldn't hear himself breathing now.

All right. He already knew the room was hexed for quiet. That was creepy, sure, but it wasn't dangerous.

What he couldn't hear, though, might be. And what he couldn't see, with the teslas disabled. He waited for his eyes to adjust. For the shadows to take on more definition. Definitely a wardrobe over there. He patted along the wall until he found a closed door beside him. The probable WC. It, like the main door, opened when he touched the panel.

Nothing came leaping out at him. No faceful of jacta bolt or monofil-swinging wichu. Of course the lights didn't work in there, either. Black as the inside of a pocket. No sound. The only smell was chemical, antiseptic, faint and permanent. The floor was—he poked an exploring toe forward—slick underfoot, like tile.

Definitely the WC, as fucking expected. Corso let his breath out in a little gust that he could only feel, and eased back. Let that door close itself, and retreated to the room's opposite wall.

Last time he'd gone into someplace that'd seemed empty, he'd found Tzcansi. But there he'd smelled the blood before he got up the stairs. He'd *known* there was something wrong, and what that wrong would look like when he got to it.

There was definitely something wrong *here*, but what it was . . .

. . . was a matter of sliding two paces down the wall until he could get an angle and peer past the partition into the main room. Chances were, anyone waiting for him was pressed against the wall shared with the WC. They couldn't see him yet. He couldn't see them.

Iari would've done it five times already. Iari would be looking at him with that *poor civ Corso* face for huddling with his back to the wall, within easy retreat to the corridor. Iari would be laughing behind her fucking visor that he was scared to go into a dark room like there were Brood hiding in there, instead of what was most likely a slagging *wichu*.

A room slathered with silencing hexes. Remember that.

Except no. Iari wouldn't laugh at him. Iari would say *get behind me* and pop out that shield.

That image got Corso to slide himself along the wall in one sharp, quick motion, jacta raised, primed, ready. Expecting to see a wichu, maybe with a weapon. Expecting that wichu to jump at him, maybe, or throw something, or scream. *Not* expecting what he did see: a sharply made bed, the cover of which was a collage of light and dark patches (they would be colorful, with sufficient light), in the middle of which was a puddle of black so dark it made all the shadows look pale and tragic.

That puddle sprouted a pentad of lambent eyes in an unbalanced arrangement. That puddle *flowed* into a collection of knife-edged limbs of asymmetrical proportions.

Boneless.

Corso fired the jacta. Whitefire arced from the muzzle, jagged and aimed by panic. It stitched across the bed, warped by the natural Brood warping effect, before ricocheting off the wall and hitting the boneless by accident.

Corso *smelled* the hit: chemical burn in his throat, in his eyes, acrid and thick as oil. *Saw* it: the spattering not-quite-flesh, burning white and raining onto the bed, raising smoke from the patchwork quilt.

The boneless (should have) shrieked. Its primary mouth irised wide, showed that coil of teeth and the triple-tongue.

It whipped sideways, uncoiling. Ricocheted off the wall and bounced at him.

This time, when Corso fired, *he* screamed.

He didn't hear that, either.

CHAPTER SIXTEEN ═══════

The boneset's chrono and the med-mecha's glowing insectoid eyes were the only real lights in the hospice. The ambient teslas, the only ones bright enough for, oh, *reading*, had powered off on some whimsical timer when Iari'd been in the middle of Book Two, Chapter Eight.

Of the things which inspire fear, there are two categories: those things beyond our strength and control, and those things over which we have some measure of the same. Among the former, we might include the shift and whim of the Elements; for who can divert a flood, or a hurricane, or lightning? Who can withstand an earthquake?

A fair question, at the time, and one with the obvious answer *nobody*. Jareth had been one of the founders of the Aedis, the First Knight-General, and first on the line against the then-united vakari Protectorate. The newly formed Aedis was starting to implement nanomecha, but the syn implants were years away. Jareth and his templars had fought the vakari without them. Iari wondered what Jareth would think of their invention. If he'd think the implants undercut all his stoicism, all his virtue. A priest *could* divert storms, with enough upgrades, or wring water out of the very air. A templar with a synned battle-rig could match a vakar for speed, for strength.

But a templar and all her nanomecha couldn't stop an automated voidspit timer that turned off all the teslas in the trauma wing.

The midnight bells came and went. Iari sang her own prayers in the dark. Tried to doze, after, but the silence was too loud for that.

The med-mecha beeped, very softly.

"I'm awake," Iari murmured. "What?"

But then she heard footsteps in the corridor. Light, quick, becoming familiar.

"Lieutenant?" softly, from outside the curtain. "Are you awake?"

Iari glanced at the med-mecha. "No. Sound asleep. Come in, Sister Iphigenia."

The curtains twitched open. "Mishka's tears, just call me Iffy. What's funny?"

"Nothing. Throat's dry. Iffy. Don't you ever go off-shift?"

"I do. I *am*, technically. Lights," she said, and the teslas overhead activated obediently. (Voice recognition? Not fair.) Iffy dragged the stool over beside the bed and perched on top of it. She had a shapeless, faded cloth bag slung over her shoulder, like she was planning a trip to the market shops. She set it on her lap and began rummaging through its guts. "I wanted to bring you this *before* first shift starts." She pulled a skinsuit, neatly rolled, out of her bag, and set it on the side table. "For later. The one you were wearing when you came in is unsalvageable. Oh, don't give me that look. I didn't break into your quarters or anything, Lieutenant. I'm just delivering it from Supply. The Knight-Marshal signed off on the order. Brother Veeda wasn't going to let me have it, otherwise. Honestly." She paused, lips pursed. "I also told

Corporal Luki when you're set for release. She said she'd be here to meet you, with Char."

Iari imagined an entire conversation, starting with *why* and including the words *Sister Diran* and conspiratorial smiles. She skipped straight to the expected, inevitable, much-deserved end. "Thanks, Sister."

Iffy's smile flickered like a damaged tesla. "And I also wanted you to see this." She produced a tablet from the bag's depths and unrolled it like she expected it to snap in half. "It's your medical report. The results of the last round of tests. Sister Diran hasn't even seen it yet, unless she's up earlier than I think she is."

"But *you* read it."

Iffy nodded. "In case you had questions."

"You don't think Dee would answer my questions? No. Don't answer that. She wouldn't. And thanks." Iari took the tablet. Didn't look at it, not yet. Iffy's face was more interesting, trying and failing at serene unconcern.

"Is it bad?"

"No." A blink. Another flickering-tesla smile. "It's actually all *good*. Your nano are fully functional. Blood alchemy is normal. Maybe even a little better than normal."

"But?"

"Just read it, Lieutenant. I'll, ah, just check the boneset."

Hrok's breath, that wasn't ominous or anything. Iari began reading. Most of the information, she already knew about, albeit from a more personal, visceral perspective. Bruises, breaks, the usual damage templars got in battle. It was the second half of the report, the part concerning her implants, framed in numbers and alchemy, with charts and color-coded results, that needed closer examination. The word *infection*, for instance, describing the failure of nanomecha—a cascading effect that had, at one point, taken almost all of hers offline. Almost. And then they'd recovered, words accompanied by a new onslaught of numerical explanation. Iari skimmed past those, looking for a probable cause in plain Comspek.

"A *battle-hex* took down my nanomecha?"

Iffy stopped fussing over the indifferent boneset and folded her hands. Stared at them, like all the answers to the multiverse were written on her knuckles. "That's the turing's best guess, based on probabilities and the initial damage. This was definitely an arithmancer's doing. Someone with knowledge of battle-hexes."

"Someone. You better not mean *Gaer*."

Iffy's chin jerked up. She flashed wide blue eyes at Iari. "No one thinks that! I mean. It's obvious it's not the ambassador's fault."

It was what Iari wanted to hear. Exactly why she didn't trust it. The anger settled back to nausea. She borrowed Gaer's tone. "Why is that obvious?"

"Whatever breached your nanomecha got in because its code *looked* Aedian. There's no way the ambassador could write something like that. No vakar could. Lieutenant. I repeat: no one thinks it's him."

"The turing ran that probability, though, didn't it?"

"Yes. Of course."

Which Gaer would expect. He *lived* here, in the middle of an Aedis compound, one of, what, five vakari on the planet, and the only one in B-town? Damn sure he was accustomed to suspicion. Chaama's cold bones, no wonder he wouldn't come down to the hospice to see her. He didn't want anyone to take him apart, sure, but he didn't want to give anyone cause to think they should, either.

"You said *our* code." Ptah's unblinking eye. Gaer had also said the code in the riev chip had looked like Aedis hexwork. "Does that mean this . . . infection . . . could hit priests, too? Not just templars?"

"That is the theory."

Iari thrust the report back at Iffy. "Thanks for letting me read this."

"That's . . . all? You don't want to ask anything else?"

Oh, void and dust. "What's got you upset?"

"The part about your nanomecha rewriting their basecode."

"That's what they're supposed to do, isn't it? Adapt?"

"In theory. It's just—they've never had to. We haven't *had* a security breach like this since . . ." Iffy waved her hands. "I can't even name a date. The beginning. Before the Weep. Not since the very *first* nanomecha—wichu-artificed to be weapons, but they overwrote their own code when they colonized the very first person to carry them. That was before we had implants to interface with them, and before we'd even invented the syn."

Iari knew the bones of that story: pre-Aedis, an early encounter with the Protectorate, the groundwork for what became the templars in its details. She *hadn't* realized, though, that the initial nanomecha had been wichu-made. Like the riev.

She remembered the pyrotechnics in her HUD when Sawtooth and Swift Runner had come crashing into the warehouse cellar. They'd been *infected*, Gaer's own word for it. But by Brood, not by . . . code. Unless the code included Brood? And even if that were possible, she didn't have a chip. Sawtooth did. How would any infection have jumped systems, its code to her nanomecha?

Iari scanned again through the report. No sign of Brood-rot in her. The Aedis would *know*. But Brood-rot was physical damage. Corruption, corrosion, natural processes derailed and disrupted. What if it could be somehow woven into a hex? Gaer said his voidspit arithmancy, numbers, underpinned everything. Why *wouldn't* someone be able to find a way to describe Brood-rot with numbers?

Pinjat's workshop, wrecked as it was, so obviously battered by Sawtooth—she and Gaer hadn't gotten any Brood emanations off of it. She hadn't been rigged, so that excused *her* from catching it; but Gaer wore that optic, and he hadn't sensed anything either. So either he'd missed it, or it hadn't been there. That would mean Sawtooth hadn't been infected when they had gone after Pinjat.

Or, *or*, the infection had been in a stage early enough Sawtooth hadn't been showing the effects. Pinjat's murder had been what, less than a full day before the cellar encounter? And Sawtooth had been *oozing* then.

Iari looked at her numbers again. It'd been twice that long now since she fought Sawtooth, and she wasn't showing signs of rot. So whatever the riev had gotten, her nano had beaten it back.

Or it was just taking a lot longer to manifest, and all the priests were wrong. And that still didn't tell her how infected code could jump from a chip to her nano. *If* it could. (How could it? Could nanomecha . . . fly?)

Ungentle Ptah, she needed an arithmancer's perspective. She needed Gaer.

Of those things which we fear that lie beyond our strength, then: only fools careless of their own lives would battle with these, or people insensible of their own limits, or the insane. The one possessed of courage knows when to yield ground, and when to hold it.

When Jareth had said it was all right to *fear that which is beyond one's power to overcome*, he'd meant external forces. He hadn't said what to do if the irresistible forces might be *inside*.

Iari heard Dee coming. Brisk strides, and hard, like she was mad at the stone floor for some transgression. Like she was making sure it knew, every step, she was in charge. It was exactly twenty-nine hours, fifty-five minutes. Iari didn't expect Diran to *defy* the Knight-Marshal's orders, exactly; but she wouldn't yield up a minute of Iari's incarceration, either. Or her own authority. Literally, not one slagging minute.

You saw that, sometimes, pissing matches between the priests and the templars. Usually it was Reverend Mothers or Fathers in conflict with their Knight-Marshals, each jealous of their personnel, their jurisdictions. They were supposed to be balanced partners, the arms of the Aedis; but there was always one arm a little bit stronger, a little more in control.

This, Diran's behavior, wasn't symptomatic of a larger problem. The B-town Aedis worked like it was supposed to, a partnership of mutual respect between Quellis and Tobin. No, this was purely Diran, purely personal.

The med-mecha beeped softly and rearranged its legs. Metal snick, metal whisper. It had stationed itself over Iari's cubicle, never mind she didn't need the attendance. She'd thought it was spying for Diran at first; but when it hadn't set off any alerts when she'd tried to walk in the boneset (bad idea) and when it'd helped her back into the bed when she'd proved she could *not*, she'd decided it was just lonely. Bored. An impression further cemented by its company *after* Iffy got the boneset off.

Diran would sniff at the very idea of a mecha's emotional matrix, but Dee would sniff at Char having opinions, hell, Dee sniffed at *anyone's* opinions, unless they agreed with her own.

"I hear you," Iari muttered, for the med-mecha's benefit. Then she sat down on the edge of the bed. Standing would've been most comfortable, but Dee would read that (rightly) as a challenge.

"All right, Lieutenant, let's evaluate your condition—" Diran swept into the cubicle with a dramatic pulling-aside of the curtain. She looked at Iari then, and frowned. "You're already dressed."

That was Diran's way of asking *how did you get that skinsuit?* Or, knowing Dee, *who got it for you?*

Iari said nothing.

Diran pursed her lips and tapped her stylus on the rim of her tablet. "Sister Iphigenia." Not even asking.

"Templar-Initiate Char brought it," Iari said, which made Diran's face pucker up, trying to think how she might've missed a one-armed riev coming into the trauma wing, trying to think when. Iari was just glad Dee didn't read auras. Hers would be glowing with whatever color lies were. "I didn't want any unnecessary delays for my discharge."

Iari patted the square-cornered bundle of hospice robe, stacked a precise fingerwidth from the pillow, which was as close to perfect center in the bed as the med-mecha and Iari had been able to manage. Tobin's copy of *Meditations* sat beside it. Iari kept her gaze on its cover, on the title, on Jareth's name.

That which differentiates an animal from a sapient is the capacity for reason. For any beast may feel anger, or joy, or fear. But it is reason which affords us the power to control our reactions, and sets us apart from the beasts.

"Mm." Diran pretended great interest in the tablet's screen. "Well. You may've gotten dressed for nothing. The thirty-hour medical hold was a minimum, not a guarantee."

Iari ground her teeth together until they creaked. Keep her mouth *shut*, that was the trick of dealing with Dee. Give her nothing to hold onto. Say *that's neefa-shit* or *Ptah's burning eye, Dee, come on* and she'd be in here that much longer.

Instead, she sat still as a riev while Diran examined her—which the med-mecha could do, but which Diran did because, oh, she could.

"I wish you'd waited to change out of the robe," Diran said, as she crouched and felt her way along Iari's newly-out-of-the-boneset leg. "Examination is easier without fabric in the way."

Yeah. Everything had been easier when it was just skin between them. It was the rest of the time, the majority of the time, they had trouble.

Diran sat back on her heels and drilled Iari with a glare. Color crawled up her cheeks. Nothing as elaborate as Gaer's chromatophores, no blues and pinks and yellows. Just good old-fashioned mammalian blush, which turned Diran's tawny skin almost bronze.

"Any pain, Lieutenant?"

"No." Another aura-combusting lie.

Which Dee recognized for the neefa-shit that it was. She was a senior healer. She'd heard variations on *I'm fine* a thousand times before. She pretended to read over the tablet, frowning and poking at the screen with a stylus.

Iari hung her gaze just past Diran's shoulder, on the dangling med-mecha (which blinked its panel of teslas at her, almost like a wink), and endured until Diran made a frustrated noise. "All right. You may return to active duty, Lieutenant."

"Thank you, Sister." Iari stood up, nose to nose with Diran, chest to chest. They were of a height, the pair of them. But Iari had tenju breadth, while Diran was human-slender, despite her mixed heritage.

Iari held her breath and walked out. Mishka's tears, it hurt. Little bolts of lightning and plasma shot along nerve-channels without warning, sudden and terrible and gone before she could draw breath to swear.

Just as well. One good *voidspit* and Diran would drag her back into the hospice and this time, Iari might just fail Jareth's test of sapience.

Iari aimed herself toward the courtyard rather than deeper

into the Aedis. The outer hospice doors were a double-wide, automated modernity of metal and sliding tracks, hexed to respond to motion from both sides. They also had a panel of transparent polymer in the center, through which Iari could see the coming sunset. Sky gone streaky, shadows spreading liquid across the courtyard. She could also see Char, standing just far enough to one side that they wouldn't trigger the motion-hex. Char saw Iari coming and squared up. Their teslas got brighter, blue verging on white.

Jorvik had been busy. Char had part of a new arm, all exposed metal framework, bolted to their shoulder, though that arm's elbow was fused at ninety degrees, the hand partly crooked. There might be servos coming, or—blessed Elements, *how* did you repair lost riev limbs? A graft, probably, which meant somebody *else's* part, and no, better not to think about that.

Char saluted, left-handed, as the doors rolled open.

But it was Luki who said, "Welcome back, Lieutenant," and levered off the wall, where she'd been waiting out of sight. She saluted, while her dark eyes flicked over Iari and then past her.

"No one followed me, Corporal."

"Making sure, sir." Luki made eyelock and grinned, sharp as Gaer's talons. "Sister Iffy wasn't certain you'd escape. Not *her* words, sir. She just said there might be a delay with your discharge, and if there was, I should send Char in to get you."

Mishka's tears, that was a sense of humor. "I escaped without incident. Char. How are the repairs?"

"Adequate." Char lifted their shoulder. The arm lifted with it. "Brother Jorvik says this immobility is temporary until he and the ambassador can agree on the hexwork required for animation."

"I'm sorry about Brisk Array."

Char's teslas dimmed. "Yes."

And Elements, what did you say to that? Iari looked north, up near the top of the wall, where a rounded corner apartment stuck out like an afterthought over the courtyard. The window glowed like a warm yellow eye in the deepening shadow.

"I'll go speak to Gaer about the hexwork now, then."

"Yes sir," said Luki. Because what the hell else could she say? New assignment, new squadmate—who was riev—and a new officer who referred to the Five Tribes ambassador by name, not title.

Iari glanced toward her own window, barely visible across the courtyard. She wanted a shower, her armor, her uniform. She estimated how long it would take, there and back. If she could do it before the prayer bells rang, or if she'd put herself back in the hospice (or collapse in a corridor and lie there, on Chaama's cold bones, until things stopped hurting).

"Sir?" Luki peered up at her face. "Is everything all right?"

There were glib answers to that. Casual ones. Instead, Iari said, "Did the Knight-Marshal brief you on our current assignment?"

"Only that it requires the utmost discretion, sir."

Which Tobin evidently expected from Luki. Or he'd just had no one else to assign.

Wish for Gaer, Ptah's eye, she did, with his intrusive optic and his ill-gotten insight. Luki looked discreet enough: not as young as Iari'd first thought, either, when the failing sunlight hit her just so. There were lines around her eyes. Around her mouth. Though age didn't guarantee wisdom, only experience (Corso was proof of that). And, truth, Iari just didn't *know* her, except as a fellow exile to nightwatch. Only the templars who didn't have a formal unit got nightwatch rotation. Iari'd gotten a sideways promotion to Gaer's security detail. Luki was just someone else Peshwari hadn't picked for his unit. Maybe that was her best recommendation.

Of the two templars standing in front of her, ungentle Ptah, it was Char that Iari *knew*. So she looked at Char, tried to read them: tenju mask of a face, tesla eyes. Cracked chestplate, twice patched, with a templar initiate's badge in fresh paint on the upper right and on both shoulders. That framework arm, still gutless, still needing a limb, flesh or mecha, to fill it and a hexwork patch to Char's neurochemistry to make it work. Luki, Iari noted, seemed perfectly at ease with a massive, broken riev at her shoulder. And Char, looming beside a human woman, seemed, well, *relaxed*, which should've been impossible for someone who could neither slouch nor stand hipshot. But Char wasn't watching Luki, wasn't angled toward her like Char always angled toward anything they read as a threat.

So that was something, too.

Iari eyelocked Luki and nodded. "All right. I owe you a briefing, then." She hesitated on *after prayers*, because void and dust, she wanted to talk to Gaer first, see where they were on everything, but that might send the wrong message to her new corporal. *You come after the vakar.*

The bells saved Iari and damned her at once: pealed out their summons and cracked the echoing quiet of the courtyard, ricocheted off the walls. Luki looked that way reflexively, expectantly. Maybe with a little relief. This was Mishka's time, the liquid fluidity of twilight, and a dozen other pretty poetic notions. It was also one of the most popular services, being most chronologically convenient, positioned just before evening meal: the end of the daywatch, the first gathering for nightwatch, when just about everyone was in the same room (Hrok's dawn services were equally convenient, for the same reasons). Luki had *been* nightwatch until, oh, some thirty hours ago. She'd have friends in there, probably full up with questions about her promotion.

Because by now everyone knew about Brood in B-town, the

explosion, whatever had Peshwari's unit on full-duty rotation, walking street-patrols like it was the surge again. By now everyone knew Iari'd been in the middle of all of it. So walk in there now, she'd have a lot of curious faces. Maybe questions, before and after the service. Probably a half-dozen dinner invitations, too, when most times it was cordial nods and a benign indifference to where she sat, with whom, whether she said anything at all.

She did not want to face a temple sanctum full of curiosity. She also didn't want to walk up and hand Tobin his copy of *Meditations* in front of everyone. And truth, she didn't want to kneel on the voidspit stones (sorry, Chaama) on a leg fresh out of a boneset.

Virtue must be an act of choice. If one acts from compulsion— out of fear of the consequences, or fear of shame—then that is not virtue.

Jareth hadn't had a lot of patience for indulging desires. You made choices based on *right*, once you figured out what that was. Not out of reflex, or habit. Not even out of duty, because that was another kind of yielding up of choice.

She imagined Jareth's face—human, male, cold as the space that'd spawned him. All angles and icy eyes. An ascetic's face.

The person who faces that which inspires fear, but yet lies within her strength, may be called brave.

Jareth would not count fear of discomfort (kneeling on stone) as worthy of fear, or of courage; but Jareth hadn't ever been smashed by a tunneler either, because Jareth had never *met* Brood. He'd written *Meditations* in the middle of the Expansion war, before the Schism that spawned the Five Tribes and before the Protectorate cock-up that'd made the Weep. To him, the vakari were the ultimate enemy. That which should be feared and faced anyway, for virtue's sake.

So Jareth might have an opinion about templars and vakari

being—*what*, exactly? What was she, to Gaer? Allies, but that was a political word. What made a vakar (anyone, really) run *toward* trouble for the sake of someone else? SPERE oaths, whatever they were, wouldn't say *run face-first into Brood without armor* for a templar. Templar oaths *did* require running at Brood, and Iari had always assumed that applied to *everyone*; but Jareth might not've agreed. Jareth might've said, *let the Brood take the vakari*. (Other Confederate voices had, during negotiations for the Accord. Wichu voices most loudly.)

Damn sure Jareth had never known any vakari personally, never listened to them go *on* about third-rate bands and the minutiae of arithmancy. Much less fought beside them. Or for them. Or, *or*, had them fight for *him*.

Say she and Gaer were *friends*, then.

Jareth might have (would have) disapproved of that. Tobin—also human, spacer, ascetic, who read Jareth and *lived* Jareth—did not seem to mind. Or maybe he just trusted Iari's discretion here, too. He was giving her wide latitude with this investigation. Hrok's breath, he'd given her a command and all the responsibilities that went with it.

Iari cast one last look up at Gaer's window. Willed him come to the glass, look out, swear at the bells he always complained about. He didn't. But—oh *voidspit*. There was something coming over the wall, a glittering pattern too bright and too early to be stars, too regular.

That was the keel of an aethership.

Barely, *barely*, Iari could make out the masts jutting up, and the tilt of flat-paneled sails catching the last spangling of sunlight as they steered the ship over the courtyard. *Aethership* was a poetic inaccuracy; it was plasma coils and physics and hexwork that battled gravity, just like a hopper, no sailing at all. Gaer would be able to see the emissions from the plasma ports, with that optic of his. See the equations describing the lift, the momentum, the force required to keep several tons of polysteel and amalgam from smashing into the courtyard. Iari saw only faint rings of bruise-black blue.

The ship swung around, maneuvering over one of the two docking slips. Then it hovered, patient, until the tesla floodlamps illuminated that slip, marked out a target for the aethership's pilot and nav-turing. Those floodlamps blasted the courtyard white, bleached and leached of color and shadow. They lit the ship's hull from below, too, splashed over the dark holes of the plasma ports, over the painted registry. *Rishi 1701-A-TNC.*

Aedian protocol said once you were in temple for prayers, you stayed there, barring Brood alerts or emergencies. But there were faces at the temple doors now, peering up at the aethership. Priests in robes, templars in armor, people in off-duty skinsuits, and civs. Alwar and human and tenju features, curiosity and excitement laid bare by the floods. An aethership might *be* an emergency, except the temple bells were still tolling *business as usual, get your ass in for prayers*. If something was really wrong, the bells would change their song.

But. *But.* Aetherships didn't just make casual visits. If there was an aethership here, it meant cargo or passengers or information too sensitive for the comm tower dispatch officer. Arrival during prayer guaranteed fewer witnesses. This arrival looked deliberate, planned, which meant—almost certainly—that Tobin had known it was coming, and he hadn't told her.

He was coming out of the temple now, never mind protocol and custom. Easy to spot him, even among all the other bits of uniform armor and Aedian red, even though he wasn't the tallest person, or the widest. Everyone got out of Tobin's way when he moved like that. Like a bolt from a jacta. He aimed for the aether-ship and marched, almost no limp, almost like Saichi hadn't happened. He didn't look Iari's direction, no reason he should, no reason he'd even know she was over there by the wall; but her guts tightened anyway, and her chest, her whole body locking up like a malfunctioning battle-rig. Void and dust, she wanted to be where he was, following him to that aethership to meet whoever was here.

She also—more practically, more coldly—wanted to know who was on it, and why, and where it had come from. As a rule, Iari didn't concern herself much with the Aedis superiors in Seawall. She liked to think it was above her pay grade, and it *was*, because those people—Senior Knight-Marshals, Mother Superiors—dealt in decisions that went wider than B-town. They oversaw a whole Weep-fractured planet. They sat on the Synod—back bench, maybe, but still lending a voice to the governing of the whole Aedis, and by extension, the Confederation.

But if Tobin *had* mentioned Brood in a report—and he'd have to, wouldn't he?—and if Mother Quellis had mentioned the altar—or if Peshwari had, because Peshwari came from old money in Seawall, and had friends in the Seawall Aedis—they'd have to send someone to investigate, and that someone might object to Gaer's involvement. It might even be Five Tribes embassy people on that aethership.

Hrok's breath. Ptah's eye. *Stop.* Templars—or regular troops, for that matter—weren't supposed to worry about what the Up Aboves thought. Execute orders, mind your own duty.

And Tobin had given her a command, and a mission, and until

his orders changed, her duty was clear. Prayer right now would be not a virtue, but a misplaced priority. A comfort.

"Corporal," she murmured to Luki. "I need you and Char to go to my quarters and get me a uniform and armor. Use the override gamma-three-five-three-six on the door panel. *Don't* close the window. I'm going to find Gaer. Meet me at his apartment."

CHAPTER SEVENTEEN ≡

ronic fact of the multiverse: a man could maneuver his career into an assignment on a planet with a Weep fissure, spend *eleven months* watching that Weep fissure do nothing, spend *eleven months* writing versions of the same reports to SPERE command (no changes to the fissure, no sign of Brood), and then suddenly, in the space of a day, have a dead wichu artificer, two Brood sightings, evidence of riev corruption by Brood, an altar covered in impossible equations, *and* a damned-to-the-fifth-hell stack of k'bal script. None of which he could report (no: none of which he *would*), all of which demanded his time, all of which needed to be handled *right now*.

Access to the library, Tobin had said, in trade for watching Iari's back when she went to talk to the riev. A fair offer, except that Iari had a tendency to dive face-first into Brood and fights she couldn't win, and *granted*, Gaer had made a mess of the last job of back-watching; but on balance, he thought he'd kept his side of things. He'd crawled around under that altar, scanned its surfaces, brought all that information back and fed it to the Aedis turing—and it gave him exactly nothing back.

There just wasn't much out there on k'bal, that was truth; they'd been gone since the Expansion, and the people—his people, vakari—who knew the most about them (as much as patrons knew about clients, which obviously didn't count for much; the wichu had changed sides, after all) lived on the vakari sides (Protectorate, Five Tribes) of the Confederate border. So because he was the only vakar in B-town, he *must* be an expert, and he simply wasn't. Arithmancy and special ops wasn't history and languages. Gaer knew there were better k'bal resources at home, but he couldn't just ask SPERE command to send along a few dictionaries, unless he was willing to break promises to Tobin and report everything, which he wasn't.

Tobin was trying to help. The Aedian library had actual, physical books from before the Confederation, in paper and hard covers made with what looked like leather, in languages human and alwar and both native tenju and spacer-clans. There were even facsimiles of pre-Landing Tanisian tenju texts, in their crabbed and jagged script. Left to right, top to bottom, rows mashed together. Languages for which Gaer had no aptitude or knowledge. There were Comspek dictionaries that tried to make sense of the linguistic drift across seedworlds. K'bal dictionaries, too, such as the Confederation had compiled. He needed a *setatir* linguist. He *needed* Yinal'i'ljat, but—Gaer glanced at his tablet—there was still no word from Corso. B-town wasn't that big. There weren't a lot of wichu. And Corso had let slip he had a contact in the PKs, someone with authority, with all the efficiency that would imply.

Two days with no report seemed *excessive*. Maybe Corso was looking for a corpse, and Yinal'i'ljat was dead already. That arithmancer, the phlogiston-igniting *setat-m'rri*, might've gotten her.

Maybe Corso just didn't want to report that. And really, so what. If Corso said *come now, I found her*, Gaer couldn't. He'd need templar escort, and Iari was still in the *setatir* hospice.

The door chimed, followed by a meat-hollow *thud*.

"Gaer. Open the voidspit door."

No. Iari was right outside his quarters.

Gaer crossed the room in one talons-scraping-furrows-in-the-floor bound and yanked the door open.

"Iari!" he said, like a damned idiot.

She stared up at him. Her eye, he noted, was only a little pinkish now, and only in the corner. Ferocious tea-green otherwise, and locked onto his. "I'm fine, thanks for asking. Let me in."

He did. Truth: she looked not at all fine. A skinsuit was aptly named, thin as skin, everything visible. The bunch and glide of muscle over bone (so *much* bone). Knobs at the top of her hips, knobs all the way down her back. Every *setatir* rib. The book folded into her elbow looked like it had more padding than she did.

"Didn't they feed you?"

"Through a tube. Gaer. Elements. I'm *kidding*. They fed me solid food in the usual way, with utensils and plates. The nanomecha burn through a lot, when they're making repairs." She crossed his room, back stiff, hips stiff, *everything* tight and brittle. She stopped by the window. "Turn off the light and come here."

"What? Why?"

She looked at him, lip drawn up over her capped tusk in a grimace or a smirk (or both). "There's an aethership in the courtyard."

He switched off the lamp. The room sank into gloom, lit by stars in their ubiquity, the embryonic moon, and a blue-white glow coming up from the courtyard that Gaer hadn't noticed before, from the very large flood-teslas on the very tall poles on the second landing pad, over which hovered an Aedian aethership.

Gaer flattened his hand on the window.

"*Rishi 1701-A-TNC,*" he said, as if reading the registry would magically reveal its point of origin, its purpose, its passengers. "*Se-tat*, I thought Tobin wasn't telling anyone about the altar."

Iari took a matching position on the other side of the window. She let the book drop and hang from her fingers like a weapon. "Yeah. Neither did I. Here they come."

Rishi's hull irised open. The ramp slid down. A set of two templars, human or tenju, obvious honor guard to a third templar, *definitely* tenju, wearing a voidspit battle-rig, met Tobin at the base of the ramp and clasped forearms.

Iari let out a breath with enough force to fog the glass. "I think that's Keawe. She's the Knight-Marshal from Windscar. That might say why the aethership's here. Might be nothing to do with the altar. We've seen Brood action in B-town, and Windscar's closer to the fissure. Maybe that's all it is."

"You don't even believe that. But you want to."

"You're reading my aura."

Fractured shards of blue and violet and a deep, throbbing maroon, a knot of greenish worry. He flared his plates, indignant. "Of course I'm not."

Two more figures appeared on the ramp. Small, casting very long, narrow shadows, with another templar in their wake. Iari pushed her forehead against the glass. "Wichu? Maybe an artificer. *Probably* an artificer. That makes sense. If Tobin made a request to Seawall, they'd want to know why, and there'd be reports. Keawe probably asked why, too, but she's . . ." Iari groped for words. "Windscar's *local*. It's us and them, front line to the fissure."

"You mean, Keawe's spacer like Tobin, not dirtsider like everyone else in command on this Brood-riven rock. *And* she's not an alw." Gaer puffed gently, laughter and exasperation together. "Oh, don't look at me like that. You know what I am. You think I wouldn't read reports on Aedian command? Keawe's got a service record as long as Tobin's, and she's from one of the tenju spacer clans. I can *guess* that if she's assigned to Windscar, and not commanding a voidship-unit, it's because she's got a reputation for independence, which is a diplomat's way of saying she probably pissed someone off in the Synod and they dropped her off here."

"I was going to say—she's more interested in practicalities than in orthodoxy."

"So she's not here just to play escort to an artificer. Tobin *did* mention the altar."

"Maybe. But I think she's here for support with the Brood. Look."

Keawe and Tobin had started back toward the administration wing, side by side, trailing Keawe's escort trio of templars. The wichu and *their* templar escort aimed toward the barracks, probably for guest quarters.

More templars had appeared on the ramp. Only four; but add them to the ones already disembarked, and that made a whole squad. These were hauling gear with them, four crates of smooth-cornered metal, familiar shape and dimension. The templars crossed the courtyard at a brisk trot, the anti-gravity hexes on the bottom of the crates throwing a dim indigo glow onto the mostly dark stone.

"Battle-rigs," said Iari. "Two rigs per crate. That'd be enough armor for all of them."

"Oh. Well. That's probably not good."

"If they were looking for a fight straight off the ship, they'd've come wearing them."

"Knight-Marshal Keawe did."

Iari shrugged, as if that knowledge would slide off her shoulder. "Tobin would've too. That's a war-commander thing. We're short-handed. Peshwari's people are guarding the altar. It makes sense they'd bring rigs." Iari paused. Took a short breath, held it. Said, with a resolution Gaer didn't entirely believe: "It makes sense Tobin would ask for more troops, too. I mean—a boneless killed four people. We had a tunneler in a residential neighborhood."

Gaer's stomach knotted around a fistful of cold spikes. "Or they're here for me. I mean, I know they can't arrest me, exactly. But I could be detained. Questioned."

"No." Iari made eyelock. "Tobin *wouldn't*. Listen. He's given me oversight of the whole investigation. I've got two people on my team now. If Keawe and her templars have anything to do with what *we're* doing, I'll find out."

"*Which* two people?"

"Char and Corporal Luki."

She didn't mention Brisk Array. Gaer supposed someone had told her. It seemed . . . *wrong* not to acknowledge the loss. "About Brisk Array. I'm sorry."

"Yeah. Me too." Iari dropped her gaze to the book she was carrying. *Meditations*, the cover said, just that word. She touched the letters like they were fragile, brittle, prone to breaking. Then she stopped, and made a fist of that hand, and eyelocked him again.

"You still have Sawtooth's chip?"

"Of course. In there." He turned his head partway, jerked his chin back toward the bedroom. And realized, as her eyes widened, that he'd left the door ajar, and that she could see his shrine from here.

It was *habit*, that shrine to the Five; it was custom, not *faith*. Shame made him want to step between her and the door. Block her view. Explain—words already crowding behind his teeth— that he was an arithmancer first, but you went through the religious motions, if you wanted to get anywhere in the Five Tribes.

You *performed*. But Iari *didn't* perform, so maybe that wouldn't impress her. Might offend her. Might—

Iari was already done looking, one blink, no comment. "Well. Just keep it secure. Deny that you have it, if someone comes and demands it that *isn't* me or Tobin. No one from the Aedis can touch it. No one with nanomecha. Priest, templar, doesn't matter. Whatever's on that chip isn't just dangerous to riev, it's dangerous to the Aedis at large."

"Wait, what?"

"Listen. Iffy brought me the voidspit medical report. A *battle-hex* attacked my nano, probably through contact, *probably* from Sawtooth. It took a large percentage of my nanomecha temporarily offline. That's why I didn't have the syn. The nanomecha turned it back—there's nothing left of it, not even fragments, to reverse engineer. But they changed some of their own basecode in the process. The report calls that a proper response. I just don't know."

There were members of SPERE who'd very much like *that* information. If Gaer delivered it, he'd be able to choose his next assignment (a bigger Weep fissure, on a less backwater planet). But SPERE wasn't void-sealed. The Protectorate had agents inside. Everyone *knew* that. And dear dark lords, what would *they* do with a code that could take the templars offline, even temporarily?

Iari had to know all of this, so, "Why are you telling me this? *They* can't want you to be telling me this."

"My discretion. My command. And you're the only arithmancer I've got right now." Iari crossed her arms, pinning the book against her belly. The motion tugged her skinsuit collar askew. Bared a smudge of green-purple bruise just below her collarbone. Same color as her aura. "I *do* know neither you nor I sensed any Brood emanations where Pinjat died, and we know that Sawtooth was there. And yet a day later, that riev set off every alarm in my rig. So clearly the infection progressed in him, and it didn't in me. Or that basecode change *is* the infection, and it's just going slower in me."

She was asking, without asking, if the report could be wrong, if what happened to Sawtooth could happen to her: oozing Brood-slime, going mad. Asking *him*, because he was the arithmancer who'd examined that chip. Her arithmancer.

Reflex, instinct, said *say no, reassure her.* That was diplomacy, wasn't it? She would believe him (probably). And he would be right (also probably). But she deserved more than a one-word platitude.

"Brood effluvia gets into a body, the body breaks down. That's Brood-rot. You know this already. Sawtooth could—probably did—have that direct contact, from the chip if nothing else, so any infection could've gotten into the hexes that way. In theory. Point is, *you* never came in direct skin-on-slime contact with Brood. If this so-called infection needs an organic vector you should be fine. If it doesn't—well. Your nano have recovered. They rewrote their own basecode. That's like throwing off an infection, isn't it? And if there *was* a danger, would Tobin have given you a command?"

"Maybe." She curled her lip over the capped tusk, a not-smile that made her scar twist like k'bal script. "My new authority means any meetings that touch on this investigation, I'll be part of, as a courtesy. So I'll know if there's voidspit about to come down on Char, or if someone from Seawall or offworld decides to lay claim to that chip." Her eyes went back to that book, to *Meditations.* "Then it lands on me how to react. Whether or not to comply with any orders I think run counter to the Aedis's interests."

"Tobin's put that on you. Defy your superiors, if necessary. Defy *his* superiors." That was, Gaer thought, all five *hells* of a burden.

"If something happens. Doesn't mean something will."

In Gaer's experience—mandatory military service, then SPERE—the unexpected had a nasty habit of happening if there was a large bureaucracy involved. Let some nebulous Aedian superior, already upset about riev, discover the Five Tribes not-really-just-an-ambassador was hip-deep in proprietary arithmancy—all that data, everything he *hadn't* sent to SPERE command, that was *right there*, on his tablet and his turing, and that would let loose a political firestorm. The Confederation could charge him with espionage, just for having that.

Let his mind travel this road long enough, he'd have the plot for a vid series (involving expensive hex-effects) and an ulcer. What was true: Iari was here when she did not have to be, warning him about an aethership, claiming responsibility for the investigation, and, obliquely, for him. And if *someone* sent people for him—templars, high-ranking priests with their wretched implants and alchemy—well. Cross that fissure when he came to it, and hope he didn't fall in.

Trust Iari. That's all he *could* do.

The bells rang end-of-prayers then, interrupting conversation. People streamed out of the temple's double-wide doors. Iari couldn't really see faces from this height and distance, with the contrast of light and shadow. Couldn't see expressions. *Could* see how everyone paused or detoured past the aethership, on an inefficient and cold autumn outdoor walk to the mess hall.

"Why are you still here?" Gaer's voice was quiet. His burnt-sugar smell was much stronger now, sharp enough to sting the back of her throat.

"Because I told Corporal Luki to meet me here with my armor."

"With your *armor*."

"They might not call for me. Or for you. But if they do—"

"They. *Tobin.*"

"—then I want to be in uniform."

"Ss." Gaer moved away from the window. He didn't seem angry. Anger, on Gaer's face, was a sunset spangling. This time—smudged by the reflection, but still bright against the darkness outside—his chromatophores flashed like plasma, like stars. A faint whiff of hot metal joined the burnt-sugar nerves. Might've been fear, or anger. Might've been, oh, just how vakari smelled. Might've just been *Gaer*.

Iari's gut ratcheted tight. Vague scenarios played out in which battle-rigged templars appeared at the door, sent by someone other than Tobin. Those templars—strangers from Windscar, people she didn't know, insisted that she go with them. That the investigation had been turned over to someone else. That she no longer had a unit to command.

Which was all absurd. She'd done nothing wrong, first; and second, she'd hadn't even issued an order yet, except *get me my armor*, so the idea of losing a command she'd barely had shouldn't make her guts turn to cold jagged shards. She had nothing to protect, here. Nothing really to lose.

Except Char. *They* wouldn't do well under another commander.

And Gaer, if someone (who? Keawe?) decided another templar should be assigned to escort him. Or—ungentle Ptah, Hrok, every Element in their most martial aspect—they decided to arrest him, or detain him for questions. She didn't believe Tobin would order that, but Tobin might not (be able to) stop Keawe if she had Seawall's orders behind her.

Her vague scenario acquired details: putting herself between any arresting officers and Gaer. The syn tingled down her spine and into her fingertips and offered itself as an option. Iari wished it back, down, impossible. Templars didn't fight with each other. *Brood* was the enemy.

She flicked a glance at her own window, just visible from Gaer's. Impossible to see if there was anyone inside, moving shadows that would say *Char* or *Luki*. They should be arriving soon, they should be—

The door chimed.

Gaer crossed the room in a fluid bound that reminded Iari *why* the Confederation had been losing the Expansion war until the Aedis developed the syn.

"Gaer," she said. "Easy. Let me."

He ignored her. Drew himself up to his full vakar height and wrenched the door open: chest out, plates mostly flat, teeth bared in an etched blue grin.

"Corporal Luki. *Do* come in. You, too, Char. Or should I say templar-initiate? Congratulations."

"I'm here," Iari said, before Luki could manage more than a dry-voiced *Good evening, Ambassador.* She stepped into line-of-sight. It was, yes, Luki and Char at the door, and only those two. Char had Iari's gear balanced in the crook of their prosthetic. Chestplate, gauntlets, greaves. Not the battle-rig, Iari hadn't expected that— but still, her gut dropped. The templars on *Rishi* had rigs. They'd've had time to outfit themselves by now.

Luki managed to come in without flinching, though Iari worried she'd roll an eye out of her skull, trying to watch Gaer without turning her head.

"Lieutenant. We've got your armor, sir. And, ah. The Knight-Marshal wants to see you at your earliest convenience."

"Thank you, Corporal."

Char ignored Gaer. Marched straight to Iari and offered the uniform with a murmured, "Lieutenant. We did not close the window in your quarters, as you ordered." The riev paused. Then, thoughtfully: "There was a black cat on the bed."

"That's Tinycat," said Iari. "Thanks, Char." She cast around for a place to put *Meditations*. Ended up offering it to Char, in trade for the armor.

The riev took the book carefully, balanced it in their massive palm and tilted their head to look down at it.

Luki, having no convenient book to stare at, was pretending not to watch Gaer. Pretending not to watch Iari putting on armor. Pretending, and failing, and probably giving herself a headache, trying to stare all directions at once. She was taking little breaths through her mouth. Well, sure. It smelled like vakari sweat in here (burnt sugar, hot metal), and whatever voidspit incense it was Gaer burned at the shrine he had in the bedroom. Templars got briefings about vakari, learned about them, but no one ever said they came with odors.

"Corporal," Iari said, and Luki's eyes snapped to hers with something like relief. "What do you know about that aethership's business?"

Luki made a face halfway between wince and grimace. "Nothing official, sir. On the way back from your quarters, we ran into Sister Iphigenia on the stairs. She was looking for you, too. That's what took us so long."

Iari raised a brow. Well, that was interesting. Maybe she'd managed a better ally in Iffy than she'd thought. "She say what she wanted?"

Luki licked her lip. "I think she wanted me to tell her where you were."

"Oh," Gaer murmured. "I'm sure she guessed."

Luki did not look at Gaer with every fiber of her discipline. "I thought if you wanted her to know, you'd've said something. So I told her that. She didn't seem upset. She *did* want me to tell you there's a pair of wichu on the aethership, along with the Knight-Marshal from Windscar."

Iari made a sound a lot like an irritated vakar, air squeezed through her teeth. "We saw from up here. The wichu, I mean. One of them an artificer?"

"I don't know, sir." Luki's face decided on *frown* as its default and settled accordingly "Sister Iphigenia didn't say. She also wanted me to tell you that the Knight-Marshal from Windscar came with Knight-Marshal Tobin to the hospice, and that they talked to Sister Diran. She didn't say about what—"

"Oh," Gaer murmured again. "I'm sure we can also guess the subject."

"—and *then* while we were in your quarters, the comm went off. I saw it was the Knight-Marshal's ID, but I wasn't sure if I was supposed to answer." Luki side-eyed Char, who managed to convey a casual blink despite having no eyelids. "Char thought I should. So I did."

"That was the right call. The Knight-Marshal was looking for me, and this time of night, with the *Rishi* out there, you can guess it's important."

"Yes sir." Luki's shoulders relaxed a jot. "Sorry, Lieutenant. I just—I'm new to this."

"Yeah. Me, too. All right." Iari jerked her chin at Luki's belt. "That for me?"

"Wha—yes, sorry." Luki pulled a very worn, scarred, familiar axe-shaft out of its ignominious place, thrust under her belt. "Wasn't sure if you'd want this, you know, in *here*."

Custom said templars always went armed in uniform: symbolism, mostly, of constant readiness to defend Aedis and Confederation. Truth was, most templars on compound duty short-handed that part of the uniform to a monofil or some small and conventional melee weapon. A plain leather sheath hung off Luki's belt with what looked like a bone handle poking out of it, on the end of what was likely a plain metal blade. Looked more like a blade ready for trimming an errant shrub than defending anyone.

Truth: most templars here in B-town hadn't seen the last surge, either. The ones who had carried whitefire weapons all the time, on and off the compound.

"Thanks," said Iari, and took her axe. She ran her hands over the haft, cursory check to make sure the safeties were on (no one wanted an unexpected deployment), familiar grooves and ridges of hexwork, and the place where a slicer had tried to disarm her (in all senses) and scored grooves in the polysteel.

She slid it through the ring on her belt. Adjusted the belt and winced a little at the knobby ends of her hips jutting up. Void and dust, no wonder Gaer's face had gone pyrotechnic when he'd seen her. She'd offended vakari aesthetics with an excess of visible endoskeleton. She realized belatedly there was no mirror in *this* room. She weighed the embarrassment of misaligned insignia with the awkwardness of asking to use the Five Tribes ambassador's personal mirror in his private chamber in front of her subordinates—ungentle Ptah, there were at least three bizarre things in that thought. Tobin would forgive crooked crests, and if Knight-Marshal Keawe didn't, well, voidspit to her.

But then Gaer—who must've been watching Iari's aura, or maybe just her expression—swooped in and, with just the tips of his talons, tugged her chestplate down and over to the left. She felt the heat coming off his skin (hide? what did vakari call it?) through the layers of her skinsuit, crossing the short span of aether between them. Smelled the burnt-sugar of him, the hint of hot metal under that.

"There." Gaer met her eyes briefly. "Now you're presentable." And, as his pigments shifted into a violet so dark it made her eyes ache, "You had trouble with getting the insignia straight before, too."

Iari felt Luki's stare on the side of her head. Damn near heard the thoughts grinding through: *When did the ambassador adjust the lieutenant's insignia? Is this sort of thing normal?*

Iari gritted a smile at Gaer, every tooth she could show. "Thanks."

"Give the Knight-Marshal my regards, Lieutenant."

She wasn't going to answer that. Swallowed a mouthful of air that tasted like Gaer and turned toward Luki. "Corporal, let's go."

Luki was looking at Gaer with a mixture of apology and chagrin. "The Knight-Marshal wants you to come, too, Ambassador. He wants to see you both." She jerked her chin at his tablet. "And he says—bring the research with you."

CHAPTER EIGHTEEN

So it was the four of them arriving together outside Tobin's office some short time later, Gaer having had no armor, no necessary changes of clothing; but he had insisted, nonetheless, on shutting them all out of his chambers while he "prepared" himself and then emerged, looking exactly the same, ten minutes later. Probably setting hexes all over the place, in case someone tried to come in. Hiding the chip. Hopefully those things, and not comming SPERE with a report.

Three of the Windscar templars were waiting in the corridor, standing casual sentry, hipshot and sloppy and bored (and, merciful Mishka, unrigged). They saw Iari and jerked straight, shoulders back. The highest rank was corporal. The other two were young privates, barely initiated. Probably their first assignment. Escort to the Knight-Marshal, which would make them potentially competent, people Keawe wanted with her, to see whatever she saw. Except there were another four templars Iari *didn't* see down in the barracks. Unless this corporal *was* the leadership—and that was as likely as Gaer growing feathers—that meant Keawe had left her unit commander to oversee the equipment.

Which suggested to Iari, who might've done that same thing,

that the really dangerous templars were down in the barracks, prepping battle-rigs for whatever reason Keawe was here.

The corporal and her two privates saluted, all snap and precision, gauntleted fists clacking into chestplates so shiny Iari could see herself in the steel.

"Lieutenant." The corporal's eyes tried, and failed, to stay locked on Iari's face. Skittered sideways, taking in Gaer and Char. Hrok's breath, you could *hear* her brain breaking from here when she saw the riev's templar-initiate badge.

"Corporal," said Iari. Blessed Four, she was the ranking templar in the hallway. Time to act like it. "As you were. Corporal Luki, Templar-Initiate Char," for the Windscarrans' benefit, to be clear, "you wait for me out here."

"Sir," said Luki.

And from Char, a rumbling, "Yes, Lieutenant." The riev had been carrying *Meditations*. Now they offered it back.

Iari took the book. Closest thing to a shield she was going to have for this encounter. She went up to Tobin's door—*Knight-Marshal Tobin*, on the brass plate on the wall—and knocked on it.

"Sir. It's me."

The door opened fast and hard. Knight-Marshal Keawe stood on the other side, still holding the handle, so that her arm blocked any entrance. She was *massive*, void and dust, damn near Char's size. Older than Tobin, lined and scarred, tusks overlarge, visible, and sharp as anything Gaer had in his mouth. She stared down at Iari with eyes that might have been golden, if there'd been any warmth in them. Cold and flat yellow and curious: a hard-eyed sweep. Iari was glad, suddenly, that Gaer had straightened her insignia.

Keawe's gaze snagged on *Meditations*. Those cold yellow eyes warmed a degree or two, and when she looked at Iari again, it looked like she'd found at least one thing she approved. "Lieutenant."

Iari straightened. Snapped a salute. "Knight-Marshal." What was the voidspit protocol? Probably Tobin should do introductions, but she couldn't see him past Keawe, and Gaer was *right there*, so: "May I present Ambassador—"

"Ambassador Gaer i'vakat'i Tarsik," Gaer said, in a tone as spiky as his elbows.

"Huh." Keawe's gaze shifted like tectonic plates. "I know who you are, Ambassador."

"Lieutenant," Tobin called from inside. "Ambassador. Come in, please." And, barely audible, "Keawe, please *let* them come in."

Iari expected Keawe to yield up her place and go back to her chair, which was obviously the one canted out of true to the others, so that someone with long legs could stretch them out, and pulled closer to the desk than the others. But instead Keawe stood sentry next to the door, while Iari and Gaer filed past, before she slammed the door shut, creating a gust that unsettled the curtains and circulated two days of Iari's hospice sponge-bathing and nervous vakar through the room. And then she *stayed* there, blocking the door.

The syn prickled the length of Iari's spine, socket to sacrum, implants looking for a needle and an attached battle-rig. Iari sympathized. She wished for two things: eyes in the back of her head, to see Gaer's expression, and the skill to read auras. And since those two were already impossible, might as well add an impossible third: to ask Tobin right now and out loud, *what does Keawe know, what did you tell her?*

Instead, she made her fingers relax, where they'd clenched around *Meditations*. She set the book on the near corner of Tobin's desk, two-handed and gently.

"Thank you, sir, for the loan."

Tobin had been watching Keawe, face masked down to spacer stillness. Now he glanced at *Meditations*. His jaw flexed. "You're most welcome, Lieutenant." His gaze dusted across hers for a moment. His eyes creased at the corners, brief as a breath, and Iari's chest loosened a notch.

Then Tobin looked past her, and the mask dropped back into place. "Ambassador. Thank you for joining us. I believe you just met Knight-Marshal Keawe."

Keawe grunted. "Pretty sure the ambassador knew who I was already, if he's worth spit as a spy. And I bet he is."

Tobin sighed faintly. His fingers moved, not the spacer-shrug Iari recognized—some other pattern, two fingers in sequence, curl and flex.

"Oh, fine." Keawe dropped back into her chair with a rattle of armor against wood. Tobin controlled a wince. Keawe controlled a grin, with less success. Her chestplate bore evidence of old damage, dents hammered not-quite-smooth, gouges a little too deep to be polished away.

"Brood breached my rig during the last surge," Keawe said. "That what you're looking at, Lieutenant? Wondering why my armor's marked up?"

"No sir. I'm wondering why you're wearing a battle-rig inside the Aedis."

Keawe tilted her chin up, eyes screwed to slits. The lamp on Tobin's desk, and the glow from his turing, splashed over her features, turned one eye brass-bright and dropped the other into eclipse. "I'm wondering why *you* aren't, Lieutenant. Given the company."

Gaer moved into Iari's periphery. Almost, *almost* on his toes, and the pigments in his cheeks burned like hot coals.

"You want to provoke the lieutenant, Knight-Marshal Keawe, you'll have to try harder. She is very patient. I'm an easier target."

"Ambassador." Keawe made it sound like *veek*, lip curled, voice deep in the back of her throat. "Don't give a dead neefa about you, except that you're evidently up to your jaw-plates in whatever's going on in B-town. I don't want you at this meeting, but Tobin says you should be, so here you are." She gestured at the second chair. "Sit down. You're too tall to stare at."

"I believe it's Knight-Marshal Tobin's command here, and not yours, and *I* don't give a dead neefa if your neck aches."

Iari inserted herself between Keawe and Gaer, just a notch. She touched Gaer's arm, a pair of fingertips above his wrist, in that patch of reasonably flat terrain before the spurs and spikes started. Vakari skinsuits were thicker than everyone else's, reinforced panels to cover the general roughness of vakari hide. She pressed hard enough to get past the oilslick surface, to the heat and the pebbly texture underneath.

Gaer let his breath out in a hiss. But he didn't move for that chair.

"Enough," Tobin said, even-voiced, quiet, with enough force to make even Keawe look at him. "Ambassador, *please*, sit down."

Iari pressed Gaer's arm again. Added her thumb this time, to the underside of his wrist.

"Knight-Marshal," Gaer said, in tones of respect, and there was no doubting which one he meant. He squeezed a hiss through his nostrils, jaw-plates being too clamped and furious. And then, with Iari maintaining herself as a barrier, he angled into the remaining chair. Iari stationed herself between them. She *might*, maybe, have a prayer of holding Gaer down, hand on his shoulder, if he decided to get up in a hurry. She hoped he wouldn't. She *really* hoped Knight-Marshal Keawe would remain where she was, and make no threatening moves. The syn twined down her limbs, tingling, while her heart tried to beat its way out of her chest.

Keawe was watching them both, now, with equal measures of cold-eyed appraisal. "Vakari arithmancers," she said, "are the reason we *have* a Weep."

Iari took a bite of air, spat it out. "The *Protectorate* arithmancers are the reason we have a Weep. Sir. Gaer's Five Tribes."

"I'm aware of his political affiliation." Keawe's lip curled and unleashed a web of wrinkles that reached all the way to her eyes. She side-eyed Tobin. "Your lieutenant's got guts."

"Yes, Kea," Tobin said, with great patience. "I did tell you."

"You did." Then Keawe lurched forward, planting her elbows onto her knees. Gaer *didn't* move; but his plates flared until Iari, from her angle, could see the faint outline of teeth clamped tight in his jaw.

Keawe either didn't notice or didn't care. Bet the latter. "I know why you're here, Ambassador, and I know why the Synod allows it. Fine. That's politics. I don't *like* that you're in the middle of templar business. But I trust Tobin's judgment, and"—her eyes flicked to Iari—"I'm going to choose to trust *yours*, Lieutenant."

"Sir," Iari said. Damned if she'd thank Keawe for that endorsement. Out of the corner of her eye, Gaer—not quite relaxed, but at least gave that impression—settled a little more deeply into the chair, and spread his fingers wide on the arms. His chin came up. His plates stayed stiff and flared—that was anger—but his pigments turned grey again, ferociously controlled neutral.

"I'm not your enemy, Knight-Marshal Keawe."

"Don't know that yet, Ambassador. But I know you're not the lieutenant's, or Tobin's, and that'll do for now."

Tobin, too, seemed to relax, unless you knew him. He leaned

forward on his elbows, folded his hands. His gaze caught briefly on *Meditations*, for the length of a measured breath.

"Ambassador," he said, "Lieutenant. In the interests of brevity and what's left of diplomacy, let me tell you why Knight-Marshal Keawe is here, and why you are. I asked Keawe if she had an artificer on staff whose services we might be able to borrow. As happens, she did. And as *happens*," Tobin locked eyes with Keawe, briefly, "that artificer, Su'seri, was *also* the victim of an attack very much like the one that killed Pinjat, albeit entirely unsuccessful. One of the riev in an arriving caravan required repairs. The caravan," Tobin said, and looked at Iari, "came from B-town."

Iari closed her eyes for a double-long blink. Chaama's bones, *what* was that other riev's name, the one who'd gone off on a caravan right around Pinjat's murder—

"Neru," Gaer said softly. "Was that the riev's name?"

"I don't know." Keawe sat back in her chair. Her fingers flexed in their gauntlets, made the leather squeak against the wood. "I *do* know that it put three of my templars in medical before we put it down. And by *down*, I mean Sister Maraleh had to open the fucking ground up underneath it to make it stop. Riev don't burn, but they bury."

"So you, what"—Gaer wiggled his fingers—"just hexed the dirt back on top, buried it alive?"

"Not alive." Keawe grimaced. "And not dirt. Bedrock's close to the surface up there. Maraleh sealed that riev in stone. Crushed it to powder and slime."

"So much for examining the corpse, then. Pity."

Tobin cleared his throat. "I thought, in light of what Keawe said, that she should know about *our* recent encounters." He gazed steadily at Iari. "That was my judgment."

"Sir." Tobin didn't owe her any explanations, or any apologies. That he offered both, in those four words, made her chest hurt. She looked instead at Keawe. "Did Neru—the riev that attacked Su'seri—give off Brood-sign, sir?"

"Like the voidspit fissure itself. My templars who ended up in hospice weren't rigged up. They were the first responders. The riev knocked them around hard. The second group who responded *was* rigged, and that thing lit up our HUDs like a whole pack of boneless. Which I understand you've also had here in recent days."

Hrok's breath, Ptah's heart, what she wouldn't give to know what Tobin had already said. Iari tried looking for clues in his face. Got only a steady stare back, dark-eyed and level, serene as if he were hearing what the kitchen had planned for dinner.

And so, same tone she would've used to give him that dinner report, same dead-even quiet: "Yes, sir. We've also had a tunneler, a boneless, and a small swarm, some of which fled into the sewers. The tunneler is dead. The boneless—which we believe is a single entity, not a pack, but we're not sure—is still at large, having killed a family of alwar. We suspect the Brood is using the sewers under B-town to move around."

"And Tobin says you had two riev go bad, too."

"Yes sir."

"They put *you* in the hospice."

"No sir. The tunneler did that. Or rather, the phlogiston leak that exploded while we were subduing the tunneler did. The corrupted riev came from the earlier encounter, and they would have killed me if Char and Gaer hadn't been there."

Keawe grimaced. "This would be *Templar-Initiate* Char?"

As if there were two riev named Char in B-town. "Yes sir. At the time, they were just Char."

"Right. And now they're out in the corridor wearing insignia."

Credit to Keawe for using the pronoun without missing a beat. No credit for saying, "That seems unwise, with riev going bad."

"Char shows no sign of contamination," Tobin said, with the weary force of something already repeated. "They had no contact with Pinjat. Neru, evidently, *did.*"

"Or with whoever, or whatever, contaminated Sawtooth and Swift Runner. I'm not convinced it was Pinjat." Gaer held out his tablet. The equations seemed to writhe on the screen, probably an effect of that dark red text color Gaer seemed to like, that strained Iari's vision. "These hexes look nothing like typical artificing. They look like the bastard offspring of a tesser-hex and Aedian alchemi—"

"And how does a vakari arithmancer know about Aedian hexes? Void and dust, Tobin, what're you letting this vee—this *person*—into?"

"The library," Tobin said dryly. "The ambassador's been extremely helpful in these investigations so far."

"Oh, yes. I'm sure. Vakar arithmancer. Fucking SPERE operative, too, or I'm an alw matron." Keawe made a gesture at Gaer's tablet, halfway between dismissive and threatening. "This, your research, isn't all going straight back to your commanders? I'm supposed to believe that?"

Gaer bristled: plates flattening, nostrils squeezing to slits. "Knight-Marshal Tobin is satisfied that I haven't sent any reports. And if you don't trust my word, which clearly you do not: anything I send has to go through the Aedis router. My communications are logged, even if the contents are encrypted. You can check those."

"I'm supposed to believe you have no way around that."

Iari stuck her arm out. Not a fast gesture, not aggressive, but a barrier. She turned her palm back toward Gaer, made sure the Aedian crest on the back of her gauntlet faced Keawe.

"Gaer's not sending reports to SPERE, any more than you're reporting all this to Seawall."

"Huh." Keawe squinted at her. "All right, Lieutenant. *Ambassador*." She drilled a scowl at Gaer. "I'm listening."

It took Gaer only a breath to recover. His voice came out even, steady. "Thank you, Knight-Marshal. I thought, in the beginning of all this, that it must be Pinjat doing something with the riev. Char and Brisk Array spoke about Pinjat's efforts to restore something they called Oversight to the riev who used his services. Presumably at their request."

"Shit," said Keawe.

"But upon further examination of the, ah, *data—*" Gaer tapped his tablet, brought up a second set of equations. "I think we're dealing with another, separate arithmancer, probably the same one who blew up the house. I think that person was working with Pinjat, or had access to his workshop and his riev."

"Then why kill him?"

"Perhaps Pinjat discovered the Brood contamination and objected. Perhaps he wanted a bigger payoff. We have no way to know."

Keawe thrust her jaw at Gaer. "What *kind* of arithmancer?"

"Not a vakar, Knight-Marshal, if that's what you're asking."

"You'd say that."

"No vakar knows Aedis hexwork that well. This person has either worked with the Aedis, or has access to people who do."

Keawe had gone still and straight in her chair. Spacer-blank features, now, eyes cold and all-seeing as Gaer's optic. "And how does this hostile arithmancer figure in with this Brood-tainted altar you found, Lieutenant?"

"*Setat*," Gaer murmured, and then something else in Sisstish.

Yeah, *setat*, with voidspit on top. Tobin *had* told Keawe everything. Had to be reasons for it: to keep Keawe from running to
Seawall, maybe. To protect the riev. Because he needed an ally.

"Lieutenant." Keawe's voice cracked like a hot stone, and Iari
came back to the room, to Keawe's eyes staring holes. She didn't
dare look at Tobin. He'd given her a command. Trusted *her* judgment. And was letting her answer, so:

"Sir. We aren't totally sure. The altar's covered in k'bal script.
Gaer hasn't been able to translate. We don't have much on them."

"You could ask the Five Tribes for *official* assistance, of course,"
said Gaer. "We have linguists. Or you can make do with me."

Keawe turned to glare at Tobin. "Well, shit."

Tobin nodded. "I did tell you."

"Let me tell you about the altar's hexwork," Gaer said, and proceeded to brief the Knight-Marshals on what he'd already told
Iari, except this time he deployed every polysyllable in his arsenal,
every marker of expertise. Void and dust, that *pride*—if Keawe
didn't already know he was a SPERE battle-arithmancer playing
diplomat, she knew it now. But Iari noticed he said nothing about
Sawtooth's chip.

"I'd like to talk to this artificer of yours, this Su'seri," Gaer said
when he'd finished. "About the anomalous equations on the altar.
Presumably he's one of the wichu who came with you on the
aethership."

"Watching, were you?"

"Gaer was with me, sir, yes."

"Huh." Keawe transferred that yellow glare to Iari. "Well.
That's part of why I dragged Su'seri down here. Though I don't
know how much help he'll be, *especially* if the ambassador's asking. Little neefa's scared spitless of vakari. What he has told me so

far is that your man Pinjat's a bit of a pariah. Su'seri said Pinjat got himself expelled from the artificer's guild. Wouldn't say why, though. Said it was proprietary information."

"Then I'll ask him *nicely*," Gaer said, and grinned. Keawe looked momentarily startled. Then she grinned back.

Ungentle Ptah, *that* was an unsettling display. Just let their alliance hold.

Iari eased back a step. Let herself lean, just a little, on the back of Gaer's chair. She'd been on her feet tonight more than the last two days combined. Her leg ached in a razor line from ankle to knee, along the healed line of the break. That would continue a day or so, perfectly normal, but unpleasant in the meantime. A battle-rig would help, if anyone ever let her back into one.

Bet she would get her wish. She had a feeling there'd be a fight coming, sooner rather than not.

"You get something out of that little neefa," Keawe said, "I'll buy you a drink. The *other* one has done nothing but talk. She's Pinjat's cousin. Not fond of him, sounds like."

Gaer sat up, same time Iari forgot about the ache in her leg and stood straight. The chair, no longer pinned between their respective masses, skidded an angry centimeter on the stone floor.

"His cousin," Gaer repeated. "What's her name?"

"Oh, something unpronounceable. Yina, oh hell, Yin-something."

"Yinal'i'ljat?"

"Yeah. If you saw Su'seri get off the ship, then you saw her, too. That's—what, Lieutenant?" Keawe shoved her chair back, eyes wide.

Iari supposed she'd turned some unhealthy color, or maybe the look on her face was enough to alarm a battle-hard tenju Knight-Marshal. "That wasn't Yinal'i'ljat, sir. At least, the woman who got off the ship with you wasn't the Yinal'i'ljat we met in B-town."

Silence, throbbing and furious and crackling like the moments before thunder. Keawe had *who* building behind her eyes, and was just as clearly clamping her teeth on the question. That was the problem, *who*.

Gaer answered it partway, as much as anyone could. "Sss. Our second arithmancer. A wichu would also explain any knowledge of Aedian hexes. Perhaps even how they got past the riev hexes—" It looked like he might've said something else—mouth still ajar, eyes half-lidded—but Keawe plowed over him.

"Where is this person now?" *At* Gaer, not asking.

Which earned a not-unexpected hiss and scowl and probably would've produced a classic Gaer retort if Tobin had not intervened.

"Presumably still in B-town. The PKs were officially in charge of the investigation until very recently. We've requested all the files, with a priority on the explosion. Some of the precincts have been more prompt than others."

"*I'll* show them prompt," muttered Keawe.

Tobin pretended not to hear. "Lieutenant? Could you go and retrieve everything the peacekeepers have on Yinal'i'ljat?"

"I'll go get them, sir. Right now."

CHAPTER NINETEEN ≡

The main peacekeeper HQ occupied a renovated mansion on a side street off the main market square in B-town's Hightown district. The area was obviously alwar, obviously restored to its prewar glory after the violence of the last surge. All that fluted stonework, the panoply of statues carved into walls and sills and crowding under the eaves. A series of artfully placed teslas illuminated the doorway and windows and the big, plain-lettered sign over the door.

PEACEKEEPERS

It was dark otherwise on that street, and quiet. Rain spat in irregular gusts from the low-bellied clouds. Rattled on the windows, the old-style metal gutters. The main doors—double-wide, a good polymer copy of wood, inset with narrow windows—swung open on automated hinges. The hallway beyond looked less historical, more utilitarian-modern. Off-white tiled floor and walls, benches lining both sides. The reception desk sat at the far end of that hall in its own small office, separated behind a presumably impact-resistant window with a hinged slot at the bottom that looked wide enough to pass documents and tablets and ID chits through. That window was closed now, and latched from the interior. One officer on duty back there, who looked up as the doors opened.

"Officer," said Iari. "Good evening."

The officer's (un)welcoming frown deepened into a scowl. The two shapes in his doorway—templar, vakar—were obvious, and troubling enough. But then those shapes came inside, trailing water on the tile. He stood as they approached. He had a little sidearm jacta, standard issue, toward which his hand drifted.

Iari walked past the empty benches lining the wall and leaned on the counter. The rain that had beaded up on her rig threaded into minuscule rivers and puddled on scuffed polymer surface.

"Lieutenant Iari, here on Knight-Marshal Tobin's orders. The Aedis is assuming jurisdiction over case files Q-1745 and LN-B7. You were told we were coming to get them."

The PK was having a hard time meeting her eyes. Too busy staring at Gaer. She took the time to study him. Human, somewhere in his thirties, with an arrogant chin and unlined eyes. Thin, wiry, uninspired blond hair. Eyes like chips of summer sky, when he *did* manage to look at her, almost as blue as Iffy's. He seemed familiar, in that way people did sometimes. The glare he was giving her seemed more personal than *just-met-you* resentment.

That arrogant chin stuck out just a little bit farther. "Lieutenant," he said, lifting his voice on the last syllable, turning it into a question. Of her name, or her worthiness to bear that particular rank. And then, grudgingly, "Ambassador."

"Officer Arlendson," Gaer said, smoothly and poisonously. "What a *delight* to see you again."

Oh sweet sizzling Ptah. *Now* Iari recognized him. This was one of the PKs who'd pointed a jacta at Gaer and threatened to arrest him outside of Pinjat's house.

Iari made a fist of her gauntlet and thumped it gently on the counter. "The files, Officer. Please."

"A moment, Lieutenant. They're in the back." Arlendson made a great show of crossing the little office area as slowly as possible. He pressed his hand on the lock-pad to the very modern, metal door on the back wall and held it there long enough someone could've hand-drawn his palm-print, long past the panel turning green and beeping. The door opened as he lifted his hand. Quick, efficient mechanism. He dragged himself through. The door flicked shut again, and stayed that way.

Silence. No one came back. One minute, two, five.

Behind them, the main door swished open. A gust of wet autumn chilled the little vestibule, snaking around into the open visor and settling around the back of Iari's neck.

She did not turn around. Pointedly.

Gaer twisted his head *just* far enough. He laughed through the sides of his plates. "I think Char's losing patience."

"I'm losing patience," Iari said, *not* softly. She found the very obvious surveillance camera in the corner of the reception area, perched where it could see both sides of the desk, and stared up at it. "Officer Arlendson. The Aedis called ahead. You knew we were coming. Your prompt cooperation is appreciated."

The camera stared back, one of those rounded black half-globes, shiny and blank as a neefa's eye.

There was another modern, metal door to the left of the poly-alloy reception window, presumably for admitting visitors, arrestees, whoever might come in from the street and need access to the back offices. There wasn't a keypad on this side of it.

Iari laid her palm flat against it. A web of hexwork flared, sizzled, produced a cascade of sparks. That would hurt on unshielded flesh. Barely registered on the battle-rig.

"There are surveillance devices," Gaer said. "Decent hexwork. Not impossible to bypass."

It was an offer. And it was tempting, if only because Iari was tired, hurt, and feeling more than a little out of sorts.

But, "Not starting a war with the PKs today." She flicked a look at the camera. "Yet."

Gaer hissed, which could be *fine* and was probably some variation of *setat*. He was unhappy because he'd left his tablet in Tobin's office—at Tobin's request, not from any loss of memory—and he seemed certain something dire would happen to it. Probably would. Keawe and Tobin would read it.

No one's going to erase the data, Gaer. Most they'll do is find you a linguist.

That's my research! Oh, sss. You don't understand.

True. Iari didn't. What she *did* understand was the need to know, oh, *now*, who this false-Yinal'i'ljat was and how she fit in with murdered artificers, hacked riev, targeted Brood. And maybe—Ptah forfend, she didn't want to think too closely about it—*Corso*, because Gaer said he'd sent him out looking for her, after the explosion at Tzcansi's sister's house, and hadn't heard back.

A fact he'd dropped on her—much like that house—on the walk down, because he wouldn't have said it *in* Tobin's office, no, not where Keawe could hear and ask questions. So yeah. She was a little worried about Corso, whose silence since then might be nothing, and might be dead-in-a-gutter or Brood-food.

"You come out with those files," Iari said, staring at the camera. "You do it *now*, or I ask the templar-initiate behind me there to open this door so we can assist you in finding them."

The interior door reopened. Arlendson came back through, but he wasn't alone. A woman followed him, alw, dark-skinned, light-haired, medium build. Sidearm jacta in a shoulder harness. *Not* uniformed, which meant she ranked higher than patrol officer. Some kind of commander, maybe. Iari made a tentative, positive judgment: the woman was straight-backed, neat, neither smile nor scowl on her face. She held a tablet embossed with the Peacekeeper logo and the B-town seal in both hands.

Very deliberately official. Very deliberately slow, like Arlendson had been, crossing the tiny office. She looked at Iari. At Gaer. Past both of them, at what was presumably Char and Luki standing at the end of the corridor, forcing the outer doors to stay open to the rain.

"Lieutenant," said the woman. She had a B-town native's accent, same as Iari. "I'm Chief Inspector Elin. B-town is under *council* jurisdiction. The Knight-Marshal sits on that council as a courtesy. I have already registered an official complaint. I'm repeating it now. This is another example of Aedian overreach in local affairs."

Oh, blessed Elements. Relations between the PKs and the Aedis were supposed to be cordial. Elin's attitude seemed personal. All right, *fine*, an exploding house and murder-arson looked high-profile, important; a chance for a chief inspector to prove herself, maybe, get a promotion, rise in the ranks, and here was some templar lieutenant coming in to take all the glory. Or maybe Elin just didn't like templars. That happened. Iari wondered what Keawe would do with a recalcitrant PK. Probably put a gauntleted fist through that alloy window. Tobin, though, would stay calm.

So Iari swallowed temper and impatience and said: "Confederate law states the Aedis takes over all matters in which there is Brood activity. This is standard procedure, Chief Inspector."

"Only the house-fire on Tenth Street involves alleged Brood activity. File Q-1745 concerns a murder, Lieutenant. Multiple witnesses report a riev in the area right before the attack." Elin's eyes flicked past Iari. "A large one."

Oh, for the love of the Four. Iari held out her hand: gauntleted, rigged, palm scuffed with years of use and abuse. "May I please have those files?"

Arlendson stepped around his boss and opened the slot in the window. Held it like a voidspit doorman.

Elin didn't look. Didn't move. Her fingers tightened on the file. "I'm responsible for the safety of the citizens of B-town, Lieutenant."

"So am I. *And* everyone else in the Confederation, if and when it comes to a surge. Chief Inspector, listen. I'm the templar who was buried under the house on Tenth Street. I am the reason the Aedis locked down the crime scene and kept your people out. And I am just as dedicated as you are to finding out what happened, who's responsible, and making sure it doesn't happen again."

Elin blinked. Some of her tension drained out. Less stiff-knuckled gripping of tablets, fewer lines around eyes and mouth. "I see. And why were you there, Lieutenant?"

Elin didn't expect an answer, clearly. Expected some evasive *I am not at liberty to divulge that information.* Maybe the question was just an investigative reflex; Elin was an inspector, and it had to be all kinds of maddening to have questions with no answers, no hope of answers, and some battle-rigged templar coming in to take all her work.

But the asking, Iari thought—that seemed like, if not an offering, then an opening. A willingness to talk. So: "I was there because I was looking for a woman named Tzcansi. Local ganglord. Small time. You know her?"

Elin laughed, dry as dust. "Not *so* small time. Tzcansi had business all over B-town. Fingers everywhere. A little black market dealing, a little enforcement. Never loud. Never messy."

"Never? There's a district in Lowtown says otherwise. Businesses burned out. People gone missing."

"You mean that fire in the public house in Ward Seven?"

"You *do* know about that."

"It wasn't my case, and it's not my district, but yes, I know about it." Elin pursed her lips. "Organized crime isn't something the Aedis usually bothers with, unless it's interstellar operations. We don't have anyone on all of Tanis who's that connected. Certainly not Tzcansi. So what's the Aedis's interest?"

"This isn't about organized crime. It's about Brood. That burned-out tavern had Brood nesting in the back room. I doubt Tzcansi *didn't* know about them. We wanted to ask her, but then she turned up dead."

Elin's brows rose. "Tzcansi's dead?"

"She knew that already," Gaer murmured. Barely a breath, meant to carry as far as Iari's ears and no further.

Huh. All right. "Thought you knew that."

Elin blinked. Her throat worked around a swallow, as if she had glass in her throat. "No, I did not."

"Sss." Gaer drifted close to Iari's shoulder. Brought that whiff of burned sugar, and a slightly louder, "That's a lie. And she's *worried* about something. Some . . . one? A certain P.R.I.S. maybe?"

Good thing Elin couldn't shoot jacta bolts from her eyes—at Gaer, at Iari. "What did he tell you?"

"What did *who* tell me?"

Elin pressed her lips flat. "Nothing. Never mind. If that's all, Lieutenant." She pushed the file through the slot in the window: unfolded, stiff, screen off. "Here are your files."

Iari took a breath. Let it go slowly as she picked up the tablet. "Thank you." She woke the screen and flicked through the pages. Wasn't too hard to find Yinal'i'ljat's name. Chief witness, interview as yet unconducted, current address and contact information—

Ptah's flaming left *nut*. "This isn't complete."

The Chief Inspector had begun to turn away. She froze, with the promptness of the guilty. She stared resolutely at the wall. "Of course it is."

"Yinal'i'ljat. The murdered artificer's cousin. Your primary witness? There's no contact information here."

Elin controlled the flinch. Arlendson didn't.

Gaer drifted close to Iari's shoulder. Brought that whiff of hot metal, and a slightly louder, "Apprehension. Recognition. *Guilt*. That's interesting."

The inspector puffed up like an affronted cat. "I don't know how you think you know that, Ambassador, but—"

"He's an arithmancer, and he's reading your aura."

Elin recoiled. "Get out."

Iari put on her best *I'm rational* mask. "I can't leave without information about Yinal'i'ljat, Inspector. I think you know that. Last known address, comm channel, anything you might have. This woman is linked to both cases."

"*You're* linked to both cases," Elin snapped. "That vakar is, too. You *have* your files, Lieutenant. Everything pertaining to the investigations the Knight-Marshal requested."

Iari gathered up the frayed remains of her patience. "I can file an official request, and we can waste time, or you can help me now and maybe save some of those B-town lives we're both responsible for."

Behind her, behind Gaer, the wind gusted, as if Hrok, too, was exasperated. And then no more wind, and a faint vibration through the floor tiles, as two large, heavy shapes—riev and battle-rig, more or less equally massive—came all the way inside. Rain rattled on the door like a tossed fistful of pebbles. Iari stared at the alloy window until she could make out the faint reflection of Char and Luki behind her.

"Problem, Lieutenant?" Luki asked, mildly enough.

Char said nothing. Char wouldn't have to.

Iari blinked her focus back *through* the window. Elin remained adamantly, furiously unimpressed. Arlendson, however, looked nervous. That chin-jutting arrogance had given way to lip-nibbling. Maybe he knew something about the missing information. Or maybe it was just the Aedian battle-rigs, the Aedian sigils, the recollection of what templars were designed to fight. And, yeah, probably Char.

Iari drilled her stare into Arlendson. "Anything you can add, Officer, would be appreciated."

Arlendson coughed. He slid an apologetic glance at Elin. "We *had* a last known address for Yinal'i'ljat, Lieutenant, and a commsign, but there was a fire at her hotel. We don't know where she is now. Comms aren't responding."

"*Another* fire?"

Elin cut Arlendson off. "There was no sign of Brood, and no fatalities. You want access to that file, Lieutenant, you go make your official requests."

"That's also not totally true," Gaer said. "She's not sure no one died. She's *afraid* someone did. That's the source of her guilt."

Elin stared at Gaer, incredulous and indignant. "All right. There were no *confirmed* fatalities at the hotel. But we haven't been able to contact everyone registered there. This Yinal'i'ljat is one of those missing persons."

Gaer's optic flashed like a mirror in sunlight. "There's someone else missing, too."

And oh, Iari wanted to ask who, was it Corso, was this straight-backed Chief Inspector feeding information to a P.R.I.S. on the side, maybe for bribes, maybe for friendship or personal reasons or *whatever*. But if it wasn't, name Corso to this woman and she'd chase him down, find him out. Jack up all his clandestine business.

If he *wasn't* already dead somewhere, he wouldn't thank her for that.

So Iari chewed her worry back down, swallowed it. Waited until it hit her gut like a hailstone and sat.

"Thank you," she said. "Now, please. We'll need the address."

CHAPTER TWENTY ═══════

The rain had intensified into a fully formed storm by the time they reached Wichutown, blown sideways in sheets by a wind that, had Gaer been unrigged, might have threatened his balance. As it was, he felt . . . *wet*, which was simply impossible. His battle-rig was sealed against—well, not atmosphere, exactly, it wasn't an e-rig, but certainly *rain*. But it still felt damp inside the armor, and cold, like this wretched rock of a planet's even more wretched weather had somehow wormed past the environmental seals.

He balanced what he *knew*—no leaks, no breaches in his seals—against what he *felt*—constricted, short of breath, and occasionally blind—and kept walking, *slogging* (splashing, sometimes) through run-off beyond what the gutters could manage.

His HUD kept track of Iari (in front), Luki and Char (in the rear), on the occasions they'd turn a corner and a malevolent gust of wind-water would smear his visor blind. Then he gritted his teeth and waited until the hexes did their job, his visor cleared, and he could once again follow Iari by sight: the blurred light from her headlamp smearing the pavement, the tiny white teslas marking points on the back of her armor, the wet gleam of her rig—Aedian red turned black in the storm light. She'd said exactly nothing since leaving the Peacekeeper annex, except for a call back to the Aedis informing the Knight-Marshal(s)—because Keawe would be listening—of this new wrinkle in the investigation. Gaer imagined that he could see her aura through her rig (red, oranges). She was so buttoned-up angry he'd bet that *her* rig was working hard to keep her cool.

Then the storm took a breath and almost stopped, wind and rain both, for one of those pockets of false-calm, and Gaer got his first look at Wichutown.

Oh, wichu. So neat. So precise. Every *setatir* building square with the next, symmetrical. Everything *just* a little too small, a little too . . . wichu-y. They had been the pre-eminent architects in the Protectorate, before their betrayal. Gaer had seen pre-Schism 2Ds and video footage of Kikitar, the vakari homeworld and Protectorate capital. The streets had looked a lot like this, scaled up for vakari. Gaer wondered if they'd torn those buildings down after the wichu defection, or if they'd left them as a lesson about trusting one's client-species too far and relying on them too much.

You *could* argue—and scholars had—that the wichu defection during the Expansion war had led directly to the Schism. No one argued at all that it was wichu ingenuity behind the first nanomecha—some biological weapon that attained something like sapience and fused with a human physiology—that had become, in less than a generation, the slagging *Aedis*. And that had *certainly* led to the Weep; so maybe it was all their fault, everything wrong in the multiverse, those industrious wichu.

Their destination was obvious: lit by flood-teslas, marked off by the blue glowing borders of holotape, a two-story structure with a gaping hole in the second floor. Gaer was gathering breath to observe that any evidence would've already washed away when he noticed the faint shimmering dome over the charred, open space.

"Force-shield," he said, on the exhale. "That's . . . unexpected."

"Huh." Iari did not sound particularly cheered. "That's standard procedure for ongoing investigations. Keeps things reasonably undisturbed. They're PK, Gaer, they're not *idiots*."

Let that comment go, yes, he would. Iari was in no mood. She stomped—even in the battle-rig, it was obvious she was using more force than necessary—to the hostel entrance. The signage was dim, off, sulking over the doorway. The name was written in plain Comspek, but the lettering was far more ornate.

Iari raised a gauntleted fist and banged on the door and waited, while the storm came rattling back for another round of itself. Gaer, glad of his visor's protection, peered up at the force-shielded open wound of a crime scene. From street level, he couldn't see much. The lightning flashes only showed him blast-white glimpses of blackened walls, broken furniture.

Broken. That was interesting.

"Note the sign's design, Ambassador." Char moved up on Gaer's side with considerably less sound than Iari's rig had made. "It mimics wichu script. Note particularly the shape of the double-s."

Which looked very much like the k'bal script on the altar, *yes,* they'd established a wichu had written it. Void and dust. "Are you saying *I told you so* to me, Char?"

"I am drawing your attention to the pattern, Ambassador. That is all."

He heard, with half his attention, the door open. Heard Iari's voice—"Hvidjatte? I'm Lieutenant Iari, B-town Aedis"—unfiltered by the helmet comms, which meant she'd raised her visor. Gaer wasn't sure her face would be *less* alarming to whoever answered the door than a visor. Wichu weren't brave. And *he* was along, which wouldn't help.

But the wichu who answered—on the high side of middle-aged, in a jacket that looked as if it were made of flower petals—did not blink, at Iari, or Gaer, or at all. He bowed, showed the top of a wispy-haired head.

"Of course, Lieutenant. Inspector Elin commed ahead to tell me you were coming. Please, come in, any assistance I can render—ah."

The wichu was staring at Char. That would have been unremarkable—that patchwork skeleton of an arm, the Aedis badge, worth staring at—but the look on his face, and the monochromatic yellow of his aura, was stark fear.

Well.

"Problem?" The rain had gotten into Iari's helmet, streamed down her face in rivers as she turned to follow the man's stare. Might've been cast from the same metal as Char's face, for all her expression.

"No. Except—I do not think the, ah, stairs will accommodate the, ah." Hvidjatte blinked unhappily at Char's badge. "The templar-initiate."

Oh, wichu manners. Gaer grinned, behind his visor.

"Then the templar initiate and the corporal can wait downstairs."

Hvidjatte wrung his hands. "It is a small space, Lieutenant!"

"Oh, for the love of—fine. Corporal. Char. Wait out here." Iari glared down at Hvidjatte. "The ambassador stays with me. I trust your stairs can accommodate *him*."

"Yes, Lieutenant."

Hvidjatte retreated back into the hostel then, fast as a fish. By the time Gaer ducked under the *setatir* doorjamb, *stupidly* short, and followed Iari inside, he had taken up a defensive post behind the reception counter.

Gaer raised his visor, now that they were out of the rain. Peered around the lobby, which was arranged with chairs, a table, a vase with cut flowers. Peered at the stairs, which looked even more wretchedly narrow than the door. Hvidjatte hadn't exaggerated. Char *wouldn't* fit.

"I'm surprised the peacekeepers are letting you stay in residence during their investigation," said Iari. She, too, was looking around. Up, mostly, at the ceiling. Gaer followed her glance. Elaborate scrollwork carved into the beams—wichu did everything with ornamentation—criss-crossed the plaster, interrupted by drop-down tesla fixtures that looked like some kind of colorful, bulbous fruit.

"They're being reasonable." Hvidjatte sniffed loudly, from rain or cold or indignation.

"I meant because of the likelihood of structural damage from the fire. But I don't see any from down here."

Another sniff. Hvidjatte blinked very large, very pale eyes. "The damage was very limited."

"You must have excellent fire-suppression hexes, then." Iari flicked a glance at Gaer.

Gaer cycled the optic. A web of equations sprang up, marching over the scrolls and the teslas, glowing in every corner. "Yes, he does."

Hvidjatte stared at Gaer with a mix of fascination and loathing. "I—yes, Lieutenant."

"What kind of damage did you sustain?"

Another flurry of sniffing and blinking. "This is all in the peacekeeper report."

"I'm leading a separate, Aedis investigation. What kind of damage?"

The wichu looked like he wanted to argue. One puffed-up moment, cheeks starting to bulge, eyes round. Then Iari leaned forward, and he crumpled.

"One room entirely destroyed. Minor damage to the two surrounding rooms."

"We need to see them."

"Of course." Hvidjatte leaned across the desk and pointed. "Up the stairs, on the right. The teslas are off on the second level, though. It will be dark."

"Not a problem," said Iari. "We can manage." She stopped midturn, as if snagged by an afterthought. "Just one more thing. There was a woman staying here, Yinal'i'ljat. You know the name?"

"That would be in the records, which I turned over to the investigators."

Oh, liar. Such pretty greens in that aura, like the rainforests on Harakai. Gaer snorted. "He recognizes the name."

Hvidjatte shot him a poisonous glare (yellow aura, with a bit of malevolent red). "Ah, yes. I recall her now. I'm sorry. Your accent confused me."

"Oh, well *done*. Insult the lieutenant *and* lie to her."

Iari ignored him. "I'd like the keycode to her room, too, please."

"I—can't give it to you. I mean, you don't need one." Hvidjatte looked back and forth between Gaer and Iari, fear and confusion as bright on his face as in his aura. "There's no door anymore to her room. That's where the fire started."

Gaer followed Iari up the steps, leaving behind the bulbous-fruit lamps and watery teslas in reception, ascending into a murky dark night punctuated by flashes of lightning. It was a slow, cramped climb. Iari was moving like she expected Brood to come leaping out any second.

Well. That might be a fair worry. Gaer rocked up on his toes and peered over her shoulder at the walls, the floor, the ceiling. "Hvidjatte was wrong. This staircase *would* hold Char's weight, if not their breadth. It'd hold a hundred riev. I also see the expected fire-suppression hexes. And anti-insect, anti-fungal, anti-leak, anti-everything. Point is"—because Iari had cranked her head around to glare at him, her headlamp blinding white—"there shouldn't have been a fire at all. There are a great many *very* good hexes here."

Which were giving him all five *hells* of a headache, not helped by the blinking alert lights on the rim of his helmet. That particular cadence and sequence meant his rig sensed an excess of arithmancy, no surprise and not helpful. He didn't need machine confirmation of the obvious.

Also obvious: where the fire had begun and ended. The visible damage began perhaps a meter from the afflicted doorway. Blackened bits of wall-frame jutted out like broken bones. Iari rubbed her fingers over one spar. Gaer squeezed around her—not easy, in wichu-sized spaces—and stepped into Yinal'i'ljat's room. There were even more hexes in here, laced and layered over every surface. *Bright*, too. He squinted, as if against sunlight.

Iari thrust her hand in front of his face. "What do you see?"

Gaer screwed his left eye all the way shut, both sets of lids, and cocked his head at her. "I see a battle-rig glove and a very scowly templar."

"Void and dust, Gaer, *look*."

"I am looking. For arithmancy. Of which there is a great deal, as I already mentioned—ah. I see. There's no soot on your glove."

"Right. And there should be, if there was a fire."

"There was *definitely* a fire. Look around."

"Yes. I see lots of blackened plaster. Lots of lumpy black things that could've been furniture." Iari panned her headlamp across the debris. "And a lot of really jagged edges. I think something happened in here before the fire, and I think the fire happened just fast and hard enough to scorch things, and probably burn off any organic residue, and *why* is your eye closed?"

"Because these hexes are too bright. Because my optic is either malfunctioning or—" Or. Gaer hissed and snapped the helmet's visor back up. The blinking yellow light on the helmet's rim bloomed into a whole HUD of hex assessments, analysis, and counter-measures.

Iari was still staring at him. Bits of her hair stuck to her forehead, plastered by sweat or rain or both. "Or *what?*"

"I am an idiot. These are *battle*-hexes all over the room, in the sense that they're meant to scramble equipment. Specifically *my* equipment. Specifically my optic, which means someone knows I have it, which means someone's seen me or knows about me, and that same someone expected us to come here."

"The arithmancer from Tzcansi's place?"

"Fake Yinal'i'ljat. Yes."

"We don't know for certain they're the same person."

"Sss. True." Gaer rebooted his optic. Flash, then blank, then a slow, dawning sparkle. "But they know how to scramble vakari arithmancy. Give me half a minute."

Half a minute was generous: ten seconds, no more, because the arithmantic interface on his battle-rig was more powerful than the optic's, if somewhat less precise, like the difference between throwing a rock into a pond and lobbing a boulder. Gaer's awareness expanded (punched through) half a dozen aetheric layers simultaneously. He sifted through the ripples, chasing the glowing hexwork back to their *exact* layer—one of the thinner ones, harder to access. Fine work, very precise, very exact. Also very delicate, when attacked by a set of SPERE counter-hexes.

The glowing equations twisted, loosened, wisped away. Left the muted normalcy of the hotel's already extensive hexwork in place. Well. Except for the *holes*.

"There shouldn't have been a fire in here at all," Gaer repeated. "But our arithmancer took the protective hexes apart. I don't mean disabled. I mean *dismantled*. And then, when the fire was over, she cleaned up by putting her own equations in place. You asked about the soot. Well. *Yes*, it was scrubbed. And so was everything else in here. That's what these new hexes were doing: removing all traces of the occupants. The PKs won't find any evidence because there isn't any left to find. *Maybe*, if they'd had a good arithmancer with them in the first few hours. But not now."

Iari turned around slowly, panning her headlamp over every surface. "So there might've been Brood here."

"There might've been a *setatir* Weep fissure in here. Or a Kreeshan Blue concert. These hexes are *that* good." The back of Gaer's throat burned like he'd swallowed acid. "I'm sorry. I keep underestimating this arithmancer. We're not just dealing with a professional. This is military-grade expertise. I'd say it was *setatir* SPERE work, except it *can't* be another vakar, for all the reasons I told Keawe. But it's someone who's done war-work."

Iari had been peering at what had been the bed (a slagged lump of synthetic fabric fused to the sootless, splintered frame). Now she straightened and turned, with that deliberate slowness that said *thinking*. "How long would these hexes take to finish erasing everything?"

"I don't know. Evidently less than two days."

"And you're sure this is the same arithmancer who blew me up?"

"Pretty sure. Unless there are two of them this skilled."

"Yinal'i'ljat could be a victim here."

"A victim who assumed someone else's name and just, what, happened to be at the site of Pinjat's murder?"

"A victim and not someone who lied to us both, *to our faces*. We *had* her, Gaer, and we let her walk."

"Be fair. We didn't know. We couldn't know. I wasn't even reading auras that night—"

"Good as she is, she might've been able to lie to you anyway."

Gaer had been trying not to read Iari's aura. Now it was hard not to. That particular shade of suspicion, the jagged pattern, like a plasma core going critical. He squeezed his left eye closed again. Iari settled back into a single dimension. Scowling, lip curled, eyes narrow. Apparently angry, but he knew her better.

Gently, carefully, as if probing a wound: "We don't know if Corso even made it this far."

Iari made a fist, raised it, threatened the wall. And stopped. Her aura settled, so rapidly and vividly, that Gaer blinked and suspected his optic again. She began uncurling her fist, one finger at a time. "No. And we also don't know why, if this arithmancer is so good, she would leave hexwork so obvious that *you* wouldn't miss it if you came here, actually *tailored to your rig*, and then make it easy to remove."

"*Easy?*"

"Easy. If this neefa's as good as you say, she could've made it harder to detect the hexes. Certainly harder to remove. We're supposed to be congratulating ourselves right now on having found something, instead of noticing what we *haven't* found." Iari might've been Char, stiff-faced and cold-eyed. "The owner Hvidjatte knows something. Maybe who Yinal'i'ljat really is. Definitely if Corso came up here." Her voice caught, steadied. "Whether he told the PKs or not, he'll tell *us*. You just make sure he tells me the truth."

"I assume that means *read his aura*, and not something more, ah, physical?" Knowing how she'd answer that, even before she grimaced at him.

But before she could say the expected *void and dust, Gaer, of course just the aura*, her helmet-comm squealed. Luki's voice squeezed out, thin and thready with distance.

"Lieutenant? You need to get down here!"

CHAPTER TWENTY-ONE ≡≡≡

Corso thought at first that he was dead. That was only because it was dark—*really* dark, no light-at-all-dark, eyes-gouged-out-oh-fuck-I'm-blind dark—and the impression only lasted a heartbeat. Because then came the *second* heartbeat, and all the proof of not-dead came flooding in. Aches and sharp pains and a sticky metallic certainty of a mouth that had been full of blood. That was dry now, saliva gone thick, like he hadn't had any water in a long time.

How long?

A good question. The blood had come from his nose, mostly—sniff, swallow, *nasty*—but also from his lip. He checked, mapped the contours of chin and cheek. Yes, that was some kind of gash and *fuck* yes, he'd broken a tusk. But all that blood was old, dry. Crumbling under his fingers, except when he snagged a scab and got a fresh source.

His fingers told him, when he checked—carefully, because what the fuck would he do if he found empty holes?—that his eyes were still there. They strained at dark nothing, sure, but they blinked. He probed gently around the sockets, pressed the quivering lids. Didn't feel like damage. But fact was, he couldn't see a slagging thing.

The first sour panic sloshed up the back of his throat. He held it down, only just, with deep gulping breaths and by holding tight to the guardrails of Confederate militia training that told him the fastest way to die in a battle was lose his shit first.

Not that this was a battle. But there *had* been one. He had very clear recollection of the boneless ricocheting off the wall at him. Very clear recollection of firing his jacta until the whitefire core overheated. (*That* explained the sting on his hand. Burn.) He'd—had he held onto the weapon? He patted the area immediately around him. Cold stone, rough on his palms (especially the burn-raw part). No jacta in the immediate circumference. He licked his lip—more old blood—and patted himself down.

No jacta, but he had his monofils. The small one in the sheath on his chest, for quick stabbing, and the larger one stashed at the small of his back, under a coat that was still mostly there. He fingered the shredded hem. That was the boneless's doing. He remembered firing at it, and missing. Remembered stitching whitefire across the walls and the bed. Remembered the bloom of flame.

So there'd been a fire. The scratchiness in his throat, the raw feeling under the blood-slick and metal—that could be smoke or heat damage, or both, in addition to dehydration. He wasn't hungry, but he had that hollow-skull ache and lingering nausea that said *post-fight*.

A fight he'd won, evidently, if he was waking up at all. So where had the boneless gone? He was pretty sure he hadn't killed it. This place, this very *dark* place—damp air, stale and cool, no breeze, a faint liquid gurgle—could be full of Brood, except it if was, they'd've gotten him by now. They wouldn't be waiting for him to figure his shit out. He dragged his legs under him, into a squat. Started listening—held his breath, turned his head, sniffed like an alley rat looking for scraps. He smelled smoke and petrichor. A strange chemical tang he didn't recognize. And echoes, like the room was big and stone-walled. Not the cramped little warrens of Wichutown. Not even a regular room.

He crouch-crawled, balanced on hands and balls of his feet, until he found what he thought was a wall, rising out of the floor. Also stone, also cool, also damp. But it wasn't a wall. It had rounded edges. It was a slagging pillar, just a little bit wider than he was. He followed his hands up the side, straightened slowly, was relieved to discover he could stand all the way upright. He kept reaching, feeling for the top. He thought from the way the circumference expanded as it got taller that the ceiling must be close, even if he couldn't quite touch it.

He had a good idea where he was, in the most basic sense. Old-style stone building, the kind with the domed ceilings to bear all that weight, which meant the oldest parts of B-town.

How he'd gotten here from a second-floor Wichutown hostel remained grimly mysterious.

Corso leaned against the pillar. Felt better, having his back against something solid. He probed his lip again, and the tip of the broken tusk. Oh voidspit, that hurt. He couldn't remember when *that* had happened, either. Seemed like he should. Might've come from a faceful of stone floor when he landed here. The nosebleed could have come from that, too. Like someone had dropped him, or thrown him, without much care for his landing.

His eyes were beginning to adjust, or at least, they were trying to make sense of the darkness. That *might* be a less black area over there. Corso pushed off the pillar and shuffle-slid along the floor: push a foot out, feel around, then commit the other to joining it. Repeat, repeat, until yes, that was a vague blacker-than-black shape rising off the floor. He dropped back into a squat and hop-shuffled toward it. The floor sloped a little bit here, and the liquid gurgle was louder; probably a drain. His throat spasmed—not quite a swallow. There might be water. That'd be nice.

But light coming out of a cellar *floor* made no sense. A drain didn't glow.

His skin tightened, prickled. His braids, stuck to his head and each other with sweat and blood, seemed to lift off his scalp like raised hackles.

Corso froze, mid-step. Swallowed his heart back down his throat and felt with cold fingers for his larger monofil. His hand didn't want to close on the hilt: a combination of flesh scorched raw and aching joints. So he drew the monofil with his left hand, and swept out with the blade—slowly, carefully. Wouldn't want to hit something solid on the edge and break the slagging thing—

The tip of the monofil poked into something, not solid at all, which at first yielded and then seemed to solidify and then actually *pushed back*. Sparks burst from that point of contact, momentarily blinding, showering Corso's wrist and hand with little pinprick burns. Light rippled out from that same initial point like he'd dropped a rock in a pond: a patchwork of symbols, numbers, all briefly and brightly glowing, moving as if stitched to a whole, transparent cloth.

He kept hold of the monofil and blinked hard, trying to clear the flash. He'd just poked a set of hexes, clear enough. Didn't need to be an arithmancer to figure that. Some kind of ward, behind which sat something darker than black, something with alien angles that didn't reflect any light. Something that made Corso's breath dry up in his throat.

He dropped into the smallest possible crouch and jabbed the wards again with the tip of his monofil. This time the ripple of disturbed hexes went all the way round, sketching a bubble perimeter of wards around that blacker-than-black thing on all sides—or no. Not quite. It was a broken perimeter. There was a hole in it, ragged, undulating on the edges as if it were laundry on a line caught in a breeze. He saw more sparks on the far side, a raw cascade of white and blue light, ozone and petrichor and something charred.

Corso thought, in the moment before the light exhausted itself, he saw a second shape on the floor beside the very black thing. An unmoving, raggedy shape, like a pile of clothing.

Or like a body, albeit a small one. Maybe a child, or a diminutive alw, or a wichu.

Corso took another deep sniff of the stone-and-damp. Smelled himself, sweat and blood. But not a *lot* of blood, like there would be if that heap of cloth had a bled-out body under it. If that pile of cloth was a body and not just *stuff*, they hadn't died like Tzcansi had.

Or they hadn't died at all.

Corso retreated from the Very Black Thing and the lump of rags and the broken ward in more or less the direction he'd come, shuffle-slide-step. Past the place where he'd landed (he thought, counting steps), and then farther. He found his jacta finally, by tripping over it, and picked it up, stuffing the monofil back in its sheath. Paused in his retreat to check the charge. Its indicator teslas were faint, two bars of seven and those two flickering. That meant he had maybe a handful of shots left in the cartridge.

He finally stopped when he reached a set of stone steps. He couldn't see any light-leak from the top. Either they went up a very long way, or it was dark on the other side and he didn't need to go running up and brain himself on a trap door. He pushed himself up one step at a time, his burned hand raised overhead and leading the way, his left curled tight around the jacta, pointing it in the direction of that Very Black Thing in case something moved over there. He kept looking that way, too—because you looked where you pointed your jacta (one of the early lessons) and because he couldn't see much anyway.

His mind, his eyes, tried to fill in the darkness. Tried to tell him that something was moving over by the Very Black Thing. His ears told him better. No scraping. No rustling. Just quiet. Brood made *noise* when they did things. Slime-slick slapping, whispers, scratching sounds. There wasn't anything happening across the cellar, no matter what his traitor eyes said. No matter how hard his heart beat and how many flashes it sent across his vision. Those were panic-lights. Those weren't anything real.

Until his eyes settled on a consistent message. *Red*, they told him, *dim red, like the charge teslas on your dying jacta.* Corso squinted. Blinked. Pushed himself up another step, blinked, and tried again.

Definitely a faint red glow over there. The Very Black Thing had become the Dull Red Glowing Thing.

Corso shoved himself up the last couple of steps fast and discovered they *were* the last few steps when his hand bumped into a solid surface. Metal, from the texture and chill. A trap door? He took eyes off the Dull Red Glowing Thing long enough to look (uselessly) into the absolute dark and pressed his raw right hand on it—pain and rising panic, potent combination—and pushed. No. So he tucked the jacta into his coat and added a second hand, and his shoulders, and all the strength that he had.

The trap door wouldn't budge.

Because, oh void and dust, it was a hatch, a real fucking *hatch*. His hands found the outlines of a metal wheel at the door's relative center. Corso grabbed hold of the wheel and threw his whole weight into the twist. Got nothing at all, not even a squeak, which meant either he was weaker than he thought, or it was braced on the far side.

Because, *think, idiot*, whoever had thrown hexwork around the Dull Red Glowing Thing had damn sure locked the hatch when they left.

Which meant someone had thrown him down here—a theory supported by the bruising, the bloody nose, the broken tusk—and then they had locked him in.

He made a mallet of his fist and banged, hard, on the metal. The impact rattled the bones of fist and forearm. Bruised the flesh of his hand. And made a noise. Muted and meaty, but clearly audible.

Please, *please* there was someone up there.

Corso liked the idea of the old religion well enough. The Elements and the Aedis were so fucking antiseptic, so inclusive, like a tenju was exactly the same as an alw, no difference, all part of the ubiquitous Four. And maybe that was fine for the alwar and the humans and even the responsible tenju: spacers, all of them, who'd invented the Aedis in their voidships and stations. But he was Tanisian, dirtsider-born tenju, and all that aether-liquid-solid-plasma voidspit didn't *speak* to him. He and Iari had argued about it, long and hard and irreparably. But, truth: banging on a hatch, trapped in a cellar with something *bad*, Corso didn't call on those old tenju spirits, the iotun or Inanak or Axorchal One-Eye. Just *please*, thrown at large into the multiverse, to whoever, whatever, was listening.

He struck again, one-two-three. Then rest, then *again*, one-two-three. Then a rest, then one, hard and solitary. Then repeat,

repeat, repeat. It was Confederate code, a pattern, to be used with light or sound or whatever lay closest at hand. Acute distress, render aid, for the love of all good things, *help*.

He beat out the distress pattern again. Then he stopped and pressed his ear against the hatch, the boltwork biting patterns into his cheek, whitefire pressure on the broken tip of his tusk. Then he started again.

And someone hit back.

The *clang* shook the hatch in its frame. Rang like a bell through the cellar's close confines. Something *far* heavier than a man's hand coming down on the hatch from above, damn sure. Like a battle-rig's fist. And no one wore battle-rigs in B-town except the Aedis.

Corso shrank away from the hatch. Stuffed his bruised fist between his knees. Shot a look at the Dull Red Glowing Thing. There was also no way templars had thrown him down here. They were up there, that meant they were watching the place, that they knew about the Dull Red Glowing Thing, which was *exactly* the sort of neefa-shit the Aedis concerned themselves with. So then they were going to open that hatch and ask him how the *fuck* he'd gotten down here, and he wouldn't be able to tell them.

Because—how *had* he gotten down here? Or had he been down here long enough that templars had just discovered the place? Void and dust. Didn't matter. Templars up there might, *might*, let him call Iari. Or the veek. And they might know how he'd gotten down here, and more importantly, what to do about the Dull Red Glowing Thing, which was rapidly becoming the Bright Red Glowing Thing, and acquiring edges and a crouched silhouette that made Corso's guts turn cold and watery.

The hatch overhead grated, metal on metal. Corso retreated a step down. Cast a nervous (oh, truth: *terrified*) look back at the (now) Very Bright Red Glowing Thing. Slagging templars were taking their time up there.

The hatch seal cracked. Cool air leaked through the gap. Sound came with it: a battle-rig's metallic whine in close proximity, raised voices.

"The Knight-Marshal's orders are *not* to open this, sir."

"I'm aware, Corporal, but there's someone down there."

"But *how*, sir?"

"We can ask when we get them out."

Corso wedged his face into the gap of fresh air. "My name's Corso Risar. I'm a P.R.I.S. on retainer for Lieutenant Iari."

"All right, Risar, easy." A human voice, male, pitched low and condescending and kind. "I'm Lieutenant Peshwari. How'd you get down there?"

"I don't know. But there's something *else* down here, and—"

"What do you mean, you don't know?"

"I mean—" Corso squeezed his eyes shut. "I was fighting a boneless in Wichutown and then there was a flash, and now I'm here, with *that* thing."

"What thing? Do you mean the altar?"

The—what? "Maybe. It's glowing. Red. Something's *happening* with it."

Then came a flash from up there, leaking around the edge of the hatch, lightning quick and lightning bright and maybe imagined, on the cusp of a blink. Corso smelled petrichor, and ozone, and that dead air that meant Brood. Brood *up there*.

He wasn't surprised to hear a third voice, more distant, pitched high and urgent: "Sir!"

Corso pressed himself against the hatch. Pushed, and thought for a moment he'd get somewhere. But the mechanism jammed on *something*. Or, *or*, that voidspit slagging templar was holding it down.

"Private, what is it?"

The voice drifted away. Corso tried the hatch again. It was like pushing solid stone. "Hey," he called through the gap. "*Hey*, please. I need to get out of here."

Nothing. A smear of voices he couldn't make out. Then the bang of heavy footsteps, coming fast.

"Stand by," said the condescending voice, only now Peshwari sounded stretched tight and tense. "You're safer down there for the moment. We'll be back."

The hatch slammed back into its frame with an echoing bang. The voices, the wisps of fresh air, ceased. Corso was left with his own heartbeat, his own salt-sweat-and-blood on his lips.

He hooked undecided fingers around the wheel on the hatch. They hadn't sealed it again. He might be able to push up and get out—

He jerked his hand back with a hiss. Flexed fingers gone instantly, ominously numb. The skin felt burned. He sampled a fingertip. Felt the pillow-plump of a blister under his tongue. Cold like that came with Brood. And what *else* would make templars drop everything and slam the hatch on him? Safer down there, they'd said.

Cold sweat collected on Corso's forehead, his temples, began carving a path down his cheeks. His heart threatened to crawl out his throat, bring his guts up along with it. This was not, *not* a battlefield. (Worse than a battlefield: he had no battle-rig, no longcaster). All he had was retreat.

He half slid, half fell, down the stairs to the cellar floor. He sucked in a lungful of basement-damp air, tasted metal on his tongue. That had to be the Very Bright Red Glowing Thing's fault, that taste. And now he was stuck in here with it. He looked that way, more from reflex than any hope of new information.

There *was* something moving over there. For a stuttering heartbeat, he was sure it was the boneless, that he hadn't killed it; then sense and vision caught up on the backsurge of adrenaline. A boneless would've closed the distance already. Would've killed him while he slept. He'd been down here *hours* at least.

The reddish glow had tilted toward purple, collecting at the bottom (the belly, Corso thought, it looks like a belly) of the Now Purple Glowing Thing. (The lieutenant had called it an altar.) Maybe it was that color shift that was fucking with his vision. Right. Except color shouldn't warp the shape of things, shouldn't make the pillars look like bending elbows. That's what Brood-presence did. Bent light. Fucked with physics. He'd learned that at Windscar, early on.

The idea of being down here, trapped with Brood, made his guts crawl into his throat. His heart pounded hard enough he saw white flashes on his vision's periphery, like plasma discharge.

Oh, fuck that. More like a fucking stroke.

The anger helped. Gave him an anchor. Something to hold onto besides fear. He fumbled for the jacta, left-handed, and got it raised and leveled, got it braced with his wounded right hand.

The hex-bubble-wards around the altar stuttered and flared at irregular intervals, in irregular locations, like something was poking them from the inside. He smelled petrichor again. Smelled something burning. The former pile of cloth was—oh shit—not where it had been. It was over by the Glowing Thing now, more upright, moving around over there, shadow on shadow behind the glow. Rough, uneven movements, like someone tired, or in pain. Maybe both.

Oh, void and dust.

Then it moved again, and his eyes carved details out of the purplish glow. A woman. Wichu. Eyes like bloody moons. Maybe the one the veek had sent him after, another victim, *what* was her fucking name?

"Yinal'i'ljat," he blurted, and the shuffling stopped.

ari took the stairs three at a time and thank you Elements for the stabilizers on her rig. Wichu-sized stairs were shallow. She skipped the last five steps entirely and jumped, landed, pivoted.

The front desk sat empty and abandoned.

Blink, *look, find* Hvidjatte, please Hrok, he hadn't bolted into a back room, out a back door, was there a kitchen in this place, *where—*

Ah, there he was, frozen halfway between the desk and a side corridor like a rabbit caught in the open. He had a coat fisted up in one hand, not yet on his person, clearly snatched in some haste.

Luki stood a little past the middle of the lobby. The rug rucked up where her rig had skidded across it, delicate little chairs from the lobby knocked askew and scattered around her. Her rig streamed water onto the carpet, made puddles on the floorboards. "Sir," she said. "He tried to run."

"I see that."

And Hvidjatte could've made it, Iari thought. Even synning, Luki wouldn't have been fast enough to cross that space before he'd gotten into the corridor. Something had made him lose nerve. Iari followed his stare to where Char filled the narrow doorway, turned slightly sideways to wedge themself through. The lintel sparked where their hexes touched, armor to wood. Char was even *less* able to cross that tiny space, but even the threat of the riev coming in had stopped Hvidjatte like someone had nailed his feet to the floor.

The wichu moaned faintly. "Keep it outside. Please."

Huh. Iari glanced at Luki—whose expression, now that her visor was up, was pure puzzlement. "Char's no danger to you, sir, they're a templar."

"Just keep it outside!"

"All right. Initiate—out, please." Iari dragged one of the lobby chairs around and slammed it down between her and Hvidjatte. She gestured. "Then sit. We've got some questions."

"Start with why you tried to run," Gaer said.

Hvidjatte wrung his coat and stared at the chair as if it were live snakes. "I'm not under arrest."

"Not yet," Iari said. "But answer the ambassador's question. Why did you try to leave?"

"It's late. My husbands will worry."

"Lies are the *prettiest* green, sometimes," Gaer drawled. "Like spring foliage."

"What? I'm not lying!"

"Just like caranda buds. *That* color."

Iari tried to catch Gaer's eye so that she could glare *shut up and let me handle it* at him. He might be looking back. Hard to tell, in this muted lighting, and his eyes sunk to featureless black. She pointed at the chair. "Hvidjatte. Sit. Now. Or I call Char back inside."

Hvidjatte did, clutching his coat to his chest like a shield. "You need a warrant for aura-interrogations. This is illegal."

Gaer hissed what she knew was vakar laughter, what Hvidjatte clearly interpreted as an intent to devour the nearest wichu, *look* at that flinch. "Obstructing an Aedian investigation is illegal. Concealing evidence of Brood activity is illegal. It's also really stupid."

"I don't know anything about Brood!"

"Ssss. Not entirely true."

"Hvidjatte." Iari was aware of just how big she was, in a battle-rig. Of just how small Hvidjatte was, perched on a wichu-sized chair in his own hostel lobby, feet drawn up so that he made the smallest target. She thought about crouching down, getting closer to eye-level. Sometimes that worked for building rapport. Sometimes it just made things worse. She remained fully upright. "Were you here when the fire started?"

A blink, obvious relief. "Yes."

"Truth," said Gaer.

"Do you know how it started?"

"No."

"You've got extensive hexwork in this establishment. What can you tell me about that?"

"I don't know anything about hexes! I'm not an arithmancer! I'm not even an artificer."

"Half-truth, truth, truth."

"I don't care if you're the secret heir to the Fyrte-Femte fortune. I need to know what happened up there."

"I don't know!"

"*Technically* true." Gaer squinted. "He's very afraid. But I don't think of you. Or even me."

"Who, then? Char?"

"Oh yes, them too. But they are not his primary terror. And it *is* a terror." Gaer cocked his head. "Although I think it's related, somehow. Char and whomever he's scared of."

"All right. Did you see someone go up there, before the fire?"

"Yes." Hvidjatte lifted his chin and kept his face pointed at her. Hard to tell where a wichu was looking, with blank white eyes. He might be looking at the wall behind her, for all she could tell. Or side-eyeing Gaer. "There was a braid-wearing tenju thug in a long coat."

Oh, ungentle Ptah. Iari breathed past a sudden surge of cold in her chest. That had to be Corso. But never assume—

"Man or woman?"

Hvidjatte was definitely looking at her now. "Man. He threatened me."

"Sss. No, he didn't. He was looking for Yinal'i'ljat," Gaer said, perfect pronunciation, "wasn't he?"

Hvidjatte flinched. "Yes."

"Truth." Gaer's plates flared. "Was she upstairs when the tenju went up? And *don't* you lie to me."

"Yes."

Gaer's nostrils clamped almost closed. Breath hissed softly through the gap. "*She's* the one you're so afraid of. Perhaps you should tell the lieutenant why."

Hvidjatte retreated to the limits of chair, his neck craned as far back as bones would allow. He raised his hands, palms out. A futile gesture. A pathetic one, like a man trying to hold up the sky. "She kept asking about the riev. Where to find them. How many there are in B-town. I thought at first that she was an artificer, which is the only reason I even mentioned Pinjat, said *he'd* know about the riev since he worked on them. I didn't know she'd kill him. And then when he ended up dead, I thought if I said something, she'd kill *me*. Now can I go?"

"Did she threaten you?" Iari asked.

Hvidjatte's face whipped toward her. Wisps of sweat-dampened hair clutched the sides of his face. "Yes."

"Partial truth."

"No, that's all of it, I swear—"

Gaer had been standing a little behind Iari. Now he stepped around her, liquid-quick, so that the syn jolted up her spine and made her lose breath. Reflex made her reach an arm out, half grab, half deflection, which Gaer avoided like she hadn't moved at all. He thrust his face up close to Hvidjatte's. His chromatophores had sunk to black, featureless and flat as his eyes. "Try again," he said. "*Setat m'rri—*"

And then came a sudden, surprising flood of Sisstish, danger-quiet, pitched too low for Iari to catch even one susurrated syllable.

Then a pause, a pregnant moment, punctuated by the rain outside, by Hvidjatte's sobbing breaths. By Gaer's slow, through-the-plates-and-teeth exhale. By the rain beating on pavement, on Char, outside.

Then Hvidjatte answered Gaer, in Sisstish, ragged but fluent, like a man running hard. And at the end, one more word, short and desperately sincere and repeated, repeated, until Gaer hissed and straightened, full vakari height, the top of his helmet a hairs-breadth from the criss-crossing beams. Hvidjatte contracted even more on the chair and shivered and stared, unblinking, at the floor.

Gaer turned his back to Hvidjatte and leaned close, until all Iari could smell was angry vakar. Until all she could see were his eyes, one hazed behind the optic, the other naked and black and cold as the void.

"Truth: the wichu pretending to be Yinal'i'ljat has a name. Jich'e'enfe. She told Hvidjatte who she was when she got here and asked for his help, which he gave her in the form of a room and board and someone else's identity. He knows Yinal'i'ljat, the *real*

Yinal'i'ljat, doesn't leave Windscar often, and has no contact with her cousin, so he figured her name would be a safe loaner."

"He told you all that just now. *All* of that."

"Sisstish is an efficient language." Gaer's anger was cold and thin as spring ice. "He sent Corso up to her, expecting that she'd kill him."

Iari squeezed her eyes closed. Held her breath. Then she stiff-armed Gaer to one side, stepped forward, and stared down at a crumpled, sniffling Hvidjatte. "Do you know where she, this, this Jich'e'enfe, is now?"

"No. Please, Lieutenant—" He left the sentence unfinished. *Please don't let that vakar kill me, probably.*

"Is Corso—the tenju who went up there—dead?"

"I don't know," said Hvidjatte. "He wasn't there after the fire. Neither of them were."

"Gaer?"

"Oh, *truth*. And you're right. She has to be *the* arithmancer, because that's the only way she could've gotten out of that room. She must have hexed herself a portal."

Another breath. Two. Three. Iari turned around slowly. Gaer was still standing behind her, arms loose, hands open, a voidspit portrait of control. But his chin had dropped, and his plates were flat, and his chromatophores were a fixed, deliberate grey.

"Explain." Iari marveled at her tone. At how cool she sounded, while her vision washed red and the syn clawed along her nerves.

"It's a wichu innovation on old k'bal tech, related to the old tesser-hex gates that ships had to use for void-travel. The Protec-torate banned the practice on vakari planets on religious grounds. What the wichu did on *their* territory was their business. Point is, a portal requires fixed points and substantial preparation—having those points already chosen and secure, all the hexes worked out in advance. They're not something that can be done spontaneously. She would've had to have a portal-point already in that room. Which, if she was staying there, she would've had time to create."

"A portal-point you didn't find."

"Correct." Gaer cocked his head. "Fire is an excellent way to dispose of hexes that are inscribed on a flammable surface."

"Void and dust." The fire at the public house, the fire at Tzcansi's, the fire *here* could've all been points on the network, places this Jich'e'enfe had used. "So if she fled, like you think, she needed to have a fixed point already, somewhere else."

"Correct."

"And is there an easy way to detect these fixed points?"

"No. I'd have to search for them specifically, and even then my optic might not be able to detect them, if she's concealed them well. At the very least, I'd have to be in the vicinity. How near depends on how well-concealed the hexwork is. Given what we know about her operations so far, my guess is I'd have to be looking *specifically* for a portal, which I haven't been. If I did find one, I might be able to see how many others are on that network, and to trace where they are."

"Might. Maybe. Not reassuring me, Gaer." She took a steadying breath. "Could an arithmancer send Brood through a portal like this?"

Gaer's jaw-plates clicked, open-shut, open-shut. "In theory, one can send *anything* through a portal, although Brood originate in the void, and to cross that, you need . . . oh, *setat.*" His un-opticked eye widened, the second set of lids fluttering at the corners. "You'd need actual tesser-hexes on the portal."

"You found tesser-hexes in the warehouse. So that altar could be a portal-point. Or near one."

Gaer hesitated. It was hard to read him sometimes: those features didn't move much. But that narrow-eyed, both-sets-of-lids-pulled-halfway expression, that was pretty clear. "Yes," he said slowly. "That's possible. But besides the issue of how you'd power a *real* tesser-hex without a plasma core, which I did not find, I also put up wards. She couldn't use any portal on that altar now. Unless," he added, "she's just better than me *again*, and she gets through them."

Iari let that float unanswered and sealed her visor. Closed her eyes and leaned her forehead against the HUD. "Comm," she murmured. And when the light greened and steadied: "Aedis dispatch, this is Lieutenant Iari. Patch me through to Corporal Heph, or whoever's holding the warehouse location."

"Copy that. Stand by." There was a fistful of dead-comm seconds, and then dispatch came back online. "Sorry, Lieutenant. I can't raise them."

She stepped around Gaer, around Luki. Char moved aside as she poked her head through the doorway and looked up at a storm-blackened sky. Lightning flickered up there, slivers of blue in folded shadows. "Storm interference?"

She could almost hear dispatch shaking her head. "Possible. You're coming in clearly, but Lieutenant Peshwari's in Lowtown. Might be some local storm intensity. Or, you know. Just normal trouble."

"*Peshwari's* on duty tonight?"

"Yes sir. But it's been quiet. No alerts."

"Copy." Iari hesitated. "Try to raise them for me again, will you? And patch me through to the Knight-Marshal. Urgent."

"Copy that, Lieutenant. Stand by."

A moment of dead comms, and then Tobin's voice filled her helmet.

"Lieutenant. Report."

"Sir. We're in Wichutown." She told him, in brief strokes, what they'd learned. What they guessed. "Not sure where this Jich'e'enfe is now, sir. We think maybe in Lowtown."

Or wherever Corso was. Guilt gnawed at her, and worry, and *anger*.

"Copy that, Lieutenant. Stand by," Tobin said. A moment's dead-comm silence, enough for, oh, one Knight-Marshal to speak to the other one in his office. Then Tobin came back. "Are you sure of the name? There's no Jich'e'enfe"—almost no mangling—"on the artificer registry."

Iari squinted past her HUD at Hvidjatte. At Gaer, who'd gone back to staring at the wichu, plates flared, photopigments controlled to dead black. "Gaer's sure."

"Acknowledged. I'll need to file a request for information through the Synod, if we want access—"

Keawe's voice rose in the background. "Let me ask Su'seri what he knows. We won't need a slagging RFI."

"—to wichu records in more detail. I'll inform the peacekeepers we'll be assuming this investigation as well. Can you bring this Hvidjatte up for questioning?"

"Yes sir. Stand by." The comm tesla blinked *incoming*. Iari flicked between channels.

"Sorry," said dispatch. "Still can't raise anyone. Can't raise the local patrols, either. Too much interference." Dispatch laughed weakly. "Just a bad night, Lieutenant."

"Copy that. Thanks. Iari out." She switched channels again. "Sorry, sir. I can't bring Hvidjatte up yet. Dispatch says Peshwari's not responding at the warehouse. Could be storm. Might be something else. I think we need to check it out."

Tobin took a sharp inhale, and let it go. "Acknowledged. If

conditions allow, keep me updated. We'll send someone down to pick up Hvidjatte."

"Yes sir. Iari out."

She pivoted, eyes on Gaer. "We're moving out. Corporal! You and Char take point. We're going to the warehouse."

Gaer had not moved. He was still staring at Hvidjatte. "We're just leaving him here?"

"We are. Templars will be down to collect you for questioning at the Aedis," she told Hvidjatte. "You should be here when they arrive. If you're not, they'll find you, and then there'll be charges. Understood?"

Hvidjatte nodded.

Iari stepped around Gaer. The rain might be letting up a little. She could see the stubby little streetlamp at the end of the block. *There* was a monument to wichu political influence: they'd gotten a waiver from the (mostly alwar and human) city council to make the lamps in their district a half meter shorter. She sealed her visor in prep for stepping outside. Her HUD showed green blips for Luki, for Char.

The blip that was Gaer, on her HUD, wasn't moving.

"This is a mistake," he said so flatly, so furiously, that her syn tingled. That was *anger*, beyond Gaer's usual, typical vakari prejudices.

She made a face entirely wasted on the wrong side of her faceplate. "Now, Ambassador. Or stay here." Then she spun on her heel and started walking. Let him follow or not. (He would; she was sure of it.) Let him seal his visor, get him on comms, she'd explain. Gaer was usually susceptible to reason.

And there, yes: her HUD showed his rig moving, coming up fast on her flank.

The click of plates clamping tight. "Can we take this to a private channel?"

"A moment, Corporal," she said, and did as he asked.

"All right, Gaer. What?"

"You are making a mistake, leaving him."

"We can't raise the templars in the warehouse. You know, the ones guarding the altar you just said might be a portal. That seems more pressing than keeping Hvidjatte in custody."

Silence from Gaer, for just long enough that Iari thought she might've won. They turned onto Main, heading toward Lowtown, and the streetlamps reverted to standard dimensions. So did the buildings, the doorways, the gutters. Hrok's breath, *imagine* what it must have been like, wichu and vakari living together before the defection. Damn sure the vakari wouldn't've issued any exceptions to building codes. Iari looked again at Char as she passed under one of those standard-sized tesla lamps. No matter the base-frame, riev were massive. Armored. Resistant to arithmancy. The perfect anti-vakari weapons. The perfect revenge, maybe, from a client-species to their overlords.

"Listen," Gaer said, and she sighed.

"What?"

"There are several separatist groups—Wichu First, Seven Strike, The Eyes of A'am, and names more pretentious from there. Mostly they're all neefa-shit, but sometimes they do more than post inflammatory manifestos on public networks. They go after vakari ships or stations, or hack the turings. Sometimes there are actual explosives and people die. They're a nuisance, mostly, but they're a nuisance with a body count, so vakari intelligence tracks them. Five Tribes *and* Protectorate. It's one of the few areas in which we cooperate painlessly, us. And you, too," Gaer added, in that same down-a-long-hallway voice: "The Confederation works with us on this. No one likes a terrorist."

You could argue (which historians did) that without the wichu defection, the Expansion would've ended far differently. That without artificing, the Confederation and the infant Aedis—presyn, the priest-alchemy in its earliest stages, only a handful of people carrying the proto-nanomecha—would've lost the war with the Protectorate outright. Wichu had made the riev (don't ask for the alchemical *hows*) to combat vakari. (From the bodies of their new allies. You didn't see wichu riev. *That* was something to think about.) They'd helped streamline the Aedis implants, adapting the nanomecha for interface with a battle-rig. Customizing them for the Elements, for priests. No one ever said wichu *hated* vakari, but it was implied.

So was the reverse.

Iari turned her head. Gaer had drawn even with her. She stared hard at the contours of his visor, of his rig: extra joints and accommodations for spikes and that oilslick armor plating.

"You knew about these separatists before?"

"Sss. Everyone in SPERE knows. But I didn't know they were *here*. This is *Tanis*. There's nothing here for them. Or there shouldn't be. They work on the fringes of *our* territory, not yours, and I never got any warnings in my briefings about them."

There were things Iari wanted to throw at him (some spy you are, Gaer), things that did not need to be said at all, things that might make her feel temporarily better. She was frustrated, and Peshwari wasn't answering, and her gut had knotted around a certainty that there was trouble at that warehouse, and she *still* didn't know what was going on, except Gaer had more in his bone-plated head than he was likely to share with her, ever.

But then, it wasn't like knowledge rained down from above in the Aedis, either. No one had told her about wichu separatists. You knew what you needed to know, when you needed it, and you managed the rest of the time. So yelling at Gaer, *temper*, that was all noise. Distraction.

What mattered here (deep breath, *center*): "Char said Pinjat was trying to reconnect Oversight among the riev. That sound like something your wichu separatists would want? How would they use that?"

Gaer's response carried that peculiar distortion of syllables that meant his lips drawn back flat, teeth bared, behind an indifferent visor. "I'm a SPERE arithmancer and Weep specialist, not counter-terrorism. I have no *idea* what they want. I'm sure they could use it, but I can't tell you how."

Well. That made two of them, then, left in the no-one-tells-me-voidspit dark. She threw Gaer a look he couldn't see, through layers of battle-rig helmets. Filled in his profile from memory. Imagined his pigments charcoal-neutral, the wink of his optic as it snagged on the light. Aimed her voice at the ridges that ran from temple to skull-spike, under which lurked vakari ears.

"Jich'e'enfe wants to kill vakari. Fine. And she wants to somehow reconnect the riev to each other and control them. Great. Control the riev, maybe use them on the vakari? Still making sense. But she *hasn't* been doing that. She's been hacking the riev and infecting them with Brood. And she's been using Brood to prop up a voidspit local ganglord on a planet in the Confederate hinterlands, and using some altar with k'bal script to do *something*. Open a tesser-hex to the Brood layer of the void? That's a very circuitous way to commit genocide. I don't think she's a separatist at all. I think she's something else. And I think you, *we*, better figure out what."

ari stopped talking after that. Gaer still had the green light in his HUD, she hadn't cut him off, but—all he could see, when he looked, was her battle-rig, the visor striped silver with rain.

Possibly, *probably*, Iari was angry with him. Fair enough. *He* was angry, too. He'd never suspected Yinal'i'ljat wasn't who she claimed to be. Never suspected she was Jich'e'enfe, never *thought* about wichu separatists on Tanis until Hvidjatte had sworn in Sisstish that's what he wasn't, but that he'd been more afraid of Jich'e'enfe than Aedian displeasure. (But not more, in the end, than he feared Gaer.)

If he had not been so obsessed with the contaminated riev chip and the arithmancy and the mystery of it, if he had reported the Pinjat incident to his superiors, *maybe* he'd've gotten some advisement, some note of *oh, yes, the separatists are doing this sort of thing now.* Maybe he would have connected *riev* with *reactivated Oversight* with *wichu,* and he might not be trotting through a *setatir* storm in the middle of the *setatir* night with Iari's silence. Maybe she wasn't angry at all. Maybe she had other things to think about than *his* perceived failures.

He looked ahead, at her back. Jorvik had put a new graft on her armor. A bright polysteel square in an otherwise scuffed, scarred landscape. If he shifted his rig sensors one notch into the aether, he'd be able to see seamless hexwork.

Char's repairs were not so seamless. He and Jorvik together had managed to armor-hex their prosthetic arm with a hybrid tangle of Aedian alchemy and vakari arithmancy, to (mostly) match the effects of the original artificing. They had been less successful patching those two sets of hexes together. It wasn't seamless, it was *ugly*, but it would hold under combat. Probably.

Ahead, Char had slowed down a little bit. Gaer recognized this pattern of streets and buildings. This was the same route they'd taken into Lowtown the day they'd found the warehouse and the swarm, at the beginning of this whole business. The day they'd walked Brisk Array into a riev trap. He supposed that Char remembered that, too. The riev's plasma-blue teslas winked like stars as they swept their gaze back and forth, up and down.

They. That was apt choice for pronoun. Char might've started as tenju, might still be *mostly* tenju under that armor; but they were not necessarily the *same* tenju anymore. What Gaer had learned about riev construction had come in the past several days, and would fuel nightmares the rest of his life.

Which might be a very short life, if he didn't, as Iari had admonished, figure this out.

Gaer considered asking Char their opinion. Maybe a riev would have the best insight into how another riev could be—not repurposed, exactly, their purpose had always been *weapon*—used to achieve Jich'e'enfe's ends.

Which, truth, they didn't really understand. Iari was right: there was no *reason* for a wichu separatist to be propping up some local ganglord and using riev (and Brood?) to do it. There had to be some heretofore undiscovered reason why the chip in Sawtooth's head had allowed—no, invited!—Brood contamination. Contaminating riev seemed like a rather large mistake, otherwise, in Jich'e'enfe's meticulous and brilliant hexwork. Of course one *made* mistakes when one was innovating with hexes; but Gaer was beginning to think the Brood contamination was the *setatir* point of the exercise. Not a side effect. The goal.

That would put Jich'e'enfe on Tanis explicitly for the Weep fissure. There were fissures all through Protectorate and Five Tribes space, a whole *border* of Weep. But the primary border—populated, massive seedworlds on either side—was patrolled, guarded, always watched. Tanis was a tactically insignificant planet, its fissure a little splinter of the Weep in a single continent watched by a scattering of Aedis compounds and a couple of Confederate military units.

But think it through—Jich'e'enfe wanted to reconnect the riev to some version of Oversight, and *riev* existed on just about every Confederate outpost, ship, base, settlement. And if somehow that reconnection also contaminated them, then every Confederate outpost, ship, base, settlement would have riev infected with Brood.

Dear five dark *lords*, the damage they could do.

That was a long chain of supposition, for which he had limited evidence. Iari might call it paranoia, but she'd want to hear it.

Gaer jog-stepped until he pulled even with Iari again. Hesitated, and then keyed the comms on the open channel.

"You're right. Jich'e'enfe's not a separatist. I think she's a nihilist. I think she's going to reconnect Oversight in order to infect *every* riev, all at the same time, with Brood."

Char stopped abruptly. Iari stopped too, and then Luki. Iari put out her left hand, like she wanted him to stop, to wait. But then the shield deployed out of her gauntlet like an exploding flower: whitefire frame first, marking the edges, and then the faster-than-blink sheet of hexwork before the shield filled in solid. Aedian red, the black and white crest in the center, the whole thing glowing but somehow still giving off no light at all.

He looked beyond the shield's rim. His HUD compensated for the rain-glare flash and ruinous brightness of streetlamps. The last time they'd come through these streets, it had been daylight. There had been people in the windows, looking out; there'd been that alwar gang with their substandard riev trap challenging them in the streets.

Now the only thing up there was Char, who had stopped statue-still in the middle of the street.

Oh, dark lords of the void.

"Hold here," Iari murmured. Then she walked toward Char, cautious but not hesitant. "Char. Report."

"There is something in this alley. I cannot say what."

To the naked, unarithmantic eye, it was just an empty street. Puddles, noxious and rainbow-slick even in *this* light, collected in corners, in the cracks of the pavement. Rain was supposed to wash things clean; but in Lowtown, it just pushed all the filth to the edges.

"Gaer," said Iari. "What do *you* see?"

Presumably that meant *get up here.* He approached with more hesitation than Iari had shown. Char would go for *him* first, if they turned bad.

Filtered through visor and optic, the alley was a wash of hex-work, shards of code glowing and throbbing where they'd landed.

"There was some kind of arithmancy," Gaer said. "Wards of some sort. Broken, now."

Iari's faceplate flashed in reflected light like a mirror. "Riev trap?"

"Hard to tell. If it *was*, it's in pieces, now, and the riev inside has moved on."

Iari angled around Char, shield first. "Char, Luki, fall back. Gaer and I will take point. In case there are more traps."

"Yes, Lieutenant," Char said promptly.

A beat later—a portentous beat, leaden with unspoken opinion—Luki said, "Yes, sir."

It was because he knew Iari so well that Gaer noticed the briefest hitch in her movement. He filled in the grimace behind her visor. Convinced himself he heard the faint sigh on his comms.

"Gaer's got different scanners on his rig. He sees hexwork. *That's* why I want him on point with me. Last time we came through this neighborhood, there were gangs and black-market riev traps, and we don't need Char walking into one."

"I understand," Luki said. Then, in a rush, "But sir. Riev trap means *riev*. Why would they even come here? Tzcansi was using them as enforcers—I read the report, sir—but she's dead. So is someone *else* using them?"

"Or it wasn't a riev trap at all, but some other ward," Gaer said. "*Or* Jich'e'enfe managed to reconnect Oversight, and she's called all the riev down here."

Iari edged a little bit more forward. Her headlamp swept up the walls, over windows shuttered and dark on the edges. Now she turned back and spot-lighted Char. "Templar-Initiate? Thoughts on that?"

Char's head turned. Those plasma-blue teslas drilled not into Luki, no. Into Gaer, straight through his visor. "I am not subject to Oversight. The damage to my frame destroyed my connection before my formal decommissioning, and my repairs since then have been nonstandard."

Gaer blinked. He'd been there when Char had asked Jorvik to build the prosthetic, when they said they did not want a graft. Then Char had explained to *him* what that actually meant, *graft*, in a detail he thought they'd enjoyed. He hadn't asked then *why* they'd made that choice. He'd assumed some conflict between the Aedis Catechism and using traditional riev repair methods. A shortage of limbs, perhaps.

And now it sounded like Char had refused tradition because they didn't *want* to be reconnected. No more Oversight.

"If Jich'e'enfe *has* reconnected Oversight," Gaer said, "can she issue orders? I mean, would you have any *say* in it? Char? Can riev refuse?"

"With the proper protocols, she could issue orders. The riev would obey."

"And then she could, one imagines, order the riev to accept chip implants in their heads, like Sawtooth."

"Perhaps. That would require overriding other protocols. Brood have replaced vakari as the primary enemy. But if she has the command codes, she could."

It was hard to see Iari's expression through a battle-rig, impossible to read auras; there was something about the attitude, the cant of head and helmet, that said she was thinking hard. Then she turned, without saying anything. She unclipped her axe, deployed it, and got back to prowling the street, shield raised as if she thought a riev might come leaping out of the dark.

It wasn't an illegitimate fear, really, except that in Gaer's experience, riev didn't do ambush especially well. They tended to crash into things, or through them.

Iari paused at an alley mouth, and stabbed into the shadows with her headlamp. "Gaer. Something down here."

Yes, *something:* one of the large, steel-sided refuse containers that dotted B-town sat partway down, set crossways. It, like every other one of its kind Gaer had ever seen, was piled to overflowing. Beside it, what looked like a sack of wet rags and wasn't. Blood, viscera, a lot of a man's insides on the outside. But the face was intact.

Luki sounded a little pale, behind her visor. "What *happened* to him? I mean, ah." Her voice steadied. "That doesn't look like a normal murder."

"Well, it's certainly not riev. Looking at how *shredded* he is, I'd say—"

"He looks like Tzcansi. Boneless did that." Iari's voice was as bleak and pitiless as her headlamp, blasting the body into stark relief.

"Except I'm not getting any Brood readings on my rig. Are you?"

"No."

"No," Char echoed. The riev had drifted—*how* did something that big move so quietly?—into the alley mouth.

"Is this some new voidspit hexwork?" Iari retracted her faceplate. Her aura spilled out: a resolved cobalt marbled with crimson, only barely flecked with a queasy chartreuse. "Maybe something off that altar, Gaer? Some *reason* our rigs are blind?"

"Maybe." He cycled his optic through the aetheric layers. "There are more fragments here, made of the same hexwork as I saw on the street last time we were here. Amateur, black-market arithmancy. I can say, though, that these fragments weren't part of a riev-trap. It was definitely a shield of some kind, probably personal, meant to turn aside impacts. *Presumably* that means jacta bolts. I'm not sure this one would've turned a well-thrown stone. But it shattered because *something* hit this man with a great deal of force."

Iari's voice was cold as the corpse, and as ragged. "That fits. Boneless attacks come fast and hard."

"Not *this* hard, unless someone threw the boneless at him, or otherwise propelled it at very high velocity. Or dropped it." He looked up. Got a faceful of rain before he remembered he'd raised his visor. He blinked and blew water out of his plates. "Truth, Iari, I don't know how this happened."

"Thrown, dropped. The boneless still tore this guy apart."

"There is something across the street, in the lee of that building," Char murmured. "I do *not* sense any Brood, and I cannot *see* anything moving, but I am certain there is something there."

Gaer avoided—narrowly, fortunately—the edge of Iari's shield as she whipped around. She was as fast as any SPERE op he'd ever trained with. As fast, damn near, as the riev.

Synning. *Bet* she was synning.

"Gaer? How many?"

Gaer bit back a *how the* setat *should I know that* because, well, he already had an idea. He pointed his rig where Iari wanted and sifted through the aetheric layer. As far as he knew, no one had ever bothered to check whether Brood had auras. No one had needed to . . . but in fact, yes, now that he was looking—they did. Or something did, back in that alley. The colors were . . . wrong. Off in their texture, their intensity, as if they'd been diluted with petroleum, colors breaking down on the edges.

"Got one something," he said, "and it's angry. It's also *scared*."

"Good." Iari stepped into the alley mouth and raised her shield.

For a moment the boneless hesitated. Then its aura flared bloody fury, and it covered the width of the street in one liquid leap. Touched down with three of six limbs (the center three, one of them folded almost in half) and leaped, this time into an arc meant to bring it over Iari's shield.

Which was low, *too* low, she had to know better—

Iari tilted the shield at the last moment, came up under the boneless and caught it solidly on the shield. For a split second— point-seven-three seconds on the chrono on Gaer's HUD—the boneless paused there. Then the shield's hexwork flared, recognizing what was in contact with it. Equations flooded Gaer's optic.

The boneless, realizing where it had landed, bunched its limbs, turned that five-eyed head back the way it had come, tried to jump. Iari yielded, knees flexing, and the boneless slipped on the shield instead. Sparks and Brood effluvia sprayed onto her rig, onto the pavement. Then she brought her axe around, one hard slice, and the boneless came off the shield. Came off four of its six legs, too (all the biggest ones); *they* slid straight to the pavement. The boneless tried to catch itself on its remaining limbs. Crashed onto its . . . did they have chins? Onto its face, then. The part with the eyes and the mouth. Iari came after it, syn-quick.

And then it was over. Iari chopped down one more time and stood over the smoking puddle.

Luki, who had been charging forward, lowered her (full-length, double-edged, interspecies-universal-shape-for-a) sword, having *almost* gotten close enough for a strike. Gaer imagined she looked somewhat chagrined behind her faceplate. *He* did.

Iari prodded the boneless with her axe. "My rig's still not saying it's real. But it is, right? Not some voidspit hologram?"

"No." Gaer dragged the word out. "My optic registers something recently dead—auras sort of *smoke* when something dies. And I can see that there's non-native material on the pavement. Organic, almost."

"Same. Luki?"

"Nothing, sir, on my HUD."

"Char?"

"No." Char, Gaer noted, had not even moved from their post on the corner of the alley. Either they had a great deal of faith in Iari's warfare skills, or—

"Char," Gaer asked. "Did you *see* the boneless?"

The riev paused. "No."

Iari retracted her visor again. Squinted at Char as if her plain biological eyes could see more than battle-rig sensors. "Something wrong with your hexes?"

"Unknown. But it is likely the same phenomenon affecting templar battle-rigs."

Char's aura was laced with fear; Iari's was a vivid blend of vigilance and trailing anger.

"Dispatch. This is Lieutenant—oh, Hrok's fucking *breath*. Luki, your comms dead?"

A breathless moment, behind Luki's visor. Two, three—"Yes sir."

Iari flicked a look sideways. "Gaer?"

He tried, even knowing, from the grey little tesla, how useful that try would be. "Dead as that boneless."

"Right. So no backup. No way to detect Brood except by looking with our fucking *eyes*," Iari said. For Luki's sake, Gaer thought. Certainly she was looking that way, as if she could see through her corporal's faceplate.

"Maybe not," said Gaer, and both Aedian headlamps turned on him like malevolent suns. "Char knew there was something down here."

"I did not know. I suspected. With no evidence."

"That's called intuition. Congratulations. You're the first of your kind to develop it, that we know of." Gaer stepped around the boneless, around Iari, into wide open, rain-slashed streets. "I don't know what the *setat* this effect is, but it's affecting everyone's technology. Let's suppose it's working either by alteration of natural law, or—well, this isn't necessarily *not* that same thing—some kind of hexwork I've never seen. Something *Char's* never seen. Something the priest-alchemists who designed your templar battle-rig never imagined. What fits *that* description?"

"The altar," said Iari. "And if it's working, then Jich'e'enfe's already there and so much for your wards."

"My wards might be working. You don't know. Perhaps we should be buried in boneless right now. Or a small family of tunnelers. My wards might be all that stands between us and the void itself." Pure neefa-shit, that; templar weapons, templar shields, and Char were far more likely to be their saviors.

"Well," said Iari, after a considered moment. "If it's the altar causing all this, we know where it is. Come on."

CHAPTER TWENTY-FOUR

The syn crackled up her spine. Iari pushed it back down, imagined it sinking back into bones and away from muscle and nerve. An arithmancer who could do what Jich'e'enfe could required a more nuanced approach than shield-bash-and-slice. She concentrated on the ache in her leg, which the syn had (almost) erased. Pain was an anchor. Right now, she needed the focus. The syn slowly withdrew its chemical courage, like the ebb of sunlight at dusk.

Very poetic. Iari grimaced at herself. The thing was that her HUD chrono said it was crawling toward dawn now. There should be some kind of brightening in the sky. But instead it seemed even darker.

And it wasn't just the sky. The streetlamps, too, had been growing steadily dimmer the nearer they got to the warehouse, as if the grid that powered them was weakening. This was *not*, thank the Four, a residential district. But still. There should have been more activity, even this time of night. It was as if everyone knew to stay away.

Or, awful thought, the Brood had already moved in and done their work. Every shadow could be stacked with them, swarm and boneless and slicer—

Except no, *no*. That many Brood—surge-level numbers—wouldn't just stay inside. It was dark, it was raining, they'd be out. They'd've spread into Midtown. There'd be *noise*. There'd be evidence, beyond the odd corpse in the street, of their presence.

Besides. Gaer could sense their auras.

That meant there weren't many, and they weren't ranging far. Someone was controlling them. That, as much as the failed rig sensors, told Iari there was some arithmantic, alchemical hexwork at work.

"What's wrong with the teslas?" Luki pointed with the tip of her sword at a flickering streetlamp. "Is that more arithmancy?"

"It is not." Gaer's helmet glowed with dim, dark blue light, at the far edge of comfortably visible. "Note that all of the teslas are losing force. Your headlamps, for instance. Mine, too. It's like a fog." He pointed his faceplate at Iari. Her (yes, dimmer) headlamp flared back its reflection like a dying sun. "I've studied the effect, but not as closely as you have."

"The hell are you on about?"

Gaer did not answer; Char did. "Lieutenant. It feels like Windscar. It feels like *Saichi*."

Which meant: the last push of the surge, when one of the massive, intelligent Brood had come through the fissure, bringing with it a dozen smaller, semi-intelligent sub-commanders and legions of boneless and swarm and slicers. Brood only fought at night; but that day, at Saichi, they're brought the night with them. The sun had gone dim like an eclipse made of black fog.

Except there was no fissure in B-town.

"Lieutenant." Char had stopped again. Was looking backward, drawn up and stiff. No, not looking. *Listening.*

"What is it?" Gaer asked. "And tell me it's not the thundering footsteps of twenty-some riev coming at us."

"No." Char took a careful step. "But it is battle."

So they didn't go straight to the warehouse, after all: they diverted instead up a side street and from there into an alley, Char on point and leading the way, until Iari *saw* the flash of a whitefire weapon through the unnatural dark, and the glint of a shield.

Oh, *here* were the slicers. A whole pack of them, and they'd gotten themselves around a—how many? Iari's HUD lit up with *contact, friendly,* and a scrolling list of designations that Iari didn't have time to read. She counted, instead, the flashes. One, two, three, four templars, one of them showing as *down* in the HUD, all their vitals yellow and dropping toward red.

"On me," she said, because she had people to lead now, and Elements help them.

Then she triggered the syn and charged.

After the fight—because there was always an *after* (there wouldn't be, one day, but not this one)—Iari scuffed through slicer guts and Brood slime and her rig's yellow *toxic environment* flash-warning.

The templar down was a private named Goran; he'd been on point, and the slicer pack had triple-teamed him. But he was still alive, and therefore lucky.

Iari didn't say that out loud. Said instead, "Well done," and "Report," and squeezed as much information out of the templars as she could. Out of Heph, mostly, who snapped his faceplate up at the first opportunity and tipped his face up into the rain and gasped like he hadn't been breathing.

Iari murmured, "Gaer," on the private channel, and "Aura," as Heph reported.

Heph and his team had been out on patrol when all the

streetlamps, all the windows, had gone dark. There'd been a flash from the warehouse first, or maybe just after.

"He's not certain of that," Gaer murmured, private-comm. "I don't think *he* saw it."

Heph had tried comming back to Peshwari (the lieutenant, Heph said, *the* lieutenant, like there was no other), but *those* comms had been down, too. He'd tried to go back to the warehouse, but—

Heph shook his head. "You see what we found, sir." His eyes wandered over Char, who was systematically stomping slicer skulls into paste on the pavement. "Something's wrong with my rig. I can't *see* the Brood. I didn't even know they'd hit us until Goran went down."

"We're having that same problem," Iari said. "Is Peshwari still there? In the warehouse?"

"Far as I know, sir. Madi—Corporal Madi—was on comm with me. Said they'd heard someone in the cellar." Heph's eyes bulged a little bit, white on the edges.

Gaer cleared his throat on the ex-comm, which sounded like an eruption of static. "Tell me, Corporal. Did Lieutenant Peshwari *open* that cellar hatch, do you know?"

Heph turned those fish-round eyes on Gaer. "No—ah. Ambassador? I'm not sure. Madi didn't say.—Sir, we have to get back there."

"We're not leaving anyone," Iari said, and Heph's eyes resumed normal proportions.

The *how* of that personnel retrieval might be tricky. The templars had been attacked in the middle of a small cross street maybe ten minutes (at a walk; at a templar-jog, say half that) from the warehouse. The wounded templar, Goran, was back on his feet, propped up in large part by the wall and one of his squadmates. The slicers had breached his rig at the knee joint. Private Goran wouldn't be walking around much without help, and that help took another templar out of the action. Luki was over there, on one knee in the muck, slapping a patch on the rig, acting as if this sort of thing happened *every* day. Iari's mouth quirked behind the visor. Her new corporal was working out just fine.

She rounded on Heph. "Collect your squad and move out. I want you to follow *this* route." She shot him a map, HUD to HUD. "You see that? We just came that way. There shouldn't be any Brood to slow you down. You get clear of the comm-block, you call up to the Aedis, you report to the Knight-Marshal. Clear?"

Heph wanted to argue. His neck stiffened. His chin came up. Iari retracted her faceplate. Stared down at him through the curtain of rain and the lingering smoky gloom that Brood carried with them. "The Knight-Marshal needs to know what's happening. Private Goran needs medical attention. You get to where you can transmit, you call code red, and you *report*, Corporal." Iari made eyelock. "We'll get Peshwari."

He believed her. She didn't need Gaer's whisper-soft affirmation of that. Conviction damn near glowed on Heph's face, *faith*. Corso would sneer at it, *had* sneered, when he'd taken his discharge and she'd joined the Aedis instead.

Only thing you should trust is yourself. Can't believe you haven't figured that out yet. Thought you were smarter.

And some other sentiments, mostly shouted, mostly profane.

Well, faith or training or stupidity, Heph was moving out, and taking his people with them. Her orders. Which left her, and Luki, and Char, and Gaer, and—

"Someone in the cellar." Gaer drifted alongside her. "You might be, ah, right, about Jich'e'enfe getting past my wards. Could be her down there."

"More worried about what she's doing with that altar. I don't

think all these Brood and this Weep-fissure dark is coincidence."
Iari rolled the syllables in her mouth—*you need to handle it, Gaer,
you're the arithmancer*—and swallowed them. He already knew.
Behind that oilslick shell of a faceplate, she'd bet his face was a
rainbow of worry.

"And here you are, sending away half our fighting force."

"Yeah. Tobin needs a report, and if they *do* run into leftover
Brood up there, they need to survive it. They need all their numbers for that."

Gaer's comm clicked. Or maybe that was his jaw-plate. Click-
click, disapproval, something unvoiced. "Why not send Char with
Goran? Keep the rest of them with us."

"I'd rather have Char." Iari side-eyed the gleaming black visor.
"You don't have to come. You go with Goran, make sure Tobin gets
the report, and then I'll keep Heph and the other two with me."

"Ss. I'm worth more than those three, if there's arithmancy.
And there will be."

Yinal'i'ljat came around the side of the Red Glowing Thing.
Touching it, looked like, leaning on it. Corso controlled a reflexive
shiver. Nothing on this side of the aetherless void would induce
him to touch it. Rather stick his arm in a vat of hot oil. Or into a
hungry swarm. Or wrestle that tunneler he'd seen at Tzcansi's,
which he'd fucking tried to do before that veek had stopped him.

Instead the veek had sent him after Yinal'i'ljat, and now here
he was, having found her.

"Who's there?" Her question sounded so normal, so expected,
he *wanted* to answer. Almost did, before cold sense (fear) slapped
him silent.

Corso sucked himself into the smallest possible shape. He

shouldn't have said anything, slagging stupid to do that. Hope, pray (to the Elements, the old gods, whomever) she could not see very well through that ward.

"Are you one of Tzcansi's people? I thought the templars had chased everyone off." She swayed forward. Touched the bubble and flinched back. He heard a hiss like water on hot metal. Smelled burning meat.

Her pain made him brave. He bared his broken grin at her. "I *am* a templar."

She laughed. *Laughed*, high and sharp as the sound glass makes when it smacks into stone. "No. I don't think you are."

Anger bubbled up in his chest, boiling away the chill. "I know who *you* are. You're the slagging arithmancer who—" He shut his mouth hard. If he was right—and his gut said he was—then she was the person who'd blown up Iari, and that meant she had skill enough to get past the veek. Maybe don't poke too hard at her. Maybe try to figure out, "Why am I here? Why are you?"

She didn't answer him. Of course she didn't. She made a pushing motion at the hex-bubble. "I'm on the wrong side. This needs to go away."

He forbore mentioning the very obvious *hole* in the bubble, on the backside of the Glowing Thing. Was it even slightly possible she didn't know it was there? That she couldn't see that? He blinked. Maybe she couldn't. Maybe he should pretend he couldn't, either.

"Wrong side of what?"

"*Terrible* liar." She moved a little left along the bubble's perimeter. Four abortive little steps and she reversed direction. He would call it pacing, except she was moving like something held together with string and wire and spit.

And she could tell if he lied. Probably some voidspit slagging neefa-shit arithmancy, because don't forget that's what she was, that's why the slagging veek had said *go find her.*

(And remember, for next time: nothing good ever came out of veek territory. Not veek, not wichu. Probably not k'bal, either, but they were all gone so who knew about them.)

"I see, I don't know what, some kind of bubble. Some kind of slagging hex. I can't *do* hexes."

She turned to look at him again. Her featureless wichu eyes caught the Glowing Thing's redness, borrowed it, made it their awful own. "I don't need a hex out of you. I need you to cross the ward, from *your* side to *my* side."

"The fuck would I do that?"

"Because the riev are coming."

That was . . . probably not good. Maybe that's why the templars had retreated. "Let them get you out, then."

"They can't cross this barrier either." She held out her hands to him, palms out. They were smudged, dark, as if she'd been rubbing her hands on soot. "It takes someone living. Riev aren't alive. Let me out, and I'll keep you safe. But if you don't, *if you don't*: then they'll come, and they'll rip you apart."

A faint grating sound came from the hatch, like something dragged across it. Corso caught himself turning to look. Blinked and gritted teeth and *made* himself keep staring at Yinal'i'ljat. "Riev don't kill people."

"I think you know better."

That dead wichu artificer, Pinjat, smashed flat by riev. That had been *her* doing. She'd made that riev kill someone, which should be impossible, because riev only killed Brood and veeks and not even them anymore.

Great time for a revelation. Corso worked backward up another stair. The chill seeping through the hatch found him again.

It prickled over his scalp, through his braids. He reached back and up, right-handed.

"Don't," she said. "You'll die if you open that hatch. There are Brood. Boneless and slicers. I opened a fissure up there."

Cold sweat slicked his face, a fresh wave of it. He sucked air into lungs gone tight and small. "The fuck would you do that? Seems like a bad idea, Brood up there, you down here. Seems like you're trapped."

"Not if you cross the wards. That will break them, and let me out."

"What, you going to control the Brood, too, like the riev?" He shook his head. The hooks in his braids scraped over his coat, too loud. "Better work on that. I saw what happened to Tzcansi."

Yinal'i'ljat staggered away from the bubble's edge, back to the Red Glowing thing. She leaned both hands on it. The Glowing Thing redly illuminated the line of her cheekbone, her nose. She looked—not angry, exactly. Frustrated? Grim.

"I liked Tzcansi. But she got ambitious. I told her, wait, I didn't have Oversight yet, the riev might be unpredictable, use them for *show*. Then she smashed up that bar. I said I'd handle Pinjat, *she* said she could scare him. And then all these fucking templars show up." Her hands moved over the Glowing Thing. "But I have Oversight *now*."

The fuck was Oversight? Something else Iari probably needed to know. It sounded important. And bad.

Corso shoved a shoulder against the hatch. The metal shifted a fraction—not resealed, then, just blocked. It was too much weight for him to shift on his own. And the metal was cold as the void. His shoulder ached after, through coat and clothing, all the way down to the bone. Brood up there already. Riev coming. At least riev would kill Brood. Keep each other busy.

But—templars up there, too. That meant the Aedis would know about the fissure. They'd come. The templars always came. All he had to do was—wait. Keep this crazy bitch talking.

"I don't care about Tzcansi," he said. "Did me a favor, killing her. Not here because of her."

Her hands stilled. "Then why?"

"I got paid to deliver a message. The Five Tribes ambassador's looking for you."

Her lips curled back. Her teeth looked bloody. White stained red by the Glowing Thing. "Always the vakari. Do you know, they used to power their voidships by *splitting* the void? They thought Brood were just unpleasant side effects. Pests to be managed, contained, destroyed. And then, even after they knew better, they kept doing it. Keep *poking*. Vakari are the reason we have a Weep. This multiverse would be better off if we eradicated them."

"B-town has one fucking veek in residence, *one*, and you're trying to tear the place apart to kill him? That's a little extreme."

"B-town is proof of concept," she said. "You don't understand."

"Then explain it to me."

"Come here and cross the barrier. Break it. Let me out, and I'll tell you."

Metal banged overhead, something slamming (being slammed) into the hatch. "Not happening."

"There is no *reason* to help the veeks or the templars."

"There's no reason to help you, either."

"Of course there is. Self-interest. I told you. You won't survive out there, without me."

"Then I'll die out here, and you watch from in there. How's that?"

She stared at him. Then she struggled back to her feet. Slowly, slowly—but not like it hurt her to stand. Deliberately, defiantly, the

way people accustomed to getting their own way did after someone told them no. She snarled something in a language he did not
understand, and the Glowing Thing flared bright as arterial blood.
She lurched back toward the bubble's perimeter, made fists of both
hands and *punched*. The barrier flashed, bright as daylight off mir-
rors, blinding and whitefire hot. The wave of that impact blew
Corso backward, slammed him spine-first into a step, sent a whole
new blast of whiteness sheeting across his vision.

Windscar-winter cold blasted up from the direction of the
Glowing Thing. He knew what was coming. *Knew*, because they
had a particular smell, because he'd *been* in the surge, even if he
hadn't made it to Saichi.

She was opening a fissure down here. She was calling Brood.

Black fog met them at the warehouse doors. It seeped from the
inside, like ink turned to aether. It coiled along the pavement,
smoked up the walls. Iari reckoned it was a good half-meter deep
in there.

"The *hell*." Luki kicked at the pavement. "Sir, that's *ice*."

And snow, too—frozen crystals of rain, anyway, spraying
white and collecting on the pavement. Iari's HUD reported a pre-
cipitous drop in ambient temperature, from damply unpleasant
autumn to the killing cold of a deep winter in Windscar.

Char, impervious, drifted alongside—not quite point, but not
bringing up the rear, either. "Lieutenant. There is a Weep fissure
nearby." Iari could see every line and glowing stroke of the riev's
hexwork.

"Sss. That's *impossible*."

Iari grunted. "You're the one who said Jich'e'enfe could've
made a fissure in her room at the hostel."

"I wasn't *serious*. Not a real fissure. I just thought she had control of the Brood and oh, *setat*. What if she can?"

"Seal your rigs," Iari said, because that was the obvious order, unnecessary and comforting because of that.

"Char," she said. "Get us inside the warehouse."

The locking mechanisms were offline: dead grey panels, no spark when Char jerked the doors open.

Iari raised her shield like she could push back the void, the fog, whatever. Her headlamp stabbed into the murk. Peshwari had set up a wall of crates, presumably meant as a barrier in case someone tried to force entry. Iari hugged close to them, noting the rime collected on the surfaces. She checked her HUD readouts. Still deadly cold out there, but creeping warmer.

"Peshwari!"

The fog swallowed the name. There were no movement alerts on her HUD, either. Dread throbbed in her gut. This kind of quiet meant disaster had been and gone already.

Oh Ptah, oh Hrok, it really was more than a little like Saichi. Then, the fissure-smoke had spread into the surrounding valleys, rendering everything permanent twilight, sending the temperatures into deep winter even though it had been spring. That fog had rendered the aetherships largely useless. That had been high command's reason for sending a unit of templars into the valley. Reconnaissance, and perhaps some judicious sabotage.

Both goals accomplished, but at a cost.

Memory washed red behind her eyelids. The syn responded, sheeting under her skin. She swallowed dust and bitter. This wasn't Saichi. There wasn't some hulking Brood in this warehouse, ready to crack her rig.

"I was wrong," said Gaer then. "There is a very, *very* small fissure, over by the trap door."

Iari moved that way, around the barrier of crates, and yes, there. The fissure hung near the trap door, several meters over the warehouse floor: a darker-than-black gash out of which the not-fog did not so much spill as coagulate, dripping into gravity and atmosphere. A tunneler—or something like a tunneler, limbless and segmented and apparently blind—lay in shiny coils on the floor beneath. There was evidence all along its body of whitefire damage, of battle, of wounding: segments pried apart, piles of steam and slime where its guts had spilled out. Its hide was already starting to smoke as the atmosphere began eating it away.

"Oh, Chaama's bones. Someone's under that thing." Luki's headlamp centered on a fragment of battle-rig just visible under a coil. A greave, looked like, and part of a knee-joint. She knelt beside the tunneler and jabbed it with her sword. The whitefire blade sank a few centimeters into the hide. A little more of its insides came spilling out and spread black and smoking onto the floor.

"I think that's Ly's rig, but where's the *rest*?"

Of Ly, of the rest of the templars. The answer was likely the same. Inside that Brood. Under it. Eaten away entirely in a flood of effluvia.

Ungentle Ptah. Luki was young enough she hadn't fought in the last surge. She'd never seen this before. There was no kind way to teach this lesson.

And no time for mourning, not now. Iari said sharply, briskly, "Get up, Corporal, and stop poking that thing. Those guts touch your rig, you'll have your first rig-breach. You and Char, sweep the warehouse. See if there's anyone else."

There would be, and they'd likely be dead, too.

"Yes sir." Luki lurched away from the fissure, and the tunneler. Char cocked their head—at Iari, then at Luki, at the fissure. Then, no comment, the riev followed Luki.

Gaer edged around the tunneler. "If that fissure spits anything else out, we're in trouble."

"You think it will?"

"The temperature readouts indicate it's warming up, so I guess that means it's resealing. But truth, Iari, I have no *setatir* idea. This is not arithmancy of any kind I recognize, wichu or vakari. Perhaps Jich'e'enfe prayed to whatever gods that altar is meant to represent."

"Prayer doesn't work like that." If it did, if it ever had, Saichi wouldn't've happened. Windscar, either, or the dozen battles won and lost along the fissure in the waning years of the last surge. "Can you do something arithmantic to hurry the fissure's closing?"

"Not a prayer."

Unfunny laughter clotted her throat. She squeezed her eyes closed. The syn throbbed under her skin, through her bones. Dead templars and dead Brood and a voidspit *fissure*, and she was still alive. Saichi all over again.

"Sir!" And then Luki choked on whatever she meant to say next, so Iari knew what she'd found, if not a specific *who*.

"By the hatch," said Char.

Peshwari's battle-rig lay across the cellar door, sprawled and twisted in ways neither rig nor body inside had been intended to bend. There was a crack in the plating just under the dorsal power cell. Frost had collected there, where the venting air inside had frozen on its way out. There was—oh, ungentle Ptah, *other* fluid frozen there, too. A lot of it. Almost black, in spite of Iari's headlamp's best effort (still watery, still weak, in the fissure-effect).

Iari retracted her shield and turned him partway over, gently as she could. Oh, *try* the impossible. Sometimes the Elements delivered a miracle. "Peshwari? You hear me?"

Gaer came and squatted beside her. He touched Peshwari's rig with a fingertip. "No aura."

Not today. She'd used up her miracles at Saichi. Tobin's rig had looked like this, except the runoff there had been liquid, and obviously, unmistakably red as it ran out of him. Iari pressed her hand over the gap in Peshwari's armor (she had then, too, with Tobin). Crystals of frozen blood crunched under her gauntlet, squeezed up between her fingers. The rig yielded a little bit to her pressing, sank further into the wound. At Saichi, Tobin's rig had been pierced and then peeled. Claws, not impact. And Tobin had been *breathing* in there, conscious and issuing orders.

One of which had not been *get me out of here*. Peshwari wouldn't've said that, either, if he'd survived the initial hit. The man had been an ass most the time, always a little bit of a bigot, but he'd died fighting. Had, by all evidence, flung himself at something— that tunneler, the fissure, whatever came running out—and been flung back hard enough that he broke on landing.

She started trying to move him, one-handed—because *damned* if she'd put her weapon aside with that fissure still open, no matter Gaer's suggestion it was trying to seal.

Gaer added his efforts to hers. "It looks like he bent the door when he landed. It also looks"—as Peshwari shifted aside, leaving a smear of bloody ice—"like the wheel was already dogged. Whoever, or whatever, was down there, they were letting it out."

Iari darted a glance back, at the fissure. "Luki," she said. "Char. I need you to stay up here. If something goes wrong down there, or if that fissure tries to get big again, you close this hatch and you make sure it won't open. Then you get out and report to Knight-Marshal Tobin."

"Sir," said Luki. She didn't sound happy.

"Yes, Lieutenant," said Char. The riev had eyes only for the fissure.

Iari caught her breath on the last name she meant to say. Gaer was—Hrok's breath, Gaer was, had been, just her assignment. Someone to escort on his diplomatic (and more often, recreational) forays into B-town. Someone who complicated her evening hours with requests to *experience the local culture*. It wasn't his job to come with her into *whatever* was down there. It was hers. He wasn't even part of her unit.

"Gaer—"

"I know. Yes. I'm with you, you have point." Lightly, easily, as if this was a small matter not worth his attention.

"Can't ask you to do this."

"Sss. You're not. I'm volunteering." He pointed his visor at her. His tone slid into serious. "Though you should let *me* go first. I'm the arithmancer. If you trust me."

Iari took hold of the hatch wheel with both hands. "Fine. You take point."

CHAPTER TWENTY-FIVE

A gust of cold came out of the hatch. Gaer eased himself through the gap. Not even all the way inside, his HUD lit up with *motion detected*. Not unexpected, and also not a problem. He had an array of battle-hexes preloaded on the rig for *just* such occasions, which involved things generally lethal. Then his arms-turing told him it had acquired a target, something his jacta could hit. It couldn't be Brood, then, because his HUD hadn't seen *them* all *setatir* night.

Jich'e'enfe, he thought next. Then he saw a whirlwind of hook-studded braids and a fluttering leather coat. Corso—that man had the blessing of all the dark lords, every Element—scrabbling across the cellar floor, careening off pillars. He sprawled flat, suddenly, tripping over apparent nothing, and whipped around to stab (with a *monofil*?) at what Gaer's visor said was empty air.

Which meant Brood. And yes, *there*, when he squinted past his HUD's display, using his flesh-and-blood vision: a darker-than-black flicker at the limits of his headlamp, asymmetrical, with a glowing pentad of eyes like malicious moons. Gaer unclipped his jacta and fired a whitefire bolt over Corso's head—please, let the man keep *flat*—and missed the boneless, *fine*, that was expected with Brood, but he startled it. It slewed into the dark, toward the source of the cold, said the HUD, which was where Gaer's memory placed the altar.

Gaer tucked his shoulder and dove, skipped all the stairs and rolled back to his feet at the bottom (Iari's rig wouldn't do that; but SPERE liked a more flexible frame). He landed almost on top of Corso—who could scrabble *very* fast, having crossed a swath of cellar floor on hands and slipping boots and sheer terror. Gaer grabbed a fistful of shredded leather coat and hauled him upright. Corso was bleeding, Gaer noted. Nose. Ears. Both hands.

Then came a flash of an Aedian shield, and Iari shouldered past Gaer and advanced into the cellar. Behind her, the hatch banged shut.

So much for letting *him* take point.

Corso howled as the hatch closed, and clawed at Gaer's wrist. "Don't, let me out, you *can't*—"

"Corso!" And what should he tell the man, relax, he was safe? Not *setatir* likely; but, "Iari's here, I'm here, we'll handle the Brood."

Corso's eyes—wide, white-rimmed and shot with red—locked onto Gaer's visor like he could see through it. Sense came seeping back, pushing the Brood-panic aside, letting a whole new flavor of fear rush in. "Don't let Iari cross that barrier, that's what she *wants*, she needs someone to cross from the outside to break it, don't let her—"

Too many of the same pronouns, *she* and *her*. But Gaer could guess well enough who was meant. "I'll stop her. Let go, yes?"

And then Gaer realized, with a sudden queasy twist, that it was still void-cold in the warehouse. That Corso's sweat-and-blood hands were stuck to his rig's metal skin.

Corso realized it too. He grimaced, then ripped himself free. He flung himself toward the steps, feet kicking and slipping in yes, blood, plenty of it, running from under the shreds of that coat, before it congealed in the cold.

Which left Gaer free to help Iari. She'd put her back against one of the supporting pillars. There was one boneless hanging off her shield, another circling around behind. A third testing the edge of her axe. A fourth in the shadows, trying to flank her.

Iari's voice punched through his comms, low and fierce and just this side of gleeful. "I got this. Get *her*."

Right, the other *her*. Gaer spun toward the altar. Easy to find it: the sole source of light (except for headlamps) in the cellar, red and purple and hazy as dawn fog off the Rust. A shape that looked wichu and female stood at the edge of his wards, which were not the solid bubble they should be. Bits were flapping and fluttering like Corso's coat. *That* was unexpected. How would you do that to a perfectly solid ward—ah. Yes. Materialize inside them. Which meant the *setatir-m'rri* must've put her portal signs inside his perimeter, which meant he had been close enough to scan it before, and certainly was *now*—and yes. There. A modest, sensible distance from the altar, a neat little grid just inside the edge of his wards, visible now that he knew what to look for.

Spare the self-congratulations. He hadn't noticed those sigils at the time, not even a glimmer. That was stupid. It was *luck* that he'd laid his ward around them. (If he had real luck then the wards would've cut her in half, and this would all be academic.)

And wards or not, she wasn't helpless, *obviously*, with fissures upstairs and Brood running amok and his ward partly shredded. But how, *how*—

Jich'e'enfe smacked the inside of the ward with open palms. White light spiderwebbed away from both points of impact. It looked painful—she appeared to be screaming—and it *had* to be doing damage to her bare hands, but that gesture wasn't going to bring down the wards, so *why*—

"Gaer!" It was Corso. "Behind you!"

Gaer whipped sideways, spun and raised the jacta. A boneless, five-eyed and open-mouthed, came slither-running from a section of the cellar he'd thought was empty.

Gaer launched one of his pre-loaded hexes: bent the light from his headlamp, distilled it to a cutting beam, sent it spearing into the boneless. He caught it in the solid middle of its pentad of eyes. The boneless's head—the flapping sack on which it kept its eyes and its mouth, there was no skull—shredded outward. Gaer's HUD reported absolutely nothing to see, no Brood. But it *did* note a patch of excessive temperature variation, over *there*, in the cellar's far corner.

Gaer spared a look, ran magnification on his HUD, and yes! There was another fissure (which explained where Brood were coming from). Except this fissure had materialized a meter below the plane of the cellar floor, as if the stone had simply ceased to be for a snaggly little gash of nothing. His HUD reported an incremental rise in temperature. That little fissure was already closing, too.

Jich'e'enfe was watching him, hands splayed, ready to slap the wards again. Ready to, what, open another *setatir* fissure? Two problems with that. One, she shouldn't be able to hex anything through the wards, and she clearly was, so she wasn't just using arithmancy. There was something *else* to her equations. And two, worse by far, a tesser-hex was meant to bore a tunnel *through* the void, point to point. The vakari battle-hexes that had made the Weep had been a mistake (no anchoring equations, no destination, just opening void), and here was this *setatir* Jich'e'enfe replicating that stupidity. On purpose. *Weaponizing* it. Micro-Weeps on demand, stocked with Brood from their source.

How rattled around in Gaer's head, *how is she doing this?* She'd beaten him at arithmancy twice already, more than twice. Dropped a whole fucking *house* on Iari, killed Brisk Array, and now she was making fissures past his wards that should have prevented *anything*. Not because he'd made them, but because of the *setatir* equations, the math, the numbers that described reality. You could reshape reality (there was a whole Aedian priesthood that made a habit of that), but there were *rules*, too. Jich'e'enfe was cheating: some *setatir* trick he didn't know, some way around every rule of arithmancy he'd ever learned.

Jich'e'enfe pressed one hand to the inside of the wards. He saw the sparks where flesh touched hexwork. The altar flared briefly, glowing brighter. Then the sunken micro-fissure squeezed out another boneless. It clawed its way out of the void-gash in the floor as the fissure widened a jot and the cold readings on Gaer's HUD stabilized at *damned lethal.*

Then like a jacta bolt (not whitefire, just a conventional, solid projectile) to the forehead, Gaer got it. She was practicing some heretical variant of Aedian alchemy, but instead of taking one sort of thing and making it into *some other* thing, she was making *something* from apparent nothing. Except it wasn't nothing: she was using organic matter as the fuel. Herself, at the moment, her blood. Probably why she'd wanted Corso to cross the wards. If he died on them (because he would have, messily), she could have used his death to widen the fissure to fuel some sort of hex with that altar. Pre-Landing tenju myth was full of things dying in bloody and inventive ways to appease imagined gods. Only maybe the gods weren't imagined (Vakari heresy, yes, but that didn't mean it was not true). Maybe something *out there* took that death-power and gave power back. Or maybe it just really liked blood.

Whether that *something* was really the old tenju gods, or whether this time the Brood had answered some heretic prayer instead, or if this was another new and unholy wichu creation—was a matter for further study. Later. *After* he didn't die here.

Gaer retracted his visor. The cold bit in deep. His breath plumed out, crystallized, sprinkled out like snow. Iari shouted something at him, having to do with seals and what the *fuck* was he doing. He couldn't spare breath to tell her; he needed his optic unimpeded by a battle-rig's sensors, when that rig couldn't even see the *setatir* Brood right over there.

He cycled the optic through the layers of aether until living and nonliving and Brood became mathematical abstractions. Equations, variables, formulae. The optic didn't have all the battle-hexes preloaded. Well. That was all right. *He* was perfectly capable. He hexed himself a simple energy-dispersing shield on the most outer aetheric layer. Then he walked up to the wards, aiming at Jich'e'enfe, who took a reflexive pair of steps back. He could feel the not-really-heat coming off the barrier. It wasn't *really* plasma, manifestation of Iari's beloved Ptah, but rather electricity, that fifth element that ran through all the states of matter. That kind of power meant these wards could stop his heart, or burn his body from the inside out—and would, unless he managed to match his hexwork shield oscillations to the ward *just so*, for *just long enough*.

Gaer closed his naked eye, and synced his shield equations with the ward's through the optic, and—

Flash-white sheeted over his rig, flared behind one closed lid. The same flash made no impression on his open eye behind the optic, which saw a phalanx of equations slide into each other, mesh, *match*.

—stepped through.

He opened his other eye and stared down at Jich'e'enfe. Blink, and he brought his optic back through the aetheric layers, until her aura blazed every shade of outrage and hatred and—as her feral grin pulled one side of her mouth—*fear*.

Wichu didn't like hand-to-hand combat.

Gaer sprang at her, swiped—missed, when she dodged (sprawled) out of the way. She landed on her back, shoved herself onto an elbow, and thrust her free hand out at him (the palm shredded, blackened, flesh hanging in strips, like Corso's). His optic saw the sudden concentration of phlogiston, every *setatir* particle within the radius of the broken ward coming together at once, at her bidding.

Oh. *This* trick again.

He threw himself sidelong, dropped his visor (too slow, both of those things); closed his right eye and slapped a cobbled-together deflecting hex at the explosion. The phlogiston ignited and ripped away all the breathable air, replaced it with skin-bubbling heat and lung-searing *nothing*. Gaer felt himself hit the altar (a whole *new* sensation, a wrongness rather than pain, that started somewhere deep inside bone and organ). Then his face-plate sealed and he could breathe again. The explosion burst against the interior wall of the ward, a ball of lightning and fire that somehow missed Jich'e'enfe entirely.

Gaer picked himself up. She was a better arithmancer. Fine. But unlike the Brood, she hadn't hexed herself invisible to his HUD. Which meant his arms-turing could target her.

He ripped the jacta out of its clip, leveled, *fired*.

Jich'e'enfe slapped his first bolt aside with a hex, sent it across the inside of his much-abused ward, punching holes in equations already stretched to breaking. But the next bolt (*lock*, said the arms-turing) hit her in the belly. Burned through. Smoke, little licks of flame from her shirt, her coat. She screamed and convulsed. Gaer shoved himself off the altar (alert, his HUD told him: radiation spike) and onto one knee. *Target: acquired*, said his HUD, and he squeezed off a third shot.

Or almost did. His optic flared blind with alerts, and his HUD did the same a sliver of a second after that with impossible warnings.

He thought she was making another fissure at first, but then he saw the equations. Oh dust and void, oh five dark lords. She was sketching a tesser-hex, a real one, a genuine hole in the void to *some other place*. She wasn't just a better arithmancer than *him*, she was better than anyone he'd ever heard about, read about. And she was about to kill him, because a tesser-hex made connections between locations in the void, which made a tunneler's suction seem like baby's breath, suction against which his dirtside-certified battle-rig would offer no protection, and no atmosphere when his rig came apart.

That it would kill her, along with him, was no comfort.

The tesser-hex opened: a whorl of purple-black-blue, a confetti splash of equations and variables and airless, murderous cold. His faceplate ruptured first, the weakest point, blowing outward. He squeezed eyes and nostrils shut against the suck of vanishing atmosphere, and pushed his awareness into the aether, until he could see Jich'e'enfe's equations, burned white on the backs of his eyelids. And all he had to do was smudge just *one* of her variables, that was all, and he could close the *setatir* thing.

It would take seconds, but he didn't *have* those: the tesser-hex was already dragging him in, as it reached for its second anchor, as the *nothing* tried to fill itself with—

—*Something* slammed into him, with speed and force enough

to throw him sidelong. Numbers slipped loose from his mental grasp as he landed hard on the stone, partway onto his back, partway under Iari (because it *was* Iari). He felt the grinding through the plates on his rig, she was going to crush him flat—but she was pushing off him, keeping one knee across his gut, and most of her weight. As *if* she could hold them down, as if an Aedian battle-rig and a templar could stand against a tesser-hex's pull.

And then Gaer realized he *wasn't* sliding anymore. And maybe that was partly because Iari's rig was just that heavy (or that hexed), or. . . The tesser-hex was still growing, reaching, and Gaer snaked his awareness through the aether and roiling equations and yes, *there*: the second anchor point. There was something like gravity on that side, something that equalized the drag on *this* location. He chased the numbers a little further, because there must be coordinates, a place on a *map*.

He found—no, *not* void, not that aetherless place where spacers lived in their ships and stations, though it was the same blinding black. This was the layer of the multiverse where Brood lived, the place Gaer had studied most of his adult life. Which meant Jich'e'enfe had what, anchored her tesser-hex into the Weep? That the Weep had actual interior coordinates? That was impossible. *All* of this was impossible.

Gaer seized those impossible numbers (one for each dimensional point on the grid, just like any location). He stored them in his optic. In his rig, too, in case. This was data. Important. He was still breathing (somehow), but that might not continue. But if he saved those numbers, maybe *someone* would recover that data and use it.

His rig's alert dragged him back into his body, into the mundane aether, into smeared vision and oh *setat*, his face hurt. Iari had gotten off him, finally, damn near cracked his armor with the force of her departure. As he tried to breathe (not going well), she raised her shield and crouch-walked toward the gaping hole Jich'e'enfe had punched in the cellar's reality. He couldn't see Jich'e'enfe, just this impossible hole. A massive wound, bigger than her fissures, same bottomless dark. That *was* the Weep, believe that.

Iari said something, an unidentifiable smudge of sound. (Make note: not much air in the Weep, but *some* air, for Iari to be audible.) Gaer kept blinking, everything gone smeary and dim. Fingers (tentacles? *something*) reached over the rim of her shield: boneless and impossibly long and huge and *barbed*. Iari's rig sparked, all those heretical hexes coming online, burning the Brood even as its slime chewed into the alloy, even as it wrapped its limbs (so *many*) around her legs, over the shield and around that wrist. A tentacle coiled up her weapon-arm, sliding like hot tar, raising smoke and sparks. The hexes *should* have made it let go, but instead its grip coiled tighter, oh *setat*, like it was going to rip her apart.

Gaer tried to cycle his optic, to sink back into the aether and gather up numbers and equations and *do* something. He heard (thought he heard) Corso shouting, and the shriek of stressed battle-rig as Iari tried to twist loose (no luck, the Brood was too big, too determined). But he was watching when she jerked her axe up for one final strike, before the Brood got that arm pinned.

A brightness started to gather on her axe's edge, a whiteness as brilliant as the void was dark. Some final build-up of whitefire, Gaer reckoned, that would burn out the weapon, that might make the Brood let her go. Too bright to look at, even through the optic—

But *all* of Iari looked like that now, every seam on the battle-rig bleeding that same brilliance, as if the woman inside had gone nova. As if the light was going to split the armor.

The axe came down, *chop*.

A column of plasma erupted, punched up, into (through? void and dust, yes, *through*) the ceiling, presumably through the floor. Through the Brood. For a heartbeat Gaer saw its silhouette, tentacles and fluttering sucker-mouths, the whole of it (bigger than the cellar, still sliding out of the tesser-hex field) fluttering like a canvas in strong wind. Whitefire picked out every contour of it, lit the Brood from the inside. A web of what must've been vessels backlit like a map, and a fistful of pulsating hearts. Then the whitefire leapt even further, and spread across the tesser-hex portal like flames across alcohol, blue and hissing.

And then came a *crack!* that Gaer felt all the way to his bones. The plasma column vanished. He was left with the Brood's afterimage burned on his retinas, and the sick certainty he really *was* blind now. The tesser-hex closed with an audible *bang* as the atmosphere rushed into the gap it left. Smells came with sound: ozone and petrichor, charred meat (oh *setat*, was that *him*?), hot polysteel.

Gaer's left eye came back in stages, behind the optic (his right eye stayed resolutely screwed shut). He saw a blank sheet of stone where the altar had been, as if it had been blast-melted smooth. Jich'e'enfe was (of course) gone. The tesser-hex, in its closing, had cut off large parts of the tentacled Brood. What was left seemed more asymmetrical than usual, and very dead. Iari was methodically chopping its remnants into smaller, smoking fragments.

Her rig had reverted to normalcy. No glowing seams. No blinding light. Just the headlamp and the small constellation of teslas on her backplate, so templars could find each other in the dark.

Gaer pushed himself onto his side. Then a wobbly crouch. He swallowed. Tried to flare his plates and lost all breath, all vision, for a moment. Something was very wrong with one side of his face. Burn, maybe, from the radiation. Or impact, from when Iari had landed on him. He couldn't remember it. But whatever, whenever, his optic had taken damage, too: his vision all spiderweb cracks and fracture-white lines, in the only working eye. He tried to say Iari's name and coughed instead, wheezed, drooled something dark and wet (not unlike that dead Brood) onto the stone.

Oh, that wasn't good.

"Gaer," he heard, as if down a long tunnel. That was Corso's voice, Corso pulling at his rig, Corso's face thrust into his. He *must* look bad, to earn that kind of look from a man who looked like Corso did.

"Oh fuck." Corso turned, all the cords in his neck standing like cables. "Iari!"

And seconds (forever) later, she appeared over Corso's shoulder. All Gaer could see was Aedian templar, a rig sealed and glowing with hexwork, and for a heartbeat Gaer was sure *she* wasn't under there anymore. That Iari had burned up in plasma, that it was just the rig working out the very last orders it had gotten through the needle-socket from her nanomecha.

Then her visor snapped up. Her headlamp chipped out her features, casting them as bone and shadow. Gaer's gaze snagged on her capped tusk. He stared hard at it. His concentration felt . . . leaky. Like if he *didn't* stare, he'd dissolve, bone and flesh and everything, into a puddle beside the Brood-slime.

Iari crouched beside him. She should have been firing off questions, *where did Jich'e'enfe go? Where is the altar? What happened?* Instead she said his name, "Gaer," like *I'm sorry.*

So he was in bad shape, then. Well. He knew that already. What he did not know, what he *needed* to know, was: "What was that? What did you do?"

Because he had seen footage of templars in battle, and priests, and had *never* seen something like what she'd done, ever, not even in fiction's imaginings.

"Don't know." Her voice came out level, cool. Only a little rough on the edges. Her features were stark in the headlamp's backsplash. "Killed the Brood, though. That's what matters."

"More than that." Corso sounded a lot like Gaer felt. "You closed the fissure. You turned into fucking *lightning*."

She glanced at him. "*Gaer* closed the fissure."

"No," Gaer said. "I didn't."

Iari's jaw flexed. *Now* there was fear, just the littlest raggedy bit of it, eroding the edge of her calm. *Now* she asked the obvious question: "Where's Jich'e'enfe? Did she escape?"

"She's dead." Please, five dark lords, that was true. A tesser-hex needed stupid amounts of power. Usually that meant a ship's plasma core; if she'd been using *herself*, like she had with the altar, she'd be nothing but ashes. And even if that hadn't killed her: "She opened a tesser-hex into the Weep. She couldn't survive in there." Please, dark lords, *that* was true, too. Jich'e'enfe, twice dead.

"And the altar? Did she take it with her?"

Oh, excellent question. "Destination stored in the optic. And the rig. *Numbers*." Gaer tried to lift a hand and point, for emphasis, and almost fell on his face.

Iari caught his arm, just below the spike-concealing fin. "Great. Now shut up. Can you stand? Don't answer. Just nod."

Nodding would hurt worse than speaking. He was sure of that. He clamped his teeth, defiant. "Ss. Yes."

He thought so. Maybe. He clawed himself steady on her gauntlet and let her haul him upright. Hung there, while he found (while his rig found) balance.

Which was how he heard Luki's voice, breathless, leaking through the comms in Iari's rig.

"Lieutenant?"

"We're alive. How's your fissure?"

"Gone. But sir. The riev are here. All of them."

CHAPTER TWENTY-SIX ≡≡≡

Iari's syn rallied. Tried to, anyway: sparks instead of lightning, stuttering along her nerves. "Coming." She ached, bone to skin and back again, and still she wanted to drop Gaer and sprint up there. Except drop him now, he might *stay* down. And Corso was in no condition to help anyone—

Corso. Huh. He materialized beside her, hands on her rig, trying to grip and pull and slipping from the blood. There was blood on his face, too, and the shattered root of a tusk jutting up. "Iari, listen. That wichu called 'em. Said she controlled 'em now. Said *Oversight.*"

Wonderful. "Luki. What're they doing? They hostile?"

"No. Not . . . yet?" A gulp of air. "They're just *standing* there. Lieutenant?"

"Right.—Here. Take Gaer."

"No, no." Gaer rolled his naked eye at her. "I can hex riev traps."

That seemed optimistic. He couldn't fight off a wet neefa kit at this point. What remained of his left jaw-plate dangled on strands of raw meat. It looked worse (please, Ptah) than it was, in the blast-blue of her headlamps. It didn't seem like someone should be able to talk with that kind of jaw damage, but this was Gaer.

"Default setting for riev is *kill vakari*. You stay with Corso."

She pelted up the rest of the stairs and burst out into the warehouse—dim-normal, and absence of light instead of void-bleed from a fissure. Which was, yes, closed, thank the Four.

"Luki," she started to say; but then she got clear of the dead tunneler, of dead Peshwari, and her voice dried up.

Char stood alone, puddles of melted ice and the last tendrils of fissure-fog curling around their legs, all their hexwork lit up and glowing. And beyond them: the rest of B-town's riev, a hedge of glowing tesla eyes, blues and greens and one lone, startling purple. They'd come in hard. The doors looked like Gaer's visor. Peshwari's barrier of crates was just splinters. The riev ranged the width of the warehouse, curved in a half-circle around Char. They hadn't come a step beyond them, like they'd drawn a line across the floor. Might've been crates themselves, except for the slow glowing throb of their hexwork.

"Why'd they stop?" Luki had her voice mostly under control.

At a guess: "Riev don't kill riev."

Riev had always been on the same side, always linked, always moving as one. And now there was Char, standing alone. It had to be habit stopping them, or confusion. Or, Blessed Four, *loyalty* to another one of their kind.

Iari heard scraping behind her: the hard *clang* of polyalloy as Gaer shambled and staggered, the softer rasp of Corso's boots.

The riev didn't move, exactly; but their focus shifted, and their intent with it. From neutrally menacing to hostile.

"Char," said Iari. "Can they hear me?"

"Yes," said Char, and at the same instant:

"Yes," from twenty-odd vocal apparatuses, same cadence, same pitch.

Iari brought her shield arm around, raised it—deployed the

shield, in a crackle and flash of officialdom. Templars held rank on the field. "Why are you here? Report."

"Oversight commanded."

"*Setatir* Jich'e'enfe."

"Gaer, shut up." Iari's heart rattled harder than anything the syn had ever managed. "*What* did Oversight command?"

That awful chorus again: "Oversight said come here."

"And now?"

"Oversight is silent."

Oh, ungentle Ptah, let that mean Jich'e'enfe was dead. "Good. Then you can stand down." Iari jabbed her axe-shaft at the decomposing tunneler. "Fissure's closed. Brood are dead."

The riev rippled like a field of lethal wheat in a sudden breeze. "There is a vakar."

Char shifted. "Vakari are not the enemy."

Silence. Take that as riev disagreement.

Iari stepped even with Char. The rig's visor resealed itself: rig-reflex, guided by implant nanomecha, because that's what a battle-rig *did* when surrounded by enemies. Her syn was sure she was in danger. Her arms-turing was more ambivalent: it found the riev, and mapped them to her HUD, but their icons remained stubbornly green-lit. Riev were *friends*.

Please, gentle Mishka, that was still true.

"Vakari are not the enemy," Char repeated, as if there were exactly one enemy at any time. Maybe there was, for riev. "Check protocols."

And again, the riev chorus: "Code incomplete."

Which meant—what? Jich'e'enfe had been rewriting command codes to make riev kill vakari again? Void and dust. If they got through this, *if*, she'd make Gaer teach her basic theory just so she could follow along in the fucking conversations.

Not a templar's job, though. Conversations. Negotiations. And yet, here she was. "Riev. Stand down. The vakar is no threat. That's an order."

"Ss. They *can't* stand down. They don't get *choice*. They're weapons."

Half his face hanging off, and he still wouldn't shut up. Iari raised her voice for the riev audience. "Char can choose."

"*I* am a templar initiate." Char's voice rolled like distant thunder.

The pronoun caused consternation: a buzz among the riev, like twenty-two processors whirring into overdrive. Iari half expected curling smoke, sparks from the hexwork.

"Stand down," Iari repeated. "You have been decommissioned. The command codes you've got are false orders. Oversight has been compromised. Acknowledge."

Silence. A few of the riev shifted position. One of them—midsized, features stylized human and sexless and oddly beautiful—leaned the barest fraction forward, as though trying to get a better look at Gaer. It was surreal, like a scene from the end of a heroic drama. Argue with riev. Persuade things that were maybe people but maybe not that they didn't need to do what they'd been made for.

The alternative was, what, fight? So choose surrealism.

"Hrok's breath, you *saw* the ambassador, *this vakar*, with me already in the city. You know he's a, a *friend*."

The humanoid riev tilted its head a fraction. "Oversight identifies all vakari as enemy."

"And what does Oversight say about Brood?"

"Corso, shut him *up*."

"You want me to rip the rest of his jaw off?"

"Maybe." But it was a good question. "Riev—the one in front. You. Yes. What's your designation?"

The humanoid riev lifted its chin a fraction. "This one is Winter Bite."

"All right, Winter Bite. What *does* this unauthorized Oversight code say about Brood?"

Winter Bite hesitated. "That Brood are not." A pause, where something with lungs would've drawn breath. "The command code is not complete."

"Extrapolate the code. *Guess.*" Gaer sounded worse. Weaker, threadier. *Wetter.* His face was bad, all right; but he might have damage she couldn't see, too. Might be filling that battle-rig with blood. Or his lungs.

Winter Bite tilted its face toward Gaer. The barest adjustment, which echoed through twenty-one other riev after a beat.

They *had* moved simultaneously, just a minute (three-point-two seconds, said her HUD) ago. They were dropping out of sync. Or, happy thought, developing twenty-two separate desires to kill Gaer.

Winter Bite dropped each word out, with a beat in between. "Extrapolation: that Brood are no longer the enemy."

Gaer made a sloppy hissing sound. Laughter. Pain. The last gasp of a dying vakar.

"That's fucking neefa-shit." Corso was *not* laughing. "Fucking *fissure.* Fucking, what is it, a tunneler over there? Dead templars all the fuck over? You think the Brood are your fucking *friends*?"

"Sss's what Jich'e'enfe wants them to think." Gaer got the words out. Somehow. "The chip. This is what it was *for.* Make riev into *vessels* for Brood. With Oversight, she could *make* them take it."

Ptah's left fucking *eye.* Iari risked a glance back, at Corso, at Gaer draped over him like a battle-rigged cloak. At Char, who did *not* turn their head—being wiser, perhaps, about what their fellow riev might attempt.

One of the riev on the periphery—smallish, bipedal, the top of its skull a faceted sensor array like a crystal tear—took a half step out of formation, back and sideways. "Brood are hostile."

"Concur," said a second riev.

"Concur," said a third.

And then they were all saying it, overlapping syllables that died, finally, with Winter Bite's final, bitten-off *r*.

"Brood are the enemy," Winter Bite repeated. "Templars are allies."

"And vakari? *This* vakar?"

Winter Bite said nothing. Oh ungentle Ptah, let them defy their command lines one more time. Let them *choose*.

Then, *then* Iari heard it: the bone-deep thrum of an inbound hopper engine. A blinding-bright circle of light stabbed down into the alley. The riev turned toward the alley, all of them, pointing with whatever optical attachments they had. And then, ragged as a new line of recruits, they peeled back and opened a corridor to the warehouse doors just as the hopper finished its descent.

The hatch opened before it touched pavement, and Keawe dropped out: scarred rig, massive, visor raised. She aimed for Iari, with barely a sidelong glance at the riev. More templars came spilling out in her wake, Windscar insignia painted on armor almost as battered as Keawe's. *They* focused on the riev: deployed shields and weapons forming a barrier as inspiring as it would be useless.

Keawe walked down that templar corridor and stopped in front of Iari.

"Lieutenant. We heard there was trouble. Seems like you've handled it."

Iari raised her visor. Should feel relief, felt reluctance instead, like cold corrosion in her belly. "Yes sir. But the ambassador's in bad shape. You bring a priest?"

"Sister Iphigenia is with us." Keawe's stare speared past Iari. Her lip curled. "And who's *that*?"

"Corso Risar," Corso snapped. "Private reconnaissance and investigat—"

"My contractor, sir. Jich'e'enfe abducted him. He needs help, too."

Corso made a choking noise. Iari ignored him. "Jich'e'enfe was impersonating Yinal'i'ljat. She was using the altar to control Brood, and she opened a fissure. Which closed, sir. The wichu, the altar, the Brood—everything gone. No other survivors."

Keawe's gaze came back, bleak and black as any fissure. "Understood. What are the riev doing here?"

"Oversight, sir. Apparently Jich'e'enfe turned it back on, but she hadn't finished rewriting the code."

"Huh." Keawe's spacer-stiff features softened, just around the eyes. "You did good, Lieutenant. Get yourself and your people onto the hopper. We've got it from here." Her visor dropped. Comms and commands must've happened, closed-channel, because three more templars detached from riev-watching and trotted into the warehouse. Keawe followed them.

So that was it, then. Mission complete. Not *accomplished*, because this wasn't a victory. It was the same hollowed-out feeling Iari had felt at Saichi, except her syn was still sputtering, sending little jolts through her limbs, her skull, across her vision. Part of her wasn't sure the fight was over.

Not sure that part wasn't wrong, but even so. Iari willed the syn to stand down, be at least as reasonable as the riev. A pair of Windscar templars broke ranks to take hold of Gaer, and began helping (dragging) him toward the hopper. Iari beckoned to Corso. "Come on."

He rolled his eyes at her, but he went. Iari could see Iffy

waiting at the top of the hopper's ramp, bouncing from foot to foot. Keawe must've given her orders to stay on board.

"Luki. Char." Iari gestured them to follow. She took a last look at the warehouse—the tunneler, Peshwari, the riev waiting behind a hedge of templars.

One of Keawe's larger templars (tenju, bet on it) detached from the barricade line and moved to intercept Char before they could walk through the door. He thrust his axe between Luki's back and Char's chest and just missed, *barely*. Char's hexwork flared up and threw sparks, it was that close.

Char stopped. Luki got another step before *she* noticed and turned back.

And by then Iari had closed the distance, riding a spike of syn and temper. She retained enough sense—*just*—to retract her axe and clip it to her rig en route, so that when she struck the Wind-scar templar's weapon aside she used just her empty gauntlet. One hit for his arm, to knock his axe out of line. A second hit with her fist, syn-quick and syn-hard, in the middle of his chestplate.

"Corporal"—she could just read the battle-rig's insignia through her syn-red haze—"stand *down*." It was becoming a voidspit mantra. "The hell are you doing?"

"Orders, sir. Detain the riev."

"Char's a templar. *My* templar. So stand aside."

The corporal's visor was down. No telling his expression; but her voice said, "Sir," after a moment. There should've been a *sorry*.

The syn wanted (blood, violence) further conflict. Iari settled for crowding the corporal aside so that Char could get past. Iari stared at herself in the other templar's visor: capped tusk, scar, narrow eyes.

Then, when Luki said, "Sir, we're on board," she turned and went up the ramp.

Iffy was already working on Gaer. Iari made herself busy with Corso, who'd scrunched into the furthest corner of bench farthest from the hatch and ramp.

"I think that templar got orders from Keawe," he said, as Iari grabbed a roll of polymesh from Iffy's kit and knelt in front of him.

"Of course he did. Give me your hands."

"You hear me? What happened out there, on the ramp with Char. That was orders. They've got comms in those helmets."

"I know how battle-rigs work." The damage to his hands looked skin-deep, mostly; but it was burn-ugly, and wrapping them would be too fine for battle-rig gauntlets. Iari started to strip hers off: triggered the seals, got the *breach* warnings all over her HUD. Her syn was still online. There were protocols against removing battle-rigs in those conditions.

Settle, she wished the syn. She couldn't override until her nanomecha stood down and they, like everyone *else*, seemed to be having trouble with that.

Corso jerked his hand back. "Leave me for the priest."

"Now you don't object to the Aedis?"

His gaze skidded off her face. "She's the healer, and you're not, and that Knight-Marshal's going to fire on the riev, soon as we're all clear. Blow this whole warehouse."

Iari stared at him. "What? You can't've heard that on their comms."

Corso leaned forward. He smelled battle-sour, sweat and fear and fury. "Look at the pilot's station. Tell me what you see."

Hrok's breath, *that's* why he'd come all the way forward in the cabin. So he could spy into the cockpit. Iari bit back a *paranoid neefa* comment and shifted sideways and looked.

And blinked. The hopper's arms-turing was active, expected and normal in these conditions; but there was a target-lock engaged, and the targets were all in the warehouse, clumped together. Twenty-two of them. The hopper had whitefire cannons. It could level the warehouse and, with containment hexes, avoid taking the whole block with it. But it would obliterate the riev.

Iari eyelocked Corso. Cracked tusk. Blood all over his face where the lip had split, where he'd smacked a cheekbone on something. He'd got through his enlistment and the whole surge with his face intact. Not so much on the inside.

But he was looking at her now like everyone looked at templars: expecting her to do something, unspecified what. Not sit here beside him and wait for her syn to ebb enough she could bandage his hands.

Not sit here at all.

There were twenty-two war-forged weapons with mangled command lines and fledgling sapience in that warehouse. Decommed and disarmed, but dangerous. Jich'e'enfe could come back online. Or someone else could. Keawe's solution was the simplest, and the safest.

Iari set the roll of polymesh down on the bench beside him and stood up. "Iffy, when you're done with Gaer, Corso needs some help. Make sure they both get to the hospice safely."

Iffy made a grinding noise in her throat. "Of course I—wait." She paused, turned her head. Her hands, gloved and stained and holding Gaer's face together, never moved. "Where are you going?"

Iari ignored her. "Char. Luki. You're with me."

Iari could see questions moving around in Luki's eyes, in the flexing of silent lips.

"The riev, Corporal." Iari walked past her. "We're going to get them."

Char asked nothing and followed her down the ramp. After a beat, Luki came too, probably choking on questions. Or concerns.

Or wondering what the hell her lieutenant was up to now, when they'd just gotten to safety.

Iari wondered that herself, as she walked back to the warehouse.

"Sir," Char said, in what passed for a low voice. "Corso is correct. I heard the Knight-Marshal's orders."

Oh, Ptah's unkind mercy.

"Over comms, you heard her."

"Yes." Char hesitated. Then, more softly, "There are riev scouts with more advanced surveillance than I."

So that meant the rest of the riev knew about Keawe's orders, too.

Iari gagged as the syn flared again. She held its (her) panic down to a brisk march, not quite running back into the warehouse.

Keawe met Iari two meters inside, forewarned, no doubt, by the hopper pilot and the templar who'd tried to stop Char. She jabbed a finger back toward the hopper.

"Lieutenant. I thought my orders were clear."

"They were, sir." Iari was very aware of Char behind her. Of the riev clumped together in the ruins of what had been Peshwari's barricade of crates, that they had destroyed on their way inside. She pitched her voice to carry—the riev would hear it, *let* the riev hear it. "Sister Iphigenia has the wounded in hand. I'm here to collect the riev and return them to the Aedis."

Keawe's visor was still raised. Her face might as well have been Char's, for all its expression. "We've got the riev handled."

Luki made a strangled noise. Keawe shot her a puzzled glance. Refocused that narrow stare on Iari.

Who said, much more quietly, "I know what you're planning, sir. I'm asking you *not* to do that."

Keawe was so very much bigger. Hulking. Almost Char's height and breadth. She took a step closer, then two. "That decision's been made."

Templars didn't fight each other, Iari reminded herself. They were like the riev that way. Iari's syn wasn't convinced. It sparked along her nerve and tugged at her breath.

"Are those Knight-Marshal Tobin's orders, sir?"

What Iari would do if they were, Chaama's bones, Mishka's blood, she didn't know. Stand down. Stand aside. Go back to the hopper.

Courage is facing that which is within your strength to face; but doing so does not guarantee your victory.

But then Keawe said, "Knight-Marshal Tobin's not here, Lieutenant. I am," and Iari let her breath go. Cold, clear relief flooded through her.

"Yes sir. But where it concerns the safety of B-town, my directives come from *him.* These riev are citizens of B-town. I'm going to bring them back to the Aedis for their safety. Sir."

Keawe's lips went white where they pressed against her tusks. "*Their* safety. You look around, Lieutenant. Look at the doors. If they'd met resistance here, what do you think would've happened?"

"But they didn't, sir. They aren't dangerous. They're not like Sawtooth."

"Yet. You said they had Oversight again."

"Yes sir. They did. I don't think it's working anymore. There's no one giving orders." Iari choked on a mouthful of honesty: she had only the riev to confirm that. But if there *were,* then Gaer would likely be dead, and this conversation wouldn't be happening.

"We've lost custody of both the altar *and* the wichu who

presumably activated their Oversight. What's to stop her from re-activating it?"

"We can't kill them because of what they *might* do. We owe them better, sir. They fought in the surge, same as templars. Same as soldiers." She kept back what Gaer would've said: that they might've *been* soldiers, before wichu artificing. "Some of them are older than we are. Char is. Some of them were at Saichi."

"I don't need a history lesson. Void and *dust*, you are so very much Tobin's." Keawe's gaze broke. She speared a scowl at the riev, who stood like it was another day at the docks, and they were waiting for day labor. Except for the wall of templars, they might've been. "So your solution is to *ask* for their cooperation."

"Yes sir." Loudly. Let the riev hear it. "It's worked so far. Asking."

Keawe glared at Char, standing silent and conspicuous on Iari's flank. "All right. *Ask.* If they'll go with you, fine. If they don't." She spread her fingers, spacer-shrug. "Then my orders stand. Are we clear?"

"Yes sir. Th—"

"Don't fucking thank me." Keawe made a slicing gesture. "Void and dust." Then, "Fall back," she said louder, not bothering with helmet comms. A battlefield shout, for when comms failed and visors broke. "Fall back. Let the lieutenant through."

Iari stepped around her then, and marched up to the templar line, which drew aside and made room for her, for Luki, for Char.

The riev were waiting. Only their optics moved, tesla eyes or sensor arrays or whatever they had. If Char could hear through helmets, then the riev would've heard *everything*.

Iari picked a familiar face, and the only name she had. "Winter Bite."

The blank mask-face tilted toward her (all the riev did, out of sync). "Lieutenant."

"Did you hear?"

"Yes."

"Then will you come back to the Aedis with me?"

Winter Bite's head moved. They might've been looking at Char, or at Keawe. Or just at nothing, while the riev did their internal, networked consultation. Then Winter Bite's chin dipped again.

"We will go to the Aedis, Lieutenant."

We, now. Pronouns spreading like plague.

"Excellent." Iari swallowed a mouthful of dust. "Corporal, you've got point. Riev next. Char, you and I will bring up the rear. Let's move out."

CHAPTER TWENTY-SEVEN ≣≣≣

The aethership *Rishi* hovered over the dock in the Aedis courtyard. Heat waves shimmered at the plasma ports, but the big coil-drives were offline. That was just venting, that heat. All the ship's buoyancy now depended on hexwork.

Iari couldn't see the equations, but she knew they were there, same as she knew the stars were, above the brassy blue, daylit vault of the sky. That was faith, maybe. Gaer would say it was *knowledge*; faith was in what you couldn't see, couldn't touch, couldn't prove.

If that was true, then what Jich'e'enfe had done in the cellar with the altar and the fissures would fall into the realm of prayer, because damn sure it wasn't arithmancy or alchemy. Let that premise hold, and what Iari's own implants had done—that white-fire column, that *smite*—was prayers answered.

She hadn't told anyone. Not Diran (rather eat the shattered remains of Gaer's visor than do that). Not Iffy, which was a little harder, because Iffy had those big blue eyes. Not *Tobin*, which made her guts knot up with guilt whenever she saw him.

Yet, she consoled herself. *I haven't told Tobin* yet.

Neither had Gaer or Corso. Not a planned conspiracy of secrets, exactly; when Keawe had arrived with that hopper full of templars, there had been too much else to do—secure the site, collect the dead. And *after*—Corso had stayed in the Aedis long enough to get his hands seen to, his tusk capped, before returning to B-town. Gaer, whose face was all over polymesh, who had a concussion and two cracked ribs and all manner of soft tissue damage and med-mecha's near-constant surveillance, hadn't said anything either for the eight days he'd been in the hospice.

And, truth, why would he say anything? He'd expect *her* to report it. Good templar, dutiful, who attended prayers in temple even at the inconvenient hours, who *believed* those prayers. Who *had faith* in the Aedis's basic goodness and rightness. She should've reported it first thing.

Templars scuttled in the aethership's shadow, moving crates out of the hold. Armor, gear, belongings. *Rishi* had just gotten back from a run to Windscar to retrieve templars to reinforce—replace, absorb—the remains of Peshwari's unit. Keawe had said they were a loan, but Iari thought they might be more permanent. A hand-picked transfer between Knight-Marshals, with the approval of the involved Aedis Mothers, didn't need Seawall's approval (or interference). And bypassing Seawall meant no political assignments, no *let's-send-the-fuck-ups-north-to-B-town*. Keawe's people were experienced templars, or at least well-trained, Keawe-trained amateurs, to pad out B-town's garrison.

The templar in charge of the unloading barked orders and stomped around and side-eyed Iari. He'd stripped down to his undershift, bare-armed and bare-chested, as if it were high summer and not watery autumn. He might be trying to identify rank—*she* was uniformed—from that distance. Or, no. He was grinning at her.

Sweet sizzling Ptah.

"He's certainly fit," Iffy observed, and sipped her mug of tea.

Steam came off the cup, reminding everyone (except that Windscar templar) that it was autumn, not high summer, and the sunlight was more light than heat. "He's trying very hard to impress."

"Huh." Iari studied the empty bottom of her own mug. "You or me?"

"Oh, please. You. There are stories going around the barracks about you. *His* name is Notch, by the way. Not his *real* name. But that's what everyone calls him, including Keawe. Lieutenant Notch."

"The hell do you know this?"

"I hear things. Are you going to ask what kind of stories they're telling?"

"No."

"How you took down a tunneler. How you fought off a whole pack of boneless in that cellar. How you killed a rogue *riev*."

"There were four boneless, which barely counts as a pack, and Gaer helped. Char killed Sawtooth and Swift Runner."

Iffy rolled her eyes. Iari pretended not to notice.

From here, in the lee of the kitchen doors, she could just see the pair of small, temporary flood-teslas, now dimmed for daylight, and the hastily erected tents across the courtyard. The B-town riev stood outside the tents, collected together like a sheaf of armored wheat. Su'seri, from Windscar, said they were intact, uninfected; and Char said there was no Brood taint. They were—well, not exactly free, because riev never had been. Tobin had *asked*, very deliberately, for them to stay in the Aedis, to which they had agreed. Iari suspected Char's hand in that decision.

There had been debate about fences. Barriers. Tobin had insisted that *guests* were not confined anywhere. Mother Quellis had concurred. Keawe had called them both reckless.

Iffy shifted a little closer. Her eyes floated over the rim of her mug like blue moons. "So. I hear there's a meeting this morning."

"You hear a great deal."

Another eyeroll, this one with a side of smirk. "Is it about the stasis chest in quarantine?"

Sawtooth's chip. Iari shrugged and looked for a place to put her own mug. "What do you know about that?"

"Oh, give it to me." Iffy took the mug from her and fit it, somehow, in her tiny hands. "I don't *know* anything. That's why I'm asking. Sister Diran acts as if Mishka herself delivered a directive of secrecy."

"Not Mishka. Knight-Marshal Tobin. People get them confused sometimes." Iari shrugged. "The contents are classified. For once, Dee's not being dramatic."

"Yes, she is." Iffy waved a hand. "Don't tell me, then. Fine. I understand."

"No."

Iffy stopped, mid-wave. "No?"

"No, the meeting this morning is not about what's in the stasis chest." Prior meetings had been. Su'seri had looked at Sawtooth's chip and demanded to take it to Windscar. Diran had objected. Now the chip sat in stasis, to Su'seri's dismay (and promise to protest, through official channels). "*This* meeting's about the ship coming from Seawall and the Five Tribes embassy delegation on board. They want to take Gaer back for medical treatment."

Iffy stiffened to her full height, plus a centimeter of pure indignation. "What, *now*? It's been eight days! If Gaer were critical, he'd be dead already. He's getting *better*."

"I think that's exactly why now."

"They can't recall him. Or reassign him. Or, or *take* him. I'll put a medical stop on his transfer."

Trust Tobin, Iari wanted to say. *Trust me. It'll be okay.*

But it might not be. Gaer was in trouble for reasons that had nothing to do with *reason* and everything to do with *politics*.

So all Iari said was, "I'll see you later," and started the not-nearly-long-enough walk to Tobin's office. The tea felt solid in her gut, as if she'd swallowed stones.

The templar-on-loan (Notch. Hrok's breath, what a name) grinned as she walked by. Elements help everyone, he started to walk toward her.

Iari's syn twitched, like a cat's ear when it hears something but doesn't care enough to open its eyes. Iari raised a hand, greeting and warning, and this *Notch* stopped like he'd slammed into Char. His stare followed her long after she passed under the aethership's shadow.

Tobin had rearranged his office. There were three chairs now in front of the desk. The new addition, conspicuously in the center, was smaller and less aggressive and of a decidedly Seawall design: all whorls and smooth waves and the shapes suggestive of fishes. Oh, Blessed Four. That meant *Quellis* was coming to the meeting, which meant something official, Aedian, something beyond Knight-Marshals shuffling troops.

Iari's guts curdled. "Am I early?"

"No. I wanted to talk to you first." Tobin pretended serenity, fingers folded on his desk, face blank. *Pretended*, because his fingertips were bloodless where they pressed his knuckles. "Iari. I need you to be honest."

Her guts coiled, clenched, turned cold and solid. Oh Ptah, oh Hrok, he *knew*. Maybe Corso had told after all. Or Dee had seen something on the med-mecha's scans. Or Gaer had—no, not Gaer. He wouldn't.

"Yes sir."

Tobin gave her one of his flickering half-smiles. "I don't mean to suggest that you'd lie to me. I mean, I need an accurate opinion."

Dust in her mouth. Ashes. "Sir."

"How well do you trust Gaer?"

Iari blinked. "He's kept his word to us so far."

"Yes. To the Aedis." Tobin's gaze drifted toward the door and hung on nothing. "But now things will become more complicated. How well do you *personally* trust him?"

Gaer was SPERE, an arithmancer, an *alien*. As a group, no, trust vakari as far as you could throw them into the Weep. That was historical precedent, and Jareth's advice, and *sense* if you'd read any history, ever.

But Gaer wasn't *any* vakar. He was arrogant and capable and currently hanging in the hospice wing in one of those vakari slings (you don't put someone with dorsal spines in a *bed*) because he'd acted when he did not have to act, and risked his life in so doing. That was bravery, by even cold Jareth's standards. Bravery was a virtue. And where there was *one* virtue, there would be others. Loyalty, maybe.

Faith, again: "Sir. I trust him. Completely."

"All right." Tobin's face gave her no hints. Full spacer mode. But before she could ask him what he meant, what this was about, the door rattled under Keawe's knock, and when Tobin called *come in*, Mother Quellis was there, too, waving Iari back to sitting.

"As you were, Lieutenant. Please. Knight-Marshal Tobin. A pleasure, as always." Quellis climbed into her smooth-sided Seawall-shaped chair and perched, templar-straight. She fired a jacta-bolt smile at Tobin. "I appreciate *all* of you taking the time to attend this meeting, although I thought, Knight-Marshal Tobin, that it would be just the two of us."

"I thought Knight-Marshal Keawe and Lieutenant Iari would bring useful perspectives to our conversation."

Keawe dropped into her chair. She fired a look at Iari over Quellis's head, eyebrows up, and scowled. "Conversation about what?"

Tobin's face didn't move. "We have two requests for custody of the ambassador. We need to discuss which one to honor."

"There is nothing *to* discuss," said Quellis, "except the accommodations for the Five Tribes delegation while they are here, and the degree of access we will allow them to the ambassador while the Synod decides how to respond to the charges. This is not *our* decision to make."

"Wait. What charges?" Keawe's hand spasmed, spacer for something very emphatic, ending in a fist. "*What* are you talking about?"

Tobin's own hands stayed knotted together. "The wichu representatives to the Synod charge that Gaer murdered the artificer Jich'e'enfe on orders from Five Tribes Special Tactics and Reconnaissance. They are demanding we arrest and remand him into their custody. To the *Vashtat*, as happens."

Iari's guts stopped their clenching and dropped, stone-hard, stone-cold, through the floor. *Vashtat* had been a prison ship during the Expansion, before the treaties and the Weep. A specifically vakari prison.

Keawe snorted. "Su'seri's in a knot because we won't let him have that riev chip, and he's gone whining up the chain. Tell me you're not going along with this."

Quellis turned completely around in her chair now, to look at Keawe. "Knight-Marshall, however . . . suspect . . . the accusation, the wichu are members of the Confederation. They have a right to bring charges."

"*Provisional* members. All this neefa-shit about self-governance and independence they keep spouting. Separate ships. Separate districts. There isn't even *one* of them in the Aedis." Keawe pointed at Quellis, half accusatory, all anger, no deference. "The wichu are on their *own* side."

Iari had heard similar sentiments over the years. Muttering in the regular army, mostly, and most of *that* from Corso, who saw wichu self-segregation as evidence of assumed superiority. *They think they're better, the fuckers,* which, truth, was Corso's litany about near everyone.

Tobin, Iari noted, was just watching. Saying nothing. Letting her and Keawe come at Mother Quellis from both sides. Now it was her turn. Reason to Keawe's force.

"We can't honor that request, Mother. Gaer didn't assassinate anyone. First, Jich'e'enfe attacked *us*. Second, we're not even sure she's dead. And third, Gaer's a diplomat. There's immunity from prosecution."

Quellis turned her head slowly, as if she wanted Iari to reconsider saying *can't* to an Aedis Mother. "To your last point, Lieutenant: ordinarily, yes. But these are exceptional circumstances. The ambassador volunteered to assist with the investigation into Pinjat's murder in his capacity as arithmancer. Then he specifically retained the services of Corso Risar to locate Jich'e'enfe. And *yes*, Lieutenant, I read your report, and I know that Jich'e'enfe's true identity was unknown at that point—to you. But there is no proof she wasn't known to *Gaer*." Quellis shook her head. "I think we're all forgetting that, no matter how fond we may be of him, how charming he seems—Gaer is a SPERE operative."

Hrok's *breath*, did everyone know that? Was it just common

knowledge around the Aedis now, *hey, the ambassador's Five Tribes special operations, pass me the cream?* Iari knew her face was loud, shouting; but her voice came out cool, even, flat as the cover of *Meditations* on Tobin's desk.

"Mother, there were Brood in that warehouse. Jich'e'enfe was responsible for the deaths of templars."

Quellis looked like Iari imagined Iffy might, on the far side of middle age. Silver threads in her hair. Fine lines. Except please, gentle Mishka, Iffy's eyes never got that hard. "That in no way changes the fact that the ambassador was responsible for killing a Confederate citizen."

"Allegedly," Tobin murmured. "The lieutenant has pointed out that there is no body. We *assume* Jich'e'enfe is dead, but what we may have is a fugitive."

"Perhaps. But we can't just ignore the charges."

"No one's saying ignore them," Iari said. "*Deny* them. Jich'e'enfe was acting *against the Aedis.* Gaer was acting in the Aedis's defense. In my defense. On my orders. It's my responsibility. That altar—"

"That altar is missing." Quellis raised her voice. "And the only record we have of it are Gaer's notes—"

"And my testimony. And Char's. And Luki's. And Corso's." A breath. A beat. She had just interrupted *the Mother.* Void and dust. "Gaer didn't *make up* the Weep fissures. I certainly didn't. Lieutenant Peshwari is *dead* because of them."

"I am aware. But we cannot say for certain that the altar, or Jich'e'enfe, created the fissures. We have only Gaer's word on that, as an arithmancer."

"We *asked* him to help us, *as an arithmancer.* Why would we doubt what he says?"

Quellis pursed her lips. Not angry, Iari thought, but unhappy.

"Despite what you may think"—and she included Tobin and Keawe in that *you*, unspoken, with a dagger-sharp side-eye—"I am aware that there may be ulterior motives for the charges against the ambassador. Gaer has, after all, discovered a flaw in wichu artificing." And when Iari blinked, "Sawtooth's chip. The wichu have requested that, too—a request we have outright denied—*and* all of Gaer's data."

"Oh, for the love of the Four. That little neefa Su'seri." Keawe grimaced. "Tobin, *tell* me we're not going to comply with any of this."

"We are certainly not giving up any of Gaer's notes." Tobin was still dead-faced, full spacer-lockdown. "On that, Mother Quellis and I are in complete agreement."

"Well, then we can't give up Gaer, either." Iari leaned forward. The edge of the chair bit the back of her thighs. Bright line of pain, something to keep the syn busy. "He knows what's on the chip. He's got information locked in his *head*."

"Which is exactly why we can't just return him to his embassy, either," Quellis said. "He would report what he knows to his superiors. The wichu request saves us a major diplomatic incident."

Keawe made a slicing gesture. "Except the wichu are going to want what Gaer knows about that chip, too. And they'll get it, unless anyone thinks they'll follow Confederate interrogation laws with no oversight on their own fucking ship, on someone they've accused of a capital crime."

"And then once they get that information," Iari said, as the syn sensed her distress, her anger, and sent sparks and lightning down her limbs, "you have to ask *who* will see it and what they will do with that data. Unless Jich'e'enfe was acting totally alone, she's aligned with people who are using arithmancy no one's seen yet.

Gaer's familiar with all of that. Hand him over to the wichu, and we lose access to all of that knowledge. It's bad strategy."

Tobin's left brow had climbed. He had probably never heard her say that much at once—well, fair enough. Especially without a *sir* or a *mother* to buffer the honesty.

Quellis was frowning now. "You think the *wichu* are a threat to the Aedis, Lieutenant?"

"I think some of them are, yes. Jich'e'enfe. Others like her."

"More of a threat than SPERE?"

"More of a threat than *Gaer*. Mother, you've read the reports. You've seen the comm-logs. Gaer hasn't sent *anything* about the corrupted chip back to SPERE. He said—that knowledge would be worth a lot to people in his government, but it was dangerous, too, if it got out. It could destabilize the treaties. He's been loyal to *us*—"

"Don't know about loyal, but that vakar has to stay in *our* custody." Keawe sat back in her chair. "Let me take him up to Windscar. If we let Seawall have him—their embassy *or* ours—*someone* down there will turn him over to the damned wichu."

"No." Iari looked directly at Keawe. No *sir*. No *Knight-Marshal*. "Gaer stays here. I'll take responsibility for him."

Keawe's jaw slid and locked forward, eyes down to slits. Mother Quellis frowned, and looked at Tobin with a clear expectation that he'd intervene and discipline his lieutenant.

He might. He could. Iari swallowed a rush of panicked *what if*, and had faith.

Tobin took a slow, deliberate breath. Let it out. "The ambassador is in *my* Aedis, and as this is a military matter, he is under *my* jurisdiction. He is involved in this at all because *I* asked him. Lieutenant Iari is correct. We are not going to arrest Gaer. Nor are we relocating him." He glanced at Iari. Now, *now*, she saw a faint, grim smile. "I have something else in mind."

———

The hospice hallways were cool, dim, after the courtyard. Empty, too, after the furious closeness of Tobin's office. Mother Quellis had yielded, finally—*had* to, because Tobin knew the intricacies of Aedis authority and treaty subsections *and* because Keawe had, after some sputtering, backed his plan. Templar response to Brood was the province of Knight-Marshals, not Mothers.

Iari's presence hadn't loaned any weight to his arguments, but she was the reason for their shape, and for the result. And so it was her duty (not pleasure, oh no) to deliver that result to Gaer.

Vakari dorsal spines didn't lend themselves well to lying flat. Healthy vakari, according to Iffy, slept on a sort of perch, leaning forward onto a cushioned surface or into a sling, for support. But given the extent and placement of Gaer's injuries, they—Iffy and Diran—had rigged up a sort of sling in place of the usual hospice bed. Iari could see the apparatus hanging off the ceiling, sharing space with the med-mecha tracks.

She stopped outside the curtain.

"Gaer?"

Silence. What might've been a faint sigh. "Iari. I thought I recognized your stomping."

Take that as a *come in*. She twitched the curtain aside. Gaer hung in his sling, a familiar book cradled between his hands. *Meditations*. Her copy. Iari squinted. Looked like he was somewhere in Chapter Three.

He closed the book carefully and set it aside. "How do I look? Sister Iphigenia will not give me a mirror."

"Better than you did. And she says, call her Iffy."

Gaer's eyes narrowed. Amusement, she thought, not ire. "Now

I know it's serious. You're being diplomatic. Help me out of this *setatir* sling, will you?"

"Why?"

He poked his chin—carefully, no sudden movements—at the side table. "I need my optic. I trust you've repaired it."

"You have a concussion. No optic allowed."

"I suppose Sister Iffy told you that?"

"She didn't. I read the report."

"Sss. Patient confidentiality doesn't mean much, does it?"

Iffy had made much the same argument, very briefly, before Iari had pulled out the words *official* and *report* and *Hrok's breath, Iffy, Tobin knows, fifteen people in the Five Tribes embassy know, let me read the slagging thing.*

Iari shrugged. "You're not supposed to be arithmancing. Not for another day, at least."

"Which is exactly why Seawall's sending a ship for me *now*. Oh, don't look at me that way. I'm a spy."

"You mean Iffy came in and told you."

"Yes. But she wouldn't help me out of this sling. For that, I need you." He stretched out a hand. "*Please*, Iari."

Oh, ungentle Ptah. Iari gave him her forearm. He smelled like antiseptic. Like metal and blood. And under that, faintly, the scent of burnt sugar that she thought was vakari sweat, or maybe just Gaer.

The med-mecha whirred unhappily and shuttled back and forth on its track. "I have him," she told it. "Don't worry. Gaer, about Seawall—"

"I know. They'll be sending Karaesh't to collect me. My direct superior. Very polite, and very SPERE. Very *arithmancer*, yes? Karaesh't will probably insist on a transfer back to the main embassy.

I think I can talk my way back up to B-town eventually, but if not—ss. I don't know, *if not*. Karaesh't might reassign me to a listening post on the edge of alwar territory and assign you some other vakar less susceptible to B-town's charms. The point is—as soon as she gets me alone, she will have questions. My condition will allow me some, ah, liberty in the depth and accuracy of what I report. I'll try to stay focused on Jich'e'enfe and that *setatir* altar, but the chip might come up. *Will* come up." He craned his head around until he could pin her with both eyes. "You do have it in custody?"

"It's in a stasis-chest down in quarantine."

"Good. It's Aedian property. No one from the embassy has a right to even *look* at it. Just don't touch it. You heretics and your nanomecha. You could be contaminated."

"Gaer. We know."

"You should *also* take custody of my tablet and my notes."

"They're in Tobin's office."

"The embassy will demand their return. My advice is wipe them. *After* you copy the data. You *have* copied the data, yes?"

"Yes. But we haven't wiped anything yet."

"Tobin's having a conscience about it, is he? Worried about offending the Five Tribes? He won't. Karaesh't will expect him to destroy the data. If *I* had you in custody, and your tablet full of sensitive data, that's what I'd do. Although I suppose I'm not technically in custody, whatever evidence I see to the contrary." He plucked at his hospice robe. "It might be better if I were. You should arrest me. Really. Iari, I'm telling you. Arrest me. Destroy my notes."

He must be feeling better. So many *words*. Or he was more scared than he was in pain. At least he'd stopped for breath.

"Shut up and listen. I just came from a meeting with Tobin. The wichu reps to the Synod are charging that the Five Tribes—that SPERE—put a bounty on Jich'e'enfe. They're saying that SPERE—that *you*—assassinated her, on orders. They're demanding we arrest and detain you, pending extradition."

Gaer recoiled, damn near let go of her arm, damn near dumped himself on the floor. His chromatophores washed vivid crimson. "They are full of neefa-shit."

"I know. Tobin knows. Mother Quellis knows, too."

Gaer's pigments bleached, then greyed neutral again, colorless as his voice. "If Jich'e'enfe's figured out how to get through Aedian hexes *and* how to weaponize the Weep, then other people will, too. The Aedis will need arithmantic help—*our* help, Five Tribes help—" His voice dried up and came back as a ghost of itself. "The wichu will take me apart. You know that. They will know *everything*. You might as well just give them the chip."

"*Gaer.* Ptah's own sake. Will. You. Listen. Tobin knows his way around the treaties. He found a clause about seconding foreign assets to the Aedis if, quote, possession of those assets is deemed integral to sovereign defense, unquote. Jich'e'enfe had possession of a device that can open Weep fissures, and we've got neither her nor that device in custody. Therefore, we have a credible, acute threat to the Confederation, and you're the closest thing to an expert we've got. So—you're now a foreign asset, and we're seizing you."

She braced for a protest. An argument. Even a disapproving hiss. Gaer only looked at her. The socket work around his left eye glinted in the stark hospice teslas like tiny stars.

"I'm . . . property, now? A prisoner?"

"No. You're free to leave the Aedis grounds, with an escort."

"What, *you*?"

"I could assign Char, if you'd prefer."

"I do *not* prefer." He let go of her arm and lurched (threw himself) for the side table. Caught himself, by some miracle, and hung there. "Tobin found a way to refuse my embassy without causing a political incident. *Clever* Knight-Marshal."

"Tobin has no intention of refusing any requests. If Karaesh't wants to take you back to Seawall for questioning, then fine. You go. But we go with you. Me, Luki, and Char. And you come back here, afterward."

"Oh, Karaesh't will *love* that. I'll end up assigned to a listening post for certain, once this is over." His talons scraped across the table. Flex. Release. "Do I get any say in this?"

"Do you get a—no. You just *said* we should arrest you."

"That was when I thought you wouldn't."

Void and dust, ungentle Ptah: this was the *one* time she wished he'd read her aura. She willed *believe me* (what color was that?) into her voice. "Listen to me. Tobin had me and Keawe in that office, arguing with Mother Quellis. We *both* said the wichu couldn't have you. But Keawe wanted to take you to Windscar. I said she couldn't. Tobin backed me."

"You argued with Keawe?" Gaer's plates (one plate, the one not meshed immobile) flared. "Jareth says it's madness to attack that which is beyond your strength."

Iari breathed past the weight in her chest. "Yeah, well. I wouldn't've let the wichu have you, either. No matter what anyone said."

Gaer reached for his optic. He flicked her a look, daring her to protest, and then he pressed it into place, fitting it over his eye socket, securing it to ridge and bone. The seals engaged, hiss and click. The optic blued translucent, then opaque. "Thank you for that, too. We would make terrible fugitives, you and I."

CHAPTER TWENTY-EIGHT

"You look terrible," Karaesh't said, which wasn't a lie. Unkind, but honest, and clearly a poor attempt to unsettle him and set him on the defensive. Gaer expected better of Karaesh't (a'ratakt'a Tirak, whose foremothers had come late to the Five Tribes heresy, and whose descendants had been trying to redeem themselves ever since). She was usually more . . . subtle. Barbed. *Clever.*

So read her clumsy insult-honesty as proof of her discomfiture, or perhaps her fury.

Gaer, who had just acquired permission to stand from Sister Iffy, absorbed the insult (it was the truth, really; he'd seen a mirror) without comment and told his first lie of the day.

"I'm glad to see you, Commander." He gestured at the chair opposite his, across the solid expanse of a Tanisian wood table. "Will you sit?"

The invitation crossed into insolence, subordinate to superior, hedged up on treasonous, as if that were his table and not the Aedis's. Then Gaer compounded the challenge and bared his teeth in, well, a dare. One of *his* foremothers had started the Five Tribes heresy: she had been the sub-commander on the Protectorate warship *Sissten*, and refused to start a war by breaking her word and murdering hostages, even *if* one of those hostages was contaminated by wichu-built nanomecha—nanomecha which was ancestor to the stuff floating in templars and priests. That might be something the Aedis didn't know. Might be something they'd forgotten, except the scholars who made knowing obscure facts their business.

It was not knowledge *Karaesh't* had mentally misplaced, no. She remained stiffly upright, glaring, and jabbed a hand at the closed door. "There is a *riev* in the corridor wearing templar insignia."

"Winter Bite," said Gaer, with more serenity than he felt. "And his pronoun is, well, *he*, not it. Honestly, I would have preferred Char, but they had other duties."

"A *second* templar riev."

"The first, technically. I think there are five now. You'd have to ask Lieutenant Iari for more exact details. They are all her initiates."

"Iari is the other templar out there? The tenju? She's your keeper?"

"Not my keeper. My escort."

"Sss." It meant the same as one of Iari's noncommittal grunts: disagreement not worth the breath or effort to articulate. Karaesh't swept the room, head tilted to best angle her optic. She was looking for any surveillance devices the Aedis might have planted. Probably frying them blind, if she found any, which Gaer hoped she did not. Tobin alleged to trust him; Keawe made no such declarations. Let Karaesh't go around dismantling Aedian tech and Keawe's arguments (to incarcerate him in Windscar, maybe bury him in the Weep fissure) might gain strength.

He cocked his head, too, to gather Karaesh't into the scope of his optic as if he were reading her aura. Which he wasn't, rot her, because she had herself hexed to invisibility. Might as well be a block of stone standing across from him, if stones scowled. Or one of the new riev, none of whom had half of Char's charm or emotional complexity. (They *had* auras. Just faint. Dim. Like the aurora borealis on a bad night.) His own aura was less well-concealed. There was that moratorium on practicing arithmancy Sister Iffy insisted upon, yes, and he'd ignore that directive if necessary, but there were the remnants of self-preservation, too. He'd already stepped over the line with Karaesh't. No need to add to it by challenging her hexwork *directly*. Stealthy sidelong challenges were still possible. Likely. She'd expect them.

Karaesh't hooked one of the chairs, jerked it out, dropped into it like a sack of knives and bone. "How much do they know, Gaer? Your templar keepers. What have you told them?"

He was glad of the table between them. Less glad that Iari had been exiled to the corridor—a concession Karaesh't must've wrung from Quellis. He wondered if Quellis and Tobin had waited until the aethership's landing to break the news to the Five Tribes delegation—Karaesh't and four, count them, *four* embassy security officers, *two* of them f-primes, for *setat's* sake—that they wouldn't be transferring him back to Seawall. That he'd been . . . what was the term Iari'd used? Seconded. Saved.

Truth: he had expected Karaesh't to insist he return to Seawall for this interview, where the surveillance was all SPERE, if only to mark him as her territory, no matter what the Aedis might claim. That she hadn't was unexpected, yes, and good, yes, but also worrying. It wasn't kindness. Karaesh't wasn't known for that. There must be some other reason that superseded SPERE surveillance.

He told her the truth. "I haven't told them anything compromising or traitorous to SPERE or the Five Tribes."

"Sss. And yet you've made no reports to us, either." Karaesh't had come into the room speaking textbook high Sisstish, for which the Aedis could be expected to keep dictionaries and translators on hand. Now she shifted to SPERE cipher-cant.

"So make those reports to me *now*, Gaer. I'm listening."

And probably recording. Guarantee that she was.

Gaer flared the jaw-plate that still worked—the other still swathed in poly-mesh, mending and mostly immobile. Be a trick to even speak that cipher, with his face like this. Karaesh't would know it. Wouldn't care if it hurt. Would expect him to do it anyway.

If he did, he'd reassure her. If he did, he might discomfit the Aedis. Because they *were* listening. They'd be fools not to, and Tobin and Quellis were anything but. Karaesh't knew that. How he answered her now—might affect more than any future posting. Might affect his life, when the seconding ended.

"The details you want," he said, stubbornly in Sisstish, "I can't render in cipher. Not and be understood. And besides. It's not like they don't know what I'm going to say to you. There's no need to antagonize them."

"Sss. Are you refusing my order to report?" Karaesh't was relentlessly average, in appearance, vocal range, bodily dimensions, disposition of features. Her best camouflage. All that average made people careless. You overlooked the intellect behind those unremarkable eyes. Underestimated her arithmancy. She must be reading his aura. She'd know he was telling the truth. She could probably (assume she could) rip through any hexes he tried to deploy. She'd certainly notice them.

"I am, Commander, for reasons of Five Tribes security. The Aedis is our ally in this. They need to trust us. Without them . . ." He gestured, a flare of fingers, a flutter, like something wisping away. "If you believed me a double agent, you wouldn't waste your time on an interview. You would send assassins."

"Mine aren't the only beliefs under consideration in SPERE command. To your *great fortune*."

Karaesh't was ordinarily, well, stone-faced (the expression translated surprisingly well). Her chromatophores stayed neutral no matter the storm and ebb of her emotional state. Gaer had never, in all his years of service, seen her face betray her. But here, now: a display of scarlet, vermilion, a sunset of hues.

So assume that Karaesh't intended to make that display. Who was the audience for it? Anyone who knew anything about vakari would read those colors as anger. Anyone (vakari) who knew Karaesh't *well* would read them as uncharacteristic overacting. A signal. A message. She wanted to offer the appearance of personal distrust, commander to subordinate. To present him as dancing on the edge of disgrace. And she wanted him to know it.

Maybe a performance for the Aedis? That made no sense. For *her* superiors, though . . . that might. Or the people who eventually got hands on her recording of this meeting, who would not be SPERE.

Oh, *setat*, but he'd worried about this. Warned Iari that *all this*—the holes in Aedis hexwork, riev perfidy, wichu involvement—would attract attention from people more focused on short-term gain. Some egg-stealing isolationist in the Five Tribes Parliament, or someone on the SPERE oversight committee, sensing an opportunity to put some distance between the Five Tribes and the Aedis. Some xenophobic Reunionist on that committee, worst case, who'd make nice with the slagging Protectorate because vakari were *vakari* and the rest of the multiverse could rot in a Brood-flooded hell.

The priorities were clear and simple here on Tanis. There was a fissure. Brood came out of it. *That* was the problem. Iari understood that. Tobin and Keawe did. And everyone-*setatir*-else—

Had to be managed. For the Five Tribes, that was Karaesh't's unenviable job. Which he wasn't making a bit easier for her by failing to file reports. Maybe *that* was why she hadn't dragged him (and Iari) back to Seawall. She didn't want him within reach of someone else.

(Or, *or:* she really did think he was a traitor, and was unable to act because of Tobin's maneuver. It might just be that.)

Well, he could ameliorate some of that concern. Gaer plucked a rolled tablet from a pocket of his skinsuit and slid it across the table. A secondary report, to augment the first official one he'd sent—through the Aedis dispatcher—earlier, which he had intended she read while she was still in the aethership. *This* report was . . . oh, let us say more detailed. More forthcoming. And it had not gone through Aedian channels.

She flicked a glance at it. Touched the display and awakened it. Studied the crabbed, distinctive columns of hand-stylused cipher. She rolled the tablet with deft fingers, stowed it. Then she audibly and obviously rattled her free talons on the table. "Your insubordination is noted. Make your report in Sisstish, then. I suppose you won't say anything they haven't heard already."

So it *was* a performance on her part, one being recorded—audio only, it seemed, or she would not have taken his tablet without comment. That pigmented display had been for him, a signal he'd read correctly. And he'd had a report to hand off, which he guessed she'd expected. Or hoped for. Maybe he wasn't on the shortlist for dishonorable discharge and prison, after all.

Gaer relaxed a notch. That explained the choice of venue. Conduct the interview *here*, she could be forgiven for failing to bring back video. *Setatir* Aedis wouldn't allow it, some manufactured excuse. (How she'd excuse not returning him to Seawall was her problem.)

He could perform for that listening audience, too.

"It begins with the murder of a wichu artificer," he said. And then, as he'd practiced a half dozen times in the hospice (for the med-mecha, the best and most supportive audience), he reported events: Pinjat's death, the involvement of riev, everything but the chip and its hexwork contagion.

"A tesser-hex," Karaesh't repeated, when he'd finished. "A tesser-hex *in atmosphere*."

"I know how that sounds."

"Like you sustained more of a head injury than the medical staff here is qualified to treat. And it just—closed? On its own?"

Gaer tilted his head. There were versions of SPERE cipher that did not rely on voice or symbol, versions meant to circumvent listening devices—versions that, even if the Aedis had camera-bots in the room, they wouldn't readily decode. Spacers of all species had some version of hand speech; SPERE cipher took that speech and, well, *ciphered* it.

The downside was limited vocabulary.

"On its own. Yes."

He gestured with two fingers. *No. Wichu hex. Wichu arithmancy opened tesser-hex.*

"That seems . . . impossible. The tesser-hex itself, first, and that it would simply—close on its own?"

His face hurt from so much talking. He was glad of the seat. Of the solidity of the table under his forearms. "I believe it closed because it anchored itself to a second set of coordinates in what I think is the Weep itself. I have included a copy of them in my official report." *Not* the one in SPERE cipher. The one Karaesh't had received while in transit, which meant Seawall would have it by now, too.

"Which the Aedis has no doubt copied."

"They did not have to. I shared it with them. We would not have those coordinates at all if not for their aid. Lieutenant Iari is the reason I got out of that cellar alive."

Karaesh't spread her fingers, both hands. *More.*

Templar closed tesser-hex, he signed back. *New battle-hexes.*

Which was skirting right up on the edge of Iari's secret, maybe straddling it, certainly not entirely true. He wasn't sure what to call what'd happened in that cellar. Corso said she'd turned into living plasma. Iari might say, *I channeled Ptah.* Gaer supposed the science was less romantic than that, less dramatic (possibly not even in conflict): that Aedian nanomecha had evolved new abilities, and he'd *bet* (without proof; there were limits to the access a foreign asset could get) that evolution had come in response to whatever hack-hex-job Jich'e'enfe had done on the riev, whatever had gotten into Iari from fighting with Sawtooth.

Karaesh't was staring at him now, eyes wide, second lids fully retracted. Jaw plates just a little agape, like she'd forgotten to finish a breath.

Well, yes. That would be big news, wouldn't it. The Aedis hadn't produced new battle-hexes since the last surge. Had not, to anyone's intel, updated their templars. That was exactly the sort of information SPERE was supposed to acquire. That *he* was supposed to acquire, stationed here in B-town.

Which he had. And which he'd just reported.

So, having given, Gaer decided to try and get, too. He folded his hands—no more cipher, that betrayal was done—and composed the ruin of his features into what he hoped was a reasonable expression. "The wichu Jich'e'enfe. Commander Karaesh't, do you know if she acted alone?"

"You're asking *me* questions. That's not how interrogation works."

"I'm asking because if she didn't, then more of her sort will wash up someplace. Here. Some other fissure. We need to know that. We, all of us. Not just the Aedis."

"Which *are* you right now, Gaer i'vakat'i Tarsik?" She bared her teeth, down to the last etching's flourish. "Aedis or SPERE? Confederation or Five Tribes?"

"Alive," he snapped. "*Not* Brood. That's what I am. And you. All of us here. That"—*are you listening, you bureaucrat with polit-ical ambitions?*—"is the priority."

"Thanks to *you* and your uncovering of this alleged altar, which we don't actually have."

"Thanks to the Aedis, mostly. And you have the images I took of that altar. It's in my report."

"We have no images of this Jich'e'enfe, there's no body, no proof—"

"Sss. Please. *Please.* The wichu want my extradition, you know this. That alone means Jich'e'enfe's not some private citizen." Never mind corroborating testimonies. Iari's. Corso's. Hvidjatte, who was in Aedis custody right now.

Karaesh't waved her fingers—not cipher, this time, just irrita-tion. "Are you saying she's a *wichu* agent? That she has, what, offi-cial sanction from a member-species of the Confederation? Do you have proof?"

"No. I don't know if she is. But I also don't think our allies, the Aedis, are in any position to make those inquiries. *We* are."

"We. You and me? Not likely."

"We, Five Tribes, which we are. SPERE, which we are."

"What you are is an Aedis asset by some archaic treaty provi-sion. We could protest that move. This isn't a *setatir* surge."

But you haven't protested, Gaer thought. So he told the proba-ble hostile audience—*bet* it was that new Chair of Oversight, may her teeth rot and fall out of her head. Gaer couldn't summon a name, just a face, at which to direct his ire. "It's damn near as bad as a surge. Imagine all the riev left in the galaxy, all infected with Brood, all moving in concert. *Imagine that.* Jich'e'enfe almost did that to all of us. She cannot have acted alone, Commander. She can*not* have. That kind of arithmancy—it's a revolution. It redefines what we thought we could do. We. *All of us.*"

"Arithmancy is *mathematics*, Gaer."

"Sss. You and I both know that mathematics does not mean fixed, static, and predictable. She was using k'bal script. Possibly k'bal theory. We have to investigate that."

Karaesh't flattened her plates. Hissed through pinched nostrils. You forgot, being around all the soft-skins, how much of vakari communication happened through scent, to which the soft-skins seemed mostly blind. Gaer tasted her frustration on the back of his tongue, bitter and slick. Tasted . . . not fear, exactly, but anxiety. Stress.

"The k'bal are dead." But her chromatophores flickered. Faintly, what was that? *Green?*

She was lying. And she wanted him to know that she was. But about *what?* Of course the k'bal were dead. The Protectorate had committed genocide during the Expansion, before the Schism, as punishment for k'bal aid to the wichu defection—

Unless they weren't all dead.

The k'bal might not all be dead.

He repeated that, in hand-cipher.

Karaesh't's fists remained unsurprisingly, resolutely immobile. But she cocked her head at him. Flared one plate just a jot. The equivalent of a raised eyebrow, among the faces surrounding Gaer these days.

"A better question," Karaesh't said, "is why Jich'e'enfe was *here*."

"The fissure."

"There are many fissures."

"The security around this one—" Gaer cut himself off. Don't rattle responses like a recruit looking for praise. Think. (It would be easier if his face didn't feel like it was going to crack off his skull. He should've accepted Iffy's offer of medication. Had wanted his wits sharp, instead. Pain was just as corrosive as alchemy to his wits, he'd discovered, and far less pleasant.)

So truth, *think*: this fissure was small, yes, but it had a formidable Aedis presence. All the fissures did. Far away from the major fleet routes if there was some kind of uprising—the riev, maybe, except Oversight should've connected them *all*, across the whole Confederation.

"I don't know what her reasons were."

Karaesh't leaned forward onto her forearms, a careful balance between spikes. Then she reached up, slid a talon between the ridges on the left side of her skull. And, as Gaer's attention followed her motion, paused and pressed.

"I rebooted the transmitter," she said, in case he couldn't figure it. She stabbed a look at the room's high corners and shifted to Comspek. "I have a few seconds that I can blame on Aedian interference. So listen." (Still looking at the corners, at the probable 'bots, at the probable templar watchers.) "The k'bal did not wait for the Expansion to kill them. They also did not fight. They ran and they hid on planets with minimal technology, planets unaligned with greater powers. They came *here*, to Tanis, the far side of this continent where there weren't many settlements. The alwar colonial government allowed it. Top secret location, need-to-know.

The Protectorate found them anyway, eventually, and killed them. That's the official record." She flexed her hand on the table. Began to gouge into the polished surface a string of numbers. Of coordinates.

Location? He signed at her. *Base? Settlement?*

Ruins, she signed back. And aloud: "If you'd reported earlier, I would have passed this information along. Then you were seconded, and I was not sure about your loyalty. Now—sss. You're what we have in the field." Her voice was crisp and judgmental. "This is very new intelligence. The Protectorate *just* admitted this to us."

"She *wasn't* alone, then. And if the Protectorate's admitting it now, they've been having similar incidents on their side of the Weep. Or they've found another altar. Or both?"

"Unconfirmed." *Checking*, said her fingers, *corroborating.* Karaesh't rolled her neck in the direction of the transmitter. She made a fist—time up, reboot finished—and shifted back into Sisstish mid-syllable, "—may merit *exploration.*"

Gaer nodded. Splayed his hand in a cipher-speak *understood.*

"It is imperative," Karaesh't continued, "that the altar is found and recovered and its nature studied. Your data said it had seven faces?"

Right. Not talking about k'bal ruins on Tanis. Talking about the altar. Gaer scrambled to recall the threads of the conversation before Karaesh't's contrived interruption and gathered them up in shaky mental fingers. "Yes. Seven faces which appeared to double as sacrificial surfaces."

"Perhaps an affiliation with Seven Strike, then. They have some numerological superstition attached to that number."

"And seven rumored leaders, if I recall my briefings." Of which

Jich'e'enfe might have been one. Assuming she was dead. *Surely* she was dead.

Karaesh't pushed herself back from the table, to the limits of the chair's dimensions. "Sacrificial surfaces on the altar, you said. Elaborate."

"Sacrifices. Living things made dead. There were blood-gutters. And stains. Jich'e'enfe appeared to be fueling her arithmantic endeavors with some kind of *exchange* of energy."

"Some kind of . . . exchange with another power? As in . . . a god? We've got no evidence Seven Strike is anything other than a secular, political organization."

"She could be part of one of the other insurgencies. Or"— awful thought—"a new religious organization."

Karaesh't's face said she'd thought of that, too, and she found the idea no more palatable. "Gaer. I do understand you believe that SPERE cannot function without your oversight, but I assure you— we are looking into such things. Even *before* your report. Your *very* overdue report."

"My apologies, Karaesh't. I was remiss. I won't repeat that error."

"Best you don't." *Report on schedule*, her hands told him. Hand cipher didn't have words for *or else*. Karaesh't's expression, and the acrid sting of her sweat, made that sentiment clear enough.

Then she thrust the chair back with more force and noise than was necessary. "That will conclude our interview. It's a long flight back to Seawall, and I do not wish to impose on Aedian hospitality."

He inclined his head. Started to stand, hands braced on the table, but she waved him back. "No need. Stay where you are." Her expression softened (so to speak: a relaxing of eyelids, of jaw-plates), a spangling of genuine sympathy across her cheek pigments. "You really *do* look awful."

"K'bal were *here*? On Tanis?" Corso sat back in his char. He bounced a look between Iari, seated across from him, and massive, impassive Char looming at her shoulder. "That's a joke. The veek's joking."

He cut himself on the serrated edge of Iari's scowl. Right. "I don't mean *Gaer* is the veek, he's all right, I mean—"

Char interrupted. "SPERE Commander Karaesh't did not seem like a vakar who jokes."

Which was ironic, considering the company. Not Char, Corso didn't expect *them* to have much in the way of humor. But once upon a time, before the Aedis, Iari'd had a sense of humor. He remembered a much younger version (of her, *of him*): uncapped tusk, no scars, teasing what-was-his-name, Melhak? Melhik? who'd had an aversion to being dirty and who'd died face-down in the mud that winter. No. It wasn't the Aedis that'd changed Iari. It was the voidspit, slagging surge and the fucking Brood.

Now there was clear exasperation on Iari's face: pursed lips, narrow eyes. Voice cool and hard as Char's stylized face. "You could shout louder, maybe. I don't think they heard you all the way at the Aedis."

"They didn't hear me out in the hallway." Corso's office *looked* like neefa-shit, he knew that. But the hexwork was good. Iari knew it, too. Bet that's why they'd met *here*, despite the attention her battle-rig got in this district. Her battle-rig, and every hexed centimeter of Char. Iari wanted a face-to-face. Didn't trust this information to electronic missives.

She could've called him up to the Aedis, though. He would've gone. But maybe he wasn't the sort she could bring through the gates more than once.

Whereas a P.R.I.S. associated with anyone who walked through his very well-hexed, surveillance-proof (as much as anything could be) door. Even templars outfitted for war.

"SPERE," he said, coming back to the point. "Fucking *SPERE*. They're your source? The hell are you talking to them for?" Oh. *Oh.* Now he got it. "That's who Gaer works for."

"You sell *that* information to anyone, you *breathe* it outside these walls," Iari said, light and colorless and entirely earnest, "I will find you and kill you myself."

"Wouldn't tell me at all, you think I'd do that." The threat stung a little bit anyway. Was a time she'd known him better than that. "Why isn't Gaer here?"

Iari's gaze broke. Found some spot on the wall past Corso's shoulder and drilled deep. "Because he still has trouble crossing the Aedis courtyard."

It was Corso's turn to look elsewhere. At the patch in Char's chestplate. "He going to be all right? He getting better?"

"Yeah," said Iari. And from Char, "The ambassador is expected to make a full recovery, in time. He is a poor patient."

"He know you came to me?"

Iari's gaze snapped back to his. Locked on like an arms-turing. "He does. He told me exactly what to tell you, so that's what I'm doing."

Corso grunted. Good. He'd've helped her regardless—she knew that, wouldn't be here otherwise—but he was happier knowing she wasn't . . . whatever. Betraying Gaer, who'd thrown himself at Brood and at that wichu sorcerer (an old word, pre-Landing, but Corso didn't have a better one) for Corso's sake. Gaer had been fucking brave, a fucking hero. He *owed* Gaer.

"So SPERE says there were k'bal here during the Expansion, and the Protectorate came and wiped them out, and that has . . . what, something to do with all the rest of that shit?"

Iari stared at him, unblinking.

"Right. Never mind. Above my pay grade."

"No. We don't *know*, Corso, that's the whole point of talking to you. SPERE tipped us to a k'bal presence on Tanis, probably long gone. Now, that could be bad intel. Gaer doesn't think it is, but he's got no proof. If it's true, then we need to know *where* they were, and if they left something behind that might've been used to make that altar. Records, or, or whatever arithmancers leave behind. Or we need to know if what they left has been looted by wichu separatists intent on bringing on the next surge, and if we can look forward to more encounters like Jich'e'enfe. And if that is what's happening, or what's happened—we deal with it."

"Fuck."

"Yeah."

They stared at each other. Corso snatched up a stray stylus and rolled it between his fingers. "You got any leads *where*?"

"That's your job. You're the one who knows all the pre-Confederation trivia. The stories. The religions, the customs. Find out if there're folktales. *Someone* out there's got a gran who heard stories about when the xenos came. Maybe as monsters, maybe as—I don't know. Strange shapes in the mist or the forest or whatever. K'bal had multiple heads and cranial vents."

"You want me to find out if someone's *grandmother* knows stories about k'bal landing on the other side of the continent."

"It's not a big continent. The fissure caused a lot of social upheaval. Whole villages moved, most of them to Windscar." She grimaced. "I have to tell *you* this?"

"No. Truth, Iari, you'd be better off asking a scholar somewhere. The uni in Seawall, maybe. Some professor of obscure literature."

"The universities are almost all alwar. Not known for their native ethnographies, are they? And besides. K'bal didn't land in Seawall. Or if they did, they didn't *stay*. The Protectorate wouldn't have been able to send assassins into the heart of the capital city unnoticed, even before the Confederation."

"But the Protectorate can't cough up coordinates where they *did* land their assassins. Shorten the job for us?" Us, now. Fuck. She had him doing it.

"They haven't so far." Iari grimaced like she'd bitten something sour. "Gaer thinks maybe the coordinates are too close to the fissure. Or *in* the fissure."

Corso tapped the stylus hard on the edge of his display. Tap-tap, like he meant to crack one or both of them. In the fissure. *In* it. But that gave him a place to start looking. He put the stylus down and made a fist of his nervous fingers. "Fuck, Iari."

"If I were k'bal and running from vakari, that's where I'd've gone. North. Before the fissure, there was nothing out there but a few villages."

And Saichi, which had almost been a city before it became a battlefield during the surge. But before that—before the Confederation's annexation of Tanis—it hadn't been anything at all. A collection of rocky hills and scrub trees. He'd grown up near there, in a little hamlet that wasn't there anymore. Still had family, maybe. Friends. Memories. Didn't want to go back north. Never again, he'd said, after he'd gotten out of the army.

Iari knew it. Iari knew all of that. And here she was, anyway.

"You're asking a lot."

"I know." She grimaced again. Stopped just short of an

apology—which was good, because if she'd said *I'm sorry* he'd tell her get out, get lost, *fuck off.* She wasn't sorry. And he wouldn't tolerate condescension.

But who else could she ask? He imagined how it'd gone. Someone saying to her, Find out if the veeks are lying about something no one's ever heard before, go on, Iari, you're from Tanis, aren't you?

And she was . . . but B-town raised, in the Aedis orphanage. Never a foot in the hinterlands—the *real* hinterlands, the villages and the countryside and the places where no one spoke Comspek on purpose. Iari's own Tanisian tenju was book-learned dialect, accented.

Her superiors, that Knight-Marshal of hers—spacer. Human. Even *less* from here than she was. But they were supposed to save the slagging *world*, this one and all the others. That's what templars did.

And she was asking him to help.

Corso found himself looking at Char, of all people: patch-welded chestplate, hexes faintly visible, that half-reconstructed arm restoring their torso to symmetry. Char'd lost their original arm up there in Saichi. And most of their division. If he'd been stupid enough to re-up his enlistment after the battle at Windscar, he'd've been there, too. Been *dead* up there, like most everyone else. Like Char's friends, because he knew now riev could have those. And *they* had joined the templars, same as Iari.

Because templars were supposed to save the world.

So ask why Gaer was doing this. Because it was his job, maybe, but Corso thought there was more. Curiosity. Maybe same reason Corso was going to agree: Iari was asking.

He'd dodged dying so many times. Run from it. Iari kept dragging him back . . . and dragging him back alive, and more or less well. Maybe he should just give up, give in, go along.

"If there's evidence the k'bal were on Tanis, I'll find it for you."

"Good," said Iari. "Thank you, Corso. I mean that."

He waved off her gratitude. Worse than condescension, that. Fuck. Then he made what was probably the biggest mistake of his life, *bet* he wouldn't regret it. "But I want in on the investigation. When I find something—*when*, unless that commander of Gaer's was lying—you take me with you. You'll need a guide. A, a translator. Your tenju's shit. You'll get yourself lost up there, you templars. Fall into a crevasse."

Looking at Char when he said it, because Char was safer. Char offered no argument, which *might* be deference to their lieutenant, but Corso thought the riev was . . . smiling, though that was impossible. Something in the cant of their head, the sudden glimmer in those tesla eyes. Approval.

So then he dared to look at Iari. Who sat back. Who blinked at him. "Huh."

Not a yes, but not a no, either.

To Corso, that felt like a victory.

ACKNOWLEDGMENTS

This year, y'all. This year was *rough*—but everyone knows that. And everyone also knows that writing a book is hard. But this year, everything was *extra* hard, for so many reasons, and so my gratitude to and for the following folks is even greater:

To the fantastic folks at DAW for getting this book out into the world.

To Tan Grimes-Sackett, both for all the brainstorming and for being masochistic enough to keep reading my first drafts.

To Lisa Rodgers, who wrangles deadlines and emails and phone calls *and* levels up my writing, every time.

To Loren, who knows when to switch the coffee out for something stronger.

And a special shout-out to the Friday Night D&D group, because without y'all, this year of Zoom and Doom would've been so much harder and darker.

Thanks, everyone. You're the best.